Eleven Days

Stav Sherez is the author of three previous novels. *The Devil's Playground* (2004), his debut, was described by James Sallis as 'altogether extraordinary, it introduces a major new talent', and was shortlisted for the CWA John Creasey Dagger Award. His second novel, *The Black Monastery* (2009), was described as 'dynamite fiction' in the *Independent* and 'truly exceptional' by Lee Child. *A Dark Redemption*, the acclaimed first book of his Carrigan and Miller series, was published in 2012. You can find him on Twitter @stavsherez and at www.stavsherez.com

Praise for A Dark Redemption:

'A compelling crime novel which is honest-to-god unputdownable.' *Crimefictionlover.com*

'Sherez is superb at evoking the unfamiliar world of immigrant communities . . . Although there is nothing more conventional than an unconventional cop, Sherez has beaten the odds and created an original detective in Carrigan.' *Daily Telegraph*

'Fast paced and slick, this is the first in what could well be an outstanding series.' *Guardian*

'Beautifully written and chilling.' Dreda Say Mitchell

'[A] riveting, powerful thriller whose subject matter is shocking and brutal yet firmly rooted in the real world. Carrigan and Miller are supremely believable characters and I really look forward to seeing them again.' Alan Glynn, author of *Bloodland*

'This is an outstanding book in every conceivable way. As a crime novel it's near faultless, marrying a highly original story to a fast-paced narrative steeped in intrigue and surprise. But what really sets it apart is its depiction of twenty-first-century London, the prose equivalent of a Hogarthian nightmare – funny, freakish, disturbing and all too true. Stav Sherez has given his hometown the book it deserves.' Nick Stone, author of *Voodoo Eyes*

'From the outset, *A Dark Redemption* establishes itself as a gem . . . This is powerful political and social commentary, scalding the search for simple, all-too-often violent solutions to Africa's problems . . . Expect great things from the Carrigan and Miller series.' *bookgeek.co.uk*

'The interplay of all the characters' fear, guilt and longing for justice adds both depth and sharpness to the novel. *A Dark Redemption* is said to be the first of the series, which is welcome news.' *TLS*

'Intriguing and well-written . . . highly recommended.' *Literary Review*

'An intelligent and superb read . . . Do not miss this one.' *itsacrime.uk.wordpress.com*

Eleven Days

STAV SHEREZ

faber and faber

First published in this edition in 2013
by Faber and Faber Limited
Bloomsbury House
74–77 Great Russell Street
London WC1B 3DA

Typeset by Faber and Faber Ltd
Printed and bound in England by CPI Group (UK) Ltd, Croydon, CR0 4YY

A CIP record for this book
is available from the British Library

ISBN 978-0-571-29052-9

2 4 6 8 10 9 7 5 3 1

Once again, for Jane

The first time you see a dead body it changes you for ever. You leave a little piece of yourself behind, but what they don't tell you, what they never tell you, is that in return you carry something new and strange into the rest of your life.

We arrived yesterday. I've never been so glad to land anywhere as I was after that flight. Of course, I had the window seat and could see every flash of lightning that sparked and danced across the plane's wing, the razor-tipped mountains so close below us that I felt as if I could reach out and scoop the snow from their peaks. He didn't even seem to notice when we started plunging, the air squeezed out from our lungs, masks dangling use-lessly, the crew buckled down and pale-faced and silent. Nor when we swerved and shook and rattled. He glanced past me out the window when the first engine failed but didn't say a word. Of course, he'd been popping pills since Heathrow, God knows what and how much, and so I shouldn't have been surprised at all.

The town is smaller than I expected. It is hot and dusty and ugly and not at all what I was led to believe. Chain stores and fast-food joints line the main street. Everything is in English. Everything is geared towards us, tourists, adventurers, white folk with money to burn. It makes me sick but he just laughs that cynical laugh of his, the one he

I

thinks makes him out to be cleverer than he is, and gives me that knowing nod, each Starbucks and McDonald's just further confirmation of what he'd believed all along. I never noticed it back in London but it only took one day in this hellhole for me to see him as he truly is. Maybe that's why we travel. Maybe we don't fly and drive and get boats to see new lands but only to see ourselves and our loved ones as they really are and not distorted by the mask and mesh of everyday life. On holiday all your crutches and supports are stripped away and there's only you and him and the relentless dead heat of midday.

He likes it here, I can tell, and wants to stay. He likes the late-night dive bars and small hole-in-the-wall cafes full of strange alcohol and even stranger food. We argue about this the first night in town. We're staying in a run-down hostel on the edge of what seems like the red-light district. The photo on the web looked nothing like this. This is the kind of house you cross the street to avoid walking past. The room is small and close so that we share each other's breath as we pass, our sticky bodies clinging for a second and then sliding off. There is a fan but of course it doesn't work. Cockroaches scuttle along the bed and floor. They are twice the size of any I've ever seen before and they make me constantly uneasy, the way they stop every now and then and seem to turn and face you, antennae twitching, before they decide to scamper off.

I tell him we didn't come here to be in another city, to sit in bars with Europeans and drink cheap beer all night. He looks at me like I'm crazy, like what else would we be doing here. It was his choice, this holiday, he'd bought and booked it before he even consulted me. It was the first time he'd done something like this and I was surprised, sure, and a little excited that he would do such a thing. He said he'd come into some money and had been dying to travel here since he was a little boy.

And, of course, I believed him. You're getting used to this, right? You think I should have known better?

At night we sit in the old quarter, under candlelight and mosquito buzz, in one of the identical bars that line the tourist area. He finds it easy to talk to people, to strike up conversations with total strangers and within five minutes they find they have something impossibly obscure in common. That's what he's like. It's not at all what I'm like but I pretend, for him, I do. I laugh when someone says something resembling a joke. I stare wide-eyed and drop-jawed at their tedious tales of near-death experiences and remarkable survivals. I drink the strange clear alcohol as it's poured into my glass and I get the round when it's my turn.

But I hate them. I stare at their crooked teeth as they tell me about the time they climbed K2 and had to deal with a kidney stone at twenty-six thousand feet. I watch their eyes as they gush about the ranges in Patagonia or the starving children of Africa and how their lives were fulfilled when they gave their first mouthful of food to a ten-year-old on the verge of death in the upper Gabon.

I hate them because I know who they are. I hate them because I am one of them.

At night you'd see them in the rundown bars on the edge of town. Drunk Germans sitting over steins of beer bigger than their heads as they go through their equipment, item by item, for the fourth time, making sure everything's packed for tomorrow's trek. Dead-eyed boys with blond dreadlocks and less than an eighth of their brain matter left, selling pills and talking about how this used to be a great town before all the tourists came. The history freaks with their Thermoses and pinched expressions, clipped beards and rebel neckscarves. The way they look at us. The way they turn to each other and mutter comments and point and aren't in the least bit ashamed of it.

I tell him I'm leaving town first thing in the morning. He can come with me or he can stay here. He throws a fit and hits the streets and comes back two hours later, apologetic, reeking of booze and easy women, saying he's sorry and that tomorrow we can start properly.

By then I don't care. By then fourteen cockroaches, or forty, or four hundred, have crawled across my legs and face as I lie back in bed and try to will sleep and then give up and ask him for some of his Valiums and chew them, the bitter chalky taste delicious, and chase it down with some tapwater which will probably make me sick but that's all there is in this room and, anyway, by then, as I said, I'm past caring.

We catch a bus out of town and leave in a haze of dust and chickens, the gaudy streets quickly fading behind us as we begin to climb a steep escarpment carved into the mountainside. The bus is beyond hot and the windows are jammed and there are all kinds of animals – dogs and pigs and pigeons and God knows what else – and everyone is sitting on each other's lap every time the driver hits a switchback and I am sick into my bag within ten minutes. He looks at me, pats my shoulder and goes back to his zoned-out state. I wish I could be like that but instead I'm the crying puking white woman who can't even take a damn bus ride let alone what these people have to endure for every day of their lives in this place, and wasn't that why I came here anyway?

4

The landscape rescues me. The blue steely peaks in the distance. The jagged precipices of black rock and broken teeth. This track, barely wide enough for the bus, curling and swirling around the side of the mountain like jewellery. Soon, there is nothing but rock and sky and thin wisps of straggly cloud. The temperature in the bus begins to cool and people are asleep, their heads rolling and nodding on their neighbours' shoulders, and he too is asleep and I want to scream and shake him awake and tell him look what you're missing! Look at how beautiful it all is! But I know that, even if I did, he would just take one brief perfunctory glance and mumble something and be back asleep within a couple of minutes.

So I look at the swooping landscape as it falls away beneath the wheels of the bus and it feels as if I'm the only passenger left, ascending into the sky, just me and the driver so far in front that I can't tell what colour his hair is or even if he has any.

He wakes up and says *are we there yet?* It is night and all around is a rushing blackness lit only by the smear of stars and whirled galaxies above. Soon, I say, and do not know why I say this because I have no idea when we'll get to the village, the village that he so wanted to go to in the first place, no idea when we'll get there and no reason to placate him, yet I do, which is something I don't understand at this moment and don't care to.

Something in the air changes as we round the rim of the mountain and drive through a high desolate plateau. The smell comes first. Sulphurous and hot, instantly filling the bus, everyone coughing or tying handkerchiefs around their mouths and noses. I press my face to my sleeve and look out the window but there's only the grudging slice of sky and the flat endless plain ahead. Eventually, the smell

5

decreases, or maybe we've just got used to it, and the night lulls me into broken haunted sleep and the next thing I know he's shaking me awake and grabbing my sleeve.

We get off at what I presume is the bus station but there is nothing to mark it as such. He tells me the village is fifteen minutes' walk over the next ridge. There's a wide animal track that winds through the rocky ground and we start walking, our rucksacks poking into kidneys and livers and backs, mouths cracked from too little water and the way this land can suck all the moisture from your body in two hours flat.

It's more like forty minutes but we finally reach the top of the ridge and stop to get our breath back. The village lies below us at the bottom of a ravine. There are no lights on in the houses and no movement discernible from where we stand. I look at him but can't tell if he's disappointed or if this is what he expected. He takes a torch out of his backpack and I carefully follow him down the scree slope, just wanting to get into my sleeping bag now, not caring where, just tired and sick and hungry and pissed off.

We come to the entrance to the village, just a couple of splintered stakes plunged into the stony soil. He's calling out in broken Spanish but there's no reply, no sound at all apart from the wind susurrating through the peaks. I begin to laugh – his awful Spanish accent, the long hours and dehydration, this whole situation.

I see him go into one of the houses. He's in there barely a minute and comes straight out and his body is folded in on itself like he's trying to hide from the sky. There's nothing there, he says, but a muscle twitch below his left eye gives him away. It's the first time I've seen him show this kind of concern towards me and this scares me more than anything else.

He points to a far rise and says we can camp there, it'll shield us from the weather at least, and I'm too tired to argue, don't want to sleep here anyway, that eerie sound the wind makes, the crunch of our feet on the pebbled ground, the pale dead sky.

We round a small hill and that's when we first see it.

Two dead trees, three hundred yards away, hidden in the shadow of a narrow defile. He's standing next to me, breathing heavily, saying *shit shit shit* over and over again. I strain my eyes, all fuzz and sleep-dragged, and try to focus.

At first I don't see anything wrong. At first I think it's just a particularity of the tree or the light or the long bumpy hours rushing through my veins. But then I look at the other tree, a few feet away, and see that it is the same.

A slim black-haired woman is hanging from the branches of the first tree, her eyes staring down at the ground and she is spinning slowly in the breeze as if she were an unwilling participant in some lost childhood game. The second tree is smaller, its branches more slender, but they are barely bent at all by the weight of the child hanging from them.

I

'London is a world by itself. We daily discover in it more new countries, and surprising singularities, than in all the universe besides.'

Tom Brown (1702)

'Who are you?' the old woman said, pushing his hand away, her eyes wrinkled in confusion. She looked up at the nurse. 'Who is this man? Why did you bring him here?' Her voice was thin and wheezy and she lay swaddled in bedding, her skin as rumpled and folded as the blankets covering her. A single tear fell from her left eye and when Carrigan reached over to wipe it away the old woman flinched, shrinking back and pulling the sheets up over her head.

'It's okay,' the nurse said, and it took Carrigan a moment to realise she was addressing him and not the old woman. 'Probably better if you don't crowd her, she's very upset at the moment.'

He took a step back and then another. He listened to the machines that surrounded the bed beeping away, a slow rhythmic pulse that mimicked a heartbeat. He could hear relatives weeping in the room next door, the anguished cries and stifled sobs of other people's grief.

'Keep him away from me. Keep him away . . .' the old woman kept repeating in a dry rasp, her bony fingers clutching the bedposts. 'I know why he's here. I know what he wants to do to me.'

Carrigan stepped back as the nurse tried to calm her with soft reassurances. She gently loosened the old woman's fingers from the bedposts and patted her head as if she were a newborn. The heat in the room was overwhelming, the windows barred, the radiators turned up high. The phone in his pocket was vibrating but he ignored it.

'I'm sorry you had to see her like this,' the nurse smiled awkwardly, exposing teeth straight and white, the faintest hint of gum. Her black hair caught the light and, for a brief moment, she reminded him of someone else and years ago.

He approached the bed cautiously, studying the old woman. How she'd changed. It was almost as if he were the one incapable of recognising her rather than the other way around. She seemed unravelled and trapped, lost in runaway memories, bone-pain and boredom; all the things that eventually catch up to you. He leaned over the bed and whispered in her ear.

She blinked twice and it was like she'd suddenly awoken from a deep and vivid dream. 'Why didn't you bring Louise?' she said, grabbing his wrist.

Carrigan tried to extricate his arm from her grip but it was surprisingly strong. He could feel the sharp drag of her nails against his skin, the press of flesh he knew so well, the simple entreaty communicated by this familiar gesture. These were the worst moments, when lucidity peeked through the fog of drugs and dying brain cells, when she remembered briefly who she was and who she'd been.

'Loui—' The words died in his throat and he leaned over and squeezed his mother's hand. 'She's at home with the kids. I'll tell her you asked after her.'

'Why doesn't she come to visit me any more?' his mother asked, and Carrigan had to turn away, not knowing what he could say or quite how to say it.

They stood outside the door to his mother's room, the nurse apologising for the old woman's behaviour, Carrigan nodding and shrugging, barely taking any of it in. His phone kept buzzing but it was his day off and he wasn't going to answer it. There were four messages from his superior, DSI Branch, three from Geneva, and several unidentified numbers. Whatever it was, he didn't want to know.

'Unfortunately, we see this quite often,' the nurse said, interrupting his thoughts. 'They start imagining things, almost always bad things. It's as if all the darkness they've successfully suppressed throughout their lives suddenly finds a way out.'

He turned towards her and shrugged and said, 'The brain can be a wonderful thing.'

The nurse gave him a strained smile and he could see that under the patina of back-to-back shifts and bedside dramas there was something beguiling about her face, some slight flaw in symmetry. 'She thought the attendants were sexually assaulting her. She tried to escape and fell from the bed. It's lucky she only broke her hip.'

He nodded because there was nothing to say to this, no easy answer that would make sense of why his mother's final years should be a drawn-out agony of fear and forgetting. She'd been in the nursing home four years now and it had been the most difficult decision he'd ever had to make. But, lately, she'd been getting worse – the broken hip was only the most recent in a long line of ailments and minor injuries, each taking her one step further away from the woman he remembered.

'She keeps asking for Louise, though,' the nurse continued. 'That's a good sign – a sign that some part of her is still interacting with the real world.'

He looked down at the cracked linoleum patterned with shoe scuffs and the snaky smears of trolley wheels. 'Louise was my wife. She passed away three years ago.'

The nurse gently placed her hand on his arm. 'I didn't realise.'

He could feel the heat of her body filling the cold spaces inside him and he shivered involuntarily and took a step back, glad that the nurse didn't try to console him with platitudes or empty phrases meant to make him feel better. He looked into her stark black eyes and saw storms and rages and everything she'd ever tried to forget, and he held her stare until they both looked away, slightly embarrassed.

'Thank you for taking care of her.'

'It's what I do,' she replied, her smile tempered by what had passed between them. 'My name's Karen . . . if you ever need anything . . .'

He reached out and shook her hand, feeling the warm blanketing of her palm against his cold flesh. 'Jack Carrigan.'

*

The phone in his pocket kept buzzing but he didn't want to look at it, let alone answer it. The walls were peppered with signs telling visitors to turn off their mobiles and he cursed himself for not having done so when he got here. His mother had been transferred from the nursing home to the hospital in the early hours of the morning and he felt lost and confused in these blank tunnelled spaces. He walked past rooms screened off where he heard relatives talking, arguing, sobbing behind blue curtains. Orderlies brushed past him pushing shrunken figures drowning in their wheelchairs. Wall-mounted TVs scrolled silent scenes of dusty revolution, earthquake and endless war. He looked in vain for the exit but the colour-coded signs only pointed towards the gloom of radiology units, oncology departments and the recurrent miscarriage clinic. All he wanted to do was get out of there and sink several espressos somewhere dark and empty where his thoughts wouldn't be crowded by the noise of other people's lives. He turned into another corridor identical to the one he'd just left. A wave of dizziness overtook him and he had to stop and steady himself against the wall. He took several deep breaths. The smell of fresh raisin cake filled his nostrils and he looked around, unsettled, but he could not see its source.

And then he remembered. An autumn day, the sun arcing through the windows of the house, splashing the kitchen with golden spray, each dust mote suddenly visible. His mother standing beside him, putting the last touches on his school uniform, and the smell of raisin bread as it cooked in the oven. The way you could almost taste certain smells, and the rough warm feel of her fingers as she pushed a stray lick of hair from his forehead. And, God, how she'd laughed, one of the only times he ever remembered her laughing, as he sank to his knees and knelt in front of the oven as if before some strange altar, his eyes glued to the miracles occurring within.

He tried to shut down the flashing rush of images, to focus on the next few moments, the next few hours, the slow sipped coffee the minute he got out of there, the double bill at his local cinema tonight, but it was no use.

He started back down the winding corridor, wondering if he would ever find his way out, when he turned a corner and saw the main exit, a group of people lined up in front of the admissions desk, doctors, nurses and the harried relatives of patients, and then he glanced to the front of the queue and saw Geneva arguing with the duty nurse, earplugs dangling from her neck and a can of Coke in her hand.

'I tried calling you. Several times.' She stepped away from the desk and he saw something in her expression and knew this wasn't going to be good.

'My day off,' he replied, annoyed but, he had to admit, also a little intrigued by what would bring her here. He was about to ask when he felt someone's hand alighting on the back of his jacket and his name being called. He turned round to see Karen detaching herself from a group of nurses clustered around the drinks machine.

They looked at each other mutely, a couple of feet apart, and Carrigan thought it felt like holding your breath.

'Lucky I caught you,' Karen said, breaking the silence, reaching into her jacket and pulling out a small white business card. 'I forgot to give you this.' She looked at it once then handed it to him. 'She'll probably be here a couple of weeks. If there's anything you want to discuss, just give me a call.'

He took the card and, without reading it, put it in his pocket. 'Thank you.'

She placed her hand on his shoulder. 'Don't worry. It gets better, you just have to—'

'I hate to interrupt.' Geneva stepped into the space between Carrigan and the nurse. She stared at Karen, her eyes flat and cold. 'But we really have to go.'

'Of course you do,' Karen replied softly, her shoulders dropping as she turned and melted back into the swirling crowd of giddy nurses.

'What the hell was that all about?' Carrigan snapped the seatbelt into its holder, catching the skin between thumb and forefinger, and cursed under his breath.

'Something's come up,' Geneva replied as she swung the car out of the parking space, through the main gate and back into the rush and glare of the city.

He nodded impatiently and stared up at the bleached sky, realising that while he'd been inside the hospital it had started to snow. Small white clumps fell lazily, spinning and dancing against the streetlights as the radio crackled news about a shooting in Peckham, a multiple vehicle collision on the M4, a rape in Richmond. 'How the hell did you know where to find me?'

'You told me.' Geneva almost hit a cyclist, swore and turned up the radio. 'Don't you remember?'

He couldn't but he nodded anyway, not wanting an argument, noticing how she'd closed herself down as soon as they'd entered the car. 'When did the snow start?'

'About an hour ago.' She took the Westway and they glided above the city, shrugging off the pink and brown houses, the dark wet streets and streaked parade of blurry lights. The sky turned steely and white as the snow bounced and starred on the windshield. 'Who was that you were talking to?' Geneva asked, her eyes squinted on the road ahead. 'She seemed very pretty . . .'

'It's nothing.'

'Were you visiting someone you know?'

'What the hell does it matter? Why am I even here?' He leaned forward and felt the seatbelt bite into his shoulder as Geneva pumped the brakes and swerved behind a lorry.

'Don't shout at me. Please. I'm trying to drive. This wasn't my decision.'

He took a deep breath, looked down, saw the coffee she'd bought for him going cold in the drinks holder. 'Sorry . . . Christ . . . it's been a long day.'

'It's going to get longer, I'm afraid,' she said, and this time he thought he could detect a note of sympathy in her tone. She reached for her lighter, the car starting to swerve across lanes. He took the cigarette from her mouth and lit it, the sudden taste unleashing a deluge of memories, then passed it back to her.

'Branch came to see me.' She took several quick drags, screwed up her face and threw the rest out the window. 'Wasn't happy.'

'What's so damn important he has to ruin my day off?'

She looked at him for the first time since they'd got into the car, her lips pressed tightly together. 'I don't know. He just told me to get you. He gave me an address, said there's been a fire.'

'A fire?' Carrigan shook his head, wondering if this was another of the super's increasingly irritating attempts at winding him up. Branch had never liked him and, after the events of last autumn, he no longer even bothered to hide it, sending Carrigan on wild-goose chases and waste-of-time inquiries whenever he could get away with it. 'Jesus, why us? We're not the bloody fire service.'

Geneva stared at the road ahead and said nothing; a year now they'd been working together and she was just learning to read his moods, knowing that when he got like this it was better to keep quiet and let him burn himself out. Being partners on the job was a lot like marriage in that respect, she thought, and then wished she hadn't, as the memory of Oliver, her ex-husband, came rising up out of the dark.

They descended from the flyover and splashed back into the city and suddenly it was all around them – the shuffle and hum of people, eleven days before Christmas, trying to get their shopping done, chatting and smoking outside pubs, kissing goodbye on street corners and staring up in wonder at the ghostly discs of falling snow.

But inside the car there was only silence. Carrigan closed his eyes, a headache beginning to spread across his skull, and took three deep breaths, his nostrils suddenly puckering. His eyes snapped open. He sniffed the air and checked the back seat.

'I hope that's not your cigarette.'

He'd meant it as a joke but somehow it hadn't come out like that at all. Geneva didn't answer but she rolled up her window and he knew that she'd smelled it too.

They turned off Queensway and into a narrow residential street, parked cars and spindly trees bordering them on both sides. The smell was stronger now, more acrid, and the day had begun to darken rapidly as if a curtain had been pulled across the sky.

Geneva stopped the car and they both sat there in silence. Through the murk of twisting smoke and smeary haze, they could see a sky lit up in orange and red streaks.

Carrigan stared up, entranced, everything else forgotten for the moment, and it took him a few seconds to realise that something was wrong.

He blinked but it didn't change a thing. He opened the car door and looked up at the sky unable to believe his own eyes.

Black snow was falling on the streets of Bayswater.

2

A thick column of smoke rose above the tall houses of St Peter's Square. The far end of the street was blocked by two fire engines, a police patrol vehicle and a gathering crowd.

'It's like bloody Bonfire Night,' Carrigan grumbled as Geneva parked the car on a double yellow line outside the Greek Orthodox cathedral. The black snow was coming down heavy and thick and it was getting hard to see, the lights of the fire engines and patrol vehicles streaked and smeared against the dizzy profusion of snow.

Carrigan was unprepared for the sheer noise of the fire, the crackle and roar filling his ears as they made their way down into the square, past the fire service barricades and the silent trellised homes whose residents were crowded on narrow balconies, their heads craned towards the raging spectacle, eyes wide in mute astonishment.

Carrigan searched for the uniforms but there were so many people, all moving fast, that it was hard to get a sense of the scene. Fire engines edged towards the burning building, their ladders projecting into the night, hoses unfurling, the firemen wiping sweat from their brows and conferring among themselves. A small group of onlookers had managed to get past the initial cordon and were staring up, hypnotised, while others held phones above their heads as if in supplication, pushing one another aside for the best view. And yet, above all this, there was a sense of quiet celebration, of expectancy, perhaps the hope for a sprinkle of seasonal magic to light up everyday life.

'Christ, it's a fucking circus,' Carrigan said, approaching the fire command unit. Geneva tugged his sleeve and pointed out three uniforms, standing and watching the blaze, as transfixed as the public. From somewhere, maybe the next road along, they heard the ghostly voices of carol singers getting louder and then diminishing as the wind changed direction.

'Who's in charge here?'

The uniforms turned to see Carrigan standing behind them. They quickly adjusted their postures and looked at the floor. 'Forget it,' Carrigan said. 'We need to set up a perimeter, did no one think of that?'

The three looked at each other as if they'd been caught smoking by a teacher.

Carrigan ordered them to start clearing the area of onlookers and residents. He stared up at the large detached house, now totally engulfed in flames, yellow and red and blue, silently praying that the occupants had been shopping when the fire broke out. If the house had been empty it would mean he could hand the case over to another team. 'Happy Christmas!' he told the constables, and headed towards the main fire truck.

He talked to the driver then stood and waited for the fire marshal to emerge from the burning building. They were at the narrow end of one of the elegant garden squares that Notting Hill and Bayswater were so famous for. The houses were tall and white; imposing and austere as Roman temples with their profusion of fluted columns and ornate pedestals. The burning building was two from the end. It was covered in a shawl of flame, the wind whipping it into scattering phantoms and flickering patterns. Black smoke poured into the sky. Residents from the adjacent premises were leaving in a panic, families with bulging backpacks and bewildered looks on their faces, their evening meal suddenly turned into life and death.

Carrigan saw the firemen spraying water from thick grey hoses which kept kicking and bucking in their hands. The snow kept coming down. The crime scene was being destroyed as he watched and there was nothing he could do about it.

He finally saw the fire marshal emerge from the black smoke, covered in soot and dust, his eyes tearing from the fumes, his body crumpling with each sustained burst of coughing.

Carrigan flashed his warrant card and the marshal stopped, took out a handkerchief and wiped his face, leaving it streaked like a soldier on night patrol. Behind them, Geneva was helping the uniforms set up a perimeter, the crime-scene tape screeching and mewling like a hungry infant as it was stretched across the road. Carrigan turned to the marshal. 'Any idea what we're looking at?'

'One hell of an insurance claim,' the man replied, and when Carrigan gave him a dark look, he laughed. 'Just kidding.' His name-tag said Weir above the left pocket and he was short and squat. 'It looks like the fire's been going for at least an hour. We'll be lucky if we can save anything.'

Carrigan wrinkled his nostrils at the smell, an acidic reek of burning plastic and wood that settled at the back of his throat. 'Is it safe to go inside?'

Weir shook his head. 'Too dangerous, these houses, too much wood, everything's collapsing.' On cue, a tremendous crack split the air and a burning beam sheared off from the front of the house and landed in the garden, exploding in a shower of sparks. Carrigan felt flashes of heat and light behind him and turned to see a news van parking alongside, two cameramen already out and snapping photos. 'Christ!'

The fire marshal grimaced. 'Made their day, this has.'

Carrigan liked the man's understated cynicism and was glad he was in charge. He was about to ask him something else when a muffled cry turned them both in the direction of the burning house.

Initially, Carrigan could see only smoke and fire, and then he made out the faint outline of a couple of bodies emerging from the darkness. At first, he thought these were survivors but then, as the smoke cleared, he recognised their yellow helmets and dark dusty jackets.

He followed Weir across the street. They reached the edge of the garden and the heat was terrible, unlike anything he'd ever felt before. The firemen emerging from the smoke were carrying something and, as he got closer, he could see that it was one of their own, blackened by soot and convulsing as if in the throes of an epileptic fit. The marshal immediately called the paramedics stationed nearby. Carrigan could tell that the injured man was on the verge of slipping away, his face red and blotchy, the skin already pulsating, his eyes rolling white into their sockets.

Weir spoke to the fallen man, held his hand and squeezed it gently, then stood up. 'Jesus...' he said, wiping his brow. 'He's been in the house. He's been upstairs. You better listen to him.'

Carrigan knelt down, feeling the sweat and heat engulf him, and he could only just make out the man's voice above the roar of the flames.

'What? What did you say?'

The injured fireman tried to repeat what he'd said but he broke into a fit of coughing, vomiting a thin yellow stream of bile onto the pavement beneath him. 'There's ...' his voice wheezed and stuttered and broke, 'upstairs... body... bod...'

Carrigan leaned closer until he could smell the man's burned flesh, dark and funky and familiar in his nostrils. 'There's a body up there?'

The fireman shook his head and even that small movement seemed to cause him incalculable pain, his eyes turning small and pale. 'Mm... mm... more than one.'

'How many?'

The fireman started convulsing again, his teeth cracking loudly against one another.

'All over the place ...' he coughed and spluttered and retched. 'Everywhere... there's fucking bodies everywhere.'

3

Ambulance sirens now added to the general noise and chaos. The fire continued burning, the wood cracking and breaking, the sizzle and hiss of water hitting flame filling the night like the beating wings of a thousand butterflies.

'I need to get inside,' Carrigan said, sweat dripping into his eyes.

The fire marshal was signalling his men, pointing out areas of the blaze they weren't covering. He was talking on the radio, his voice low and deep as he recounted the situation, his eyes fixed on his fallen colleague being stretchered into a waiting ambulance. He put down the handset, took off his gloves and pulled a packet of chewing gum from his pocket. 'Want one?'

Carrigan shook his head. 'When can we go in?' He was impatient now, wanting to see what was waiting for them in there, what they would have to deal with over the coming days.

'Not for a couple of hours at least,' Weir replied. 'Not unless you want to end up like him.' Carrigan followed his eyes towards the stretchered figure, groaning and gasping in pain as they raised him onto the ambulance bed.

'I need to get in there,' he repeated. 'I need to see what we're dealing with.'

Weir nodded. 'We don't get this under control in the next hour, all you'll be dealing with is ashes and dust.'

Carrigan found Geneva helping the uniforms extend the cordon. The public were swaying and cramming against the blue-and-white crime-scene tape, their mobile cameras held aloft, shopping bags discarded for the moment as they posed in front of the burning building. He pointed to a small cleared space and led her away from the noise and press of the crowd. He kept having to wipe sweat from his face and he was tired and hungry and pissed off he'd missed his movie. Geneva called for more back-up as Carrigan rounded up the uniforms.

'Stop looking at the fire,' he told the young constables, 'and start looking at the people looking at the fire.'

They stared at him, confused and disoriented. 'Start asking questions. Some of these gawpers might have seen someone running away from the scene, they might have been here when this started. They won't be here long. Once the fire's out, the entertainment's over, and they'll go back to their homes and we'll never know what they saw.' He stopped to wipe away more sweat popping on his forehead. 'Look for the usual, anyone who suddenly decides it's a good time to leave when you approach, anyone staring too hard . . . and pay close attention to people's hands when you're interviewing them.'

'Their hands?' a petite female constable asked. She didn't look old enough to get served in a bar.

Carrigan nodded. 'Look for anyone with soot or dust on their hands, but what I really want you to do is smell them.'

'Smell them?' This time it was all three uniforms who stared up at Carrigan as if a madman had taken over the case.

'Yes. The crowd are too far away to pick up the smell. Here . . .' He raised his arm and pulled on his sleeve. The cloth released its vapour and he watched with satisfaction as the uniforms wrinkled their noses. 'That's what you smell like if you've got too close to the fire. But, more importantly, look out for anyone who stinks of petrol.' He watched as the young female constable took notes. 'Do you have a video camera in the patrol car?' he asked her.

'We do.'

'Good. Go get it. I want you to circle the crowd and film them.

24

Do it several times so you get everyone.'

'Film them?' She stopped writing and looked up from her note-book.

'People who start fires like to watch them burn,' he replied, re-membering a course he'd attended on this very thing, several years back. 'They love to see their handiwork, it's what gets them off. Chances are whoever set the fire is standing in the crowd right now, watching it.'

'How do we know it's not accidental?' she asked.

'We don't, but if it's not then this is our only chance at this.'

The sound of crashing drums and squealing guitars burst through the night. Carrigan and Geneva looked up and saw a group of people standing on a balcony diagonally across from the burning house. They were passing around a bottle of champagne, smoking cigars and watching the fire with rapt expressions. 'Christ,' Carrigan muttered. 'Someone tell these jokers this isn't some bloody Christmas party.'

The uniforms nodded and avoided Carrigan's eyes. They chatted among themselves for a moment then spread out to tackle the crowd.

'You okay?'

He hadn't even realised she was still standing beside him. 'I can imagine better ways to spend my day off. Do you have any idea why Branch called us in?'

But Geneva wasn't paying attention. He saw her look past him, squint, then frown.

'You can ask him yourself,' she said, pointing over to the peri-meter and then quickly turning back. 'Oh my God, I hope that's not who I think it is with him.'

Carrigan brushed some of the dust off his jacket. It had mixed with the melting snow and now lay like an oil slick across his clothes and face. He straightened up as Branch approached but it was the other man he was watching.

'Assistant Chief Constable Quinn,' he said neutrally, as the pencil-thin figure next to Branch stepped forward. 'I'm surprised to see you here.'

Quinn came to a stop a foot away from Carrigan. He was a tall bony man, all angles and points, always neat and fastidious, with a whispery moustache perched on his upper lip, making him look more like a mournful pre-war bank clerk than the third most important man in the Met. 'And why is that?' Quinn's dry enunciation filled the air around them, crisp and hard as a whipcrack. 'Do you all imagine that I do nothing but sit behind a desk?'

Carrigan had never been able to read the man and couldn't tell if this was his attempt at humour or a rebuke. 'I just meant this is a fire, accidental for all we know. Why bring my team into this?'

Quinn sucked the insides of his cheeks, his eyes probing Carrigan's as if searching for some obscure meaning behind the words. 'I happen to live on this street,' he said, pointing behind him. 'I heard the fire engines, looked out and saw where it was. I called DSI Branch immediately.'

Carrigan was certain he'd missed something. He glanced over at the burning house then back at Quinn. 'Where *what* was?'

'The fire, young man, the fire,' Quinn replied tersely. 'Now, DI Carrigan, let's stop wasting time. What do we know?'

'Not much as of yet,' Carrigan admitted. 'Still too dangerous to go in, but one of the firemen reported seeing bodies.'

'Oh no,' Quinn said, cupping his forehead.

'What?' Carrigan saw the ACC's face sag and blanch, saw Branch shaking his head. 'What is that house?'

'It's a convent.' Quinn looked up and Carrigan noticed the rings circling his eyes, the drawn and puckered skin, late nights, smoke and booze, a lifetime of bodies and blood.

'A what?' He wasn't sure he'd heard right.

'Nuns, DI Carrigan, nuns lived there.'

'Oh shit.'

'Yes, quite,' the ACC said. 'I want you on this, Carrigan. I asked Branch specifically. The work you did last year, that dreadful child soldier thing, earned us some good points with the public. I want you in charge.'

'Sir, I think we should wait and see what the fire investigator finds . . . it's just as likely this was an accident.'

Quinn seemed to be weighing this up. 'Just as likely, yes, you could say that. But how would we look if this turned out to be intentional and we were caught behind the curve on it?' He pointed to the two white vans. 'The press are already here, Carrigan. The press are already asking questions.'

Carrigan nodded, noting that Branch hadn't said a word during the entire conversation. 'Do you know how many nuns lived there?'

Quinn turned to Branch and smiled for the first time, his lips sticking defiantly together. 'See, Jason, that's why I want him on board, already asking the right questions.' Branch's eyes turned small and fierce as Quinn addressed Carrigan. 'Ten, Detective Inspector, ten nuns lived there. My wife occasionally helped them. She's very upset, as you can imagine.' Quinn's eyes suddenly narrowed. He looked up as a blast of reggae made its way from the balcony across the road. 'What in God's name are those people doing?'

'Someone's on their way over.'

Quinn nodded curtly, conferred with Branch, then brushed some of the black snow off his suit and disappeared back into the smoky night.

'Not my decision.' Branch was sweating heavily, his face blotchy and crimson.

'Didn't think it was,' Carrigan said.

Carrigan watched the fire being extinguished. An hour passed and then the fire marshal approached him.

'You ready?' he said.

Carrigan nodded and followed Weir past the cameramen setting up their tripods, the reporters practising their lines, the sound of triggered car alarms and distant guitars wailing.

'How bad is it?' Carrigan asked as they went through the gate.

The marshal looked up at the blackened shell of the house and shook his head. 'Bad,' he said. 'Really bad.'

4

The smell was overwhelming. It was like nothing he'd experienced before; not the reek of decomposed corpses in dark basements, nor the salty tang of freshly spilled blood, but something almost physical.

'Careful,' Weir warned as they made their way through the front garden. 'They'll burn a hole right through your shoe.' He pointed to the smouldering pieces of wood spitting and hissing on the path, but Carrigan's eyes were drawn to the sky. 'What's with the black snow?'

'It's that way because of the fire,' Weir explained. 'Soaks up all the ash and dust on its way down.'

'Nice,' Carrigan replied, adjusting his safety hat and turning back towards the convent.

The main structure was no longer burning, the firemen retreating their ladders and hoses, the top of the building covered in clouds of billowing steam as water cascaded from the gutters and eaves. The air was filled with bursts of cracking and popping, loud groans and moans coming from the wood as it contracted violently against the cold water, making the house seem as if it were alive and extremely disgruntled.

They could see into the building as if it were a doll's house in some little girl's bedroom or one of those models that architects use to pitch new designs. But there was nothing new here, only staircases that led into empty space, door frames gaping like open mouths, windows blown through, the glass twisted and melted and reconfigured into nightmarish shapes.

'It's still unstable, so we can't spend too long.' Weir was chewing gum, his lips smacking against each other. Snow had collected on his hat and clothes. 'The fire investigator will go through it tomorrow morning and you should have his report by the afternoon.' He stopped and turned towards Carrigan. 'Very unusual for you guys to get here so soon.'

'Tell me about it,' Carrigan said, thinking about his encounter with the ACC – he knew that Quinn's presence meant it would be one of those cases, the kind he dreaded the most.

'We're lucky we got here ourselves when we did,' Weir said, leading him into the reception hall, but Carrigan wasn't listening. He stopped, turned back and inspected the entrance.

'What?'

Carrigan pointed to the doorframe. The wood had been badly burned but the slim metal locks were still in place. Carrigan used the sleeve of his jacket to brush away some of the soot. There were four mortise locks spread evenly along the doorframe's length, three Chubbs, and the housing for two heavy-duty bolts.

'A lot of locks,' Weir said, a low whistle escaping his lips.

'Yes,' Carrigan replied. 'Especially for a convent.'

The marshal nodded sombrely and turned back into the reception hall. The outside wall had collapsed and brought down a portion of the roof, exposing a rectangle of sky through which the snow drifted slowly down. A staircase rose steeply to their left. Carrigan followed Weir past the melting bubbling plastic, half burnt umbrellas and empty coat-stands, their metal hooks steaming in the dark.

'Can you tell if this was arson?'

Weir started to say that he wasn't an investigator but Carrigan wanted to know his first impressions and told him to continue.

'I got a good look at the flames before we went in.' He passed through a small corridor, now exposed to the night. 'You know about flame and colour spectrums, right?'

Carrigan didn't but nodded anyway, his throat dry and scratchy from the soot and dust.

'Basically, we can tell what kind of fire it is from the colour of the flame. Different materials burn with different heat signatures. Blue flames are nearly always an indicator of accelerants, which often means the fire was intentional. I didn't see any of that here. The fire burned mainly red with some yellow and only sporadic flashes of blue. It looks like no accelerants were used and the seat of fire appears to be singular rather than multiple, which is what we would expect to see in cases of arson. Then again, I'm only guessing. We'll know much more when the investigator's done.'

Carrigan stared at the ruined house, trying to visualise what it must have looked like before the fire, how the corridors and rooms connected and what their functions had been. 'Do you know if the bodies are all grouped together?'

The marshal thought for a moment and nodded. 'We haven't been in the basement yet, but the ones we found upstairs were all in the same room.'

Carrigan filed this bit of information away. He knew it could mean any number of things but it would help them reconstruct the series of events which had led to the fire. 'Where?'

Weir pointed directly above and they climbed the stairs and turned right on the first-floor landing. At the far end was an empty doorframe revealing a room shrouded in smoke and haze. As he entered, Carrigan saw a set of dark smudges aligned across the floor. 'How many?'

The marshal checked something on one of his instruments then stepped through the doorframe. 'We haven't managed to count them yet.'

The smell in this room was different. Still the acrid tang of burnt wood, the acidic reek of melted plastic, but also something else. Carrigan tried breathing through his mouth but then he could taste it and that was worse. It really did smell like barbecue and that was what made it so horrible, this close relation to pleasure, the way the tongue could not distinguish between the two, and he tried not to think about what he was actually breathing in.

'This room took some of the worst damage,' Weir said. 'The fire started in the chapel directly below, so it burned for a long time before we could get to it.'

They both coughed and spluttered and Weir took a small collapsible fan from his belt and set it down. As the smoke dissipated, the dark blotches on the floor began to take shape.

They were evenly spread out in two rows. They looked like small children, the black and brown skin snagged tight against the bones, the arms and legs curled into each other in a foetal boxer's position. It made them appear as if they'd died fighting, struggling desperately against the confines of their own skins.

Carrigan leaned down next to the nearest body, the small shrivelled form giving off steam as the eyes still bubbled in their sockets. He got up, nauseated and dizzy, and started to count.

They were arranged in an almost geometrical pattern around a humped mass of grey ash situated in the centre of the room. They were all reposing in virtually identical positions. It didn't seem like any of them had tried to escape – there was none of the scatter pattern you normally saw in a fire, the panic and fear driving the victims to try all available exits and windows – no, this looked like they'd sat and waited for the fire to consume them. Or maybe they hadn't been able to move, Carrigan thought, and made a note to ask the pathologist about that. He studied the mound of ashes in the centre and saw the silver glint of cutlery, broken china, a scattering of small black stones, the metal edges of chair supports, and knew they'd died where they'd sat, around the dinner table, gathered for their last supper.

He blinked the image away and counted again.

Just as Quinn had said. Ten bodies. The fire had got them all.

A beam cracked above him, showering dust and sparks down on his jacket. He stood up and made his way towards the stained-glass window high on the west wall. There was no way anyone could have reached it, let alone used it to escape.

He walked past Weir without saying a word and stopped and looked down at the remains of the door, using his foot to sift through the debris. Most of the wood was gone, only splinters and slivers remaining, skinny as fingers. He leaned down and picked up a darkened doorknob, still brassy under the layers of soot. He looked at it for a moment then put it down. He used his hand to sift through the rest of the ash and stopped when he felt the warm touch of metal. He reached over and picked up the object and examined it.

'You still think this was an accident?' He handed the fireman the dull disfigured lock that had once been part of the door. Weir took it and held it in his hands, turning it over several times as if confused of its function. The cylinder was engaged and the two pieces, lock and housing, were embraced in an unbreakable kiss.

'The door was locked . . .' Weir said, and then his radio crackled, making them both jump. The fireman spoke into it in short staccato bursts. He clicked off and looked up at Carrigan, his face puzzled and strange.

'What is it?'

'I'm not quite sure how to explain it,' Weir replied. 'You better come downstairs and have a look.'

The size of the chapel surprised him. The fact of it lurking invisibly in this nondescript house. Smoke obscured the far edges, the nave, altar and rood screen. Firemen were rushing around putting out small blazes erupting in corners and niches. Weir spoke to one of his colleagues, nodding rapidly, then turned towards Carrigan.

'They heard something moving in there.' He pointed to a line of confession booths against the far wall, their metal frames hissing sibilantly.

'They heard something?'

Weir nodded. 'Yes. A thump.'

Carrigan looked in the direction of the booths. There were three of them, now reduced to skeleton remains of metal and charred timber. He stood and listened but there was only the crackling of the rapidly cooling wood, the hiss and sputter of dead fires. The firemen had stopped what they were doing and were all gathered around him. He took a step forward and carefully opened the door to the first booth. A pocket of trapped smoke burst out, momentarily blinding him. He went over to the second booth and tried the door but it was locked.

'Anyone got a penknife?'

Weir passed a small folding knife over to him and Carrigan carefully ran it through the gap between door and frame, unlatching the lock. He turned and handed the knife back to Weir. He pulled the handle but the lock snagged and caught and the door jammed. Carrigan was about to give it another yank when something moved inside the confession booth, thudding against the door.

The sudden weight and pressure made Carrigan jump back. They all watched the door of the second confession booth with held breath and unblinking eyes but there was no further sound nor movement. Carrigan took a step forward and gripped the handle so tightly that he could feel his own pulse throbbing through his fingers as he waited for whatever it was behind the door to move again. He could hear Weir talking behind him but not what he said. He could feel the pressing weight against the door and he gently turned the handle and gave it a sharp pull. The jammed lock broke and the door swung open.

It came tumbling out with a breath of charred meat and bitter smoke and landed hot and wet in his arms. The smell instantly filled his mouth and nostrils. He stumbled back but the body clung to him fiercely, the weight not much more than that of a small child's.

He resisted the urge to rip his hands free and slowly got to his knees and lowered it onto the floor. He got up and quickly wiped his hands on his trousers. He felt like he was going to be sick, his forehead blazing and stomach churning as he forced himself to focus on the twisted remains lying at his feet, a slippery figure curled in on itself like a broken question mark.

He'd missed his morning coffee. As he sipped his glass of water, he looked out at the sea of faces gathered in the main room of the CID building. Flashbulbs popped and stuttered, making him squint and blink, as reporters found their seats for the morning's press conference.

It was the worst possible way to begin a case. Carrigan had wanted to start the day with an initial briefing to his team but Branch had been waiting for him in the incident room. The press conference had been set up last night on ACC Quinn's express orders. Quinn now sat to his right on the podium, the Met logo draped behind him, Branch flanking Carrigan's other side.

Carrigan took another sip of water, feeling everyone's eyes on him. His head raged with pain, his stomach flip-flopping like a rollercoaster. He hadn't got drunk for a long time but he'd got drunk last night. In the living room, in his favourite armchair, watching the cars outside his window ignite the darkness. He'd fallen asleep and dreamed of his mother trapped in a burning church, strapped to her bed, slowly disappearing into herself and into time, and woken up dishevelled and dream-haunted and itching to get back to work. Sometimes he thought the job, the obsessiveness it required, the long hours and bad dreams, was a way for him to avoid the complicated process of actually living a life. Other times he knew it was so.

He cleared his throat, stood up, waited for the cameras to find their focal point and began. 'At around six o'clock last night, a house in St Peter's Square caught fire. The fire brigade were despatched to the scene and managed to bring the blaze under control before it could spread to any adjacent residences.' Flashbulbs popped and Carrigan raised his hand to shield his eyes. 'When the firemen deemed it safe to enter the premises they discovered several bodies. The building housed a convent used by a small group of nuns. We're appealing to anyone who might have seen anything unusual in the vicinity of 33 St Peter's Square yesterday evening to contact us.' Carrigan took his seat as cameras whirred and competed with the bray of questions from the gathered reporters.

'Is it possible that this was a ritual murder? Black magic?' a young woman from Sky News asked.

Carrigan tried to find her face among the bobbing heads. 'We're not yet certain that this was an intentional fire, so to make such far-flung speculations would be silly.'

The woman frowned and wrote something down in her notebook. Carrigan pointed to a reporter from the *Times* but before the man could get his question out, another voice, painfully familiar, rose from the pack.

'Is there any truth to the rumour that this was a terrorist act?'

Carrigan scanned the densely packed crowd of reporters till he found Khan. George Khan had been working at the *Standard* for almost as long as Carrigan had been in the Met. Everyone in the department knew of his reputation for sudden non sequiturs and subtle word traps and they'd all learned to avoid him if they could.

'You know as well as I do, George . . .' Carrigan glared at the overweight reporter, his suit crumpled and stained, a bottle of Lucozade in his hand and an unlit cigarette jumping between his fingers, 'that rumours such as that have no place in our investigation.' Carrigan suspected that Khan had in all likelihood made up the 'rumour' himself just to get a quote. 'There is absolutely no evidence of anything that could be construed as a terrorist act. This wasn't a bomb, this was a plain ordinary fire that went out of control. We will, of course, be consulting with the fire investigation team as to how it started but that's all to come. As of now we are treating the fire as suspicious but no more, and I certainly won't comment on what are mere rumours.'

He sat down and immediately felt the ACC's hand on his arm. He turned to see Quinn looking even more ghostly than he had the previous night. The man obviously hadn't got any sleep. 'Good work,' he said quietly into Carrigan's ear. 'These things are never easy, son, you've done a good job.'

He was on his way out when he heard Quinn call his name. The cameras and journalists had departed leaving them alone in the cavernous hall. 'I want you to do this clean and fast, understand?' Quinn said. 'It's probably nothing more than some crazy firebug, so you know what to do.'

Carrigan nodded. He could see why Quinn had got a reputation as the most feared man in the Met – behind his polite facade there was a steely authority which made it clear he wouldn't stand for any mistakes or lame excuses.

'The timing's particularly bad here,' Quinn continued. 'The public have a lot more sympathy towards nuns during the festive period. The press have nothing else on their plates. It's imperative we wrap this up before Christmas.'

'Sir?' Carrigan said, knowing this would be his one and only chance. 'I'd rather you gave this to another DI. I'm in the middle of something else at the moment.'

Quinn coolly appraised him. 'DSI Branch didn't mention anything.'

No, of course not, Carrigan thought. 'A sixteen-year-old boy went missing three days ago.'

'Young boys go missing all the time, you know that as well as anyone.'

'This is different, sir,' Carrigan continued. 'I believe this is linked to several other disappearances over the past few years. I know this is the work of one man and I don't think we have much time if we want to find the boy alive.'

Quinn nodded quietly and sank his hands deeply into the pockets of his uniform jacket. 'You're in charge of the investigation into this fire. Did I not make myself clear?' His eyes were cold and pale as a winter sky. 'It's time to think about your future, Carrigan. Promotion to DCI. Handle this case right and I'll put a word in. This other thing, you can pass off to someone else. I want you fully focused on the fire and nothing else. The press will have their eye on you, Carrigan, remember that.'

6

The new building. They still called it that even though the Murder Investigation Team had been here almost a year now. Carrigan made his way past the main station entrance, checking the daily incident logs to make sure he was up to speed with what had transpired overnight, then caught the lift, still bristling from his encounter with Quinn.

The offices were the latest in ergonomic design. Gone were the old yellowed rooms with their institutional fug of microwaved food and stale coffee and in their place were large square spaces, each a replica of the other, fitted with beeping machines and electronic hums that guaranteed you could never get a moment's peace.

He entered incident room two and saw that Geneva was already there, sitting at a desk near the back, almost invisible in her cubicle, going through a large stack of reports and slugging on a can of Coke.

'How was it?' She put the files aside and swivelled her chair towards him. She was wearing a red blouse and a dark skirt, her lower lip swollen from biting down on it, something he'd noticed she did when she was upset.

'Quick, thank God,' he replied, and started shifting chairs to the main table where they would hold their daily briefings. 'The ACC even called me *son* if you can believe that.'

'Sounds like we may not have you for long,' she replied. 'I heard that when he calls you *son* it means you're on the way up.'

'I heard the opposite,' Carrigan smiled and pulled out his briefcase. He extracted a handful of A4 photographs of the scene and started pinning them to the surrounding walls. Behind him he could hear the team coming in, sighs short and frequent, nods and subdued greetings, a studied reluctance in every movement and gesture – everyone knew what was waiting for them courtesy of the non-stop footage broadcast and looped on last night's news.

'Thanks for coming in early,' Carrigan began, wishing he'd nipped out for that coffee now, his voice scratchy from the smoke. 'As you know, we're launching an investigation into the fire at 33 St Peter's Square. We'll have two daily briefings here as per usual.' He ignored the moans and scattered comments from the uniformed constables surrounding him. 'What we know as of this morning is that 33 St Peter's Square wasn't an ordinary family home. The building was used as a convent by a small group of nuns . . .' He looked down at the hastily scribbled notes in front of him. 'The Sisters of Suffering, apparently. Before you ask, I know as much about nuns and orders as I do about quantum theory, which is pre-cisely nothing. The diocese have confirmed that only ten nuns lived on the premises. Now, as most of you know, St Peter's Square is not your average street. It's probably the most exclusive address on our patch. Several lords, a sheik or two and, of course, our own assist-ant chief constable live there, so we're going to be treading on some toes, that's inevitable.'

'But we have no indication that the fire was deliberate, right?' DS Karlson was dressed in a tight pinstripe suit, his hair gelled back and his stubble a dark charcoal shadow on his jaw. His shoes were shiny and black with pointed tips and he was tapping one heel im-patiently against the leg of his chair.

'Correct, John, we don't know that yet.'

'Isn't it a bit premature setting up a major investigation before we know all the facts?'

Carrigan bridled at the sergeant's insolence – he knew how im-portant it was to have someone to challenge his basic assumptions and keep him sharp, but there was something else underlying Karlson's tone, something he didn't like.

'I agree, but it's not my decision. Seems that ACC Quinn has taken a personal interest in the case. I think his wife helped them out. So, until we know better, we treat this as a murder inquiry. That way we won't get caught out if it does indeed prove to be intentional. If it's an accident then we all get to enjoy our Christmas, no harm done.'

'Except to the nuns.'

Carrigan's gaze found Geneva busily scribbling away in her notebook. 'Thank you, Miller, I think we're all aware of that.' He looked up at the photos he'd pinned to the walls – burnt doorways and cracked windows, the dark smear patterns of soot and dust. 'I'm scheduled to meet the fire investigator later today at the scene. He'll have spent all morning going through the rubble and should be able to tell us whether we're wasting our time or not. I'm told the house is now more or less stable, the SOCOs have finally gone in and the bodies have been transferred to the morgue.'

He paused, slightly out of breath. 'It's Christmas – people get drunk and do things they wouldn't do any other time of year, they play dares and get careless, so keep that in mind.' Carrigan looked over at his team and sighed. He knew it was the worst possible time to start a murder inquiry – everyone looking forward to well-earned time off, Christmas all planned and prepped for, and he could see that their minds were elsewhere, little tells of daydream and stary absence. For him it was different. He knew the case would take his mind off the festivities and rush of unwanted memories that always came with them – cuddling in front of black-and-white movies, Louise's yelp of excitement as she unwrapped the tree, hot slow kisses in the rumpled morning.

He shook the memory free and continued. 'Cases of arson tend to be either easy to solve or bloody impossible. It's a crime that wipes out its own traces but, in doing so, it leaves other traces – that said, the snow isn't going to make it easier for us. Let's hope the SOCOs got there before too much damage was done.

'Now, there are normally three motives for arson.' He pointed to the photos of the smoking wreckage pinned up behind him. 'One: the perpetrator gets off on it. Two: the fire is used to cover up another crime, usually murder. And three: the arsonist has something against that particular property or institution. So we should be thinking about why anyone would have wanted to burn down the convent. Was it a drunken prank that went badly wrong? An accident? Or is the fire somehow symbolic – did someone want the nuns to burn . . . to burn in hell, even? Remember, this isn't merely a case of arson we're investigating – this is murder – someone killed eleven people in that building.'

'Eleven?' DC Singh looked up from her files.

Carrigan told them about the eleventh victim, the corpse in the confession booth. 'There were only supposed to be ten nuns in residence but we have eleven bodies. It's important we keep this detail out of the press for now. I'll be seeing the diocese later today so I'll find out if there was a cook or visitor on the premises, but we should initially focus on this person. It's significant she wasn't found with the others.' He stopped and waited for them to take this in, then turned to face the whiteboard next to him. He began jotting down names and tasks, his handwriting impenetrable as ever. 'Singh, I want you to see if you can find out whether there've been any threats or complaints lodged against the convent in the last couple of years.'

'Are you thinking hate crime? Or an abused child taking revenge?' DC Singh flicked back her lock of black hair and Carrigan was again reminded of her quick intelligence and unerring ability to get straight to the point.

'I'm not thinking anything yet,' he answered. 'Let's see where the evidence leads us first.' He pointed to the whiteboard. 'I've drawn up an initial wall-chart detailing the positions of the deceased. We need to find out the nuns' movements and routines – did they always take dinner together? Did they always take it at the same time? Why did they make no move to escape the room?'

He looked across the table at the serious-eyed young man crouched behind a phalanx of humming laptops. 'Berman, I want you to go through the video footage of the crowd watching the fire. I got one of the uniforms to film it. Arsonists hang around the scene. They get their kicks from watching things burn. If that's the case then it's likely our perpetrator's on tape. We may get lucky.' He looked at his team, trying to offer them this small comfort as they slowly came to the realisation that this investigation was going to mean disappointed relatives, refunded train tickets, and presents sitting on a shelf come Christmas morning.

'Jennings, take a couple of uniforms and start door-to-doors. I'll be joining you later. The snow began falling at six last night. People would have been looking out their windows or sitting on their balconies,' he continued, remembering the fire party last night. 'Someone may have seen something, a person running away, anything.'

He turned to his sergeant. 'Karlson, I want you checking recently released firebugs – Berman, cross-reference what Karlson finds with the video – oh, and Karlson? See if there's been any similar fires in the area recently.' He scanned the table once more, satisfied that all bases had been covered for now. 'I'm sure you're well aware that all Christmas leave will be cancelled if this turns out to be arson and we're left holding the bag, clueless.' He waited for the groans and sighs to subside. 'The press is watching us carefully. The public is watching and Quinn is watching. So let's do everything by the book. If things turn out badly at least we can say we followed every possible line of investigation.' He closed his policy book and looked up. 'Remember,' he said, 'every act leaves a mark upon the world – it's up to us to find those marks and decipher them. And let's try and not get too carried away. It could be nothing more than a simple accident, a prank gone wrong.'

'But that's not what you think, is it?' Karlson interrupted.

'If I was a betting man, I'd say cancel your appointments for the next few days,' Carrigan replied. 'And I hope you've already done your Christmas shopping.'

'So we're looking at this as arson?' one of the uniforms asked.

'Murder, not just arson. Eleven people died and this in itself makes me suspicious. But it's not only that. Three things bother me. The fact that the fire started right below where the nuns had just gathered for their evening meal. The fact they didn't try to escape. The eleventh victim.'

7

'God, you still stink of smoke,' Geneva said, rolling down her car window. He noticed she was wearing a new jacket today, one he'd not seen before, and it made her look older and somehow graver.

'Could say the same about you.' He pointed to the empty pack of cigarettes on the dash, the gaping ashtray too full to close, and smiled as Geneva turned down Westbourne Grove, heading towards their appointment with the bishop.

'Manage to get any sleep last night?' he asked as they stalled in traffic.

'Barely. Ended up watching some stupid Italian slasher film till I fell asleep on the sofa.'

'That sounds familiar.' Carrigan laughed. 'You ever watch anything apart from horror films?'

'Used to. Not much any more. I like knowing the way it's going to unfold. Horror films have a structure and that's comforting.' She risked a glance at him. 'Why? What kind of movies do you like?'

'Ones I don't understand.'

'A film Jack Carrigan doesn't understand, I'd like to see that.' Her nails clicked on the steering wheel as she drummed her fingers in frustration while waiting for the lights to change. There was that peculiar look in her eyes he'd noticed before, a rumble of contained energy written in every muscle twitch and eye flicker.

'What's bothering you?'

She fumbled for her cigarettes, then gave up. 'I didn't want to bring this up in front of the others . . .'

'But?' Carrigan said, watching her carefully. 'C'mon, I know that look . . . you may as well tell me.'

She felt her cheeks flush, embarrassed at having been read so easily yet, at the same time, secretly pleased he'd noticed such a thing. 'Dare I mention the words *mass suicide*?' she said and saw his eyebrows arch slightly as he continued staring out at the snow-covered pavements.

'I very much doubt it,' Carrigan finally replied.

'Really?' she said, her voice dropping slightly. 'It's not that uncommon to find enclosed religious sects who believe the end of the world is coming and who kill themselves in preparation for the Rapture. Heaven's Gate, Jonestown . . . the list goes on and on.'

'This is an established religious institution, not a cult,' he said a little too sharply.

'There's a difference?'

He scratched his beard and listened to the whip-whap of the windscreen wipers as he considered this. 'Yes, there is.' Something had opened up between them in the unsaid words, a space neither realised had existed. 'And I suppose you have something to back up your theory?'

'Funnily enough,' she replied, 'I do.'

The diocese's offices were located in a sprawling church deep in the heart of Pimlico. The car park was full, and priests and seminarians walked past them, hunched in conversation and thought, utterly oblivious to the two detectives as they made their way to the front door. Carrigan pressed the buzzer. The door opened revealing a young man dressed in brown monk's robes and a thick mop of black hair that almost obscured his eyes.

'Yes?' His accent was so clipped and rarefied that it only took that one syllable to evoke an entire world of country houses, tweed jackets and private gentlemen's clubs on Pall Mall.

Carrigan pulled out his warrant card. 'We have an appointment with Bishop Price.'

The seminarian nodded once, then turned and headed back down the hallway. They followed him through a twisting panelled corridor studded with saints in agony and beatific virgins, photos of monks and priests and politicians lining the walls. They turned a corner and he pointed to a wooden bench beside a large arched door. 'You can wait there.'

They sat on the bench, the wood cold and unyielding and only six inches deep so that they had to tense their feet against the floor to stay upright like dozing medieval priests perched on their carved misericords. Carrigan stared up at the coffered ceiling and tried to count the angels hiding in its folds.

'Detective Inspector Carrigan? I believe we have an appointment.'

Carrigan hadn't noticed the door next to him open and was startled, almost losing his balance on the narrow bench. 'You're not Bishop Price,' he said, quickly gathering himself together as he looked up at the man standing beside him.

'Quite right . . . which must make you the detective.' The man offered his hand. 'Roger Holden. I'm the diocese's press secretary. I'd be happy to help you with any questions you may have.'

Carrigan stood up and shook his hand, flinching slightly at the unexpected pressure on his fingers and the way Holden looked directly into his eyes as he did this. The man was in his early forties, an expensive haircut framing a bland square face, teeth gleaming white behind fleshy gums. He wore a pink pinstripe shirt that looked as if it had been squeezed out of a tube of toothpaste and he smelled faintly of soap and mint.

'Our appointment was supposed to be with the bishop.'

Holden smiled apologetically as they entered the office, the corners of his eyes crinkling. He wore a silver ring inset with a small ruby on his little finger and he kept worrying it with his other hand. 'Unfortunately, the bishop is indisposed right now, but I'll be happy to provide you with whatever information you may need.'

Holden took his seat behind a large, neatly ordered table, the papers and stationery all squared and aligned. Bookcases lined three of the walls, packed tight with leather-bound volumes, serious and grave in their uniformity. A row of metal filing cabinets stood to the left. A small oval oil painting on the far wall drew Carrigan's eye. It depicted a group of three unnaturally elongated figures sitting around a campfire and peering fixedly into the flames. The scene was lit from the centre, shadows spreading like black fingers across the canvas, and there was something sinister about the way the shadows fell, as if independent of their origin. It made you want to get closer, to see what the figures were so entranced by. But of course you would never know, that was the point of the painting. Next to it sat framed certificates and more photos of people Carrigan didn't recognise, handshakes and glossy smiles beaming from each one.

'A drink?' They both nodded and Holden cautiously poured some water from a silver jug, careful not to let a single drop land on the table. He took a small white handkerchief out of his pocket and used it to dry the lip of the jug before placing it back on the tray. 'So, you're in charge of investigating the fire?'

Carrigan nodded.

'A terrible thing, terrible,' Holden replied, folding the handkerchief neatly into four. 'We're still trying to come to terms with it. As you can imagine, Bishop Price is most upset.' He looked up and placed the handkerchief back in his pocket. 'Now, what can I help you with?'

'We'd like the personnel files on the nuns so we can start identifying the bodies.' Carrigan was surprised that Holden hadn't asked him whether the fire had been deliberate or not – it was almost always the first thing anyone wanted to know in such cases.

'Of course. That won't be a problem,' Holden replied, making a note on a peach-coloured piece of paper.

'We were also hoping you could give us some information on the

49

convent: what were the nuns like? What kind of activities were they involved in? . . . Anything we can gather may help us in determining why this thing happened.'

Holden smiled and said, 'I think only God knows the answer to why.'

'Well, since God's not going to hand in his findings, we'll see what we can do.'

Holden turned and stared at Geneva as if surprised to find her there. Carrigan had noticed how he'd studiously been avoiding her until now. Holden took a sip of water, his lips barely touching the glass.

'You won't have to look far, then. There are plenty of people who don't like us. They've never liked us, not since the sixteenth century – but of course no one says so. They tolerate us because we keep quiet and because they need our dogma to justify themselves.'

'What do you mean?' Geneva asked.

'Anglicans, the non-believers, the atheists and their ilk, they need us. They need our intransigence over contraception, abortion, euthanasia – they need it to highlight their own normality, how rational their belief system is compared to ours, how far they've progressed . . . but religion is not rational nor would we want it to be so. Mystery is the abiding nature of God. Ultimately, our roles are really not so different, Detective Sergeant Miller. We both have a set of rules we follow and we both try to stem the flow of evil in this world.' He looked at her for affirmation then, finding none, continued. 'What do you know about monastic orders?'

'Only what I've seen in films,' Geneva replied, and Carrigan felt a momentary snap of anger towards her but then noticed the look on Holden's face and kept his mouth shut.

'There are two main types of order: monastic and mendicant,' Holden explained. 'The former spend all their time cloistered and concentrate on prayer, while the latter have a greater emphasis on missionary work. The convent in Bayswater, the Sisters of Suffering, were part of a mendicant order; they were involved in good works and community outreach as well as their prayers and devotions and they subsisted on donations. You say you want to know about the nuns. Well, the convent actually has a very interesting history.'

Carrigan watched silently, letting Holden dictate the pace of the interview, allowing him to slip into comfortable routine and slick patter. He knew it was often when people were at their most relaxed that they gave themselves away.

'The convent was founded by Constance Bellhew – I don't suppose you've heard of her?' Holden looked up, saw them shaking their heads and continued. 'She was the 1910s equivalent of someone like Kate Moss, the girl everybody wanted to know. She presided over weekly salons, wrote several books of poetry, associated with Pound and Woolf, the whole Bloomsbury set. Then the war intervened and she gave it all up and volunteered as a nurse. She spent three hard years in the Dardanelles and at the Western Front and it was among the amputated limbs, shattered minds and unassailable volume of the dead that she found her place. A Catholic by birth, but never before by inclination, she began to read Teresa de Ávila and Julian of Norwich in her tent during the eerie gunless nights, and when the war ended she joined an order of nuns and, a few years after that, took her vows.

'But she soon sensed that there was something missing from her new life and she kept thinking back to how she'd felt in the trenches among the wounded and dying and realised that a life of contemplation and withdrawal was not for her. A couple of years later, in 1924, she formed the order of the Sisters of Suffering, in a disused building in a rundown part of town full of tenements and bedsits called Notting Hill. She believed that it wasn't enough to pray to Jesus, one also had to live like Him – to spend your life alleviating the sufferings of the poor. In the years which followed, the Great Depression, the millions standing in bread lines, there was a lot of work to do, and Sister Constance found her calling. She reorganised the convent and set the rules by which they would function, including the rule of ten.'

'The rule of ten?' Carrigan interrupted.

'She believed the number was the perfect balance; that too few nuns would be inefficient in their task and that too many would lead to a dilution of purpose and factional dissent.

'Unfortunately, Sister Constance died during a Luftwaffe raid in the winter of 1943. The nuns had refused to leave the convent during the Blitz and spent their days ministering to the wounded and newly homeless. After the war, the convent flourished, renewed greatly by Sister Constance's sacrifice, and was a tremendous boon to the community during the tense and racially divisive years that were to follow. More recently, the convent was headed by Mother Angelica. She's been the abbess for the past twelve years. In her tenure, the convent greatly expanded its charity works and role in the community, from the battleground schools to the homeless shelters under the Westway. Their focus over the last five years has been predominantly in dealing with the scourge of drugs sweeping through our streets, setting up rehabilitation centres and workshops and organising the community. Indeed, over the past eight years the convent received several commendations from the Vatican for their outreach work.'

'You know the history of all the orders in your parish in such detail?'

'No, I prepared myself this morning when the bishop told me you were coming.'

'So otherwise you had no particular dealings with this convent?'

'No, Detective Inspector, I did not. What exactly are you implying?'

Carrigan shook his head, 'Nothing, nothing. Don't pay any attention to me, I was just thinking out loud.' He flicked absently through the pages of his notebook. 'Now, would there have been anyone else in the convent yesterday evening apart from the nuns?'

'No, of course not,' Holden replied.

'You seem very sure of that.'

'The nuns may have done a lot of outreach work but the convent was their personal space. And there certainly wouldn't have been anyone there yesterday evening. It was the feast of St John of the Cross, an extremely solemn and private occasion for them.'

Carrigan nodded, thinking about the timing of this. 'What about a cook or caretaker?'

He caught something in Holden's expression before the man answered. 'They cooked their own meals and made their own beds. That was part of Sister Constance's rule, to ensure they never grew reliant on outside help.'

Carrigan leaned forward and placed his arms squarely on the table. 'Tell me about the caretaker.'

Holden briefly looked away. 'How . . . how did you? . . . Never mind.' He twirled the ring on his finger. 'It was against the rules but they did employ a part-time caretaker. There were some things that the nuns just couldn't do by themselves – but it was more an act of charity, I believe. He was one of their strays, one of their countless lost sheep, a wiry little man by the name of Hubbard, Alan Hubbard.' Holden shrugged. 'They always had their little pet projects.'

'Did Hubbard live on the premises?' Carrigan asked, wondering what it was about the caretaker that made Holden so uneasy.

'No, of course not. He came once or twice a week to fix things, that was all.'

'Do you have an address for him?'

Holden shook his head. 'As I mentioned before, this was not done with official sanction.'

'And there was no chance that the nuns had invited him over for dinner? Maybe felt sorry for him, one of their *lost sheep*?'

Holden looked at Carrigan as if he'd just enquired whether the convent employed a stripper. 'No, of course not. The feast of St

John was a holy and onerous occasion. There certainly wouldn't have been any guests. That's ridiculous.'

'Ridiculous,' Carrigan repeated, writing the caretaker's name down in his notebook and, next to it, the number '11' and a question mark. The pathologist at the scene had, on cursory examination, determined that the bodies were probably all female, but Holden had described Hubbard as wiry and small – could the pathologist have been mistaken in his initial assumption? Carrigan gripped the pen a little tighter, feeling a flutter-surge of adrenalin at the thought that they'd either identified the eleventh victim or found a possible suspect.

'I'm nearly finished,' he continued. 'Sorry to have taken up so much of your time. Just wanted to clear something up – your diocese has overall authority over the convent, is that correct?'

Holden smiled. 'I wouldn't call it authority, no.'

'But your office was in charge?' Carrigan persisted.

'How much do you know about ecclesiastical governance?'

Carrigan was about to say not much at all when Geneva interrupted. 'I know that the diocese is responsible for all religious orders within its boundaries and acts as a kind of governing body should conflicts arise.'

Holden studied Geneva carefully before he answered. 'Yes, quite right,' he said. 'Though that does make us sound like some kind of local council. Convents differ from parish churches in that they're far more autonomous, as you'd expect, so we don't often have day-to-day dealings with them. Generally, we only deal with problems that arise, otherwise they pretty much run themselves.'

'And . . . did problems arise?' Geneva asked.

Holden met her gaze and said, 'No, no problems at all.'

'No problems at all? No threats or complaints? You're sure about that?'

'Of course I am. Everything concerning the bishop goes through me first.'

Geneva looked puzzled as she took out a thick green file from her bag. 'Isn't it true that there was a serious dispute between the convent and the diocese?'

Holden stared at the ring on his finger, his tongue flicking briefly across his lips. 'I wouldn't call it serious, no. Nothing more than a minor disagreement.'

'Really?' Geneva flicked through her papers, dropping several on the floor. As she got to her knees to pick them up, Carrigan could see Holden's lips twitching with impatience. She finally sat back down and pulled out a single photocopied sheet from a three-month-old newspaper. 'If it wasn't serious then why would the bishop issue a writ of complaint to the order's headquarters in Rome?'

Holden almost managed to hide his surprise, but not quite. He shook his head as if annoyed at having to explain something very simple to someone for the fourth time. 'These are arcane matters of theology, Detective Sergeant Miller, I'm not sure you would appreciate the subtleties.'

'You're quite right,' Geneva agreed. 'I don't really understand much of this, which is why I looked it up earlier and, according to the *Catholic Encyclopaedia*, such a writ of complaint is only issued in matters . . .' She glanced down and paused as if reading the next sentence from her print-out but Carrigan could tell she knew it off by heart. 'Matters of urgent or extreme deviation from the Creed.'

'You seem very well informed.'

'It's my job,' she replied, bristling against the smooth purr of his voice. 'So, humour me a moment – if, for instance, the nuns believed in apocalyptic imminence, in the end of the world, then that would be a reason for the bishop to issue such a writ?' Geneva stopped, noting the crinkle in Holden's brow, the way his eyes had narrowed slightly.

'You believe the nuns killed themselves because they thought the end of the world was coming?' Holden laughed. 'Detective Sergeant, please, these nuns dedicated their lives to helping others. This wasn't some misguided cult, this was a long established and rule-bound order.' He rose from his chair and leaned across the table. 'I advise you to tread carefully here. You can't start bandying about the first thing that comes to mind, starting all sorts of rumours. This was a much loved and well-supported convent.'

'Is that a warning?' Carrigan asked, impressed by how Geneva had managed to rattle Holden.

'Merely a statement of fact,' Holden said.

Carrigan nodded blankly and wrote something down in his notebook. 'Talking of facts, Mr Holden, would it surprise you to know that there *was* someone else in the convent yesterday evening? An eleventh victim? After all, according to your statement, that would be impossible.'

For the first time since they'd got there, Holden's expression slipped, and Carrigan caught a flicker of panic and something else beneath the well-heeled charm.

'Eleven bodies?' Holden repeated to himself. 'You must be mistaken. That . . . that simply can't be.'

'Merely a statement of fact,' Carrigan replied.

8

The fire investigation officer was perched on the bumper of his truck, smoking a cigarette and reading a book. His helmet lay next to him and snow covered his blond curls and lined the curves of his droopy moustache.

Carrigan made his way through the slush, feeling his socks turning wet and cold, and introduced himself. The fire investigator nodded once and finished the sentence he was reading. He put down the book and Carrigan saw it depicted the blackened bodies of burn victims, displayed in glossy colour and intimate close-up, scrawled notes and bright yellow Post-Its covering the page.

'Kirk,' the investigator introduced himself, not specifying whether this was his first name or last. He was at least four inches taller than Carrigan and twice as wide, but he carried his size lightly, moving with a deft assurance as he offered Jack a cigarette.

'Year and a half,' Carrigan said, waving away the pack.

'Me too,' Kirk replied. He lit his cigarette and laughed, blowing smoke out into the night.

The snow kept falling, thicker and thicker clumps, soundlessly lighting on their hair and clothes, blanketing the street around them.

'You finished in there?'

Kirk stubbed out his cigarette and nodded. 'You want to grab a drink and I'll talk you through it?'

Carrigan smiled and pulled two paper espresso cups out of the take-out bag he was carrying. 'I want you to show me.'

Kirk looked Carrigan up and down as if he'd initially mistaken him for someone else.

'It's not really safe,' he finally said.

'Neither is smoking,' Carrigan replied with a smile, and led the way.

Now that the fire was out, the real extent of the damage could be seen. The blackened shell of the building smouldered and sizzled darkly in the morning air, a hissing skull with empty windowframes and gaping doorways made all the more sinister by the normality of the houses on either side.

Kirk handed Carrigan a fire jacket and hard hat as they crossed the front garden. Some of the trees had caught fire and stood blackened and skeletal, smoke rising from their stippled branches.

The change in temperature hit Carrigan as soon as he stepped inside the house. The air was thicker, dusty and sour, and he began to sweat under the too-tight hat and clumpy jacket as he followed Kirk through the hallway and up the stairs. They walked across the landing, avoiding the places where the floor had collapsed to reveal black holes yawning like pulled teeth, and entered the dining room.

The parquet flooring had turned black, blistering like sunburnt skin. The painted canvases had melted from their copper frames leaving new designs, tongues of smoke and flame, a narrative of blister and peel. Two wheelchairs sat in the corner of the room, arabesques of steam rising like probing fingers from their seats. Random mounds of ash and metal lay scattered across the floor. A large crucifix hung above the fireplace, the figure still smoking and blackened beyond recognition.

Carrigan crossed over to the centre of the room and peered down at a set of dark smudges spotting the floor. 'That what I think it is?'

Kirk squatted on his haunches and nodded. He was biting the ends of his moustache between his teeth, his jaw clenched and his eyes narrowed. 'The SOCOs took the bodies away this morning but yes, that's what you're looking at. Human tissue burns much more fiercely than wood. That's where they died.' Something cracked behind them and Kirk looked back uneasily. 'We shouldn't stay here long. The kitchen floor collapsed overnight and this one's next.'

Carrigan ignored him, bending down and examining the black patches. Each expertly traced the shape of the body that had left it, as if their very shadows had been trapped at the moment of death. He got up and began to count. He did this twice and each time he got ten. Ten black smears, ten bodies burnt down to ash and memory.

'Doesn't it seem strange to you that they're so neatly positioned around the table?' Carrigan took two steps back and inspected the mound of ashes which lay at the centre of the room. 'That's the dining table, right? And here,' he pointed to one of the dark smudges, 'and here and here and here. The nuns are sitting around the table when the smoke creeps through the door. Okay, that makes sense. But why are they all in the same position when they die?' Carrigan shook his head and scanned the room. 'You'd expect that as soon as they smelled the smoke they'd start to panic and try to find a way out. We should be seeing bodies scattered in a random pattern, or at least closer to exits and windows, but all we have here is ten dead nuns who seem to have quietly sat at the dinner table as the fire entered the room and who continued sitting at their places until the fire consumed them.'

'Perhaps they couldn't move because they were tied up,' Kirk said quietly.

Carrigan looked down at the zigzag canyon cracks in the floor. 'Could you tell from the lock whether the door was fastened from the outside or inside?'

Kirk shook his head. 'No. Only that it was locked. But we didn't find any key.'

Carrigan thought about this as they stood among the ash and

dust. 'If the door was locked from the outside, we'd still be seeing a scatter pattern, right? People still panic even if they know there's no way out. Which suggests that maybe the door was locked from the inside.'

'Why on earth would they want to do that?'

Carrigan shrugged. He thought back to what Geneva had said earlier. Maybe he needed to let her follow her instincts. She'd been right before, and it reminded him of being young and eager and new to murder work and how the years of practice and experience had dulled and withered his hunch-sense. He stared at the black smears and thought about the nuns' last remaining moments. The agony and fear and panic as one by one they succumbed. What prayers, what regrets and childhood memories flashed before their eyes in those final fleeting seconds?

He crossed over towards an alcove and checked the surrounding area but there was nothing of interest there. He looked up at the high inaccessible stained-glass window, the stately procession of pain and suffering enacted on the way to Golgotha, then turned his attention to the wall below, using the torch to run light up and down its coffered surface. The wall was empanelled with square insets made from a darker wood. The wood had blackened and blistered and peeled, the years of dust and varnish and smeary touch erased in flame. There was no way anyone could have gained purchase and climbed it to get to the window. Would the nuns have known that?

A sudden thought flashed through his head and he crossed the room and squatted in front of the remains of the table. He could see the dulled edges of cutlery poking through the debris, teapots and trays, broken glass and cracked porcelain, a fork missing its tines and a swan-shaped salt shaker, its wings tarnished black. But he wasn't interested in these. It was the small black objects peppering the ash that he now examined. Carrigan bent down and picked one of them up and rolled it between his fingers. It was still warm and when he tilted it towards the light he could see the pinprick tunnel threading through it. He put it back down and selected another but he already knew what he was looking at. When he was finished he got up, his knees cracking painfully, and pointed to the round black stones dotting the floor. 'Their rosary beads were kept under their habits, on the waist. We shouldn't be seeing them all over the place like this unless they had them out when the fire reached them.' Carrigan looked down. 'And that doesn't make sense . . . why would they all have their rosary beads out when they were sitting down to dinner?'

'Downstairs is where things start to get interesting,' Kirk explained as they exited the dining room and made their way across the landing. Carrigan couldn't help thinking there was something about the house, beyond the damage wrought by the blaze, which made it seem oppressive, as if gravity had more purchase here, a fleeting sense of agony and confinement which made him eager and impatient to get back out on the street.

As they passed the door which led down to the basement, Carrigan stopped. He looked down at the blackened set of steps disappearing into darkness.

'We can't go down there until tomorrow at the earliest,' Kirk said. 'You wouldn't last two minutes in there. If the stairs don't get you, the fumes will.'

Snow was falling in the chapel. The outer wall had collapsed and wind-blown flurries danced and scurried in front of them. Steam was still curling from the walls, white puffy coils which dissipated in the frigid air. Dotted around the room were niches and hidden cloisters, screened-off areas and the row of confession booths, making the room seem smaller than it actually was. At the far end, where the space opened up into a large hexagonal bay, stood the altar on a raised stone platform, a darkened crucifix smoking behind it. Carrigan stood silently taking in the scene, the language of niches and candle stands, the hewn syntax of rood screens and mystical vision and seared eyes.

He walked over to the confession booths and searched the skeleton remains of the two on either side, then the one where the body was discovered. Most of the wood had burned leaving only the metal doors, the spiny supports and screens, yet, despite all this, they still looked eerie and magnificent. He stepped inside the booth, the smell heavy and rich in his nostrils, imagining the people who'd sat here and poured out the worst moments of their lives into the blank and faceless screen.

Pulling his torch out, he aimed the beam at the back of the door and took an involuntary swallow of air as he saw the marks on it. He splashed the light left and right and saw that they were everywhere, up and down and across the surface of the door. He snapped on his gloves and used the back of his hand to wipe away the top layer of soot. The marks were more like scratches, you could see that now, small crescent-shaped grooves in the metal, overlapped, random and furious.

'She was alive when the fire got to her. She was trying to get out,' he said.

Kirk craned his neck and saw the frenzied palimpsest of scratches that the eleventh victim had made. He took a deep breath and shook his head. 'Not necessarily. This close to the seat of fire the flames would have got to her before the smoke could knock her out. Those scratches may have been involuntary.'

'Involuntary?'

'As she burned, her muscles would have contracted and popped and she'd have flailed and lashed out. I'm afraid it would have been an extremely painful few minutes.'

'Jesus,' Carrigan said, stepping out of the booth, trying to rein in the dread images conjured by the fire investigator. He scanned the room, the dark ceiling, the mottled floor. 'Where did the fire start?'

Kirk pointed to a large bayed niche at the opposite end of the room and they slowly crossed the nave, weaving through the scattered debris and mulch until Carrigan stopped and wrinkled his nose.

'What's that smell?' He could feel it in his nostrils, sour and caustic, an underlying stench behind the stink of the fire.

'You noticed it too?' Kirk came up beside him. 'We're not quite sure what it is.' He pointed down at the floor, to an area that was darker than the rest. 'From the amount of ash it looks like there was a large item of furniture here, maybe a chest of drawers or bureau. I took a sample and sent it off to the lab. We'll know soon enough.'

They crossed the room and the fire investigator gestured towards the wide semicircular niche in the west wall, a single blackened statue at its centre. 'That's your seat of fire.'

Carrigan looked at the dark patchwork of marks behind the icon then craned his neck and saw the burnt ceiling beams and partially collapsed floor of the room above. Black arrows of smoke snaked up the walls in twisting spirals as if they too had tried to escape the flames.

Kirk aimed his flashlight at a dense hatchwork of soot and grime to the left of the statue. 'See how the damage is worse here than anywhere else?'

Carrigan found it hard to tell one scorch mark from another, the seemingly random mosaic of burn shadows and ash smears vaguely sinister, a perpetual flicker at the periphery of his vision, but for Kirk the chaos of smudge and burn was like an open book, one whose language he could easily decipher.

'What we have here is your classic V pattern, telling us this is where the initial temperature was the highest. That was a table,' Kirk pointed to the two-inch deposit of ash spread evenly across the floor, grey and flecked with small shiny particles. Next to it stood a twisted frame of hissing metal. It was rectangular in design and composed of three horizontal sections with gothic tines of blackened metal rising from its cross-bars like accusatory fingers. 'No idea what that is. Looks like one of those medieval torture devices,' Kirk said quietly, and he was unprepared for Carrigan's throaty laugh.

'It's a pricket stand,' Carrigan said. 'You find them in most Catholic churches. They're usually dedicated to a saint, that's what the statue is. People light a candle, put some money in the collection box and say a prayer.'

'Didn't help them much,' Kirk replied. 'All these bloody candles.' He shook his head and pointed up to a set of metal rods fixed to the wall, small cylinders with empty brass rings hanging loosely from them. 'Drapes or curtains,' Kirk explained. 'Textbook fire hazard. A candle must have fallen over and ignited them. The fire would have then spread up and across. Once it hit the drapes there'd be no stopping it.'

Carrigan studied the niche then made a sketch in his notebook of the relative positions of pricket stand, table, drapes and saint. He took out his phone and snapped a few shots. 'And you're absolutely certain this is where the fire started?'

Kirk smiled broadly. 'It's physics and geometry, not a matter of opinion.'

'Any evidence of accelerants?'

Kirk shook his head. 'Not that I can see. No pool marks, no residual smell – the candles, the drapes, the painting – you wouldn't need anything else,' he said, biting the ends of his moustache again.

Carrigan nodded and stared at the blackened statue. He didn't recognise the saint. The figure was tall and thin and seemed unruffled by its present condition, an enigmatic smile planted on carved grey lips. He took a couple more photos of the statue's face and turned around, studying the layout of the room, then took several steps back and looked again at the pricket stand, and from this vantage there was something different about it, a subtlety of shade and angle revealed by the slanted slabs of spilled light.

The pricket stand had been positioned a couple of feet away from the back wall but it wasn't quite flush. The left side of the stand was closer to the wall than the right by maybe two inches. Carrigan fished the torch out of his pocket again and splashed light onto the area. He got to his knees, the floor cold and hard, and scanned the space around the stand, using his sleeve to clear the ash. He licked the tip of his gloved finger and rubbed away the fine coating of soot until the surface of the floor was uncovered.

He angled the torch in and hunched forward, running his fingers up and down the two faint scrape marks trailing from the pricket stand's left leg. He got up slowly, thinking about this, and took a step back.

'Somebody moved the pricket stand,' he said, pointing to the floor. 'Moved it so that the candles would be positioned directly beneath the drapes.'

9

'I've never talked to a police officer before.'

'Well, there's a first time for everything,' Geneva replied, slightly surprised by the tone of her own voice. She'd been put through to John Staples, the editor of the *Catholic Tribune*, and had expected someone older, stuffy, severe and impatient, but the man on the other end of the line possessed a calm reassurance. She'd spent the last hour going through the files the diocese had sent over but could find nothing about a dispute. Yet Holden had denied it strenuously and this didn't make sense. She looked at the pages and reports scattered across her desk and felt an unexpected wave of excitement. This was her favourite part, always. At this stage it was all paper and chaos – an avalanche of random and hidden data obscured in black type and binary code and she loved the challenge of it, the bloodrush when events and facts began to separate themselves from the main group and cohere into new and startling patterns.

'I'm investigating the convent fire and I was wondering if you could help me with something.' She told Staples who she was and explained what she'd found out about the convent's dispute with the diocese. 'But, to be honest, I don't really understand much of it.'

'No, that's the point,' Staples replied, his voice suddenly animated. 'They couch everything in complex language so that the true meaning is hidden. There was talk of this a few months ago,' he said, 'but the rumours I heard were that it had gone far beyond being just a dispute.'

'Really?' Geneva clutched the phone tightly to her ear, looked up and saw DC Jennings come in, scan the room and make his way towards her.

'Yes, as I was saying, there were rumours that...'

A shadow fell over her. She glanced up to see Jennings standing beside her, out of breath and gesturing impatiently. 'Just a moment,' she told Staples. 'What is it?'

'I've got an address for the caretaker,' Jennings said, trying to contain his excitement.

She picked up the phone, 'Mr Staples, I'm really sorry, but can I call you back? Something's just come up.'

*

The Westbourne Park estate looked like yesterday's vision of the future. A future that had never arrived. Long, dark and relentless, the windows like gouges in its black armature, it projected an overwhelming sense of enclosure and monochrome, a garrisoned claustrophobia Geneva felt deep in her bones. It could have been some turreted hell-prison from Mars, a place on the liminal edge of human existence, but it was right here, only a few minutes' walk from the pet clothing boutiques and designer chocolate emporiums of Notting Hill.

Inside, it was even worse. The estate was a labyrinth of shadowed corridors and locked doors, a suffocating human density stacked one on top of the other. Geneva and Jennings entered the courtyard, the sun immediately snuffed out behind the ridge of roofs from the surrounding flats. The snow covered the bare asphalt and the tops of the broken swings and abandoned roundabouts but it could do nothing to hide the sense of neglect and careless ruin.

Graffiti had sprung up like some baleful flower, splashed and spangled across walls and doors and staircases, most of it impenetrable as Arabic or Burmese script and yet just as lovely. But Geneva had noticed a worrying new trend recently – angry political slogans replacing taggers' names and lovelorn dedications; imprecations to kill the pigs, smash the system, arm the homeless.

Jennings tried to read the posted directions through the dense hatchwork of squiggles and illegible scrawls. 'Flat 134,' he pointed uncertainly to the far corner of the quadrangle, one floor up. Geneva was surprised by how nervous he seemed, almost disappearing inside his terrible suit. Field work was not his strong point and she'd often wondered how he could bear it, stuck in an office and never directly in contact with the world he was investigating. For her, the field had always been the one place where she could totally lose herself, where the spinning noise of days quietened to one whisper and anything could happen.

'We should have just got the uniforms to pick him up,' Jennings complained as they crossed the courtyard and ducked under the overhanging walkways.

'It's better this way,' Geneva said, remembering how Carrigan had taught her that one of the most invaluable sources of evidence at their disposal was a subject's flat, what they chose to show of themselves to the world. 'At least that's what the boss says.'

Jennings sniffed and coughed and stopped. 'Funny you should say that, I was going to ask you about him.' His smile was lopsided and shaded as he said this. 'You have any idea what's up with Carrigan recently?'

'What do you mean?' Geneva turned to look at Jennings and he quickly looked away.

'He seems wound up very tight . . . I mean, more than usual.' A small nervous laugh escaped his mouth. 'Karlson said he gets like this every Christmas, said it was because . . .'

Geneva shot Jennings a cold hard stare. 'I'd focus on what we're here to do if I were you and worry a little less about other people.' She saw his face drop and felt bad for snapping at him. She knew it wasn't Jennings she was mad at, and wasn't there also a little truth to what he was saying? There was something different about Carrigan recently, a slight but unmistakable tension that was always present, as if his skin had shrunk in the wash. But it was his life and he would tell her if he chose to. You couldn't force confidences. She knew that only too well, thinking back to Oliver's relentless probing of her every thought and fleeting whim, his need to know everything erasing the walls of privacy she'd spent so long erecting around herself.

They walked silently under the parapets, the net-curtained windows on either side twitching and shifting as if disturbed by their very passing, and came to a sudden stop a few feet from the stairwell.

A group of kids stood in a circle, huddled around the stairs. Loud music, seemingly consisting only of bass thumps and ground tremors, emanated from a chunky boom box perched on the second step. The kids ranged in age between twelve and fifteen, were mixed in race and gender, and glared at them with a uniform hostility as they approached. There was no fear in their eyes, just a simmering discontent. They were passing around a reefer and the smell was rich and pungent in Geneva's nostrils, a smell that reminded her of her mother more than anything else.

She saw one of the kids, the leader presumably, corn-rowed hair and track lines, turning up the volume until she could feel her organs begin to vibrate. She stood and eyeballed him until finally the corn-row kid broke her stare and spat on the floor an inch away from her shoe. She turned, seeing Jennings totally pale, eyes like rabbits, and pushed her way past the kids and up the stairs.

Geneva knocked on the door to Alan Hubbard's flat and waited. She could hear the music from the boom box downstairs, the screams of neighbouring TV sets competing in the gauzy air, words and accusations bouncing across the concrete parapets and drowning flat in the snow.

She knocked again, this time harder, looking at Jennings, wondering if he'd fucked up, got the wrong address, when she heard the sound of breaking glass coming from within. She immediately had her baton out and ready. She knocked again, stopping when she heard footsteps, each one getting a little louder, approaching the door. 'He might have a broken bottle in his hand so be careful,' she warned Jennings as they took positions on either side of the door. She heard the sound of unlatching locks and ratcheting tumblers and tensed herself.

Alan Hubbard was not holding a broken bottle or a knife or anything else. He looked as if he didn't have the strength to hold a packet of cigarettes. It took a moment for his eyes to focus and for him to look up but, when he saw Geneva's outstretched hand brandishing her warrant card, he reacted with the alacrity of a hyena, instantly dropping his shoulders, his whole body turning in on itself as his eyes scoured the ground.

'Mr Hubbard?'

The man in front of them let out a deep sigh. 'I know why you're here,' he said. 'I know why you've come.'

Geneva thought she was going to gag the moment she entered the flat. She'd smelled enough bodies, blood and rot, but this smell was something else. It was almost tangible, the air thick and hot in the cramped one-bedroom flat. Onions, sour milk, old laundry and bad breath mixed with a sickly sweet dash of booze. She concentrated on breathing through her mouth as they followed Hubbard through a small hallway and into an equally small living room. The floor was covered in yellow lino which had peeled and cracked at several points revealing the rough wooden underlay. Empty bottles of booze lay scattered across the flat and a bin had overflowed, rubbish spilling out of its top like cascading lava. Airbrushed paintings of horses dotted the walls – horses nuzzling each other in lush green meadows, cantering across a prairie, in close-up, flared nostrils and gentle eyes staring sadly into the smudged horizon. A

TV was on, broadcasting shaky hand-held images of civil war, dust and explosions and running journalists. Piles of old newspapers lay stacked around the room in various stages of decomposition. There was a shelf filled with forty or fifty half-empty pill bottles, and several umbrellas, the skin torn and frayed, silver fingers bent and poking through. Framed portraits of the queen were hanging on three of the walls as if she were a dictator or a saint.

Hubbard sank into a grey armchair and reached for a grimy bottle of Scotch that lay by his feet. Geneva could see the greasy ghost-mark of his lips on the neck of the bottle, overlapped and smudged like a set of fingerprints. He took a long pull then put it back down and sat mutely staring at his hands. She'd initially thought he was an old man but he wasn't even middle-aged, his youth lost behind a patchy ginger beard, sunken cheeks and red-rimmed eyes. He wore a grey T-shirt with sweat stains under the arms and smears of crusted food across the belly and a pair of ill-fitting jeans, bagged in a tight concertina around his waist.

'It's all my fault,' Hubbard said, finally looking up at her. 'All my fault, all my fault, all my fault . . .' he repeated, banging his fists against his thighs in time with the words.

Geneva told him to stand up. She took a step back as he did so, the stench of unwashed clothes and night sweats making her feel dizzy, and it was then that Hubbard lunged forward and grabbed her arm, moving much faster than she'd thought possible.

His fingers felt cold and wet against her skin. His face was a few inches away from hers and she could see his missing teeth and black gums as he spoke.

'You have to believe me.' His grip kept getting tighter with each word and then, before she realised what he was doing, he leaned in closer, his body pressing hard against hers, and whispered in her ear.

Jennings had stepped forward, baton out, but Geneva nodded him away, gently put one hand on Hubbard's wrist, looked him in the eyes and pulled her other hand free. She brushed her sleeve and turned to see Jennings pale and bug-eyed, looking as awkward holding the truncheon as a dog playing the trumpet. She shrugged a silent message at him and turned back to the caretaker.

'Could you please repeat what you just told me, Mr Hubbard?'

Hubbard looked at Jennings, then at Geneva, his eyes pale and runny, his voice a thin, scratchy wheeze. 'I did it,' he said, putting his arms out, palms up. 'I killed them. I killed them all.'

10

The coffee was strong and made him feel human again. He slowly savoured it, watching the snow spiralling outside the cafe's windows as light jazz played over the house stereo. He thought it might be Wes Montgomery but it had been so long since he'd listened to music that he wasn't sure. He often came here when he felt the need to escape the clang and clamour of the station. The cafe had comfortable sofas, halfway decent espresso and staff who never cleared his cup before he was finished. There was half an hour to go until his appointment with the pathologist and he needed the food and drink to fortify himself for what would be waiting down in the morgue; the sickly smells combining with the pathologist's scratchy smoker's whisper, the cloying scent of her hairspray and constant barrage of jokes at his expense.

He took another sip and stared up at the queue. Today, the cafe was crowded with Christmas shoppers taking a break from the relentless burden of choices on the high street. Everyone seemed faintly aglow with seasonal expectation. Strangers began conversations about the snow while waiting for their drinks. But no one spoke to him. They could see the dark shadows flickering behind his eyes and sense that he was immersed in his own separate world and that it was a world of which they wanted no part.

He finished his sandwich and tried calling Geneva but there was no reply. He'd detailed her with finding the caretaker's whereabouts and wanted to know if she'd got anywhere. He took out his policy book and started to jot down the things he'd just learned at the scene – the scattered rosary beads, the scratches on the confession-booth door, the way the pricket stand had been moved. He didn't like what they were finding out at all. The faint hope that it had been an accident was being chipped away with each new piece of information.

None of it made sense no matter how hard he stared at it. He flipped the notebook shut and checked his watch. Fifteen minutes to kill. He thought of Karen then, the nurse he'd met only yesterday, and how her expression seemed to reflect his own wheeling doubts and dreams. The way her smile ignited her eyes, her two front teeth emerging behind rosy lips – how it made her look sad and serious at the same time.

He took out his phone and stared at it, wondering if it was too soon to call – he'd never been very good at these things. He looked up at the whirling sky outside, the buses going by, their windows fogged and streaked, the cars sporting strange toupees of snow on their roofs, then turned back and pulled the card out of his wallet. He dialled the number before he could change his mind.

She answered on the second ring.

'Hello?'

He almost snapped the phone shut, the blood beating in his veins, but there was something calming about her voice, the swirl of her accent more pronounced than when he'd spoken to her the day before.

'This is Jack Carrigan,' he said, clearing his throat. 'My mother, Margaret Ca—'

'Hi Jack,' Karen interrupted, her voice soft and sultry as it crackled through his earpiece.

'I was just wondering if there were any new developments?'

'I'm glad you called,' the nurse replied. 'She's much better, the hip seems to be settling and we've sedated her for the pain.' There was a pause and he thought he could hear faint moaning on the other end of the line. 'I was going to ask . . .' the nurse continued, 'maybe if you were coming in to see her . . . we could have a drink or something?'

He looked down at the remains of his coffee and thought about the case; the long, relentless hours ahead. 'I'm sorry,' he said, 'this week's going to be tough.'

'I understand,' she replied, her voice subdued and hard to read.

Carrigan watched the falling snow outside, the crush and bustle of shoppers and neon stutter of Christmas lights arched across the high street like the gateway to some imperial corridor. He was about to ask her if they could rearrange but, by then, she'd already hung up the phone.

*

He stood outside the pathologist's office and wiped down his jacket and boots. The snow was falling pure and white but it turned to slush almost instantly on the grey pavements of Bayswater.

He waited in the reception area for the pathologist to come and get him. He found that, despite himself, he was looking forward to the old woman's abrasive manner and dry humour.

'Mr Carrigan?'

Jack looked up and saw a burly, barrel-shaped man approaching him. The man was shaking his head and muttering to himself. He had long salt-and-pepper hair, uncombed and wild, and a bushy black beard.

'It's Detective Inspector,' Carrigan replied as he stood up. 'I have an appointment with the pathologist.'

'I'm Milan,' the man said, not offering his hand nor any shred of comfort in his voice, which was strangely accented, a dry obduracy to it as if each word were something to be wrestled then spat out.

'And Bentley? Where is she?'

But Milan had already turned his back and was striding down a long narrow corridor towards the doors which led to the morgue. Carrigan had little choice but to follow him. He descended the stairs and blinked to adjust his eyes. The brightness of the basement always assailed him, the stuttering lights and reflective marble floors proving a potent combination. He put on a pair of blue plastic bootees, studying Milan, who was impatiently tapping his foot while humming something low and dolorous under his breath. Despite his initial impression, Carrigan realised that under the faded Deep Purple T-shirt and long hair, Milan was in his late forties, his skin cragged and wrinkled like the flesh of a walnut, his eyes sunk deep into folded pockets of skin as if they'd already seen too much of the world and didn't want to see any more.

'Is the pathologist coming?' Carrigan was starting to feel a prickle of annoyance. He didn't want to be wasting time if the old woman wasn't here. There were too many things to do, too many leads to chase up, and he recognised that peculiar mix of adrenalin and despair that often greeted him at the beginning of a major case.

Milan shrugged and used a scrunchy to tie his hair back into a ponytail, the T-shirt riding high above his gut. 'Dr Bentley's not here.'

'I can see that. Where is she?'

'She's dead.'

Carrigan stopped in his tracks, unsure if he'd somehow misheard the man through his mangled accent. 'Dead?'

'Yes, dead. You know . . . like all these people here.' Milan swept his arm across the room, the sheet-covered mounds on the metal tables eerie and still.

Carrigan took a moment to digest this information. When was the last time he'd spoken to her – a week ago? A month? He remembered her Thatcher hairdo and the constant stink of smoke on her breath but not her first name. 'The cigarettes?'

'No, no,' Milan replied. 'She walked into a bus last week. Double-decker. Squashed flat, no chance.'

'Jesus,' Carrigan exhaled. 'Who's in charge, then?'

'What, you haven't worked that out? Some detective you are.' Milan turned and headed towards the centre of the room. He wrote something down on a clipboard 'So, what do you want?'

Carrigan stared at the floor, trying to make sense of it. 'I came to get an initial report on the bodies recovered from the convent.'

Milan sighed and scratched his belly. 'I told your boss this would take at least a week – you think I'm some kind of magician?' He pointed to the metal gurneys surrounding them. Normally the pathologists worked on two or three bodies at a time but, as Carrigan surveyed the room, he could see gurneys pressed tight against each other wherever he looked, the whole room covered in a sea of shrouded bodies. Dull metal scales hung from various points along the ceiling. Each held a mass of red or grey matter, kidneys and livers and hearts waiting to be bagged and weighed.

'I was just hoping to get your initial impressions.'

'Initial impressions?' Milan repeated. 'My initial impression is that you're nuts.'

Carrigan didn't know what to say, so unexpected was the man's response and so different from what he was used to with the old woman. 'Please?'

'Okay, okay, okay,' Milan finally allowed. 'I look at them, I see some things, yes, but remember this is only, what you call it? Initial impression? Might be all wrong. You then come back and say Milan fucked the case, gave us wrong results, am I right?' Milan clicked his teeth and shook his head. He walked up to the nearest gurney and unceremoniously yanked the sheet as if he were a tired maid at the end of her shift. Carrigan took a step back. The smell was so strong and rich, so familiar.

'Smell like barbecue, right?' Milan smiled and Jack could tell he was enjoying this. 'Like barbecue I used to do with my father back in the old country – but that shouldn't surprise you, Detective Inspector, what are we? Just meat on the bone, no different from a leg of pork or rack of ribs, right?'

Carrigan tried to tune out the pathologist's words as he stared down at the shrivelled and blackened remains of corpse one. The eleven bodies had all been tagged numerically, starting at the head of the table and progressing clockwise. Corpse eleven was the one they'd found downstairs, cowering in the confession booth. Carrigan hated the anonymity of it, this last reduction into a single cipher, and knew that finding their identities so that they could be properly buried would be his first priority.

Milan crossed to another gurney and stripped the sheet. He did this until all the bodies were uncovered, small black lumps, more like children than adults. Medical assistants walked past, bagging samples and clearing the mess. Milan berated and shouted at them at every opportunity. They seemed shell-shocked by the new order in the morgue.

'This,' Milan pointed to corpse one. 'You should not think they curled up like this to protect themselves. This is fire, this is what happens, the muscles lose liquid and contract, the body ends up looking like it struggled and fought, but this all happens after they die, you understand?'

It was basic forensics, something every detective, whether they liked it or not, quickly became familiar with, but Carrigan saw no gain in antagonising the new pathologist.

'The bodies are in very bad condition. Burned for a long time. We couldn't get any fingerprints off them and dental work for only a few.'

'Do you have any previous experience with this kind of thing?' Carrigan asked softly.

Milan eyed him carefully, looking for the slight behind the words. 'Believe me, you don't want to know,' he replied. 'War has a way of making you into a very good pathologist.'

'Which side?'

'The side that wasn't trying to kill me.'

Carrigan shrugged, wishing he hadn't brought the subject up.

'What about DNA?'

'I managed to scrape some samples but the tissue is very degraded – I don't know if we'll be able to get much from it.'

Carrigan thought about this. 'Prioritise corpse eleven, have her DNA checked before the others.' He knew it was imperative that they get an ID on the eleventh victim as soon as possible. Without knowing who she was they were flailing around in the dark.

Milan nodded and rubbed his small plump fingers across his shirt.

'Did you notice anything different about her? The corpse from the confession booth?'

Milan thought for a minute, checking something on his clipboard. 'Yes, I thought you would ask that.'

Carrigan waited for the pathologist to continue but he didn't say anything else. 'What was different about her?'

He saw Milan smile, then quickly hide it, and he got the impression that he'd just passed some small but significant test. He watched as Milan went over to one of the gurneys and delicately turned the skull towards him.

'Major blunt force trauma.' Milan pointed to a shallow declivity at the front of the skull. 'She was hit hard. Before the fire.'

Carrigan thought of the body crumpled inside the confession booth, the fire investigator's description of the woman's final agonies. 'Could she have fallen forward, hit her head against the booth door?'

'Maybe, but probably not. She was hit with a lot of force. It would be very hard to do that to yourself. The blow would have rendered her unconscious.'

Carrigan flashed back to the serrated scratch marks on the inside of the confession booth's door. 'She was awake when the fire reached her.'

'Interesting,' Milan replied. 'It's possible she came to, but after such a blow she would have been very confused and disoriented.'

'What about the others?'

'I haven't had much of a chance to examine them yet. I have ten more female bodies. They range in age from early twenties to late seventies. That's more or less all I can tell you right now.'

Carrigan nodded, knowing this had been a waste of time. He'd been too impatient and should have waited for the full report. He thought about the neat pattern of bodies, the way the nuns had stoically faced death at the dining-room table. 'Anything to indicate that they were killed before the smoke got to them?'

Milan shrugged. 'Hard to say till I open them up. No external signs like on corpse eleven, but the fire didn't leave us much to work with. Why, you think someone killed them then set the fire to cover it up? Amateur hour.'

Carrigan was about to say that most criminals did not have a grounding in pathology and therefore made those kinds of mistakes regularly, but Milan had already turned his back to him and was washing his hands in the sink. He came back, pulling a green tubular packet from his top pocket. Carrigan watched queasily as Milan unsheathed the salami from its packaging and bit off a massive chunk.

'Are there any indications they'd been tied up?'

'I could find nothing that would suggest that.' Milan spoke with his mouth full, making it even harder to understand what he was saying. 'But the fire . . .' he held up his hands, 'who knows what it erased.'

'So, apart from the body downstairs, nothing struck you as suspicious?' Carrigan said irritably, thinking this was the least informative post-mortem chat he'd ever experienced.

Milan shrugged. 'Well . . . I don't know . . . I mean, it has nothing to do with the case.'

'Let me be the judge of that.'

'Okay, but this is old, maybe thirty, forty years.' Milan finished his salami, burped and snapped on his latex gloves. He walked Carrigan over to a group of gurneys crowded into the far corner. 'The skin on corpse one's legs has been totally burned off by the fire, otherwise I wouldn't have noticed it.'

'Noticed what?' Carrigan leaned closer but could see nothing unusual.

'There are several unusual injuries on the shins of the corpse.'

'What kind of injuries?'

'Striations on the bone.'

'Any chance these are related to their deaths?'

Milan shook his head. 'No, no, these are very old. You can tell from the way the cartilage has healed around it, good but not perfect. So, I think to myself, this is strange, but maybe she had some freak accident when she was young, these things happen all the time, okay? But still, I decide to check the others, just the shinbones, and yes, I'm thinking this is just some childhood accident but then I get to corpse four, corpse six, nine and ten, and I see similar marks.'

'Can you show me?'

Milan pointed with a penlight at the legs of the first corpse and Carrigan could see the black blistered surface, like something left in the oven for too long. The pathologist delicately pulled away a loose flap of skin to reveal the congealed mass of rendered tissue below.

'What am I supposed to be looking at?'

Milan switched on an overhead spotlight and angled it in. The light was harsh and unremitting and Carrigan saw the obscene white glint of bone and he wanted to turn away but forced himself to look closer and then he saw what the pathologist had meant.

There were several vertical lines running up and down the shinbone. They were rough and uneven, overlapping each other, and were about half a centimetre deep.

The pathologist led Carrigan to the adjacent table, corpse four, and aimed the spotlight down into the mess of bone and burnt sinew. 'See? Almost the same injuries. One, yes, could be an accident, something like that, but five? Five would be very big odds, the kind of odds you win lotteries off.'

'And these are also old injuries?' Carrigan stared at the small bones, marked and lined with ancient wounds, and felt a shiver run down the back of his neck.

'Yes, very old. Exactly the same as on corpse one. Same thing on the others.'

'Any idea what could have caused them?'

Milan shrugged. 'They're not accidental, that's obvious. Something very sharp and fine was used to make these. And it would have hurt a lot.'

'Could it be self-inflicted?' Carrigan asked. 'Some kind of self-punishment?'

Milan laughed. 'Oh no, Mr Carrigan, I very much doubt it. These nuns were tortured, and by someone who knew exactly what they were doing.'

11

Geneva put Hubbard in interview room number two and tried to reach Carrigan and Karlson, but neither was answering his phone. She stood and stared at the water cooler as it dispensed two cups, weighing it up. You had to take confessions when they were offered – people quickly lost the desire to talk once they'd been sitting in a police station for a few hours. With the other two gone she was now the highest ranking officer in the team.

'Would you like some water?' She handed Hubbard one of the plastic cups and closed the door to the interview room behind her.

Hubbard waved it away. 'I don't want a drink, I want to confess.'

She sat down, called for Jennings and took out her notebook. She turned towards the far wall and started the digital recorder. Hubbard had waived his right to have a lawyer present but Geneva made sure she followed procedure – if Hubbard was about to confess, she didn't want some oversight on her part getting the confession thrown out of court. She stated the date and location, 'DS Miller and DC Jennings present. The subject is named Alan Hubbard and has come in of his own volition.' She heard a weird snuffling sound and looked up. Hubbard had slumped down onto the table, his head cradled in his folded arms.

'I'm to blame,' he said, his voice muffled and distant, more like an echo than an actual voice. His smell permeated the room, meaty and sour and close. It was obvious that he'd been drinking and that he'd been doing it for the last couple of days but under the bulb flicker and whirring tapes he seemed strangely sober and lucid. 'I was supposed to do it last week. Fuck!' He slammed one fist down onto his thigh. 'Fuck. Fuck. Fuck.'

'What were you supposed to do?' Geneva moved her chair closer, spreading her arms across the table and settling her head down to his level. There was a strategy and game-play to every interview and each one required a totally different approach. You had to anticipate, psychoanalyse, and go with the beat of the moment.

Hubbard continued pounding his legs in staggered bursts. 'I was lazy. Always lazy. Sister Jacky made it clear that I should do it before Christmas. I was going to do it, I swear, I just lost track of the days.'

'What is it you didn't do, Alan?' Geneva said, starting to have a bad feeling about this.

'They told me the boiler cover needed fixing. They didn't say do it now but they never say do it now, that's not how they are. The boiler blew because the cover hadn't been fixed. The boiler blew and now they're all dead.' Hubbard started crying, small racked sobs emerging from the depths of his throat.

Geneva looked at Jennings and saw her own thoughts and doubts mirrored in his eyes. She turned back to the table. 'Mr Hubbard, we've had the report back from the fire investigator. You'll be happy to know that the fire did not start anywhere near the boiler.' It had been in the summary she'd read; one of the first things any investigator would look for. 'It's not your fault.'

'How can they know that?' Hubbard said. 'How can they know what happened when only God can know that?'

'They've looked at the evidence left from the fire.'

'But they weren't there! How can they know when they weren't there?'

She was about to say something then stopped. There was nothing to say. Evidence and fact were nothing compared to this man's guilt and need for recompense.

She thought about what she'd seen in Hubbard's flat, the gaunt grey pallor of his skin. 'When did you contract HIV?' Geneva asked quietly.

Jennings's head shot up from his notebook and he gave her a startled look.

'How?...' Hubbard used one of Geneva's tissues to wipe his nose and beard. 'How did you...'

'I saw your pills, Mr Hubbard.'

The man stared at the wall and sighed. 'A long time ago,' he said, his voice shifting down a pitch, 'I was backpacking through Russia, got drunk one night and woke up in a prison cell. Two years later they let me out.' He looked down at his crumpled shoes, the stitching unseamed and the leather curling up at the toes. 'I didn't know at the time, but they gave me this souvenir to take home with me.'

'I'm very sorry,' Geneva said.

Hubbard sniffed. 'Most people thought I got what I deserved. Me? I knew I'd got what I deserved. The things I'd done... God, I wish I could forget my life.' His head jerked up and his eyes met hers. 'Do you ever feel like that?'

Geneva was about to say no then stopped to think about it and nodded, sensing something small and important pass between the two of them. 'Was that how you met the nuns? Through the outreach work they did?'

'No,' Hubbard replied. 'I was looking for work. I just knocked on doors, that's what I did. I knocked on their door, had no idea it was a convent, must have been the fortieth door I'd knocked on that day. When Sister Jacky opened it I didn't know what to say, I must have stood there looking like an idiot. Finally, I snapped out of it and told her I'd fixed the front gate, the latch had been wonky, and that, if they needed, I could fix other things around the house and grounds.' Hubbard stopped and looked at the blank surface of the table, his mouth pursed tight. 'She was so kind, Sister Jacky. She took me to the kitchen, sat me down, gave me a cup of tea then made me lunch. Scrambled eggs, toast and bacon. She said yes, quite a few things around the place had fallen into disrepair, and that she would need to clear it with the mother superior but she was sure they could find work for me.

'I came in twice a week after that. Sister Jacky or Mother Angelica would give me lunch, then a list of things that needed to be done. There wasn't much. I think sometimes they even made things up or put things out of joint so that I'd have work to do. They gave me food to take home, they helped me find temporary accommodation and what did I do? I killed them. Like everything else I've ever done in my life, I fucked it up.' He huddled into himself, his breath raspy and strained, his curled fists pressing down into his legs.

'You mentioned two nuns, a Sister Jacky and Mother Angelica – were those the only two you met?'

Hubbard shook his head. 'Those are the ones I dealt with most of the time.'

'Can you tell us a little about Mother Angelica?' While Geneva had been disappointed that Hubbard did not seem to be the arsonist – her daydream of calling Carrigan and telling him she'd wrapped up the case, dashed – she now realised he could be a valuable source of information.

Hubbard's face darkened and a muscle on his left cheek started twitching. 'I don't think she ever liked me,' he replied. 'But she tried to hide it. She was different from Sister Jacky and the other nuns I met. As if she were floating an inch above the ground and everyone else a prisoner of gravity. She was an old woman and she'd been through a lot, you could tell by looking at her face, the way she conducted herself, how she never wasted a single word. She wore these tight round glasses that made her look like an owl.' Hubbard smiled to himself and Geneva caught a brief glimpse of the man he'd been before life had hiccuped and sent him on a different track.

'Me and Sister Jacky used to call her the Owl, it was our private joke. Sister Jacky told me that she'd written an important book many years ago, that they all looked up to her, and that I shouldn't judge the Owl by appearances.'

Geneva glanced up from her notes. 'You must have got to know the convent's routines pretty well. You didn't by any chance notice anything unusual during the last month or so?'

Hubbard's eyes looked anywhere but in her direction. 'Why are you asking me all these questions? Why don't you just arrest me?'

'We'll get to that soon enough,' Geneva said. 'But I know you know more than you've told me. You think it's your fault that the nuns died despite what the fire inspector found, okay, I understand that, but someone killed those nuns intentionally and I'm going to find out who it was. You can help me, Mr Hubbard, and you can help the nuns too by telling me what you know.'

Hubbard took a deep breath and slowly unclenched his fisted hands, laying them flat across the top of his thighs. 'My flowers,' he replied. 'Someone kept treading on my flowers.'

'That's not what we meant,' Jennings said irritably. 'This is a murder inquiry and we were looking for something a bit more . . .'

'Where exactly were your flowers?' Geneva interrupted, the edges of her fingers tingling.

'In the garden, up against the back fence.'

She considered this for a moment as she took a sip of water. 'Did you notice if the damage was worse nearer the fence or further away from it?'

Hubbard looked confused by this line of questioning and she could see him straining to remember. 'Right next to the fence, about halfway across, that's where they were trampled the most.'

Geneva thought back to her quick perusal of the convent blueprints. There was a large garden at the back of the house. She tried to remember what was on the other side of it – more houses? another street? – but it was a blank. 'Was that the only unusual thing you noticed recently?'

Hubbard shook his head then looked down at the table.

'It's okay, Mr Hubbard, whatever you say won't go further than this room. You want us to catch whoever did this, right?' Her voice softened and slowed. 'Everyone's dead. You're the only person who can tell us what went on in there, what could have led to this.'

'It wasn't the same,' he whispered.

'What wasn't?'

'The mood in the convent,' Hubbard said. 'Everyone seemed in a bad temper all the time, even Sister Jacky who was never like that. They rushed down the corridors and didn't see me. Doors that were always open now remained shut. Often the basement was locked and I couldn't get to my tools. They began to talk in whispers, in corners and alcoves, their faces shaded and suspicious as if they didn't trust each other any more.'

Geneva was writing this down so fast the sides of her fingers were turning a bright red. 'Do you have any idea what brought on these changes?'

'I don't know . . . but it started shortly after the new girl first appeared,' Hubbard replied, something in his dead grey eyes flickering to life for a brief bright moment.

'New girl?' Geneva and Jennings said at the same time.

'I first saw her about a year ago and then I kept seeing her more and more. She was often with the Owl, both of them talking, looking serious, their heads bent down over some book or other. She always smiled when she passed me in the corridor. She was very pretty.'

Hubbard blushed and Geneva could tell he was a little in love with this girl, an anonymous yearning played out in snatched looks and chance encounters. 'Do you know her name?'

Hubbard shook his head.

'Was it possible she was in training, a novice perhaps?'

Hubbard seemed to find this mildly amusing, smiling out the corner of his mouth. 'She definitely wasn't a nun.'

'Why do you say that?'

'The things she wore, ripped jeans, baggy T-shirts, big chunky black boots, but the funniest thing was her hair.'

'Her hair?'

'She had pink hair. Pink Panther pink. It looked so out of place among the nuns with their wimples and habits.'

'When was the last time you saw her?'

Hubbard closed his eyes for a moment. 'A couple of weeks ago,' he replied. 'The same day the visitors came.'

'Visitors?' Geneva said, slightly out of breath.

'I only saw them briefly but I'd never seen them before.'

'What did they look like? Men, women, priests?'

'Two men. Foreign, they were. Dark-skinned but not black. Wore suits, looked like expensive suits. They were talking to Mother Angelica. Arguing, really. Then shouting. Finally, Mother Angelica told them to leave.' Hubbard looked up at Geneva. 'Mother Angelica was shaking with anger. I'd never seen her like that before.'

'Did the men say anything?'

Hubbard sniffled and coughed into his fist. 'Only that they would be back.'

12

She was about to call it a night. She'd written up her notes from the interview and was looking forward to the prospect of a slow strong drink, the lights down low and the curtains pulled tight against the day. But something kept nagging at her. She read through the interview summary again and it didn't take her long to work out what it was.

She managed to grab a sandwich at the canteen but she ate it too fast as she made her way through the tightly packed crowds of Queensway. Her jacket wasn't warm enough and the snow was working its way under her collar, causing wet trickles to run down the back of her neck. But she didn't care, didn't care at all. She tilted her head and let the snow fall on her face, enjoying the icy slapping sting of it. She'd always loved the blank mystery of snow, from that first remembered Easter in the Baltic to the crisp white fields of wintertime Colorado where she and Oliver had spent their Christmas holidays. The thought of her ex-husband came up like the bile in her stomach. She'd finally opened the letters, listened to the answering-machine messages with their threats, insinuations and promises of lengthy litigation, and knew she would have to meet him face to face so that she could end this part of her life once and for all. She couldn't bear the thought of it but she needed the money he owed her, was sick of borrowing from her mother at the end of each month. She wished she could take Carrigan with her, there was something about him, a sense of comfort and protection, but she quickly dismissed the idea, embarrassed for even having thought it.

She turned into St Peter's Square, the scent of scorched wood still suspended in the air as if trapped by the snow. The scene was as she remembered and yet it was also different. The eager jostling crowds of the first night had thinned so that now only a few stray shoppers stumbled on this ruined skeleton of a house, staring up for a few moments, then turning back toward the chaos and noise of the high street. The blue crime-scene tape had been moved and it now covered a much smaller area, as if the crime itself was receding from memory.

Geneva thought about what Hubbard had said about his flower-beds and the girl with the pink hair, wondering if she was another of the nuns' projects, their 'lost sheep', as Holden had called them. She pulled out the map Hubbard had drawn for her during the interview, shielding it from the falling snow. She tried to imagine the house before the fire, the front garden all neat and tidy, the light leaking from arched windows and falling softly on the grained floor as the nuns sat and knelt and meditated on fate and suffering.

But she didn't stand there long. She checked Hubbard's sketch again and walked past the house. The firemen had got there in time to save the buildings next door. She could see blurry lights behind pulled curtains and the flickerdance of shadows moving within. There were two houses to the left of the convent and then the square ended. She checked the map and turned down the narrow side street.

A high brick fence enclosed the terrace and ran the length of the back gardens. She followed it until the wall curved back round into a small alley. The snow was as smooth as a well-made bed and her footsteps were the first to mark its surface as she cautiously entered. The alley was about fifteen feet wide with tall wooden fences on either side and was lit only by the weak spilled light from the sur-rounding residences. Geneva walked slowly, her feet unsteady in the deep snow. She could see the roofs of the houses above the fence-line and made her way towards the convent.

She stared up at the ruined structure as it glowed darkly against the sky, then she looked down. The snow next to the fence was unbroken. No one had been here today. She pulled out the map Hubbard had made and tried to work out where the flowerbeds were.

The fence was about twenty feet long and eight feet high. The top of the fence was crowned in snow and she was unable to see if there were any scratches, tears or other evidence that it had been climbed. Small bushes and scraggly weeds covered the ground directly in front of it, rising several feet above the snowline.

She gently kicked away the loose powder with her boots. She looked up as a light went on in one of the neighbouring houses then blinked off. She knelt down and carefully scooped away the remaining snow with her hands until she'd revealed the rough asphalt. A muffled sound made her turn round, almost losing her balance, but when she looked behind her the alley was empty. She took a deep breath and brushed some more of the snow away from the bottom of the fence. She aimed her torch into the newly cleared space and noticed something shining on the ground.

By the base of the bush there was a collection of random litter – crushed cigarette butts, chocolate wrappers, dead leaves and several small squares of silver foil. Each one had dark burn marks spreading from its centre like crushed spiders. Geneva took out an evidence bag and was reaching down when she heard the sound again. She spun round and aimed the torch in the direction of the noise. She swept it up and down the alley but there was nothing. She waited a few seconds, listening to the roaring of the blood in her ears, and then she heard it again, a soft mewling cry floating on the wind.

'Police! Show yourself!' she shouted, her palms sweating despite the cold. There was no reply nor repeat of the sound. She was about to turn back when she saw it coming towards her.

The cat stopped and arched its back and hissed at her. Its eyes were black as night, lost in ruffles of white fur, and its mouth was stretched so wide it looked as if it had been torn apart. It stood there and hissed again and curled its right claw. A nervous burst of laughter shot through Geneva.

'Get out of here, cat!' she said, feeling embarrassed and more than a little relieved.

She turned round, bagged the silver foil, then took a few steps back and studied the fence.

It was made up of several sections nailed together. One of the sections, directly in front of where she'd found the foil, had come loose. She leaned forward and ran her hand into the gap. The wood gave about an inch and she heard a faint scraping and scratching coming from below. She used her fingers to follow the crack as it disappeared behind the bushes and held her breath as she felt the sudden change in texture from the rough splintered feel of the wood to something smooth and man-made. She dropped her torch, cursed and picked it up again, then crouched down and pushed the shrubs aside.

The fence was broken all the way to the bottom and the lower half of the crack was held in place by four thick strips of grey gaffer tape. She stared at it for a long moment and then she understood.

Someone had removed the section of fence then taped it back together so that it could be opened and closed at will. Someone had turned the broken fence into a door.

*

DC Singh found her standing outside the front of the convent. 'I think we may have something,' Singh said, out of breath and a little ruffled.

'Thought you were off today?'

Singh frowned. 'Branch came in earlier, told us all leave was suspended until this thing is solved.'

'Shit,' Geneva said.

'I guess Christmas just got cancelled,' the young DC dourly

93

replied as she pulled out a clipboard and rifled through the pages. 'Haven't broken the news to Steve yet, he's going to blow his top.'

Geneva shrugged the kind of shrug women give each other to signify the vagaries of men. She looked across at the blackened silhouette of the convent, one wall still standing, the others in various states of collapse, and she was reminded of those paintings of ruined abbeys straddling impossible mountain peaks, the sense of longing and mystery in things no longer there. 'Anything on the door-to-doors?'

'Pretty much the usual crap.' Singh explained that the uniforms had spent the day going up and down the street, interviewing the residents, hoping someone had seen something the night of the fire. 'One woman, an old lady two houses across, said she saw a priest leaving the premises at about five, gave us a description,' Singh said, wrapping her jacket tightly around her as the wind came careening down from the park, icy and sharp, so cold it made their eyes water. 'We also talked to some of the other people who called it in. They were about to have a dinner party and the husband had gone outside to smoke his pipe. This was around six forty-five by his estimate. He said at first he didn't see anything unusual and then a few minutes later he noticed white smoke coming from the building but didn't think much of it. He was just putting out his pipe when the first flames became visible. He reckons that a pipe takes him fifteen minutes to smoke so we now have seven p.m. as an approximate time for the fire.'

'For the flames,' Geneva corrected, then immediately regretted it when she saw the constable's eyes drop to the ground and realised that Singh had been hoping to impress her. 'Good work,' she added, but she could tell it was too late. 'You mentioned there was something else?'

Singh nodded, hugging herself against the wind and snow. 'One of the uniforms talked to a teacher at the primary school a couple of doors down from the convent. Apparently, she said she had something to report, but that she was busy and he should come back in an hour.'

Geneva shook her head and looked down at her soaked shoes. 'And he just left her there, right?'

Singh shrugged her shoulders.

'For God's sake, they're worse than useless, these new recruits.'

Like the convent, the school was housed in what had once been a residential building and the only thing to announce this change was a small brass plaque fixed to the gate proclaiming it one of the first Montessori schools in London.

It took three rings before the door was answered. The woman on the other side looked put out and piqued, as if Geneva and Singh were the fifth set of salesmen calling that day. 'Yes?' she said, her accent totally at odds with her looks.

Geneva showed the woman her warrant card. 'You told one of the constables you had some information?'

The woman nodded and introduced herself as Gabby. She had long blonde hair tied back in a messy ponytail and chapped fingers.

Gabby studied the warrant card carefully then grudgingly opened the door a further few inches. 'Look, I'm really busy. Couldn't you wait until I've finished?'

Geneva walked past her into the hallway. Bright paintings, crude diagrams, strange versions of Disney characters and third-world leaders lined the walls on either side. 'We won't take up much of your time.'

'I've got to go through this again? Christ, I didn't even see anything important . . . I wish I hadn't told the officer now.' The woman stood there a moment as if she couldn't quite believe Geneva's impertinence. 'You mind if we do it in there? I still have a lot of work to do.'

The front room had been converted into a small classroom.

Twelve wooden desks were aligned in precise rows, the chairs all neatly tucked beneath them. A blackboard was mounted on one wall, posters, revolutionary slogans and more of the children's artwork surrounding it. A large photo stretched the length of the room and depicted two hands, one black and one white, shaking.

'You told one of the officers you saw something?' Geneva watched as the woman cleared her desk in staggers and clumps and could tell she was one of those people, more and more of them lately, who distrusted the police instinctively, as a badge of fashionable protest and self-gratifying resistance, seeing them only as jackbooted avatars of a new world order.

'*May* have seen something,' Gabby replied as if correcting a student for her errant grammar.

'Listen, we're conducting a murder inquiry so you need to tell us anything you *may* have seen.'

'Murder?' Gabby raised a hand to her mouth. 'You mean it wasn't an accident . . . oh God.' She looked down at the table then back at the two detectives. 'No one will know I gave you this information, right? I won't have to testify?'

Geneva thought she'd probably watched too many American cop shows but assured her there would be no need to testify and that this was purely for background information. Gabby stared across the classroom at a Mugabe poster splashed in red and green on the far wall. 'Because the people I saw . . .' she said, pointing to the front window. 'Look – three gates down? That's the entrance to the convent. When I'm here teaching the girls I can see who's coming and going.'

Geneva sidled up next to Gabby. From where she was standing, in front of the whiteboard, you could see the entire class but you could also see the large louvre window and everything that occurred within its frame.

'I only noticed them because they double-parked,' Gabby continued. 'We've spent years fighting the council to put up signs about it. It's a narrow road and a double-parked car is a death-trap when you have so many kids running around.'

'Noticed what?' Geneva was becoming increasingly frustrated by the teacher's digressive burble.

'It was only a couple of times, no, three I think, but it was the same two men each time. As I said, if they hadn't double-parked I wouldn't have noticed. It's just they weren't the kind of men you expect to see in a place like that.'

Suddenly Geneva's attention was entirely focused on the teacher. 'What do you mean?'

'You know . . . there's . . . there's a certain type.'

'And what type is that?'

'Black suits,' Gabby replied. 'Serious-looking people. One had this grotesque scar running down the side of his mouth. They didn't look like nice men.'

Geneva thought about what the teacher was saying and what she wasn't saying. 'And you saw two of these "types" visiting the convent more than once?'

'Yes, three times over the last month. Each time double-parking and just leaving the car there, blocking the whole street.'

'Did you notice how long they stayed?'

Gabby took a moment to think about this. 'Never more than ten minutes, a little less actually. I could see them better when they were walking out, when I knew they couldn't see me. They climbed into one of those black BMW monstrosities with tinted windows.'

'An SUV?'

The teacher nodded.

'You didn't by any chance get the registration?'

'You think I'm stupid?' she replied. 'You think I'm going to go out there and write it down? Besides, until what happened with the fire, I really didn't think twice about it, only remembered when your officer asked me if there'd been any unusual comings and goings.' Gabby shuddered and shook her head as if trying to rid herself of the memory.

Geneva listened to the furtive scratching sound of her pen as she wrote this information down. 'Did you know the nuns? Did the school have any dealings with them?'

'No, not for a while,' Gabby replied. 'They used to come and help us put together fundraisers for the kids but that all stopped about a year ago.'

'That alley behind the school, has there been any trouble there?'

Gabby's eyes widened briefly. 'We had a few problems. People dealing drugs out the back. We called you lot and a couple of uniforms came over and had a word. The next day the dealers were back again as if nothing had happened.'

'And it's still going on?' Geneva asked, some small lever in her brain starting to trip.

Gabby shook her head. 'The nuns put a stop to all that.'

Geneva's eyes flicked up from her notebook. 'How did they do that?'

'A couple of them stood sentry by the mouth of the alley. They took shifts. Gave out leaflets for rehab clinics. Prayed and sang hymns. Guess it put off the customers because we no longer had any trouble back there.'

'And what about a woman with pink hair? Did you ever see anyone of that description entering the convent?'

'Pink hair?' Gabby shook her head as if the very question didn't make sense.

They left the teacher alone in her classroom and stepped out into the snow and howling wind. Singh went off to check on the uniforms as Geneva lit a cigarette, thinking that for somewhere that wasn't supposed to have any visitors, the convent was proving to be a popular place.

She was about to head back to her car when she noticed the

cameras.

They were small, grey and well concealed. One was aimed at the front door of the school and would be of no use but, as Geneva looked up at the camera facing the main gate and followed its trajectory, she felt a surge of excitement and smiled.

13

Branch caught him on the way to the late briefing. 'A word, Carrigan,' he said, disappearing into his office before Jack had a chance to reply.

A TV had been recently installed on the super's wall and muted news bulletins about the fire, European economic collapse and a new super-virus kept flashing across the screen as Carrigan took a seat. Outside, the evening sky was white as a candle, a steady bright smudge across the horizon which forced him to squint as he faced Branch.

'Good work, Carrigan. Good work!'

'Sir?' Jack shifted uneasily in his chair. He knew his boss well enough to know that Branch handing out compliments was always the precursor to something bad.

'You have a suspect, I'm told, confessed to the crime. That's splendid news.'

Carrigan tried to read the super's expression but Branch was already flicking through the files on his desk. Suspect? He had no idea what Branch was talking about.

'DS Miller's been trying to contact you.'

'I was at the morgue and I had to give a deposition in court, you know that.'

'Well then, I've made your day.' Branch looked up and smiled. 'The ACC is on his way here, so it would be good if you had this suspect all packed up and ready. Quinn wants a press conference tonight to announce it. He's seen the papers and he's not happy.'

'The papers?'

Branch shook his head despairingly and flung a copy of the

Standard across the table. The front page had a colour photo of the flame-wrapped convent under the headline *Who Is the Eleventh Victim?* George Khan's byline appeared just beneath it. Carrigan scanned the first two paragraphs. 'Christ.'

'Indeed,' Branch murmured. 'In my experience, Carrigan, when people start talking to the press it's often because the investigation is losing focus and the rank and file are questioning their superior's handling of the case.'

It took Carrigan a moment to realise what Branch was saying. 'It could have come from any of a number of sources, could be the pathologist's assistants, one of the firemen, could be anyone.'

'Well, I'm glad you're so quick to dismiss it,' Branch replied. 'With Quinn looking over your shoulder, let's hope for both our sakes it is.'

Carrigan waited a beat. 'We have some new information regarding the nuns.'

Carrigan told him what the pathologist had found, the marks on the shinbones of the five nuns, knowing it was the last thing Branch wanted to hear.

'Quinn's not going to like that one bit. Forty years ago? I don't think it's wise to mention that particular bit of information when you see him.' Branch let out a dry, bitter laugh. 'Jesus, why the fuck did he have to choose you for this? You have no idea what you've got yourself into, Carrigan. You really don't want to fuck with Quinn. There's stories . . . I'm not going to tell you what they are . . . but believe me, there's stories that'll make your hair curl.' Branch paused and shook his head. 'This would almost be funny if it wasn't for the fact that I'm your superior and I'll get blamed for your fuck-ups. Christ, not only does Quinn live up the road, he's also the head of the bloody Catholic Police Association.' Branch stopped suddenly, his eyes squinting. 'Anyway, to get back to the point – take the suspect, I don't care how strong you think the case is, process him so that Quinn can have his press conference and leave us the fuck alone.' Branch pulled out a mobile from his jacket, signalling the end of the conversation. As Carrigan was leaving, the super looked up one last time and said, 'Under the fucking microscope, Carrigan, remember . . . under the fucking microscope.'

He marched into the incident room, the door slamming shut behind him, everyone in the room raising their heads.

'Why the fuck wasn't I told we have a suspect?'

No one said a word, gazes dropping to notebooks and knees.

'I tried calling you, sir . . . several times,' Geneva explained.

Carrigan took the phone out of his pocket and realised he'd forgotten to turn it back on after leaving court. 'Shit,' he muttered under his breath. He looked back up at the team. 'So, do I have to wait till Christmas or is someone going to tell me who this bloody suspect is?'

'We picked up the caretaker, Alan Hubbard,' Geneva replied. 'He said he'd killed the nuns. We interviewed him and concluded that he's not a viable suspect.'

'And what made you conclude that, DS Miller?'

Geneva swallowed rapidly, looking down at her notes. 'He thinks he killed the nuns because he never got round to fixing the boiler.'

For a brief moment the mood in the incident room lifted, some of the younger constables laughing and swapping incredulous looks among themselves.

'We're holding him downstairs as a witness for now. Jennings checked his whereabouts on the night of the fourteenth and it looks like he's clear.'

Carrigan didn't know if this was good news or bad. He stood up and wiped the whiteboard behind him. He pinned up the photos he'd taken in the chapel. The scratched door. The pricket stand. The statue of the saint. 'This isn't our usual case: we have eleven bodies, not one, a crime scene that's almost useless and a public relations nightmare if we don't find out who did this.' He turned around, saw the gravity of the situation sinking in and continued, 'I want updates from you as soon as you have something, even if you think it's nothing. I don't want to get sandbagged by Branch like that again.'

Geneva pulled out her notes and told him about Hubbard's description of the new girl. She felt a small measure of satisfaction when she saw his expression.

'Okay, we need to find out what we can about this woman. Jennings, I want you to take some uniforms and re-canvass the area. Do we have a description?'

Geneva shrugged. 'Not really, apart from the pink hair.'

'Any other visitors?' Carrigan asked and DC Singh told him about the sighting of the priest leaving the convent a couple of hours before the fire.

'I showed the description to Hubbard and he recognised him immediately. Said his name was Father McCarthy and that he was a regular visitor.'

'That bastard Holden never mentioned any priest,' Carrigan said, not knowing if Holden had been evasive because he had something to hide or because it was his default position. 'Do we have an address for this Father McCarthy?'

Karlson shook his head. 'I called the diocese. They confirmed that a Father Callum McCarthy worked for them, but when I asked where I could reach him they told me he was unavailable and then when I pressed them they put the phone down.'

'They put the phone down?'

'They put the phone down.'

Carrigan felt that familiar heat in his chest, the case finally beginning to break open, showering them with leads, anomalies and inconsistencies. He knew that it was always somewhere in here, in the raw data sprawl of information and recalled fact, that the solution would be found. 'Any other visitors?'

Geneva told him about the double-parked SUV, the teacher's description of the two men and the position of the school's CCTV cameras. 'Could be the same two that Hubbard mentioned.'

'Berman? Get hold of that footage, let's see if we can find out more about these men.' Carrigan updated the whiteboard and stood back. He could always see the case better when it was written down, each piece of information and stray fact sequestered behind neat columns, but with the convent nothing was that simple. Usually, any anomaly in an investigation stuck out like a loose nail, but this case was proving to be so full of them that it was impossible to recognise what was genuinely pertinent. He knew it was his job to rein in the investigation and make sure they wouldn't be led into spinning black holes of mystery and dead ends. Branch's words rang sourly through his head. 'So, we know the convent certainly had their share of visitors but we don't know if this means anything yet.'

'There's more,' Geneva interrupted.

'More?' Carrigan frowned and ran his fingers through his beard as Geneva explained about the jury-rigged fence at the back of the convent. 'Looks like some junkies were using it regularly to fix. There were rumours someone was dealing out of that alley. The local station despatched some uniforms a few months back but apparently that didn't help, so the nuns decided to take things into their own hands, stood there all day handing out leaflets for rehab clinics. I sent the SOCOs to have a look but with the snow washing everything away I'm not confident we'll get much in terms of evidence. I think we should have a uniform posted there in case anyone returns.'

Carrigan looked lost in swirls of thought, his voice strangely disembodied when he finally spoke. 'I don't think that's relevant to the fire and we're stretched way too thin as it is with all these new leads to pursue.'

Geneva looked down at her notes, her shoulders slumping. 'I disagree.'

The incident room was silent, everyone watching Carrigan to see how he would react, Karlson just managing to hide the smile that was creeping across his face.

Carrigan stared at Geneva, then said, 'What makes you think this has any relevance?'

She looked surprised and took a swig of Coke to gather her thoughts together. 'Holden told us that the nuns had their special projects, their lost sheep,' Geneva said, thinking out loud. 'Maybe the back garden was known as a safe place to fix, the door making it easy to slip in and out.' She saw the team's expressions suddenly slip into focus, a new intensity in their eyes, and continued. 'Let's say one of the junkies decided to go inside the convent, perhaps just wanting to get out of the cold, was staggering around and knocked one of the candles over . . .'

'What about the eleventh victim?' Carrigan asked, running the scenario through his mind.

'Maybe she was the junkie we're talking about or maybe she stumbled on them, tried to get them to leave and a struggle broke out? That would explain the head wound.'

'I wish it was that simple.' Carrigan could see Geneva was upset but they were in a war against time and memory and everything had to be sacrificed to the momentum of the case, it was one of the few things he believed in without reservation. 'Karlson? Talk to your sources, find out who's been fixing up in that courtyard and see if they know anything about the door in the fence,' he said, trying to placate Geneva, but the mood was sour and deflated after that. It didn't get any better when he told them about the pathologist's findings.

'I don't know if this has anything to do with the case but the pathologist was pretty certain that five of the nuns had been tortured in an identical way.' He remembered the shrivelled bodies flat on their gurneys, how every life, when put under the microscope, was a collection of shadow and rumour, inconsistencies, mysteries and petty misdemeanours. 'Now, this was done to them at least thirty or forty years ago and I don't want to waste too much time on it but – Singh and Miller – I want you to go back to the diocese and have a look through their archives. We need to know who these nuns were. Not all of them join young, remember. Some have previous lives, lives they've run away from. We're seeing the nuns as a group now and that's wrong. We need to see them as individuals . . .' Carrigan looked up abruptly, his brow creasing. 'Jennings? Can you get off the bloody phone – we're in the middle of a briefing.'

Jennings put his hand over the mouthpiece. 'It's forensics, sir. They've just processed some of the samples from the convent.'

Carrigan grunted an apology and continued. 'We don't know if the nuns were locked in or if they locked the door themselves. We need to take into account both scenarios. We also need to consider whether the eleventh victim was the intended target and the nuns just collateral damage. Maybe this was a random accident, some junkie stumbling over a candle, but maybe it wasn't. The fact the fire started directly beneath the very place where the nuns had just gathered for dinner and the presence of the eleventh victim make me think we're looking at something else. We need to get an ID for her. Once we know who she was and why she was there that particular night, we'll know a lot more about why the fire started.' Carrigan scanned the room and saw that everyone's eyes were focused and sharp. They now had something to pursue, a promise that somewhere in the confusion of random data and rumour, a killer was hiding. He was about to dismiss them when he saw Jennings putting down the phone and signalling agitatedly with his left hand. 'Yes?'

'I've just talked to forensics.'

'And?' Carrigan said impatiently.

Jennings looked down at his notes. 'There was a funny smell in the chapel. They took some samples and tested them.' Jennings hesitated, his breath short and laboured. 'The samples came back positive for cocaine.'

14

There was nothing waiting for him at home. Sleep and rest were not to be found there. Carrigan felt frazzled and frayed, his body running on empty, too many coffees and the long winding rush of the day culminating in that last unexpected piece of evidence.

Once he would have called his best friend, Ben. Once he would have walked over to Ben's house and spent the night talking until the first faint light of morning. But Ben was in prison and Carrigan had put him there. He'd never second-guessed or regretted his decision, and knew it had been the right one, but on a night like this, that was little comfort.

So he drove. From Hammersmith to Highgate, Hackney to Hounslow, through Southfields and Mortlake, across time and space and night. Three, four times a week, when sleep wouldn't come, he would circle the city, passing through neighbourhoods he'd never seen before and would never see again. There was something soothing about the deserted streets, muted pavements and darkened shops, the rough edges and unrealised hopes rubbed away into shadowplay and night. This was the city in its most essential state, the bare blueprint on which the day's events and tragedies had yet to be written, and he often felt that the city was somehow contained in these nocturnal orbits, that as long as he kept driving he could circumscribe the endless spill and burst of its boundaries.

He crossed the wintry spine of Hyde Park, thinking about the case, the spiralling flow of new information, how everything they'd learned about the nuns in the last twenty-four hours seemed so at odds with their initial impressions. The snow was coming down in heavy drifts, erasing the horizon and greater city beyond. He drove past the night-dwellers huddled in narrow doorways, shivering and junk-sick on benches, or sleeping in shop alcoves under cardboard blankets. When you reached this depth of weather only those with truly nothing left and nowhere to go were still out on the streets and Carrigan tried not to think how little there was separating them from him.

He rubbed his head and blinked as the traffic lights turned to green. So much they didn't know yet. So many blank spaces on the map. The ACC calling every hour. Branch making frequent unannounced visits. The press clamouring and hectoring with every editorial. Ten days until Christmas.

He kept coming back to the cocaine. He remembered the sour stinging smell in the chapel. What was it doing there and how significant was it?

The angry honking of a cab snapped him out of his thoughts and he was surprised to find himself gliding down Bayswater Road. Maybe it was just muscle memory, the way he'd ended up back in his own patch like a homing pigeon, but he knew it was something more than that as he turned into St Peter's Square.

He got out of the car and stretched, his shoes instantly disappearing under layers of snow. The icy chill reaching his toes gave him a welcome jolt. He ducked under the crime-scene tape and looked up at the house. The moon rained light on the ruins and the snow hid the ugly burn scars and twisted metal. But it wasn't the house he was interested in, it was what lay beneath.

The fire investigator had told him the basement would be secured some time tomorrow and that he'd be able to inspect it then, but he couldn't wait – the unexpected findings of the SOCOs, and an offhand comment from the caretaker, had made sure of that.

He passed through the gaping doorframe and into the hallway. The smell filled his nostrils instantly. Despite the howling wind which rattled through the building, it hadn't dissipated, leaking from the wood and curled metal.

The firemen had strung emergency lights across the walls. Small bulbs lay in white plastic holders as if in imitation of fairy lights. When he pulled the switch, he was surprised to find they worked. Carrigan briefly looked up at the dining room then headed for the basement stairs. He opened the door and saw that the firemen had strung the lights all the way down. He put his torch back in his pocket and examined the stairs. They'd been charred and cracked by the fire but the SOCOs had managed to make their way up and down them without incident.

The stairs wobbled as he put his weight on them, his palms curled tight around the banister, but they held and, as he descended, he noticed that the smell had become stronger and harsher, tearing at his nasal passages, a bitter snap of taste at the back of his throat.

The emergency lights emitted a foggy yellow glow so that the basement resembled something from an old photograph, a snapshot of things long gone, drenched in sepia and dust. Carrigan's eyes slowly adjusted to the murky gloom and he could see that he was in a large single space, demarcated by darkness and cloistered areas. There were no windows, and large arched transepts swept along the centre of the room tapering down into plain stony columns. The basement had been used as a crypt and three of the walls were lined with dusty grey tombs, each about four feet high. The back wall was bare and had a table at its centre, a large 1970s piece of office retro, sturdy enough to have withstood the fire. An empty chair was tucked neatly underneath. Tall metal bookcases lined the walls to either side of the table, the paint blistered and the shelves holding only the ashes of their former occupants.

The corner area was partially walled off by linked columns and Carrigan could see slant tools dangling from hooks and slots driven into the wall, screwdrivers and hammers and pliers of all sizes. He got to his knees and examined the floor underneath. The area looked like an overhead shot of volcanic badlands but, instead of black, the hardened lava was white and creamy. Carrigan picked up one of these strange congealed forms and saw it was composed of several different types of plastic which had melted and reconfigured on cooling. The ash was peppered with small burnished metal parts, cogs and springs and pulleys which had survived the fire. There were also a handful of motherboards and processors, scorched and cracked and useless.

He made some notes, then got up and examined the tombs. They were made of granite and white stone and the dates inscribed on their sides ranged from 1926 to 2009. There were no carved angels, comforting saints or words of hope, only the blank hewn stone, as austere as the lives of those resting within had been. He counted eighteen tombs, lined up in even rows along three of the walls, uniform in size and design, the marble and stone cracked and patterned with the years. He thought of the people walking by on the street outside, taking their children to school, unaware of the mute ashy bodies beneath their feet, and it made him think of all the undiscovered corpses leaking slowly away below parks and moorland, new developments and kitchen floors. Two hundred and fifty thousand people went missing every year in Britain – how many of them had been murdered? No one knew. The irony was that the killers they caught and locked away were the careless or stupid ones, the ones who'd made mistakes. The idea of a Darwinian process of natural selection among murderers was something he didn't want to think about.

He spent the next fifteen minutes walking the basement, checking through each mound of ash and dust, pressing his face against the walls, looking for marks and signs, traces and anomalies, but he found nothing of interest. He came to a stop in the centre of the room and closed his eyes and tried to imagine what it had been like when it was full of people. It was a useful trick in getting an idea of what should and shouldn't be present. He imagined the nuns coming down here to pay their respects or doing the washing, cleaning the mould from the stones, maybe using the tools he'd found in the back corner . . . and then his eyes flicked open and he looked at the far wall with its desk and bookcases and then he looked at the opposite wall, a line of three tombs running along its length, and then back again.

He scanned each wall in turn, sensing something awry, some shift of perspective, and then he went upstairs.

He looked to his left, then to his right. The light was better here on the ground floor but he was certain it was more than just that. He approached the front door, then turned and counted his steps all the way to the back door. He could hear a van or SUV parking outside, the sound of a TV from a neighbouring house, a cat screaming somewhere in the night.

He took less time going down the stairs, knowing which were weak and which would hold him, and when he was in the basement he repeated the procedure again, counting steps from front to back. He did this twice to make sure he hadn't made a mistake and then he did it once more because it didn't make any sense.

The basement was five paces smaller than the ground floor. He tried to think of any reason this might be but came up with none. He looked at the workshop, then at the opposite wall.

Three tombs lined the length of it, placed head to toe, a two-foot gap separating one from another. Carrigan ran over to the wall, almost tripping, pulling down some of the emergency lights by accident as he stumbled and righted himself. He stared at the dark dappled surface. Roamed his torch across every brick and grout but it was nothing more than a plain brick wall.

He stepped back, a little disappointed, and examined the tombs. He checked each tomb in turn, running his light down into the space where rock and wall met, and it didn't take him long to spot the fine tracery of scratches veining the floor and radiating in an arc from the far edge of the middle tomb. He thought of the pricket stand upstairs and aimed his light into the gap between the tomb and the wall but it was too narrow to see what lay behind.

He bent his knees and pressed his shoulder against the side of the tomb. He pushed, his shoes sliding on the floor, and felt the tomb give slightly. He leaned into it, encouraged, and pushed harder, certain he was about to dislocate his shoulder.

The tomb shifted. He stopped, got his breath back, then, using his legs for support, he continued until one end of the tomb was several inches away from the wall. He squeezed himself into the gap and, using this new leverage, pushed the tomb further back. The stone slid and screeched against the floor but it was surprisingly easy and he wondered if it had been designed expressly for this purpose. He got back to his feet and peered into the gap. This time he didn't need the torch to see that the wall wasn't brick all the way down.

Concealed behind the tomb, at the bottom of the wall, was a small horizontal wooden door. It was flush to the floor and about three feet high and five across. At the bottom of the door there was a single ring-pull made of brass. Carrigan put his torch back in his pocket, squatted down, his back tight against the cold tombstone, and pulled.

Nothing. No movement at all.

He curled his fingers around the ring, tensed his shoulders and pulled harder. This time there was a single muted click and Carrigan felt a rush of stale air hit his face as the door-flap swung open.

15

The traffic was backed up all the way down Vauxhall Bridge Road. Geneva was watching Singh texting in the seat next to her, the young constable's attention fixed on the small grey screen, her fingers moving in rhythmic counterpoint to her expression. Geneva couldn't begin to imagine what could be so engrossing. She turned and stared out at the snow-sculpted pavements, the shuffle of shoppers and workers sludging through the muck and slush on their way to someplace better, and tried not to think of her own flat, the letters on the coffee table and shrill demands waiting on her answering machine.

Singh was still texting as Geneva parked outside the diocese's office. She'd spoken to Holden after the briefing, having caught him on his way out, and he'd agreed to let her go through the archives tomorrow morning. She'd put the phone down and stared at the mountain of files on her desk, not wanting to go home, then glanced across the table at Singh and said, 'You up for a late one?' Singh had nodded and Geneva saw relief brighten the young constable's face. For Geneva, late nights had always been one of the perks of the job.

The seminarian who answered the door wasn't the same young man as before and yet there was an uncanny similarity between the two, as if they'd been sourced from the same mould.

'He didn't say anything to me about this.'

Geneva flashed her warrant card. 'I spoke to him a couple of hours ago and he okayed it with me. You want me to go back to the station, tell a judge you're refusing us entry and come back with a warrant?'

The young man's face blanched at the word 'warrant', despite his best efforts to hide it. 'I'm afraid Mr Holden's gone home for the day,' he said.

'That's perfectly okay,' Geneva replied. 'It's the archives we want, not him.'

The young man moved back, as she'd known he would, not wanting to brush up against her as she stepped past him. She noticed his eyes linger just a little too long on her legs and she gave him one of those smiles that always worked for her in bars. His cheeks turned a surprising shade of crimson as she held out her hand and introduced herself.

'Rupert.' His palm was soft and hot and she couldn't feel any bones underneath the padded folds of skin.

The archives were located in an extension of the second-floor library. Rupert led them past long tables populated by silent young men hunched over ancient handwritten books, a grim concentration on their faces, and into an annex full of rusty filing cabinets and dusty stacks of paper.

The silence in the room was startling. It was as if someone had turned off the city with the ease of flicking a light switch. Geneva took out her notebook, pencils, laptop and a can of Coke. She turned to see Rupert shaking his head, pointing to the can, then to a sign saying ABSOLUTELY NO FOOD OR DRINK. 'Thanks, I think we'll be okay.' Geneva waited, but Rupert didn't budge.

'I'm afraid I can't leave you in here alone.' He avoided her eyes, focusing instead on the floor, examining his shoes as if seeing them for the very first time. 'It's diocese policy.'

'You think we're going to steal these documents?'

'I don't know what you're going to do. No man can know what another man will do.'

'Woman,' Geneva corrected.

They went through the grey creaky cabinets until they found the files for the convent. Geneva was disappointed by how thin they were, wondering if Holden had filleted them after receiving her phone call. She spread the files across a table which Rupert had obligingly cleared for her. She scanned the sheet Holden had given her yesterday and matched each name to a separate folder.

There were ten folders for ten nuns. The nuns' names were Irish, English, Scottish and Spanish. Geneva gave Singh the first five off the top and took the rest for herself. Rupert sat perfectly still and silent as the two detectives spent the next forty minutes going through each folder then swapped, hoping to catch anything the other might have missed. Geneva took notes, cross-referencing and underlining, but it was so early in the case that it was impossible to tell what was pertinent and what was not. There was nothing obvious, no criminal records, no red flags, but, after going through the material for the third time, she thought she could begin to discern the faintest flutter of repetition and coincidence.

She reread the nuns' biographies, their qualifications, the work they'd done, the institutions they'd been part of, but nothing further struck her and she realised she was looking at this the wrong way. She asked Singh to arrange the files in the order in which the nuns had joined. She noticed that Rupert had moved his stool a few feet closer to the table and that there was a flicker of interest in his eyes which he couldn't hide. She waited until Singh was finished, then scanned the folders on the table, but she already knew what she would find.

'Mother Angelica had been at the convent longer than anybody else,' she said quietly.

Singh came closer and stared at the files. Geneva had placed each victim's photograph at the top of her file. Laid out like this you could see the variety of expression and personality behind the strict habits and wimples and, for the first time, Singh saw the nuns as separate individuals, each with their own distinct history, and realised why Geneva had done it this way.

'Which means,' Geneva added, 'that all the nuns who were there when she joined have since left.'

'Maybe they just didn't get on with her?' Singh said, then caught herself. 'Sorry, I shouldn't be making jokes . . .'

'No,' Geneva interrupted, 'I think you might be on the right track. There's been a lot of turnover in personnel. The last nun to leave, Sister Rose, left just over a year ago and was replaced a month later. In fact . . .' she checked the dates again, 'everyone who died in the fire had been hired during Mother Angelica's tenure. It's almost as if she'd been recruiting them.'

'Why would she do that?' Singh looked up from her stack of files.

'Maybe she knew them?' Geneva thought about the dispute and how quickly Holden had dismissed her idea that the nuns had killed themselves because they thought the end of the world was coming. It made sense of the many contradictions of the case – why the nuns had died sitting peacefully at their tables, how anyone would know the exact time they'd all be gathered together, the locked room. She turned towards Rupert. 'Always ten nuns, right?'

'Always.'

'Can you find out how many died while serving at the convent?'

Rupert was up before she'd finished asking. He crossed the room and sat down at a small table, logging on to a dusty white PC. Geneva watched his eyes, intense with concentration and excitement, as he waited for the results.

Both his eyebrows shot up at the same time. 'Only two,' he replied.

'If only two were replaced because of death then we have to assume that the others left voluntarily. How unusual is that? Does the diocese deal with such things, Rupert?'

'No, that all goes through the order's headquarters in the Vatican.' He looked as if he was about to add something so Geneva kept her mouth shut. 'Unfortunately, it's not as unusual as it once was,' he finally said. 'It used to be that once you took your vows you stayed wherever the order told you to but a lot of things like that have changed recently.'

'What's the most common reason for a nun to transfer?'

'Clash of personalities, mainly. Still . . .' he said, thinking about this, 'for that number of nuns to leave the convent would be unusual even these days.'

It gave her an idea, the slightest glimmer of an idea, and she went through the paperwork and reread the deployment records, this time paying close attention to the dates. What did it mean, if anything, that seven nuns had left the convent since Mother Angelica had become abbess?

Geneva pulled out the relevant sheets and put them next to each other, then double-checked. The records had a detailed list of all postings, foreign and domestic, that the nuns had held. Geneva scanned names and dates and places, amazed at how their reach extended across the globe. Four of the nuns had done missionary work in the Holy Land, five had been in Africa, three in the Philippines, two in China and one in Papua New Guinea. But seven of them had spent time in South America.

She wrote down the dates and locations in her notebook. She cross-checked the list again. Some of the nuns had spent years in that continent while others were there for only a short period, but there was just one place where all seven nuns' paths had crossed. Peru. 1973. August to November.

She turned towards Rupert, catching his eyes roaming her skirt then pretending to look at something else, maybe the pattern of tiles on the floor. 'And how unusual would it be for them all to have been stationed in Peru at the same time?'

Rupert looked surprised. 'Not so unusual for them to be in Peru.

Each nun normally does a few years of missionary work,' he explained. 'But at the same time? And in the same convent? That's a big coincidence.'

'Yes it is,' Geneva replied, looking down at the records again. All seven nuns had spent the autumn of 1973 in the San Gabriel region of south-central Peru. She told herself not to leap to conclusions. Maybe it was nothing more than that they'd developed a bond in that far-flung posting and that Mother Angelica trusted them, naturally giving them first refusal when a place opened up at the convent.

Geneva made copies of the files she needed, thanked Rupert and started packing her things away when she remembered something that Gabby, the schoolteacher, had mentioned. 'Rupert? That computer of yours, does it have details of the charity work that the nuns were involved in?'

'No,' he replied, seeing Geneva's face fall. 'But I can get the register from the library, that should have the details,' he offered.

Geneva smiled and crossed her legs, watching Rupert exit the annex, his body taut with excitement and hurry. 'Men . . .' She shook her head and turned towards Singh, seeing the sudden weight in the young constable's eyes that her joke had elicited.

'Husband problems?' Geneva knew that Singh had got married last Christmas – she'd also noticed that all the wedding photos surrounding her desk had mysteriously disappeared a couple of months back.

Singh nodded and stared at the bright hard ring on her finger. 'He was never like this before we got married.' She sounded sad and defiant and a little pissed off all at the same time. 'Wants me to quit the job, can you believe that?'

'It doesn't surprise me.'

'He never said a word before we got married. Said the job made me even sexier in his eyes. Now all he talks about is me quitting, settling down and, fuck, I know what's coming next.'

There was no advice Geneva could give. She'd screwed up her own marriage. She had a bitter ex-husband who was trying to cheat her out of her half of their house and a head full of bad memories. 'What are you going to do?'

Singh looked up from her files with a muted rage in her eyes. 'I'm not fucking quitting. Can you imagine me sitting at home with a baby, watching daytime TV, doing the laundry, talking to other mums in the playground? I'd rather be a nun.'

They both laughed and were still laughing when Rupert came in. 'What's so funny?' he said, blushing bright red, and they laughed even harder, unable to stop for a few moments.

When they were done, Rupert showed Geneva how to use the charities register and after fifteen minutes she found what she was looking for.

The convent had a long history of good works and philanthropy – Holden had been right about that, at least. They had run kitchens and emergency clinics during the Blitz, soup lines and doss houses in the bleak ravaged years which followed. In the last couple of decades they had opened youth centres in blighted areas of Ladbroke Grove, been involved with the Terrence Higgins Trust, run workshops for troubled teens and fed the constant army of homeless that trudged through London's streets day and night. They had also initiated drug rehabilitation programmes and organised neighbourhood watch teams to deter roving dealers, unhappy with the police's efforts to do the same. It was a large and admirable CV but it all stopped dead a year ago.

The outreach programmes had been shut down, memberships of boards and charitable organisations had been resigned, funding had ceased, and all of it over the space of a few weeks.

Geneva sat up abruptly, checked her notes and thought about this. 'We have reports that a priest named Father McCarthy was a regular visitor to the convent.'

Rupert nodded. 'Each convent has a diocesan priest attached

to it. They come almost every day to conduct masses.' He typed something into his computer, his expression turning into a frown. 'Father McCarthy was not their diocesan priest, a Father Malone was.'

'Would it be strange for another priest to visit?'

'To visit, no. To visit regularly, yes.'

'Do you have a photo of him? It would be extremely helpful for our inquiries.'

Rupert punched something into the keyboard and swivelled the monitor so that Geneva could see. A black-and-white photo of Father McCarthy took up half the screen. She looked at Father McCarthy's face but she didn't look at it for long. There was something unsettling about the priest's expression, the way his eyes were hard and cold and seemed to stare out of the computer and into her very soul.

'Can you pull up his file?'

Rupert nodded and started typing. 'Got it!' he exclaimed, and then she saw the screen flashing in front of him and the slump of his shoulders.

'The file's right there on the mainframe but it's locked.'

'Isn't that normal?'

Rupert shook his head. 'No, I've only seen this before in extremely sensitive cases – child abuse scandals, financial embezzlement, that sort of thing.'

16

The rush of stale air made him feel dizzy. The door-flap had swung
back on its hinges to reveal a narrow opening. Carrigan aimed the
beam of his torch into the room beyond and saw a bed and a grey
concrete wall. He looked behind him, distracted momentarily by
some low growly sound, then crouched down and crawled through
the gap.

The room was a disappointment. Whatever he was expecting
to find in the few moments between the door swinging open and
entering, it wasn't there. The room was cool and had been pre-
served from the ravages of the fire. Dust motes danced and spun
in the air as he straightened up and took in the space around him.
It reminded him of an old prison cell but it had been years since
they'd been allowed to be this small. The silence was absolute and
his tinnitus sounded like a gale blowing through his ears, a series
of high-pitched whines and crackles that even after twenty years
he'd still not got used to. Sometimes, mostly in the lost hours of
the night, he thought there were voices in the crackle, whispers
between the sudden shifts of tone, a constant chattering of the dead
broadcasting on some deep underground frequency.

He made sure the door-flap was still open and took out his
mobile, switching to video so that he could film the room before
disturbing the scene. It didn't take long. The room was about ten
feet by five and contained the bed, stripped of sheets and blankets,
a framed religious sampler hanging on the wall above, a bookcase
crammed with books and a small bedside table, empty of
everything but dust.

His heartbeat was finally returning to normal as he put the camera away, realising that whatever answers he'd thought might be buried in this secret room were not to be found. He remembered having read how most older churches and monasteries had rooms such as these, called priest-holes, that had been used over the centuries to hide those hounded by authority for whatever heresies they'd committed or beliefs they'd held close. He looked around the bleak dim cell and a small part of him envied them the utter blinding certainty of their faith, a faith strong enough to endure such privation and hardship.

The bed was narrow and much used, the springs sinking deeply when he sat down on its edge. The pillow had been stripped of linen and he danced his beam across it, hoping to see some trace of former occupants, but there was none. He repeated the procedure with the mattress and, apart from a couple of dark stains which he'd have the SOCOs analyse, there was nothing that spoke of its purpose or inhabitant.

He checked under the bed but saw only balls of dust, spiralled and stacked up against the far wall. He looked at the sampler hung above the bed. Jesus in a circular field with a herd of stray sheep. The embroidery was amateur but there was something unsettling rather than comforting about the lone figure silhouetted against the hill, his face caught in the process of turning away. And then he looked closer.

Initially, he'd thought the figure was Jesus, but as he examined it carefully he saw that it depicted another face. It was a face he knew.

A cold tremor ran down his back. His breath stammered in his throat.

The face of the man in the sampler was the same face as that of the statue behind the pricket stand, next to the seat of fire. Carrigan snapped several photos of the sampler.

He turned from the image and approached the bookcase. Books and pamphlets had been jammed into every available space. He looked through the titles and saw books on the Bible, exegesis, commentaries, books on politics and memoirs of mystics and prophets. Many of the books were in Latin or Spanish. He took close-up photographs of spines and titles for Geneva to examine. Each book, he knew, would have to be meticulously looked through, sifted and examined and sniffed and rubbed to see if it would give up its secrets.

He left the bookcase and scanned every remaining inch of the room, the bare floor, the walls, under the mattress, the crevices between bed and corner, but there was nothing else, and he felt a wave of disappointment as he realised this room might not have been used for years. His eyes crinkled as the emergency lights stuttered and blinked outside. He briefly wondered if they were connected to a generator or battery and knew he might not have long before they went out completely.

He'd left the bedside table for last. It was a single wooden piece, nothing antique or fancy about it, a purely functional object with one large compartment and a smaller drawer above. There was a thin layer of dust coating the surface, no disturbances that would indicate something had been sitting on the table then taken away, no fingerprints or smudge marks. The main compartment was empty apart from what looked like mouse droppings in the corner but the drawer contained a Bible and a crucifix. He pulled his gloves tighter so they wouldn't snag against the wood and lifted both items carefully out of the drawer. The lights stuttered outside and he turned his torch back on and aimed it at the crucifix.

The detail on the figure was astonishing and Carrigan could see the individual veins in Jesus's arms, the fingernails on his impaled hand, the snarled lips revealing white teeth, a single tear rolling down his wooden cheek. He took out an evidence bag from his pocket and bagged the crucifix.

The Bible was old and covered in cracked red leather. Its animal smell seemed alien in this antiseptic room and he brought it a little closer to his nose, enjoying the warm familiar scent. It seemed an ordinary Bible and he quickly turned to the front but there were no personalisations or family history inscribed in it. He flicked through the pages, hoping something would fall out, a scrap of paper, a hidden snapshot, but there was nothing but dust.

He left it for the SOCOs, then turned back to inspect the door mechanism. There was a small lever about halfway up the wall. He cranked the lever and saw the cogs and pulleys shift, lurch and lock. Whoever had stayed here had not been a prisoner.

He took one last look at the room, then crouched down and rolled through the narrow opening. He was almost all the way out when a stray hair caught on one of the springs and he let out a sharp exhalation as he felt it tear away from his scalp. He got to his feet on the other side of the door, massaging his head, and then he quickly got back down, poking his flashlight into the opening.

His hair had been snagged by one of the levers on his way out; it was probably an occupational hazard of moving through this constricted space. He leaned further in, aiming the light into the skeletal mechanism, probing the cracks and shadows. He only noticed it because of its colour, so startling in that murky darkness, and it took him a few seconds before he realised he'd been holding his breath.

He stared at it, unable to trust his own eyes. He took out his phone and snapped a photo of the single strand of hair. It was about three inches long, fine and slightly curled, and it was a bright shocking pink, the colour of candy floss or a young girl's lipstick.

It was caught between two cogs and he gently pulled the hair from its place, careful not to snag or break it, and eased it into an evidence bag. He held up the bag and stared at it. The length and colour indicated that it was probably female. Best of all, it looked like the root was still attached. The SOCOs might be able to get a DNA print off it. He was thinking about this and the caretaker's description of the new girl when the lights went off.

The basement was plunged into darkness. Carrigan snapped his head up and got to his feet, keeping his torch shielded. He placed the evidence bag in his jacket pocket and wondered where the battery for the lights was and whether there was a back-up he could engage so that he could further investigate the hidden room, but then he heard the unmistakable creak of the floorboards above him and knew that someone else was in the house.

He slowly made his way across the basement, keeping the light dim and pointed downwards, avoiding the tombs and scattered debris, trying to make as little noise as possible. He heard nothing else from above and chided himself for having been so easily spooked. It was probably just the floorboards warping and settling as they cooled from the heat of the fire.

He reached the stairs and looked up. At that exact moment the door at the top of the staircase opened and bright white light spilled down into the basement.

A man was standing at the top of the stairs, his body filling the doorframe. He seemed just as surprised to see Carrigan as Carrigan was to see him. For a moment that seemed to stretch much longer they both stood there as if not quite believing in the other's presence. Carrigan had just enough time to note his black suit and the jagged scar pulling down one side of his mouth before the man turned and ran.

Carrigan leaped up the stairs two at a time, his momentum such that by the time the wood broke and fell away beneath his feet he was already onto the next one and he knew that if he hesitated for even a fraction of a second he would end up crashing back down into the basement.

The last piece of staircase splintered and cracked as he grabbed onto the doorframe and steadied himself. He looked to his left and saw the man with the scar running down the corridor, then stopping abruptly and turning to face him. There was something strange in the man's expression, and then Carrigan watched his eyes drift, looking at something behind him. Carrigan turned and saw the

125

other man coming towards him, swinging something in his raised arm, a gaudy eagle tattooed on his neck, and then his vision exploded in starshower and light-dazzle. He waited for the floor to break his fall but there was no floor, only the black rush of the stairs like a gaping throat, swallowing him up and folding him into darkness.

II

'One cannot be in the world without getting a little dust on his shoulders.'

St Francis of Assisi

17

He dreamed they were together again. They were sitting on a bench in Hyde Park watching the children play by the pond. Louise was holding his hand and whispering in his ear. Her skin was cold and dry and he had to keep leaning closer because it was so hard to make out what she was saying. The kids were laughing and yelling, their parents chatting on mobile phones as dogs dipped their noses into the rippled water. Louise was telling him to look up at the sky, you need to look up, but he didn't want to take his eyes off her, things he'd forgotten – the slight crinkle under her right cheek, the slope of her jaw, the way her shoulders dropped when she spoke – came rushing back to him. He saw her watching the children, one small boy walking unnoticed into the pond until he disappeared beneath the calm green water, and then he turned back and she was gone and the children were gone and the sun was gone. Even the grass was gone. All that was left were her shoes, Louise's shoes, lying neatly side by side on the gravel path, cracked and worn and drenched in blood.

He snapped awake, his tongue dry and bitter, his heart thudding away in his chest. The sky gone, the park gone. He stared up at the sterile white ceiling, the riverine cracks and fissures, the dangling tubes and cables, and then he felt her hand and it was warm and soft.

'You were dreaming. The doctor said the painkillers would do that.'

Geneva was sitting on a stool beside the bed. Her hair was loose, falling around her neck in yellow folds, and her eyes had a funny squint to them as if she'd just emerged from a place of total darkness.

'What happened?' He looked around the room, the white walls and beeping machines, the tubes snaking up from under the sheets, the concern darkening Geneva's face.

'A neighbour saw two men running out of the ruins. She called us and we found you lying on your back in the basement.'

He was sitting up now, the tubes gurgling and sending fluids through his system, a glass of water next to him.

'What were you doing there?'

He tried to think back and the memories rushed him like a storm – fragments and pieces coalescing into sequences and stagger-frames, into things he'd rather not remember. 'I thought . . . I wanted . . .'

'Never mind for now,' Geneva said and handed him the glass of water. It was too cold but he drank it anyway, enjoying the sudden icy shock to his mouth. 'How long have I been here?'

'Just over thirty-six hours. The doctor said you took quite a beating.' She stopped and looked at the flowers and cards sent over by the department, each one more depressing and inappropriate than the last. 'What happened, Jack?'

The use of his first name startled him, or was it just the way she'd said it, he wasn't sure. He tried talking but his mouth felt as if it had been filled with sand and he gulped the water greedily, half of it running down the front of his gown. He gave her a brief rundown of what he'd found in the convent, the secret room, the pink hair, and the men who'd been waiting for him, the one with the eagle tattoo and the one with the scar on his mouth. He leaned forward suddenly, his bones popping and cracking, a wave of nausea washing over him. 'My jacket . . .'

She put a hand on his shoulder and gently pressed him back down. 'Don't worry about your clothes, the doc—'

He turned and something cracked loudly in his neck as he grabbed her wrist. 'It's not the damn clothes, there was evidence in there.'

'The crucifix? Yeah, I saw that,' Geneva replied. 'Thought you'd gone all religious on me, then I noticed the other bag. I sent them both to the lab. Quinn's fast-tracked it, we should get the results soon. There's also been some new developments regarding the nuns.'

'What?'

'Later. You need to rest.'

He let go of her hand and closed his eyes and saw the pink sky, the pregnant clouds, the eager smiling children, but however hard he tried he couldn't bring Louise's face back into focus. 'I need to get out of here,' he said, raising himself from the bed, then collapsing back down as the world gave way to rushing emptiness.

'Inspector Carrigan?'

She was shaking him but the dream refused to loosen its grip. He felt her hand, then tried to focus on the words emerging from her mouth. His eyes blinked open and he saw the long sad face of ACC Quinn leaning over him. 'Good to see you back in the land of the living.'

Carrigan looked around but Geneva was nowhere to be seen. He reached for his glass of water but it was gone.

'How are you holding up?' The ACC was attired in full dress uniform, hands planted deep in pockets, his hair slicked to the side, shiny and glossed, making it look as if it had been painted on.

'Better when I get the hell out of here.'

'Yes, quite,' Quinn replied. 'Not the best time for the investigating officer to get himself hospitalised.'

Carrigan looked around but Branch was nowhere to be seen. He wondered why the ACC was visiting him alone. Quinn kept standing despite the fact that there was a stool right next to the bed. 'Now tell me,' the ACC said. 'What happened in there?'

Carrigan shrugged or at least tried to, but his shoulders felt as if they'd been crushed to dust, muscles he didn't even know existed glowing hot with needle-prick pain.

'I know you're still recovering, probably nursing a bad headache, but I'm sure you've had worse. The quicker we know what we're dealing with the better, right?'

Carrigan managed to nod. He told Quinn about the room he'd found, the single strand of pink hair, the men. 'After I heard about the cocaine in the chapel I started wondering if maybe we've been thinking about this all wrong.'

'Cocaine?' Quinn repeated, his top lip trembling, his face deathly pale and bulge-eyed. Branch had obviously not updated him on this part of the investigation.

'Yes.'

'And what, exactly, does this have to do with the fire?' The words came out slow and measured but there was an undertone to them that Carrigan noted.

'We don't know that it does,' he answered. 'That's why we need to investigate the convent further.'

'Now, Carrigan . . .' Quinn's voice turned steely and flat. 'We don't want unsubstantiated rumours floating around or, God forbid, being bandied in the press – this isn't going to help us catch whoever set the fire.'

'Are . . . are you suggesting I ignore evidence?' Carrigan tried sitting up but the effort was too much.

'You're an intelligent man, I think you know what you need to do.'

'What I need to do is get a warrant to see the full diocese files on the Sisters of Suffering,' Carrigan said, propping himself up on the bed. 'Something was going on at that convent. Five of the nuns bear identical torture scars. We have reports of strange visitors when there shouldn't have been any visitors. The nuns were involved in a lot more than just prayer and good deeds. We're only beginning to scratch the surface. The chances of this being a random fire are diminishing by the day.'

Quinn studied him silently for a long moment, his shadow blocking all light from the window. 'Absolutely not,' he replied. 'That's just the kind of thing I'm talking about, Carrigan. Being a policeman isn't only about solving cases and you should know that by now. It's about understanding how to handle *all* aspects of the case. The days of steaming like a bulldozer through the victims' private lives are over. A policeman who wants to stay in the Force needs to realise this.' Quinn looked down at the dull and grimy floor. 'Perhaps it's better if you rest. I can always pass this case on to another DI.'

Carrigan started to say something but the blackness came again like a dark blanket and this time he welcomed its arrival.

He woke to the smell of coffee. He kept his eyes shut for a few seconds in case the smell was only some stray linger from the dream. He took deep breaths, savouring the aroma. And then he heard her cough and knew it was real.

She was sitting silently on a stool beside the bed, eyes closed, her face tilted slightly towards him, and he could see the curve of her lips, the sudden fullness at the centre, a scar the shape and size of a thumbnail just below her jaw.

'I wasn't sure we'd have time for that coffee later, so I thought we may as well do it now.' Karen leaned forward and her hair spilled across her shoulders as she handed him the small hot cup of espresso, their fingers touching for a brief second.

'Thank you,' he said, managing to smile. They held each other's stare for a moment, her eyes fierce black orbs, her smile soft and gentle. He was still adrift on a sea of painkillers, the hard edges of the world softened into brushstrokes, and in the spilled light she looked haloed and aglow.

A sudden panic flashed through his mind like black rain. 'Is . . .

is my mother okay?'

Karen smiled, her eyes crinkling into focus. 'She's fine, Jack. I've just come from upstairs. She's sleeping peacefully. That's not why I'm here.'

Her accent made even the most familiar words sound exotic. Carrigan relaxed back into the bed. 'I never thought I'd find myself a couple of floors down from my mother.' He looked up at Karen and all he wanted to do was fall into her life, her petty struggles, middle-of-the-night fears and small unexpected joys. To forget his own life inside of hers.

She took a sip of her coffee, her lips parting slightly. 'We never know where each moment will find us. That's why when I heard you were here I came straight down.'

The door snapped open and they both looked up, startled and gape-eyed, as Geneva entered the room. She took one step inside then stopped and stared at Karen. Her gaze went over to the two espresso cups on Carrigan's bedside table, then back to the nurse. She blinked twice as she recognised her and her mouth tightened into a perfect O.

'No one's supposed to be in here,' Geneva said. 'This room is off limits.' Her voice was sharp and brittle in the tiled white space.

'I was just checking on him.'

'I can see that.'

Karen raised her eyebrows and looked back towards Carrigan. She shrugged her shoulders, her eyes retreating, and got up and left the room.

'That wasn't very nice.'

Geneva looked down at the floor, her mobile clutched tightly in her right hand. 'I know. I'm sorry. This fucking case . . .' She trailed off, not wanting to say it was also the sight of him, so helpless there on the bed.

'Forget it,' he replied. 'We've got bigger things to worry about.'

He started to lift himself up and when Geneva tried to say

something he cut her off. 'Quinn's talking about bringing in a new DI. I need to get back to the station.'

Just then, the door opened and a young, harried-looking doctor came in. He glanced sharply at Carrigan until he lay back down on the bed. The doctor didn't say a word to either of them as he went round checking the machines and making notes on the clipboard he'd taken off the end of the bed. Finally he turned towards Carrigan. 'We're going to take you down for a few more tests, I'm afraid. Shouldn't be too painful.'

'How long's it going to take?'

The doctor was ticking something off on his clipboard and didn't look up as he answered. 'A couple of hours, give or take, but there's no hurry. We want to keep you here a few more days for observation, make sure nothing permanent got damaged. You're a little overweight and rather unfit for your age and you took quite a fall. I'll have the orderlies come for you in ten minutes.' The doctor checked Carrigan's pulse, looked under his eyelids, made a few more notes and left.

A scream came from the room next door. Carrigan looked at the tubes and clips attached to his skin, saw two orderlies wheeling someone down the dark endless hallway, and started pulling the drips out of his body.

'Are you sure you should be doing that?' Geneva asked.

'Get my jacket,' he said, ignoring the concern in her voice. 'And get everyone together in the incident room. We've wasted enough time.'

18

They clapped as he entered. He didn't know why they were doing this; he'd failed after all, the probable suspects had been in his grasp and he'd let them get the better of him. His left eye was black and swollen, and he had a square of white gauze taped to his right temple. He tried to smile but it still hurt too much, so he nodded his head and waited for everyone to take their seats. Someone, maybe Geneva, had left a chocolate Florentine by his chair. He took a hurried bite, feeling the sugar hit, and then he began.

'First of all, thank you for all this, but I fucked up. I should have called back-up and maybe we'd have those two in custody right now instead of this bloody headache I've got, so, please, no more clapping, okay?'

'We weren't clapping because you got beaten up,' Karlson was rather too eager to clarify. 'We just heard back from the lab. They managed to extract a sample, God knows how they did it so quickly. The DNA from the pink hair you found matches the sample the pathologist retrieved from the eleventh victim. I think we can be pretty certain that the body in the confession booth is the new girl Hubbard told us about. We're running the sample through the database at the moment but the server's on the blink, as usual, so it's going to take a while.'

Carrigan stared at his sergeant – was there a grudging acceptance in the man's tone? He'd never got on with Karlson, or maybe it was the other way around, but there was something about this case that seemed to transgress all personal issues. 'That's great,' he said. 'But it doesn't mean we'll necessarily be able to identify the eleventh victim – it's only good to us if she's on record somewhere, so don't get your hopes up.' He stopped, out of breath, a sharp hot pain in his left side making him buckle. 'Anyone talk to the SOCOs about what they found in the secret room?' he said, hoping no one had noticed his momentary weakness.

Singh looked up from her notes. 'A lot of fingerprints, mainly overlaid and of no use to us. They said it looked like many people had stayed in the room. I did manage to identify the statue found at the seat of fire. It depicts Archbishop Oscar Romero. The sampler in the secret room is of the same person. He was a famous church leader and liberation theologian in Central and South America and was assassinated in 1980.'

'What on earth is liberation theology?' Karlson asked.

'No idea,' Singh replied. 'The SOCOs also went through the bookcase in the secret room. The books had nothing unusual inside them. They're sending them over to us today. They didn't find anything else they considered significant.'

'The hidden room is significant,' Carrigan said. 'Many older religious buildings have priest-holes of some kind but this one was in use. Was the girl with the pink hair staying there? And if so, why? Singh – get the blueprints for the convent, see if the room is marked on them or whether it's a later addition. There was also something that looked like a workshop along the back wall – tools and machines and so forth – I want you to liaise with forensics over this, find out what the space was used for . . . it doesn't fit with the rest of the basement.' He paused and looked down at his hands, then cleared his throat. 'We still have no idea what the cocaine was doing there and that bothers me.' He looked across the room and saw Karlson smiling to himself. 'You have something to share with us, Sergeant?'

Karlson shuffled in his chair, stretched and sat up. 'The nuns were hassling dealers and moving them on. Maybe they confiscated the coke off one of these dealers. It would give that someone a bloody good motive to set the fire.'

'It seems a bit implausible,' Carrigan replied, making a note in his policy book. 'Now, how're we doing on locating Father McCarthy?'

Jennings shrugged despondently. 'I spoke to Roger Holden and he told me that, as of yesterday, Father McCarthy is on retreat and uncontactable.'

'On retreat?' Carrigan repeated, wondering exactly what kind of game Holden was playing. 'Thank you, Jennings – keep hassling the diocese, try and find out exactly where he's staying. We need to talk to Father McCarthy. We know he was a regular visitor and he was seen leaving the premises an hour before the fire.'

'You think it's possible he set the fire?' Jennings asked.

'I'm not thinking anything yet except it's bloody curious he decided to pick this week to go on retreat.' Carrigan wrote something down on the whiteboard then turned towards Geneva. 'Miller, what did you find out at the diocese?'

Geneva ran through it point by point. 'It looks like Mother Angelica recruited the other nuns. Seven of them knew each other from Peru. They were all stationed there in 1973.'

'1973 . . .' Carrigan said. 'Forty years ago.'

Geneva nodded, and there was a momentary silence as they considered the implications of this. 'They also curtailed all their charity work a year ago. Before, they were involved in organising homeless shelters and youth workshops. They set up drug rehab centres and mobilised local residents in picketing known drug houses, giving out leaflets and advice to customers – suddenly, this all stops dead a year ago.'

'And you're assuming this has something to do with the case?'

'Everything has something to do with the case until we rule it out.'

He nodded. It was something he'd taught her. 'Okay, keep looking into that, Miller, but let's focus on what we have that's concrete. Berman? Did you get anything from the school's CCTV tapes?'

Berman's face emerged from the bank of computer screens lining his desk. He blinked twice like some burrowing animal unused to the light. 'We got lucky there. Because of previous problems with paedophiles, the school keeps all the footage archived.' He stood up, taking a long black lead from his desk, and plugged it into the back of a flatscreen television mounted on the far wall. He was clumsy and uncoordinated and it took him several tries before he got it right. 'The camera is angled towards the front gates of the school. The convent is two doors down. We can just see their drive-way.' Berman nervously fingered the prayer shawl he wore under his shirt and looked up at the screen as if for confirmation to carry on. 'The uniforms spent all night going through the footage. Take a look at this.'

He pressed a button on his laptop and the TV flickered to life revealing the front gate of the school and the gently curving road beyond. Berman fast-forwarded the tape until a black SUV drove into frame, slowed down and disappeared at the edge of the camera's domain. 'I checked the number-plate. It's fake, not stolen, made up from two separate plates as far as I can tell.' He pointed to the screen. 'They're parking a couple of doors down from the school, almost directly outside the convent. See how they're start-ing to swing in?'

Berman switched to another shot. 'This is a couple of weeks later. It's the same SUV, no doubt about it. Now watch this . . .' He fast-forwarded the tape until a glimmer of black filled the bottom left-hand corner. 'This time there's already somebody else double-parked outside the convent – you can just make out the back of what looks like a Royal Mail van.'

He pressed play and they all watched as the black SUV came to a stop closer to the school gates. The driver was the first one out but his face was obscured by the top of the SUV and he quickly walked off screen. Then the man sitting in the passenger seat opened his door. He stepped out, checked either side of him, then looked directly at the school.

Carrigan stared at the frozen image of the man who'd been standing at the top of the stairs. In the light, his face was raw and curiously unformed, but the scar which disfigured his mouth was unmistakable.

'Thought you'd like that,' Berman said, punching keys with a renewed energy. 'You're going to like this even more.'

The image changed and Carrigan saw that the sergeant was running the video taken at the initial crime scene, a visual record of the frantic eager crowd who'd gathered to watch the fire. The young female constable had done a good job. There were families with kids and shopping bags, groups of teenagers swigging on cans of lager and Middle Eastern businessmen in long flowing white robes, everyone's eyes wide and agape, their faces freckled by flame, a reverent awe in their muted expressions. Carrigan found himself transfixed, realising he'd never seen this footage before, watching the rapt and stunned faces as the camera moved steadily through the crowd, past the pressed huddle of bodies and flung arms and party cheer, and suddenly there he was.

The same man. Three rows back, watching the fire and talking to another man who was partially hidden from view.

'This was taken only an hour after the fire started,' Berman said.

He paused the video and Carrigan stared at his assailant, the small recessed eyes and jagged horror-film scar. He got up and walked over to the screen.

Everyone was silent and spooked and a little excited. Carrigan's eyes were fixed on the TV. The man who'd attacked him in the ruins had visited the convent a week before. He'd been standing outside watching the fire as it blazed. Had this man followed him to the ruins last night? Or had he come there for a different purpose and just stumbled upon him?

'Karlson, get Berman to run you off some stills. Focus on the scar. There can't be too many of those around. Check through the

PNC database – if he's been in trouble before, it'll be in there.' He walked back to the table and sat down and pulled out his policy book. 'Our main focus now is getting an ID on this man. I want you to circulate the photos, see if anyone in vice or immigration recognises him, send it to all patrol and watch officers.' He stopped and waited for everyone to finish their frantic scribbling, and was about to assign the constables their daily tasks when Karlson's computer started beeping insistently. Everyone stopped what they were doing and turned towards the sergeant's desk. Karlson was staring at the screen, his face a mask of surprise.

'What?' Carrigan said.

'The system's back online. We've got a match . . .' The normally deadpan sergeant looked utterly astonished as he clicked on the link, his fingers tapping impatiently against the desktop.

'I don't fucking believe it . . .' he said. 'Our eleventh victim has a criminal record.'

19

Emily Maxted.

Thirty-two years old.

Carrigan flicked through the three scant pages resting on his lap as Geneva drove, the cars and trees and buses whipping by his window in a smeary spray of light.

Emily had been arrested in 2008 for cannabis possession. The arrest had resulted in a couple of hours in the cells and, luckily for them, a DNA sample, taken from her as part of a trial programme the Met had been running at the time. The sample matched both the pink hair found in the priest-hole door and the degraded DNA from the corpse in the confession booth.

Emily Maxted was their eleventh victim.

Carrigan felt his heart beat a little bit faster.

As they headed north, the tight constriction of Paddington and Kilburn gave way to an unobscured sky, steep hills and sudden unexpected views. Parkland spread out on either side, a brilliant blaze of white melting into the far horizon. Children ran across the road clutching toboggans in mittened hands while their parents tried to keep up, hampers and wet writhing dogs juggled in their arms. The snow fell in white swirly sheets making the world seem domed and contained as if they were trapped inside a snow-globe. Carrigan took a KitKat from his pocket and scored his nails down the foil, popping half of it in his mouth and closing his eyes for a moment to savour the taste. When he opened them again he noticed Geneva watching him. 'What?'

'Is that all you're having for lunch?'

He balled up the chocolate wrapper and dropped it next to his seat. 'Got another one in my pocket.'

She couldn't help but smile and was a little too slow to cover it up. 'You know that's not what I meant.'

'I'll eat when the case is over,' he said, unpeeling the small faded photo from the first page of the arrest sheet and holding it between his fingers.

Emily Maxted had been stunned by the flash, her eyes squinting against the sudden burst of light. But despite that, and the fact she'd just been arrested, there was something about her that would grab your attention even in a crowded room. Her skin was pale and finely textured and it made her eyes appear unnaturally green and defiant. There was a dangerous curve to her lips and her hair was dyed purple and hung across her forehead in a set of uneven bangs that concealed as much as they revealed. She seemed squeezed into the photo's frame, its strict parameters unable to contain her, but even in this single snapped moment Carrigan could see a wealth of buried history lurking in her eyes, storms and resentments and things that happened to her when she was four years old.

He put down the photo and re-checked the address on the file, telling Geneva to take the next right. They soon entered a hidden London, spacious and pristine, folded between the rolling hills and humps of Hampstead Heath. The area looked as if the last hundred years had never happened. They drove by houses that took up a whole block, houses invisible behind ten-foot walls and houses set so far back on their grounds they seemed mere specks on the horizon. The road curved and twisted as it followed the swirled spine of the heath, making the residences seem cut off from one another, distant ships on a jewelled sea. You could spend money to protect and seclude yourself from the harsh noise and swagger of the city but, as they pulled into the driveway, Carrigan knew that no amount of money could spare the people inside from the news he was about to deliver.

He got out of the car, brushed the crumbs from his jacket and stretched his legs as he stared up at the imposing Palladian facade. 'You ever done this before?' He turned towards Geneva, startled at how pale and drawn she looked.

'Once . . . only once,' she replied. 'Swore I'd never do it again.' She laughed faintly, the sound disappearing almost as soon as it escaped her mouth.

He'd been pleasantly surprised when she'd volunteered to come along. It was a necessary part of the job but it was always ugly and nothing would change that. It was the part everyone hated, the part where they suddenly made excuses or remembered important meetings they were late for, but Carrigan had always believed that he, as the investigating officer, should do it himself. No victim's relatives deserved a uniform three weeks into the job stumbling through his lines and putting his foot in it. But it wasn't just that, he had to admit, as he stared one last time at the photo. They needed to find out as much as they could about the mysterious pink-haired girl, about her life and friends and routines, before they could understand how she was involved with the nuns and why she was there that night.

A Filipino woman dressed in an old-fashioned black-and-white maid's outfit opened the door.

'We're here to see Miles and Lillian Maxted.' Carrigan showed her his warrant card. The maid looked at him in alarm, staring down at the card then back up at the man with the black eye and Frankenstein gauze.

'Maria? Is everything okay?' A woman's voice came from a small speaker attached to the maid's outfit. It was the same kind of device parents use to monitor sleeping babies. The maid winced when she heard the voice, then picked up the receiver and pressed a button. 'There's two policeman here to see you and the mister,' she said in a pleasant sing-song voice.

The receiver crackled briefly with static. 'Well, I suppose you'd better bring them up.'

They handed the maid their jackets and followed her through a hallway that was like the atrium to some eccentric oil baron's private museum. Statues of Greek nymphs and Roman legionnaires were mounted in niches at regular intervals. Wood-smoked Regency chairs stood stout and wary as guard dogs. The walls were heavy with painted faces, dark troubled portraits from another era, every available bit of space crammed with a confusion of art. The maid knocked once on a large wooden door, then, without a word, turned and left.

The woman who opened the door showed no sign of surprise when she saw them. Carrigan could tell she was far too well bred for such displays. She was one of those women whose former beauty resided just below the skin, like old paintings that still sparkled underneath the patina of years and neglect. 'You'd better come in,' she said, incurious and unrattled, as if they were delivering her weekly shopping.

The room was overwhelming in its bounty. The Maxteds had collected so many books and artworks and knick-knacks that the space seemed diminished by them, the light from the floor-to-ceiling windows disappearing in a murk of haze and obstacle. There was no sense or order to the room: Indian dream-catchers stood next to Greek figurines, Buddhas next to sculptures made from toothbrushes. The floors were covered with ornate Persian rugs and Turkish kilims, a riot of colour and squiggle. A series of paintings dominated the room. The image was almost the same in each one, a procession of anguished heads, eyeless, wrenched in agony, contorted by silent screams, the brushwork loose and furious. There were books on the floor and books on the piano and books teetering on the curved arms of sofas.

'What do we have here, then?'

Carrigan turned to see a man sitting in a deep black leather armchair. He wore a brown polo neck and ash-grey chinos and was holding a glass of red wine in his hand. His fingernails were manicured, outshining the glass, and his eyes possessed a deep probing restlessness, sizing up the two detectives in one quick glance.

'My name is Detective Inspector Carrigan . . .'

'Yes, yes.' Miles Maxted rose from his chair and put down his drink on a small, ornately lacquered side table. 'What do you want?'

'Is your daughter Emily Maxted?' Carrigan watched the man's eyes carefully but saw only a sharp intelligence and a wary cunning there, no sign of what lay underneath.

'What has she done this time?' Miles asked, then shook his head. 'No, don't tell me, I don't want to know.'

Carrigan looked over at Geneva. This wasn't turning out the way he'd planned. He took a step forward. 'I'm afraid that a body identified as Emily's was recovered from the scene of a fire three days ago.' He watched as the words sank in, noting any facial tic or tell. It was always the same in these situations – at first it was as though they hadn't heard him, quickly followed by bewilderment and then, finally, the realisation of what lay behind the words.

'A fire?' Miles Maxted tapped his fingernails against the side of his glass. 'What on earth are you talking about?'

Lillian Maxted was absolutely still beside her husband, a three-inch gap separating them. She didn't say anything but her face was pale and stretched. A grandfather clock stood sentry by the door and its insistent ticking filled the silence. Carrigan cleared his throat. 'There was a fire at a convent in Bayswater on Thursday night. I'm afraid we've identified Emily as one of the . . .'

The glass fell from Lillian's hand and shattered on the floor. She stared down at the scattered shards and quietly began to sob.

Miles Maxted turned towards his wife. 'Lillian, please!' His voice was sharp and brusque and his expression cold and weary as if he'd been through this kind of thing too many times to count. Lillian gathered herself together and wiped her eyes with the sleeve of her blouse.

'I'm sorry,' she said. 'I . . .'

'There's nothing to be sorry about.' Carrigan took her by the arm and gently led her towards a large red velvet armchair. As he passed Miles, he brushed against him and felt the man's taut frame beneath the silky skin of his shirt. 'We're used to much worse, believe me. I'm very sorry about your daughter.'

Lillian slumped into the chair and snuffled, rubbing her eyes and smearing her make-up. 'A convent? Are . . . are you sure?'

Carrigan knelt down until their heads were level and nodded, then stared down at the floor. It had been polished so many times that the wood sparkled with an unnatural clarity and he could almost see his own reflection in it. 'We have a positive DNA match.'

Lillian looked up briefly, saw something in Carrigan's eyes that confirmed her worst fears, and began to cry, quickly wiping the tears away with her hand. 'I always knew it would end like this.'

Geneva and Carrigan looked at each other as Lillian's words tumbled into incomprehensible sobs and punctured coughs.

'Mrs Maxted?'

'She means Emily chose her own path,' Miles said, his voice breaking slightly on the last syllable. 'The path she chose was always going to end badly, Inspector. You're only confirming what we knew and feared would happen.'

Carrigan stared at the man, trying to figure out if it was the shock that was making him like this or if he was like this all the time. 'Mr Maxted, we've just informed you that your daughter is dead. I think . . .'

'You think everyone reacts in the same way?'

'They usually do.'

'But some people don't, right? Some people don't behave like everyone else?'

'Yes, and that tells me quite a lot about them,' Carrigan replied.

He took out his notebook and pen and flipped the pages till he found a blank one. 'You don't mind if I make some notes, do you? My memory's not what it used to be.'

Miles Maxted shrugged.

'When was the last time you saw Emily?' Carrigan asked, his mouth tight, the breath locked in his chest.

'We haven't seen her in nearly two years,' Lillian said.

'I'm sorry to hear that,' Carrigan replied.

Miles settled himself down in the armchair and poured a large measure of Scotch, his hands unsteady, the whisky splashing on his sleeve, but he didn't seem to notice or care.

Carrigan closed his eyes and took a deep breath. The last thing he could afford to do was lose control in front of a grieving parent, but there were questions that had to be asked and leads that needed to be pursued. 'You said you knew she would end up like this – could you please explain what you meant by that?'

Miles took a long messy gulp of his drink. 'I'm afraid Emily was lost to us a long time ago, Inspector. The people she hung around with, the lowlifes and bottom feeders, those crazy ideas of her, it was bound to end up like this. It was only a matter of when.'

Carrigan leaned forward and propped his elbows on his knees. 'It would be helpful if you could tell us a little more about who you mean when you say *lowlifes*.'

'Why are you asking these questions if she died in a fire?' Maxted searched Carrigan's eyes and then he understood. 'This fire was intentional, is that what you're saying?'

'I wasn't saying anything, Mr Maxted, but yes, we do believe the fire was intentional. We have no idea what Emily was doing at the convent or why anyone would want to set fire to it, and we were hoping to find out a little bit more about her.'

'I don't understand . . .' Lillian was sitting up, she'd wiped her eyes dry of tears and make-up and there was a seriousness and purpose to her expression that had not been there before. It was clear to see that, even though this was probably the worst news she'd ever received, she was no stranger to suffering and that sudden shocking awareness of how thin life really is.

'It can't be her. Don't you see, Miles? It can't be her.' She began to laugh, her eyes crinkling with light. 'Thank God!' She grabbed Carrigan's wrists, encircling them with her palms.

'I'm afraid that . . .'

'But it can't be!' Lillian stared at Carrigan, her eyes and face each telling a different story. 'She wouldn't have set foot in a convent. That's not Emily. You're mistaken.'

Carrigan was about to correct her when Miles interrupted. 'Lillian is quite right. We didn't bring Emily up to believe in that nonsense and for all her failings and faults, religion, I'm glad to say, was not one of them.' His face was calm and composed as if he were working out a crossword rather than talking about his daughter's death but when Carrigan glanced down he could see the man's hand worrying the arm of the chair. The area under his fingers had scuffed and frayed over the years and Miles kept picking at it as if it were a scab too itchy to resist.

'That's what puzzles us too . . .' Carrigan began to say, then stopped, as he heard a door closing upstairs followed by the sharp percussive patter of a pair of high heels against a wooden floor. He looked up and he saw her and he blinked.

She was descending the staircase slowly, her eyes roaming the room below, alighting on the unexpected faces of the detectives and the muted expressions of her parents. She had sunset blonde hair, dark sparkly eyes and a small nervous mouth. Her long flowing dress covered her feet and made it seem as if she were floating above the ground. She hesitated halfway down then continued, each step taking a fraction longer than the one before, and it was clear from her expression that she knew there was nothing good waiting for her at the bottom of the stairs.

20

'Donna! Go upstairs now!'

The snap of Miles Maxted's voice broke the spell. The woman stopped halfway down the stairs, torn between obeying her father and her curiosity regarding the two visitors. 'Donna!' Miles Maxted's tone was sharp and firm, his eyes turning small.

'What's . . . what's happening?' Donna looked at her parents, at the detectives, at her parents again. 'Mum? Is everything all right?'

Lillian Maxted didn't reply. She was sitting slouched in her armchair, silent sobs racking her body, her fingers tangled around a loose knot of hair.

'Dad? What's going on?'

Carrigan looked over and saw that Miles was enjoying the confusion and surprise on his and Geneva's faces. 'Detective Carrigan, this is my daughter Donna.' He pursed his lips and seemed to be studying them as he spoke. 'Emily and Donna are twins, as you may have surmised.'

'Emily? . . . Is . . . is Emily okay?' Donna came to a stop next to Carrigan and he could feel the heat of her body in the space between them. She looked up at him and he saw the moment it clicked in her eyes and it was an awful thing to witness. 'Please. Someone tell me what's going on?' She looked over at her mother but Lillian Maxted's blank stare and slumped posture only confirmed Donna's worst fears.

'I'm afraid we found your sister's body at the site of a fire.'

Donna Maxted shook her head. She blinked. Shook her head again. Looked at her parents. Her skin was drawn tight over her cheekbones and seemed as fragile as the most delicate china. She walked over towards Lillian, her gait unsteady, catching her heels against each other, a stagger-stumble that almost made her lose her balance. She took her mother's hands and held them as she searched Carrigan's face for an answer or a joke or a mistake. 'What happened? How did she . . .'

'That's what we're trying to find out,' Carrigan replied. He knew that at this stage distraction and facts were all that kept the bridge from collapsing. That was yet to come, when the family was alone, when the sirens and phone calls stopped, when they were left with only the night and the unassailable weight of memory and space. 'We need to ask you a few questions, but it's okay if we do this later, I know this must be . . .'

Donna met his eyes. 'You said she was killed in a fire but that doesn't explain why you're here.' And then she stopped as it dawned on her. 'You mean it wasn't an accident?'

Carrigan nodded. 'I can't imagine what's going through your head at this moment, I can't even begin to imagine. There's a family liaison officer who'll be here soon and help you with anything practical you need.'

'Do you know of anyone who may have had cause to harm Emily?' Geneva's voice was sharp and clipped, cutting Carrigan off. Donna shook her head but Miles snorted, a harsh expulsion of air in the silent room.

'Miles, really!' Lillian had recovered herself and shot her husband a look dense with broken promises and bedroom history.

'Oh come on, Lillian, you've been living in this fantasy world, thinking that one day Emily will come to her senses, that she'll knock on the door and be the daughter we always wanted. But that was never going to happen and, Christ, now it never will.' Miles looked down at his feet. 'You asked me if anyone would harm her, Inspector. Well, I believe you've got your work cut out for you. The people she hung around with, the things she got up to . . . so many times I explained to her the damage she was doing to herself and to this family but she just went harder and faster down the road she'd chosen and there was nothing I or her mother could do about it.' His fingers picked at the chair with increased vigour, his lips almost disappearing. Donna's phone started beeping. She ignored it and eventually it stopped.

'Have you any idea what Emily would have been doing in a convent?' Geneva asked.

There was a look of confusion on Donna's face, quickly followed by a faint glimmer of something which almost resembled hope. 'Emily in a convent? She hated religion, always did. Are you absolutely sure it was her?'

'We have witnesses who saw her visiting the convent regularly over the last year.' The phone started ringing again.

'For God's sake, turn that bloody thing off,' Miles snarled at his daughter.

'Actually, it's mine,' Geneva said, getting up and answering it as she shuffled off to a corner of the room.

'When did you last speak to your sister?' Carrigan could see Donna falling apart by the second, a drawing in of body and spirit that was painful to watch.

When she answered her voice was choked and stumbled, air and tears and the broken-off bits of words all mixing together. 'Not for a long time. Maybe eighteen months, maybe more.' She stared down at her hands and Carrigan knew what was going through her head at that very moment – how easy it was to pick up a phone, how hard to go back and make up for the things you never did.

'Was there any particular reason that you or your parents hadn't spoken to her for so long?'

Donna looked over at her father. He returned her stare and though the meaning of his expression was hard to read, its tone left nothing to be deciphered.

'We haven't spoken since Dad cut her out . . .'

'Donna! That's enough.' Miles turned towards his one remaining daughter, his mouth small and pursed.

'We're going to find out anyway, so it's best you tell us in your own words.'

Miles's top lip curled slightly as he appraised Carrigan. 'I cut her out of my will, okay? Satisfied?'

'Can I ask why?'

Miles's mouth got even tighter. 'No, you cannot. Some things are private.'

'I'm aware of that, but the more information we have, even if seemingly irrelevant, the quicker we'll find out who did this to your daughter and punish them.' Carrigan used the penultimate word carefully, watching the man's eyes flicker as he said it.

'Absolutely not.' Miles's nostrils flared and he gripped the edges of his chair. 'What I did or didn't do is none of your business and if you have any more questions I suggest you contact my solicitor.' Miles Maxted stared up at Carrigan, his eyes simmering and bright. 'I think it's time you left.'

The maid appeared out of nowhere, silent and grey, and if she knew what had happened then she didn't show it at all. She took them through the long corridor and just as they were turning into the hallway, Carrigan heard loud, uncontrolled sobbing coming from the main room and he was glad when they were finally out of earshot.

Donna met them in the foyer. She handed them their jackets and apologised for her parents. She managed to appear calm and lucid and even a little charming but as soon as she walked away they both saw the grief and pain sag her body again as she headed back to the living room.

*

They'd driven back in silence, not much left to say to each other. Carrigan had always felt like this after delivering a notification of death, slumped and slightly soiled, the herald of slammed doors, unspoken guilt and painful longing. He parked the car in his usual spot and was putting the keys back in his jacket pocket when he felt something rustling inside. He pulled out the wrinkled piece of paper, assuming it was a stray bit of litter, a chocolate wrapper he'd neglected to chuck, and was just about to bin it when he noticed the handwriting.

He unfolded it carefully and read what Donna had written:

We need to talk. Somewhere without my parents. There's a lot about Emily I couldn't tell you in front of them.

And, below that, she'd written her phone number.

21

She held him by the throat and stared into his eyes as he strained
and struggled and moaned. She wanted them – his eyes – to speak
to her, to tell her all the things his mouth wouldn't, but they were
impenetrable as stones. She grabbed his wrist and held it firmly,
feeling the smooth skin on his forearm, the slight ripple of veins,
the weight of it lying in her palm. Then she brought it up to her lips
and kissed it softly, running her tongue across the scars on his skin,
the shrapnel bites from some dusty forgotten war, past the inocula-
tions he'd received as a child, and then she fell onto him, her whole
body forced into one deflation, spirit and muscle together, and the
room melted away from her, the day, the week, the life, everything
she thought about and didn't want to think about, everything that
was keeping her awake at night, that was running through her brain
like crazed viral screams – all of it forgotten and lost as she lowered
her head and tasted his mouth.

Blue Valentine was playing in the background. He'd brought
the LP with him, knowing her copy would be lost somewhere
among the boxes and bags, the unpacked strata of her life. She
could barely hear the music and didn't want to. It bought back too
many memories, good memories and bad ones, the whole arc of a
love affair contained on two sides of spinning plastic.

'What's wrong?' Lee said, twisting away, taking the duvet with
him, reaching out and picking up one of her cigarettes from the
table by the bed. He lit it and then passed it to her and lit another
for himself.

'Nothing's wrong.' The words came out mixed with smoke and
sting. She looked away, out the window into the falling confusion

of snow.

'If you wanted someone to lie to, Geneva, you should have picked a stranger.'

She said nothing, dragging tight-lipped on her cigarette, and continued to watch the spiralling squalls of snow. All that freedom, each flake spinning and dancing in the air, its own individual steps, but it didn't matter how well you danced, she knew, you'd always end up crashing to the floor in the end.

'I don't know if I can do this any more,' she said and was immediately aware of the weakness of that line, the way it had been said a million times before, and wasn't that partly why she was so discontented? Her life as the other woman turning her into a cliché with every passing day?

'What the hell's that supposed to mean?' Lee said, sitting up, the duvet falling and revealing his chest and she had to turn away again because it was too much.

'It means exactly what it means.' She stubbed the cigarette out in one hard stab and gasped as the cherry burned her fingers.

'Geneva?' He tried to take her hand but she retracted it, sat up, pulled the sheets over her body and shook her head.

'It means I'm sick of waking up in the middle of the night and turning around and you're not there. Slipped out like some thief or gigolo. It means I'm sick of closing my eyes and holding you and imagining your wife waiting up half the night, not sure where you are, suspecting, the baby crying for Daddy and Daddy stumbling home at four in the morning reeking of sex and booze.'

'That's not your concern, Genny, that's mine.'

'Of course it fucking is! What do you think I see when I look in the mirror? The person I wanted to be? Or the person I am? This woman breaking up another woman's life. And it's not just her. You have a son, Lee, you have a life that you can't just sunder any time you want.'

'That's my choice,' he said, and she was pleased to see a flash of anger roil through his body, the muscles tensing against the skin making him look young and hungry again.

'And this is mine,' she replied, staring at the rumpled duvet, the late falling snow, the unpacked boxes and ex-lover inhabiting her bed. 'And please,' she took a swig of tequila and lit another cigarette, her head spinning in time with the music. 'Please don't tell me it's not working between the two of you. Don't tell me you're only staying with her because of the baby. Don't fucking tell me you were going to leave her anyway. I don't want to hear it, Lee. I don't want you to leave her for me. I don't want to start it all over again. We tried that, remember, we tried it once and we both know what happened.'

All pretence at post-coital murmur and cuddle were gone. Lee sat up and swigged from the bottle. His eyes had grown small and cold. 'And what about you, Genny? You were the one who texted me tonight. You're the one who keeps calling. Sometimes I think I'm no more than a convenient excuse for you to escape your life.'

And this time there was nothing she could say because she knew he was right.

'You like this,' he continued. 'You like the fact you can call me when you want or not call me when you don't. You like it that there's no commitment on your part.'

'That's not fair.'

He slid over toward her and nodded. 'Sorry, perhaps it wasn't but, Genny, you need to find something in your life to make you smile again. Christ, I remember what you were like once, before all this fucking work of yours dragged you down. You need to find something or someone that makes the rest of it worthwhile. You can't go around like this all the time.'

She sprang up from the bed, suddenly and uncontrollably furious. Because he was wrong? Or because he was right? 'You expect me to smile and bounce and say *hi, how's your day* after I've spent twelve hours looking at dead bodies? After I've talked to the worst scum this city has to offer and watched them walk away free to ruin more lives? Jesus Christ, Lee, you know what it's like. You weren't any different when you used to come back from those trips to Bosnia, Colombia, the Congo.'

'That's exactly why I stopped, Geneva. That's why I don't do it any more. You have to make your accommodations with the world at some point. You have to stop doing the things that tear you apart and settle for the ones that don't.'

'Then why are you still here? Why are you even answering my calls?'

'I didn't say it makes you happy, just less unhappy.'

She started putting on clothes, the scatter of shirts and socks under her feet. 'I don't know what you expect me to do. The fucking day I had.'

'We all have days.'

'But did yours involve spending hours looking at photographs of corpses burnt to a crisp? Tell me. Using a magnifying glass to stare and stare at scratch marks on dead women's shinbones? That's what I've been doing. You really think . . . what?' She saw his face turn white as the sheets, his mouth hanging half-open. 'What did I say?'

'What kind of marks?' Lee asked in a whisper.

'Shallow vertical cuts along the shinbone.'

Lee sighed deeply and shook his head as if trying to shrug off a bad dream. 'Tickling the bone . . .' he said, and he said it so softly that Geneva had to ask him to repeat it.

'What the fuck is tickling the bone?' She tried to make light of it but saw something in his expression that stopped her dead.

'It's a very painful method of extracting information or of just plain hurting someone. The torturer makes a small incision in the skin just above the shinbone. He then takes an ice-pick or something similar, and gently presses it into the wound until it comes into contact with the bone. Normally, this is when he will look up and ask the first question. Then, slowly, he rakes the tip of the ice-pick against the bone, scraping and chipping away, causing excruciating pain.'

Geneva wrapped the duvet around her but it didn't stop her shakes. 'You know this?'

Lee nodded gravely. 'When I was doing my pieces on Mexico, I came up against this a lot. Tickling the bone was originally a speciality of South American dictatorships. These days it's used mainly by the drug cartels.'

22

The book was waiting for him as he'd known it would be. He saw the padded envelope and recognised it for what it was immediately. There'd be no return address, he knew, no fingerprints, and the postmark would be different from the previous time.

Each month, for the last year, he'd been receiving a book in the post. There was just the book and the envelope, his name and address typed out and pasted to the front. There was no note inside and the books were new, unhandled, even though some, Carrigan had checked, had been out of print for years. The first book had arrived just before last Christmas and he'd thought it had been mis-delivered, even after reading his own name off the front of the envelope – because who would be sending him books anonymously? That first offering had been Plotinus, the *Enneads*, and he'd pored over the text looking for some indication of who its sender may have been but there were only the words, etched out almost two thousand years ago.

He took the envelope out of the box, along with a handful of bills and a flyer for a canine cancer charity. He ripped open the envelope, unable to wait until he got inside, and pulled out a dark-jacketed paperback. *God in Search of Man* by Abraham Heschel. He'd never heard of it and it seemed forbidding, its opaque cover and even more opaque language. He flicked through it briefly then put it under his arm and entered the flat.

He'd left the lights on again. The bills would remember that. He'd left the window slightly open and blowing snow had frosted the ledge and buckled a series of newspapers he'd saved, meaning to read them when he finally had some time to himself, but they were now useless, the words melting into each other, the ink running and mixing, the pictures all but unrecognisable. There were no messages on his answering machine, no voices to greet him.

He spent a few minutes telling Louise about his day then took the burrito out of his bag and stripped it of packaging and placed it in the microwave. The beep reminded him it was there. He ate facing the window and was finished before he'd even begun to taste it. Everyone kept telling him he'd reached an age where he needed to watch what he ate and how much, but these little treats were often the only moments of calm and pleasure in his day. He turned on the TV but he couldn't concentrate, his head unable to stop spinning, running the latest facts and finds through each scenario and possibility.

Something about Emily's arrest sheet didn't make sense. It was a feeling, more than a feeling – a small black stone lodged in his brain. There had been so much new information today that he was finding it hard to keep track. But that was good. The initial logjam had been broken and now they were awash in a cascade of data, the kind every investigation needs to propel itself in the early days. He knew most of the leads would go nowhere. He knew that any life would open up to mystery and confusion if you looked at it hard enough, but he also knew that there was something he'd missed.

He cleared the dishes and then the night was all there was and he sat staring at the motorway ramp outside his window, jewelled with the lights of passing cars, a steady exodus from the choke and cram of the capital.

After the third ginger beer, he picked up the phone and called her.

'Wanted to say thanks for the coffee.'

'Oh, it's you,' she said, her voice slightly slurred, and he felt suddenly guilty, knowing she worked shifts, and wondering if he'd awoken her from a long-cherished sleep.

'I hope I didn't disturb you.'

She laughed, a carefree chuckle that crackled through the receiver. 'I just got in,' she said. 'Back on at two tomorrow but I can't sleep.'

'Me neither,' he said.

'Lucky we have the phone.'

They talked about things that were part of their daily lives, about time and space and the pressures of shiftwork, and as he heard her soft exotic voice he felt better, calmer and less hassled, and he flicked idly through the files on his desk, Emily's record, and listened to Karen telling him stories from the three in the morning A & E wards, sad tales of late-night mistakes and stumbles, and even sadder, those who had nothing wrong with them and had just come in for some company to get them through the night. She told him about her sister who'd died and how it had changed her – not in one big explosion but in a million small yet significant ways, and of the men she'd been with, both kind and cruel, and countries she'd visited and the ones she still wanted to, and he imagined her standing in some lost forgotten desert out on the edge of the world, amidst the dust and heat, her black hair crackling in the wind.

And then he stopped. Karen's voice faded to a whisper as he stared at the page in front of him.

He looked at the mugshot photo, seeing the pain and long nights of battle in Emily's eyes, and then he knew what had been bothering him about the arrest sheet and cursed himself for not having seen it earlier.

'I've got to go, I'm sorry,' he said, and she said she was tired too and the night was getting shorter and that they would talk again. He listened to the dead hum of the phone after they'd said goodbye, and then he got up, cleared the table of junk and paper, and spread out Emily's arrest sheet and warrants across the scratched plastic surface.

Emily had been arrested in March 2008, outside Whitehall. She'd been smoking a joint when a uniformed officer walked past. He arrested her and took her to the nearest station. Carrigan stared at the page, puzzled. Cannabis was a low priority for the Met and a huge waste of resources. Four hours of processing paperwork and a beat constable off the streets for half his shift over a single joint. Which was why, in most cases, a caution was often enough.

But there was something about the date of the arrest that was vaguely familiar. He noted the day, time and exact location, then picked up the phone.

The desk sergeant sounded tired and pissed off and reluctant to do anything that meant moving from his chair. He eventually grunted an acknowledgement and wrote down the date and postcode Carrigan had recited.

Jack could hear the man slowly punching in letters and numbers on the other end of the phone. He stared out at the cars gliding through the night, and then the sergeant was back on the line. Carrigan had asked him to perform a search for all arrests on the same day as Emily's and within a half-mile radius of her location.

'How many?' He leaned into the phone as if that would make the answer more understandable.

'Four hundred and fifty-six.'

'Four hundred and fifty-six arrests on that day?'

'Yes.' The sergeant paused as he scrolled through the list. 'Pretty much all of them for public nuisance or disorder breaches.'

Carrigan thanked him and put the phone down. Four hundred and fifty-five other people had been arrested on the same day and in close vicinity to Emily. He opened a new window, typed in the arrest date and location into Google, and watched as a list of web pages and news articles appeared.

The websites all belonged to student and anarchist groups. The news articles made him remember why the date had seemed so familiar. An anti-war march had been held that day which had left many police injured and half the shops on Oxford Street destroyed. Pacifists fighting against war. Carrigan had been there that day, along with every other policeman who wasn't on leave and most of those who were. The march was supposed to be peaceful and yet, within a couple of hours, it had turned into a battlefield. The police were attacked from all sides, objects and projectiles raining down, fists and legs and angry scowling students in black balaclavas wielding metal poles and Molotov cocktails.

He stared at the screen, remembering the chaos and fear. Amid all the lawlessness and looting why had Emily been arrested for smoking a single joint?

He made another coffee and paced the flat. Sometimes it was easier to arrest someone for drugs than public disorder, he reasoned. The weed would put her in a cell while they checked the CCTV to see if a further charge was warranted. It made sense and yet it didn't make any sense.

He walked over to the chair and picked up his jacket. He went through the pockets, getting rid of the amassed junk and twists of chocolate wrappers, and then he found the card. He stared at the words Donna had written – *There's a lot about Emily I couldn't tell you in front of them* – and picked up the phone.

He spent the next hour going through his policy book, making sure there were no avenues left unexplored, no timebombs ticking in anomalous timelines or misrecounted fact. He popped two pills for the headache erupting from his left temple. He went back to Geneva's notes and read through them again – her account of the nuns busting up a drug-dealing operation in their backyard, the picketing and leafleting – and he turned on the computer and waited for the PNC screen to boot up.

A couple of years back, he'd got Berman to fix access to the PNC through his home computer and he now logged on. As he waited for the system to recognise him, he opened a packet of German biscuits, half-moons dusted with crushed hazelnuts and powdered sugar. He took out exactly half the biscuits and put them on a plate. The rest he bagged and returned to the kitchen. This was how you went about a diet, in small and manageable steps, in learning to resist easy temptation. He ate the biscuits and began searching. He analysed patterns of recent drug activity in west London. The ever-shifting flowchart of alliances and feuds. He drank black coffee and trawled through out-of-date arrest sheets and old serials looking for something, he wasn't quite sure what. He finished the biscuits and got up and fetched the rest from the kitchen. He read reports of petty turf wars, stabbings or beatings over nondescript street corners in Kensington or Kilburn or Kensal Rise. Market forces and the myth of a recession-proof business. New groups coming from every part of the world to contest such rich territory, the inexorable globalisation of criminal enterprise. He finished the last biscuit and started going through twelve months' worth of drug squad reports. He was focusing on St Peter's Square and the neighbouring streets when he found mention of an altercation the uniforms had been called to a couple of weeks earlier.

A group of concerned residents in a residential street off Pembridge Square decided they'd had enough of dealers doing business in their front gardens. They organised themselves and made a nuisance whenever anyone came down the road looking to make a buy. They found out the address of the local dealer and plastered posters outside his house and all across the street, naming and shaming him in photographs and deeds. They assiduously reported all offences and suspicions to the local station. A week later, the uniforms were called to the scene of two residents lying beaten, bloody and battered on the pavement. The assailants were nowhere to be seen and the victims had been too stunned and shocked and scared to say who did this to them.

Carrigan sat back and rolled his shoulders, waiting for the welcoming pop that would untangle his muscles. There was no mention of nuns in the report but the residents' actions were very similar to the nuns' initiatives in combating drug dealing in the neighbourhood. Carrigan looked up from the screen into the starless sky. Could it be that they'd got it all wrong? That Emily and the nuns' tangled history had nothing to do with the fire? That it all came down to something as stupid and pointless as this?

He turned off the computer and stood by the window. He didn't want to think about it but it was all he could think about. He knew sleep would not find him tonight and he didn't bother looking for it. The snow was falling in thick spinning clusters, obscuring the motorway ramp and street outside. Somewhere above, he could see the faint blips of light marking another plane leaving the city and disappearing into the sky, a tiny metallic cylinder, crammed with people and hopes and histories, on the way to somewhere else.

23

The incident room was empty at this time of the morning and that was exactly the way she liked it. The antiseptic white spaces were silent but for the buzz and murmur of computers left on overnight, hard drives wheezing like exhausted workers at the end of a long and gruelling shift. Geneva could hear the splash and fizz of the Coke in her can, the steady pulse of the fluorescents above her, and popped two more pills, trying desperately to focus. She'd had way too much tequila last night and she'd woken, alone, at 4 a.m., with a blazing headache. She didn't want to think about the flung words and accusations between her and Lee last night, but she couldn't stop thinking about what he'd told her after she'd mentioned the pathologist's findings.

She fought back a wave of nausea, spread out her notes either side of the keyboard, checked her to-do list and sent out a request to Westminster and to Kensington and Chelsea for parking tickets registered to the fake SUV number plate. The chances were almost zero, the men in the SUV probably changing plates with great frequency, but nonetheless it annoyed her that no one else had bothered to check this. Once this was done she opened the box sitting at her feet. The diocese had sent further files on the convent yesterday and she went through these now, reading about their charity endeavours, anti-drug initiatives and numerous commendations. She flicked through the files until she saw a folder for travel requests. She took out the crumpled photocopies within and scanned them. For each trip out of the country, the nuns had to fill out a form requesting leave. One copy was sent to the diocese and another to the order for approval. There were nearly fifty such forms and Geneva went through them slowly, making notes of which countries the nuns had visited.

Twenty-three requests had been made for travel to the Vatican, twelve to the Holy Land and three to Ireland. The remaining eight requests were for travel to Peru.

Geneva pulled out the earliest request and scrutinised the handwriting. The form was a request from Sister Glenda Waldron for a six-day leave to go to Lima during the last week of November 2011. The reason for the trip was given as *conference*. There was an identical form for Sister Rose McGregor.

She remembered the name from the files at the diocese. Sister Rose had been the last nun to leave the convent, just over a year ago. The requisition forms had two signature boxes at the bottom, one for departure and one for arrival. Sister Glenda's signature filled both boxes but Sister Rose had only signed the departure box. Geneva briefly wondered if Sister Rose had forgotten to fill in the form on her arrival, but the records were too well kept and organised for this to be likely.

She read through the other six travel requests. Each was signed, arrival and departure, by Sister Glenda. She went back to the main set of files but there was no record of Sister Rose anywhere.

Geneva pushed her chair back and rubbed her eyes. Two of the nuns had travelled to Peru in the last thirteen months, one of them on seven separate occasions. She felt a tingle in her stomach. She knew this changed everything. The Peruvian connection was no longer just ancient history. She jotted down the dates and made a note to call Holden, then, thinking back to last night, the look in Lee's eyes, the way the words seemed so reluctant to leave his mouth, she entered *tickling the bone* into the search engine.

There were many references to comedians and funny bones but, hidden among the humour and jape, was an article about how drug cartels were getting more sophisticated and grimly medieval by the day. How the violence and torture had left the private sphere and was now occurring in the worldmesh of YouTube and Flickr. The article described this particular method of torture exactly as Lee had. The use of an ice-pick, the breaking of the skin, the point of the pick inserted through the tender flesh until it came up against the bone. She read reports from undercover DEA agents who'd undergone this ordeal. She thought about the nuns' trips to Peru, her heart beating a little faster.

There was a sidebar detailing history and uses. Tickling the bone had been the favoured method of torture used by right-wing para-militaries against leftist agitators, or folk singers, or writers, or people who'd been mistaken for someone else. This technique, the report stated, was primarily used in Central America, in El Salvador and Nicaragua, but it had also been adopted by Pinochet's men in Chile and had spread to Colombia, Peru and Ecuador.

She clicked on the word *Peru*, her breath held and body tensed, and read tales of military coups and counter-coups, repression and poverty, oil and torture and bicycle bombs in the marketplace. The phrase 'liberation theology' kept cropping up between the margins and across the texts. There was a whole section about armed insurgents in the Inca hills, a band of Maoist guerrillas called the Shining Path, led by an ex-professor of philosophy, cutting a swathe through the Andean heartlands, burning the bourgeois blight from the ground as if it were weeds and enmeshing the country in a twenty-year civil war. She sat back, the lights washing over her, as she thought about what she'd learned in the diocese archives and what she'd just read.

Seven of the nuns had been stationed in South America. Their stay had only overlapped for four months, during the autumn of 1973, in the San Gabriel province in the south-central section of the country. All seven of them had been relocated shortly afterwards.

Five of the nuns had identical torture scars. The pathologist had estimated the scars to be thirty or forty years old. Geneva looked at the flickering screen, willing to bet her salary, her iPod, whatever she owned, that the scars dated from the autumn of 1973. Something had happened in those cold mountains, up near the roof of the world, something which had followed the nuns all the way to London and the twenty-first century.

She felt a surge in her chest as she punched in the nuns' names, dates of deployment and locations in varying sequences. She came up with nothing or with so many results it amounted to the same thing. She stopped, thought about it, and recalibrated her search parameters, this time substituting the word *political* for *religious*.

There were seventeen major political incidents in Peru during the timeframe she was looking at but only one in the remote San Gabriel region. She clicked on the link and was taken to a page devoted to analysing the dialectics of the September '73 strike at the Chiapeltec mine. She cross-checked the dates, feeling more and more certain, and began reading.

The Chiapeltec gold mine had been worked continually since the days of the Incas. The Spanish had stumbled upon its natural bounty and duly co-opted it for the Crown, using native Indian slaves to harvest the shiny flecks of metal embedded in the rocks. The mine had been in operation since then, closing down only intermittently, changing hands and countries of ownership with striking regularity, bought and resold and bought again.

In 1973, the mine was in full production, the latest drilling and scouting technology applied to go even further down into the folds of compacted earth searching for the elusive dust. The death rate for miners was the highest in South America at the time, comparable to the mortality rate for slaves during the Spanish occupation. Geneva read dour reports of silicosis, cave-ins, noxious fumes, bar fights and strange cancers.

By the sizzling, scorched summer of 1973, things had come to a head. Twelve miners and two priests from the local village who'd tried to organise a strike disappeared. They were found three days later hanging upside down, naked and mutilated, in the village square.

Geneva glanced out the window, measuring the spindrift and gather of snow on the sill, trying to clear her head of the dread images the words had conjured. The phones kept ringing on the empty tables and she stared at them until the answering machines kicked in. Her private mobile hadn't stopped buzzing and she checked the display but it wasn't Lee and, despite herself, she felt a little sink of disappointment. Oliver had rung five times in the last hour and left three messages. She switched off the phone and continued reading.

The news of the murders had quickly spread from village to village, mine to mine, up mountains and down the long ancient river, and soon strangers started turning up at Chiapeltec, bearded burly men with serious brows wrinkled in righteousness and rage, priests and nuns and ordinary people. Journalists made the trek up to the high country with their cameras and microphones, their big-city certainties and beliefs safely in pocket. The village swelled and roared during the night with the megaphoned voices of political agitators, Marxists and Castroists, anarchists and liberation theologians, the crazed and God-touched. A committee was formed by a leading Peruvian bishop and a strike was called for the following day. There was a party atmosphere that night, a feeling of comradeship and unity, of purpose and prophecy, a swelling together of farmers and miners, intellectuals and holy men.

The first day of the strike went by peacefully, the workers lined up either side of the only paved road in the province, the atmosphere one of genial protest rather than anger or violence. Everyone went back to the village that night and celebrated their success with loud music and laughter so that no one heard the bomb go off.

There was a house at the far edge of the mine company's property that the owners and management used for lunch and to conduct meetings. It was only in use during business hours. The bomb had been set to explode at midnight. It destroyed the building, leaving only grey ash and fingers of smoke curling up into the dark sky. It also destroyed the lives of twelve women and thirty-four children who'd been secretly relocated there in case their homes were targeted during the strike.

No one knew who'd set the bomb and squabbling and blame broke out among the strikers the next day, all of them knowing that the stakes had changed overnight. The bosses buried their wives and children that morning, and then they called in the army but the army was busy killing leftists in the dappled Inca hills. The government sent the next best thing. A battalion of death-squad veterans.

They came with blowtorches and machine guns, machetes and cattle prods, grudges and century-old hatreds boiling in their blood, but the villagers had their own weapons, clubs and pitchforks and hammers and anything they could find lying about in the sheds or stony fields. The battle raged across the day and deep into the night.

The army was sent in on the second day and two hundred strikers disappeared and were never seen again. The mine owners shipped in workers from the mountains, tough gnarled Indians who didn't care about conditions and safety as long as they got paid. The murdered strikers' families were booted out of their homes and the village that very night.

Geneva squinted as she finished the article and skimmed the footnotes, the long lists of the disappeared, the rumours of swirling moaning pits out in the hills, the flowcharts of red terrorists and religious institutions. The government blamed the insurgency on Marxist agitators, calling the bomb a terrorist outrage, the president appearing on national TV and saying that when the body had a sore, you had to cut it out quickly or it would spread to the rest of the body.

She sat back, queasy and shaken, the story reeling through her blood. She made notes and opened another can of Coke, then logged into the Press Association website with the password she'd got from Lee last night. She searched for images from the Chiapeltec massacre.

To her surprise, there were many, taken by brave and foolish photographers, and you could tell it hadn't been an easy assignment, the shots often blurred and out of focus, a jostled sense of panic in each frame, a feeling that this was something photography couldn't capture, that it was too quick and mercurial and real. There were photos of picket lines, army gunboots, vapour trails, grinning soldiers, and one of a woman holding her screaming baby as she lay sprawled and dead on the railroad track.

There were hundreds of these photos and Geneva scanned through them quickly, her hangover coming back hard and strong, the blood and screaming faces making her feel as if she could taste her own stomach, and then she stopped and zoomed and clicked on a thumbnail of a photo near the bottom of the page.

She tapped her foot as the full-size file slowly unscrolled on her screen.

The image was of a bristling picket line, all grimaces and clenched fists, maybe twenty or thirty people standing out in the bright dusty sun, arms raised heavenwards or holding handmade banners with skulls and demons crudely daubed upon them, and it wasn't until Geneva zoomed in closer and studied the faces one by one that she recognised her.

She was much younger, of course, but there was no doubt it was the same woman.

Mother Angelica stood left of centre, wearing the full habit, wimple and cincture, and those tight round glasses that had led to her being nicknamed the Owl. Her mouth was twisted in a snarl of indignation and she had one arm raised, her fist pumping the empty sky.

Geneva looked at Mother Angelica for a long moment, then

studied the faces of the people standing beside her, time and the piled emotions of the occasion making everything seem both dreamlike and utterly vivid at the same time. Behind the nuns was a group of priests. One of them was a full head taller than the others and in his fist he held a large wooden club studded with nails. Even across forty years, Geneva recognised the penetrating stare of Father Callum McCarthy.

24

Berwick Street in the snow. The fruit sellers crying out their bargains, the dazed Japanese tourists with record bags held protectively to their chests, the rainbow-haired girls from St Martin's buying cloth for their end-of-year shows. A little further down, the porn parlours and DVD shops, lingerie emporiums and spangly nightclubs. Vegetables and lunch-hour sex side by side.

Carrigan trudged through the slush, past the doorways with their peeling paint and crude handwritten cards promising pleasure up two sets of stairs and the frazzle-eyed hipsters heading home. As a teenager he'd come here often to buy records, blithely unaware of this shadow world existing alongside. A sad reproduction of Amsterdam for people who'd never seen Amsterdam. The buildings faded and dilapidated, the girls crying out from blue velvet booths, their voices shrill and indifferent as if calling out items at a supermarket till.

After what he'd read last night, an idea had begun forming. He thought about the dealers in the alleyway behind the convent, the SUV visits, the men who'd attacked him in the ruins. He needed to know who was running drugs in his patch. Who the nuns might have upset and what kind of people they were dealing with. So, last night, he'd sent out a Met-wide request for information on drug activity in west London. A couple of hours later he'd received a call from DS Byrd who worked for the Met's Organised Crime Unit, suggesting they meet at the White Dove.

The pub could have been a museum piece, a smoked antique seeped in beer fumes and muzzy light, a last remaining bastion of the old Soho before the scenesters and media companies had taken over. You could still smell the smoke though it had been years since the last cigarette had been crushed out in the last ashtray. The windows were almost opaque and the world outside reduced to a blur of smudges and passing shadows, disappearing as quickly as dreams. Carrigan scanned the bar for Byrd but saw only old men hunched over pints of beer, their eyes already foggy and surrendered by lunchtime. You could read their life stories in the way they sat and stared at their drinks. It was the kind of place only the terminally lost frequented and the state of the decor and furnishings was testament to the fact that all anyone cared about was the level of liquid in their glass and the three feet of space which separated them from the rest of the world.

Carrigan finally spotted DS Byrd sitting at a corner table, a pint of murky ale and two clear shot glasses lined up in front of him. Byrd was in his late fifties but he was the youngest person here.

'Thanks for meeting me.'

'Was having my lunch anyway,' Byrd shrugged by way of reply. His face was long and thin, riddled with folds, his hair a lanky black shawl draped across his eyes. His left leg was constantly in motion, pumping up and down against the floor, his eyes scanning the room.

'You're on the convent fire, right?' Byrd reached for his pint and took a long deep swallow, then picked up one of the shot glasses and downed it in one.

Carrigan nodded.

'And what does any of that have to do with drugs?'

'The nuns were active in anti-drug initiatives,' Carrigan explained. 'They had quite a presence in the neighbourhood. They shooed off some dealers from an alley at the back of the convent. There's also reports of them picketing dealers' houses, approaching incoming customers with leaflets on rehab centres and the curative powers of God.'

Byrd listened intently, his eyes unblinking. He took in Carrigan's words without expression, then had another sip of beer followed by the second shot. Carrigan opened his briefcase and pulled out a file. From inside, he took out a photo of the man with the scarred mouth that Berman had printed off from the CCTV footage. Byrd looked at the photo and his eyes narrowed. He didn't say anything.

'This man visited the convent at least three times before the fire. He was standing outside watching the convent burn down that night. He also assaulted me in the ruins the next day.'

He saw the merest flicker of interest in Byrd's eyes but the sergeant managed to snuff it out almost immediately. 'Where did you get this?'

'CCTV camera outside the school next door to the convent. Who is he?'

Byrd stared into his glass in silent deliberation. 'We know him only as Viktor. He's a lieutenant for one of the top Albanian bosses, Agon Duka.'

'Duka?' Carrigan repeated, his teeth buzzing.

'Runs one of the larger Albanian gangs. Viktor's his right-hand man. If he's involved then it's something that's important to Duka.'

'Albanians?' Carrigan said. 'You mean the Albanian mob?'

Byrd nodded, got up and walked over to the bar, ordering another round of drinks. His legs wobbled slightly as he came back across the room. He sat down, took a sip of beer and swiped back a shot. His eyes glassed over and for a brief moment all the lines and long hard years were temporarily erased.

'What the hell are the Albanians doing here? I didn't even know they were active in London.'

'War,' Byrd replied, a grim smile on his face, and when he saw Carrigan's confused expression, he said, 'Do you believe in the law of unintended consequences?'

Carrigan looked at his drink but he didn't need to think about it. 'We can never know the outcome of any given action.'

'Good. Too many people think they can see the future and no

one can. Bill Clinton passed sanctions on Serbia during the Bosnian war. The traditional route for heroin smuggling into Europe had always been from Turkey via Belgrade. The war closed that route. Albanian gangs suddenly found themselves literally in the right place at the right time. They could guarantee safe transit through the war zone. They made a lot of money but, more importantly, they made a lot of connections. When the conflict was over they entered the EU as asylum seekers and put together the infrastructure we see today. Initially, it was heroin they were involved in, but they were also behind the Securitas heist in 2006, several other armed robberies and a million petty thieveries.'

Carrigan could only shake his head. Even twenty years as a policeman hadn't exposed him to the full horror running through London's veins. It was like the fabled onion. Peel off one layer and there was always something worse underneath. He looked at the old men leaning against the bar and wondered whether they realised what brave new times they'd survived into – or maybe that was exactly why they were here, folded into barstools and inner darkness, enacting a slow stunned withdrawal from the world.

'Impressive,' he admitted. 'How did they manage that? The Russian and Chechen gangs are no pushover.'

'Violence,' Byrd answered flatly. 'It's always going to be the primary currency in these cultures and the Albanians have plenty to spare. Remember, we're talking about men who come from the bloodstorms of ethnic war, from mountain villages where grudge feuds have been playing out for centuries – a lot of them are ex-Sigurimi, the Albanian Communist secret police – our homegrown gangs were no match for them and neither, as it turned out, were the Russians.' Byrd stared at his empty glass. 'You're lucky, Carrigan. With murders you either solve them or you don't. In this job you have to spend a year, maybe more, watching these scumbags enjoying their earnings, parading it in front of you, and most times when you've finally nabbed them and it goes to court, the witnesses recant or disappear, and they're back out on the streets the same fucking day.'

Carrigan took a deep breath and sipped his coffee. 'You ever think about transferring?'

Byrd smiled but there was nothing remotely mirthful in his expression. He pulled a wallet out of his pocket and flipped it open to reveal two faded photos. One was of a normal suburban house, the other of a young woman holding a little boy.

'That was my house,' Byrd said. 'That was my wife. She took all my money and the house. That's my son. I haven't spoken to him in over four years – I wouldn't even recognise him if he walked past me on the street.' He flipped the wallet shut and put it back in his jacket. 'They remind me what I've already given up for this job. If I back out now, this would have been all for nothing,' he said, and it was obvious that he carried his bitterness like an enormous weight, that he'd been both shrivelled and honed by it and that it was the only thing still keeping him going.

Carrigan drained his drink. The taste in his mouth was rank and metallic. 'This man, Duka, what can you tell me about him?'

'Duka runs most of the heavy drugs – coke, heroin, crack – through west London,' Byrd replied. 'The majority of the organised dealing in W2 has his involvement somewhere down the line. He keeps himself and his top people away from most of the dirty work, of course.'

'What about the area surrounding the convent? Anything there?'

'There's four houses in the postcode you mentioned we're keeping an eye on. Duka owns them but they're not rented and he doesn't live there. We think he uses them as stash-houses. The primary shipment gets cut and bagged there, then the mid-level dealers come and pick up their supplies. But Duka's smart. We think he's revolving the four houses randomly. Makes it almost impossible to get enough intel for a warrant.'

Carrigan wondered if any of the houses the nuns had picketed belonged to Duka. 'Where are they, these four houses?'

'One's on Gloucester Terrace, one on Prince's Square, one on Queensborough Terrace and one on Hatherley Crescent.'

'If a group of nuns hassled his dealers and pestered customers, how would Duka react? Would he go as far as burning down the convent?'

'He wouldn't think twice about it,' Byrd replied. 'But for something like that? I don't know. He'd just move his dealers to the next road along. He's not stupid, wouldn't be where he is if he were. The nuns would have had to piss him off a little more than that before he took such a step.'

Carrigan thought about this. 'Where did he come from? I've not heard his name come up before.'

'That's because he's extremely good at what he does.' Byrd ran long skinny fingers through his greasy hair and drained his beer. 'Duka was an elite member of a paramilitary group during the Kosovo conflict. He came here after the fighting was over and brought along a handful of his loyal troops. He made deals where he could and got rid of the competition where he couldn't.'

'Sounds to me like your average dirtbag dealer,' Carrigan said, the pages in his notebook filling up fast, his handwriting deteriorating as he tried to catch up with the flow of names and facts pouring from Byrd's lips.

Byrd's sudden laugh surprised him at the same time as making him feel distinctly uneasy.

'Oh, he's a lot more than that.' Byrd stared morosely at his empty glass. 'Let me give you just one example. There's a story we heard from one of our informants. Duka had a younger brother, a bit slow by all accounts, and he used to take care of him, you know, like Hitler was good to his dogs and all that.

'Anyway, one day, Duka finds out that his bitter rival, the head of a neighbouring gang, has made plans to kidnap the brother and use him as a bargaining tool. Duka invites his rival to dinner so they can talk it over. The rival is intrigued, thinks he sees a chink of weakness in Duka's armour, so he accepts the offer. They drink good wine inside Duka's house and eat the most delicious stew the rival's ever tasted. They talk of the weather and the fields and the old men who never came back from the war. Finally, Duka leans over the table and gets to the point of the meeting. "You were look-ing for my brother, I hear?" The rival stares into Duka's eyes but he doesn't deny it. "Well," Duka says, taking the lid off the pot from which they've been eating, "I sincerely hope he was to your liking."' Byrd leaned back and unleashed a blustery bellowing laugh and Carrigan briefly wondered if he'd once been an eager young police-man, assured in his mission, because all he saw now was a broken figure, plagued by failure and doubt, by the things he'd seen and the things he'd done, but most of all plagued by the darkness residing within human hearts.

'Where can I find Duka?'

Byrd shot his hand across the table and grabbed Carrigan's wrist. Despite the alcohol, his eyes were clear and focused as he spoke. 'Keep away from him, Carrigan. You don't want to get involved. He's something new. Something we haven't seen before. For some people cruelty and revenge are arts, to be practised and endlessly improved upon. There are no rules here. He'll come straight for you.'

'That's exactly what I intend.'

Byrd smiled. 'And none of what I've just told you puts you off?'

Carrigan extricated his arm from Byrd's grip. 'No,' he replied. 'It just makes me more certain that I need to speak to him. He sounds like exactly the kind of person who would have no qualms about killing ten nuns.'

Byrd's jaw tightened. 'The last thing you want is to be on Duka's radar, believe me. You've got to think about that and you need to run anything through me first before you authorise any actions, understand? We're in the middle of several long-range operations and I don't want you or your team stumbling into something you have no clue about.'

Carrigan got up from the table. 'How about you tell me what your operations are and then there'll be no chance of that happening?'

Byrd smiled but it was one of the most malevolent things Carrigan had ever seen. 'Can't do that and you know it. We need to protect our assets. Just make sure you check with us first. Wouldn't want you wading into deep water without knowing. You'll drown.'

As Carrigan stepped back out into the spray of wind and snow, the world seemed dimmer and darker and more hopeless than before. He stood and thought about Byrd's final remark, unsure whether it was meant as a friendly warning or a threat.

25

Sometimes you get lucky in the strangest of places, Geneva thought, as she scanned through the attachment Westminster Parking had sent her. She printed it out, laid the page across her table and went down the columns just to make sure. Earlier, she'd sent out a request to Westminster and to Kensington and Chelsea Parking for any tickets issued to the black SUV in the last couple of months. She'd thought it was a long shot, something that only had to be done because it had to be done, and was surprised when she got the results.

The fake number-plate belonging to the black SUV had picked up four parking tickets in the last eight weeks. Each had been settled promptly, within seven days. One of the tickets was given on Queensway, outside a Chinese restaurant that Carrigan had once taken her to. The other three tickets were all issued on the same street, a small cul-de-sac off Westbourne Grove called Hatherley Crescent. Her skin began to itch as she magnified the tickets on her screen and tried to untangle the spidery handwriting.

She looked across the incident room. DC Singh was on the phone, Berman and Jennings leaning intently over a computer screen. She looked at the parking tickets again. She didn't really trust it, this hunch of hers, it wasn't even that, just something which needed to be checked and crossed off the list, and she felt uneasy about taking anyone else away from their tasks on what would probably be a huge waste of time. Besides, she was only going to look at a section of road, nothing more.

She thought about calling her mum as she walked down Bishop's Bridge Road in the swirling snow and wind. She wanted to talk to her about what was going on in her life, Oliver, the job, but all she ever got was disapproval and distance.

She lit a cigarette instead. She hadn't seen her mother for a while, several weeks. She kept telling herself it was the demands of the job, the long hours and crashing come-downs, but she knew it wasn't really that. It was her mother's new boyfriend, Greg, a lecturer in politics at the LSE who nursed a pathological hatred for the police and goaded her at every opportunity, turning every meal into a minefield. It was the distance that had gradually grown between them since she'd joined the police force, her mother never quite forgiving her, but what Katrina didn't understand was that Geneva loved the puzzle of her days, sifting through the lies people told to others and those they told to themselves. There was an intoxication in the mystery of other people's lives and it was hard to think of another career, another life.

She dropped the cigarette in the snow and watched it disappear down a hole of its own making. She ignored the bag-laden tourists and grinning revellers surrounding her and turned into Hatherley Crescent.

It was a short, narrow cul-de-sac, with terraced Edwardian houses on one side and a 1930s mansion block on the other. The street was dark and cold and gloomy, the buildings forming a narrow canyon.

She checked her notebook, shielding the pages from the snow. All three parking tickets had been given outside numbers 46–50 Hatherley Crescent. Geneva slowly made her way up the street until she was looking across at the space where the tickets were issued. It was a resident's parking bay and, of course, if you had a fake number-plate you couldn't have a resident's permit, hence the tickets. Whatever business the driver of the SUV was on, it was obviously worth the £80 fine each time.

She looked across the street at the doors of the two houses directly behind the parking bay, wondering which one the man with the scar had been visiting – perhaps neither; maybe this was just where he'd found an empty space to park as he'd gone to pick up a takeaway from one of the many restaurants on Westbourne Grove. She shook the thought free and began crossing the road. She'd set her phone to silent and the sudden vibration against her skin made her jump. She stopped and pulled it out and read the message. She read it twice, frantically wiping snow off the display, then read it once more. She realised she was clutching the phone so tightly it was beginning to hurt. The message was from Lee. She read it again, bringing the screen closer to her face. *You're right, we need to stop doing this. I'm sorry too.* Her hands shook. Her stomach flipped. The words didn't make sense and then they did. She read the message again. It said the same thing. She put the phone back in her pocket and crossed the street.

Both houses were similarly weathered and in need of repair, both chipped and cracked and neglected, but the house on the left had three shiny new security cameras pointing at its front door.

She took careful steps through the deep drifts of snow. The door was painted brown and the paint had faded and flaked but the locks were sturdy and recent. There was only one buzzer – unlike most of the other buildings in the street, this one hadn't been cut up and converted into flats. The stone lion at the head of the stairs was missing half its face, but the burglar alarm and security system were new and high-end.

She rang the doorbell, first hesitatingly, then pushing down the square grey button with increasing force. Her hands were suddenly too hot, as if she were wearing gloves. She heard the cameras whir and saw them zooming in on her as she waited. A door slammed somewhere inside and she placed one hand on her belt.

She could hear approaching footsteps. They seemed to take

forever. She heard someone cough on the other side of the door, a long sustained hack and spit. The sound of the locks being disengaged was sharp and dry in the chill air.

The man was dressed in a black suit as if he'd just come back from a funeral. He smiled when he saw her, his eyes roving up and down and across her body, his teeth capped silver and gleaming in the snowglare.

She hadn't really thought what to say, was going to pretend that a nuisance call had come in concerning the flat, but the man's stare undid her and she stood frozen.

'Would you like to come in?' the man said, his accent cracked and heavily vowelled.

She hadn't expected this and was so surprised she didn't know what to say.

'Please come in,' the man said, extending his arm, the knuckles covered in spidery black hair. 'I make you some coffee, or tea if you prefer.'

'No, it's okay,' she replied. 'I must have got the wrong house.'

The man took a step forward, the smile creasing his face. 'No, I think you came to exactly the right place,' he said. 'Please,' he beckoned her inside with his arm, 'I would like to get to know you. Please come in.'

She took a step back, her foot sliding on the icy slick stone. 'No, thanks.'

The man continued smiling, but there was something else in his eyes now as he took a step forward. 'You sure? I think you would have a nice time if you came in with me . . . I think I could make you very happy.'

Geneva felt her entire body crawl. She shook her head, turned around and walked down the stairs, forcing herself not to break into a run, not to let the panic seep through her skin as the man's eyes tracked her all the way down the street.

26

'Emily Maxted,' Carrigan said, pinning the blown-up mugshot photo to the whiteboard behind him. 'We've managed to identify the eleventh victim but let's not pat ourselves on the back just yet – this only raises a whole new set of questions. What was she doing there? We know she wasn't a nun and she didn't have any official connection to the convent, yet the caretaker told us he'd seen her frequently and referred to her as the "new girl".'

The incident room was packed with bodies this afternoon, shuffling in from the cold, their clothes steaming and dripping melted snow, the uniforms hungover and huddled in the back. Carrigan ran down what they'd learned from the Maxteds. 'We shouldn't cling to the fact that they haven't spoken to her for nearly two years. It may be nothing to do with the case,' he warned them. 'Could be just plain old screwed-up family dynamics, but it'll make it harder for us to trace her whereabouts over the last few months.' He brushed his fingers through his beard and shuffled through his notes. 'Karlson, did you manage to find out anything about the family?'

Karlson unwrapped his long spindly legs from the stool like a spider and picked up his iPhone. 'I looked up the parents,' he said. 'They're both relatively well known, filthy rich too. The father, Miles Maxted, is a pretty controversial figure in his field, has some interesting ideas about child-raising. There's a Wikipedia page on him. His basic theory seems to be that parental love conditions the child to be unprepared for the heartless cruelty of the world – a place where this love can never be replicated, leaving the child forever longing for something that not only can he never have but that doesn't even exist.'

'Yep, a nice guy all round,' Carrigan said, impressed by Karlson's précis.

'What about looking at Facebook, Twitter . . . ?' DC Singh suggested. 'We should check Emily's social networking sites, see what she was up to.'

Carrigan chided himself for not having thought of it earlier and nodded. 'Miller? Anything new to report?'

Geneva took a sip of her Coke and updated them on what she'd discovered earlier, still unsure as to what it meant, the traces and connections all hazy and just out of reach. She'd convinced herself that there was no point mentioning the house on Hatherley Crescent or the smiling man on the other side of the door. Carrigan would dismiss it, the evidence was circumstantial at best, but she'd felt something when the door had opened and she couldn't describe it, even to herself. It wasn't the man, or at least it wasn't just the man, it was as if something dark and trapped had rushed out of the house, sensing its chance. She knew it was stupid, her feelings probably far more to do with Lee's text, and she tried to put it out of her mind as she continued. 'Mother Angelica, Father McCarthy and at least two of the other nuns who died in the fire were involved in the 1973 Chiapeltec strike. It began as a normal strike but that first night a bomb went off, inadvertently killing the mine owners' families. The next day they retaliated and a lot of people were murdered. No one knows who placed the bomb, but the Scarlet Fire, a Marxist-Leninist group whose members later joined the Shining Path, were suspected. A month later, Mother Angelica was transferred back to London, having only served three years of a five-year residency.'

'That's all very interesting,' Carrigan said, seeing Geneva's mouth tighten. He could tell she was hungover and irritable, her eyes a little smaller and more pouched than normal. 'But it's ancient history.'

'How about thirteen months ago?'

Carrigan's eyes shot up. 'What happened thirteen months ago?'

'Two of the nuns travelled to Peru.' She just about resisted the urge to smile when she saw the look on Carrigan's face. 'It gets better,' she continued. 'On the first trip, two nuns flew out to Peru but only one came back.' She shuffled through her papers till she found the right one. 'I looked up the nuns' travel records, they were in the file Holden sent us. Sister Glenda and Sister Rose travelled to Peru in November of last year. The strange thing is that there's no record of Sister Rose returning. I checked with immigration and they have her leaving the country but not coming back in. A month later the convent replaced her with a new nun.'

'Maybe she liked it so much she decided to stay there?' Jennings quipped.

'She's a nun, it's not up to her,' Geneva replied. 'And if she was transferred there, why is there a travel requisition form in her file and not a transfer request?'

'What do you think happened to her?' Carrigan asked, his voice careful and soft.

'I don't know yet, but it all ties in to the convent ceasing their charity work, I'm sure of it. They did this a few weeks after Sister Rose didn't return from Peru. It doesn't make sense. They spent years building up their outreach programmes – why shut them down? With the economic situation as it is, why did they give up their charity work just when it was needed the most?'

Carrigan stopped his note-taking. 'Do we know why the nuns travelled to Peru?'

'I phoned the diocese and spoke to Holden. He told me he would have to get back to me on Sister Rose's whereabouts but he confirmed that the nuns had gone to attend church conferences in Lima . . .'

'But?' Carrigan could see something small and mischievous in Geneva's eyes.

'I checked the conferences Holden mentioned and cross-referenced them with the nuns' dates of travel. All three conferences were on dates that didn't tally with the nuns' trips.'

Carrigan looked over at Geneva and shook his head. 'It's a good story but I'm still not convinced it has anything to do with the fire. It's far more likely that the nuns' crusading activities pissed off the wrong people and that the fire was in retaliation for that.' He saw their faces slump further as he updated them on Byrd's information. 'This man, Viktor,' Carrigan said, pointing to the photo on the wall behind him, 'is now our main suspect and we need to focus all our energies on finding him. We know he visited the convent. We know he was outside, watching, while the fire was blazing. I think the nuns pissed off this Duka guy and he sent his lieutenant, Viktor, to have a word with them. The fact he made three visits to the convent tells me the nuns were none too eager to stand down. Duka gets pissed off and sends someone, maybe Viktor again, to torch the convent.' He could sense Geneva's stare burning a hole in the side of his head and ignored it.

'Quinn's just gonna love this,' Karlson chuckled, a leering grin across his face. 'Can't wait to see you trying to explain to him how this case just got a whole lot more fucked up than it already was.'

'Thank you for that, John,' Carrigan replied. 'As you're so eager to see the ACC's reaction, I'll make sure you're there with me when I hand in my report.'

Karlson's eyes sputtered momentarily then muted. Shooting the messenger was one of Quinn's most firmly held beliefs.

But Carrigan felt no pleasure in goading his sergeant. Karlson was right – Quinn had wanted an easy solve, a firebug recently out of jail or an accident, but the more they looked into this case the more it seemed to spin out in contradictory directions, each path at seeming right angles from the others, layered and dense with history and occluded years.

'We should at least check the nuns' financial records,' Geneva said and Carrigan turned swiftly, ready to be angry at her, but when he saw her face, the seriousness and weight of her eyes, he stopped and said, 'Why?'

'For years the nuns were involved in funding all this outreach work in the community. They were spending a lot of money and then it stops dead.' Geneva looked up from her notebook, a hard bright gleam in her eye. 'I want to know what they've been doing with all the money they previously would have been spending on good works.'

Carrigan considered this. It was a good question and he was disappointed in himself for not having thought of it. 'We'd need to get a warrant and Quinn would never allow it.'

'I know,' Geneva replied. 'Which is why I took the liberty of asking Berman to see if he could hack into the diocese's server.'

Carrigan stared at Geneva then turned his attention to Berman. 'And . . . can you?'

Berman avoided Carrigan's gaze, using the opportunity to examine his keyboard. 'It won't stand up in court but it's quicker than a warrant.'

Carrigan thought about this for a moment. He looked around the room. 'Everyone OK with this?'

No one blinked or shook their heads. Slowly, everyone nodded.

'Good,' Carrigan said and turned to Berman. 'Can you get us into their financial accounts?'

'Yes, I think so,' the DC answered. 'The convent was a registered charity, it existed on donations. That means the records are in there somewhere.'

'Do it,' Carrigan commanded.

Berman typed in a string of commands on two keyboards at the same time. They all hunched impatiently over the desk as the screen flashed a long list of numbers. It was scary what was out there, Carrigan thought, every keystroke and kink of your personality, all the words you gushed out drunk at three in the morning, the fired-off jokes and offhand gossip, and it was all stored and waiting in a cold underground room for someone to retrieve it.

A couple of minutes later, Berman nodded imperceptibly and a smile crept across his face.

Carrigan almost ripped the page from the printer. He scanned the dense sheet of numbers, then scanned it again because it wasn't at all what he'd expected.

'What is it?' Geneva said, noticing the quickening in his features. He passed the account sheet across the table. 'The nuns had over a million pounds in their account as of last month,' Carrigan stated, watching everyone's eyes curl in surprise. 'Berman, can you get their monthly statements?'

A minute later more paper came crunching through the printer. Carrigan stared down the long list of figures. 'Money was coming in every month to the nuns' account. Different sums from several different payees. Berman, I need you to get a list of donors to the convent. Anything over a couple of hundred pounds.'

'No problem,' he replied, but Carrigan was too ensnared by the balance sheets in his hands to notice.

'There's a monthly standing order going out of the convent's account,' he said, each word slow and deliberate. 'Twenty thousand pounds on the sixteenth of every month. Same destination each time.'

Berman scanned his screen and copied the sort code and account number of the bank that the money was being paid into, then punched the information into a search engine.

He moved his face closer to the screen until his nose was nearly touching it. They could all hear his breathing as the data flashed up. 'The transfers are all routed to the same place,' he said. 'The sort code refers to a Banco National branch in Cusco.'

'Cusco?' Geneva repeated.

A small grin escaped the side of Berman's mouth. 'According to this, the nuns transferred almost a quarter of a million pounds to Peru this year.'

27

Geneva stood outside the small stone church nestled in a sleepy cul-de-sac in the wilds of Lewisham and smoked a cigarette as the snow filled the folds of her jacket and smudged her lenses. She'd been too tired, hungover and red-eyed to put her contacts in that morning and the weight of her glasses was an unexpected thing, it had been so long since she'd last worn them.

She'd left the briefing buzzing with theories and speculation and spent the last two hours glued to the computer screen, zooming and clicking and making notes, the case now pushing her along on its own rhythm.

But what she read only confused her further. She didn't know if the events at Chiapeltec had anything to do with the case or if they had nothing to do with it. She wasn't sure how Sister Rose, the missing nun, fitted in. Maybe Carrigan was right and this was nothing more than a feud taken too far, the nuns naively getting into deep water with some nasty drug dealers. But no, that didn't feel right. She was sure the nuns' activities in Peru were pertinent to the case despite how persuasive Carrigan's counter-theory had been. She needed more evidence to back up her hunches. This was an unfamiliar and murky world, one she knew nothing about, and she was only beginning to realise how deep and layered and alien it was. She knew she would never understand the case unless she understood the underlying contexts behind it and so she'd called the editor of the *Catholic Tribune* and asked him to direct her to someone who could help.

She stubbed out her cigarette and opened the gate to the church grounds, walking past the cracked gravestones and dead flowerbeds and up an overgrown winding path to the front door.

Her first thought was that Father Spaulding looked like a carica-ture of a monk – a ten-year-old's Disney version of a brown-robed holy man. Spaulding was extremely bald, extremely short and ex-tremely fat – a man composed of squashed circles placed atop each other. He had saggy jowls, small kind eyes and a nervous laugh.

'Detective Sergeant Miller.' His accent was the last thing she'd expected, high and tremulous, yet with a musical lilt to it, an accent only heard in black-and-white movies, dashing officers gathered to-gether in the mess hall on the eve of a momentous battle. 'Do come in.'

The silence struck her immediately. Though the church was only a few yards away from the high street with its crack dealers and boarded-up shop-fronts, in here, with the door closed, she could have been in another century. She followed Father Spaulding through a long narrow corridor, dark with paintings of virgins and popes, and into a surprisingly bright and airy front room.

'I was just about to have my lunch,' Spaulding said as he directed her to the wooden table at the centre of the room. 'You simply must join me.'

Geneva pulled out a chair, staring at the food on display. The monk was eating alone but there were several plates, enough food for three or four men. Spaulding sat down slowly, hitching his robe and sighing as he carefully placed a napkin on his lap. He pointed to a plate of sliced meat the colour of burnished mahogany. 'Those are from a small monastery in Switzerland,' he said. 'They make the best cured beef in the world. It's so good it really should qualify as a sin.' His laugh was full and belly deep, his whole body shuddering.

She looked at the food and felt sick. The last hour swirled in her mind. She'd finally called Oliver and reluctantly agreed to meet him that night to discuss the issue of the house and the money he owed her. The grease on the monk's lips made her feel queasy but he kept insisting and she forced herself, taking a small piece of black bread and a slice of meat. She bit into it hesitantly and before she knew what she was doing she was reaching for another helping. The dry and bitter taste which had coated her mouth all morning was replaced by the smoky tang of the beef, the subtle hand-rubbed herbs and peppery spices.

Spaulding watched her with amusement as he picked up an olive then studied it before placing it between his lips. 'You said over the phone you were investigating the fire?'

Geneva nodded, her mouth still too full to attempt speech, and pulled out her notebook.

'A most terrible thing,' the monk said. 'But not for them, of course. They are now sitting at Jesus' side, the problems of the world, the problems of their bodies and brains, all gone.' He picked up a dusty green bottle of wine and tilted it towards her. She placed her hand flat across the top of her glass.

'Oh, come on now, this food tastes so much better with a little wine.'

Spaulding filled her glass. The wine looked unusually dark and viscous, and when she took a sip, the flavour was rich, complex and smoky, maybe the best wine she'd ever tasted.

'I was looking into Mother Angelica's past,' she explained, pulling out the tangled mess of print-outs and scrawled notes from her bag. 'And I read about the strike at Chiapeltec, the bomb, the ensuing massacre.'

'Ah, yes,' Spaulding nodded. 'What times those were . . . priests and nuns taking up arms, the whole continent seduced by the promises of liberation theology.'

'I saw you wrote several books on the subject but, to be honest, I don't really understand much about it.'

Spaulding finished off a slice of salmon, took a sip of wine and, despite her protestations to the contrary, topped up her glass. 'No need to be embarrassed. There are not many people in the modern church who know that much about liberation theology any more.

The Vatican have been rather successful in that.'

She picked up the edge to his words, the way he said this thing out the corner of his mouth. 'Not fans of it, then?'

Spaulding laughed. 'Dear me, no, you could say that, though I would put it a bit more strongly.'

An idea started to form in her head and she wrote it down, then took another sip of wine. She hadn't meant to, was trying to slow down, but it tasted so good and her hangover was finally clearing.

'Liberation theology is exactly what it says on the tin,' Spaulding explained. 'A theology of liberation.' He leaned forward and propped his elbows on the table. 'It is also an intrinsically South American thing. It follows from the prophetic tradition of the missionaries and the Jesuit Reducciones, having its roots in great men such as Bartolomé de las Casas, Antonio de Montesinos and Brother Caneca, but it is also a purely modern phenomenon.

'In the 1950s and sixties, Latin America went through a rapid process of industrialisation. Countries that for centuries had been predominantly rural suddenly transformed themselves in a very short space of time. The new factories and sweat shops led to an increased exploitation of the poor. The villagers who could no longer afford to farm migrated towards the cities and found work, often under the most brutal of conditions. This led to a series of uprisings in search of a living wage, health and safety restrictions, an end to oppression.' Spaulding stopped and looked up at the ceiling. 'The world often works in contradictory ways and the uprisings gave the militaries and right-wing political parties the excuse they needed to wrest control of the political machine. Hence you get the years of Latin American dictatorships, the screaming bodies under the football stadium and black-suited death squads roaming the night-time jungles. Anyone who complained of injustice or tried to organise the workers was beaten, tortured and killed. The local parish priests in the villages and countryside saw this violence and oppression with their own eyes and when they met as a body they knew that something had to be done, that the church could not stand by and watch its people be destroyed. And so, liberation theology was born, Marxism no longer held a monopoly on historical change, Christ had taken over.'

Geneva looked up from her notes, trying to make sense of all this new information, to squeeze it into the gaps of what she knew about Mother Angelica and the convent. She could see the faint sparkle in Father Spaulding's eyes as he talked about the past and she briefly wondered if he'd been there, in South America, but he didn't look old enough. 'What did this theology involve? Theology is abstract, in the mind, right?'

Spaulding smiled. 'Yes it is, but the priests realised that theology needed a modification, that it was not enough to just stand and witness. Action was necessary. The theologians went back to the Bible and guess what they found? – their own predicament written in the words of the Gospels.

'Jesus himself was concerned with these issues. None of this is new, the world changes but ultimately it is the same, and as they read those familiar words they saw something freshly revealed in them. They realised that the prescription and instruction for what they needed to do was right there in front of them and had been for two thousand years.'

'I'm afraid I'm a bit lost. The Bible was never my strong point,' Geneva confessed.

Father Spaulding looked at her kindly and smiled. 'Christ speaks about the preferential option for the poor. The poor and oppressed are preferred by God because they have been done wrong to here on earth. Can you imagine how radical these ideas must have seemed in that context? What followed in the light of this reading was a general move away from contemplation towards action. This was the big break from previous theology. No longer was prayer enough. Action was needed and it was needed right here on earth.'

'Why would the church not approve of that?'

Spaulding gave a derisive snort. 'Yes, indeed, this was an attempt to replicate Jesus' ministry on earth, to help the most unfortunate, so why did they repudiate it? Good question. And the answer is, as always, politics.'

'I thought the church was supposed to be above politics?'

Father Spaulding laughed loudly. 'God is above politics but the church is the church of men and men want to sleep in comfortable beds. The liberation priests were a massive thorn in the side of the prevailing governments. They wanted to organise workers, demand better conditions, stop the exploitation. The exploitation was how these governments made their money, how they lured factories and corporations to their shores: cheap labour, no red tape and zero tax. And it saddens me greatly to say that the local hierarchy of the church had very close and unhealthy ties with the regimes. Priests and clergy active in mobilising and organising were swiftly sent elsewhere. Many saw this as their chance at martyrdom and many got their wish.'

'Mother Angelica was one of these liberation theologians, right?'

'She was quite the bright spark in the church's arsenal. Her death . . .' For the first time the monk stumbled and Geneva could see him choking back a wave of memories. He picked up a napkin and snuffled into it. 'She spent her early years studying theodicy, the idea that all evil acts are justified by a greater good that only God can see. She wrote her seminary paper on it, but there were rumours of a breakdown at Oxford, that trying to reconcile the Holocaust and the atom bomb drove her crazy. The next thing we heard she was involved in liberation theology, which made sense – rather than accept evil and exploitation as part of a greater plan, she wanted to fight it. Her first book, *Of This World and the Next*, was published in 1972, two years after she was sent to Peru.'

Geneva took only the smallest sip from her glass. The wine was far more powerful than she'd expected and she felt a little light-headed and dizzy. 'How radical were Mother Angelica's ideas?'

'The church thought them pretty damn radical. That's why they went to the extraordinary step of banning her from the continent.'

Geneva looked up. 'Banning her? I thought they'd transferred her for her own safety, that there were death threats against her?'

Spaulding shrugged. 'Doubtless there were, and it was a long time ago and who's to say now what really happened and what didn't? We go where the church sends us. Tomorrow I might be told that I am needed in a remote monastery in Mongolia and I will pack my bags dutifully, leave my fine wine and Swiss beef behind, and get on the first plane. The church wanted Mother Angelica where she could do the least damage and so they banned her from South America and transferred her here where her power would be greatly diminished.'

Geneva tried but couldn't begin to imagine this kind of life, the total submission of your desires to a higher power, the utter abnegation of want and need. 'And she only wrote that one book?'

Spaulding shook his head. 'It's the only book that got published. But she spent the rest of her life, both while in South America and then here in London, writing what she considered her most important work. Unfortunately, not many people have seen it. The church barred its publication.'

'Why?' Geneva said, thinking back to her conversation with Holden.

'Hard to say,' Spaulding replied, 'not having seen it. But there are rumours, stories floating around the edges of the theological world, that she was attempting to construct a moral calculus.'

Geneva looked up. 'A moral calculus?'

'Yes, that was how she referred to it. From what I've heard it was a totally different book from her first, moving a long way away from the precepts of liberation theology. I've heard it spans over six thousand pages and is very mathematical in nature. Allegedly, she was trying to work out a foolproof system whereby one could gauge any moral act as to its validity in the eyes of God.'

'Wow,' Geneva replied. 'Big task.'

Spaulding laughed. 'Yes, yes it is.'

'And this was the cause of the diocese's dispute with the convent?'

'Well, you could call it that, I suppose.'

'But you wouldn't?'

'I'm not sure I should be telling you this,' Spaulding said, and Geneva could tell this was a phrase he liked using and used often. 'But . . . since the fire, since what happened . . . well, there have been rumours, more than rumours in fact, that the convent was going to be excommunicated.'

Geneva thought back to Holden calling the dispute a small disagreement. 'Excommunication – that's pretty serious, right?'

'It's the strongest punishment the church can mete out. It means they can no longer perform their duties as nuns, are not allowed to participate in God's sacraments – it's like closing the door on heaven.'

'And all because of this book she was writing?'

'No,' Spaulding admitted. 'It would have had to have gone beyond that, something far more serious, if the diocese had taken steps to excommunicate them. We're talking about the entire convent here, not just Mother Angelica. It's not something the church does lightly. In that respect, the fire was very convenient for them.'

There was something about the way he'd said it that made Geneva underline the words in her notebook. She thought about what they'd found out, the nuns' trips to Peru, to conferences that didn't exist, the evidence left behind by the fire. 'What about now? What's the situation like these days in Peru? Are clergy still involved in politics?'

Spaulding nodded. 'Though the church has succeeded in pretending the injustices don't exist, they're still there. Peru now has an elected president and parliament. But nothing has really changed

– if anything the situation of the poor is even worse. The government has sold off most of the valuable land to foreign corporations. There's no regulation, entire areas are being deforested, rivers polluted, and the Indians are finding the very land is disappearing from under them.' Spaulding shook his head and took a sip of his wine. 'Add drugs to the mix and you have a terrible situation.'

'Drugs?' Geneva moved her chair a few inches closer to the table.

'Peru is the most productive coca growing region in the world. This is not a good thing for the people who live there, as you can imagine. Men with guns in open-backed trucks. Army incursions. Farmers forced to grow coca by the cartels then punished by the government for the same. It's a mess that no one has the resolve to do anything about.'

Geneva shook her head, grateful once again that she lived in a country where things were not so fucked up. 'Do you know what happened to Sister Rose?' she asked. 'The convent sent her to Peru in November of last year but I can't find any record of her coming back into the country.'

'That's because she didn't come back,' Father Spaulding said.

'What do you mean?' Geneva felt a hot rush tumble through her as she clenched her notebook tightly.

Father Spaulding steepled his hands. When he spoke his voice was lower and surprisingly grave. 'A terrible tragedy. Her body was never found. She's still missing, probably will be until some farmer ploughs his fields and discovers her body.'

'You think she was killed?' Geneva said, leaning forward. 'Isn't it possible she just decided she'd had enough of being a nun and made her own way?'

'Possible? Yes, but not very likely,' Father Spaulding replied. 'When she went missing she was on a field trip with a priest from the local parish. Two weeks later they found the priest's head. Someone had left it in the front yard of the local church.'

She stopped at a coffee shop on her way back to the station and bolted down two macchiatos, trying to stop her head from spinning. The wine was sitting hot and deep in her belly and her head felt pleasantly light. Father Spaulding's words streaked through her mind, the worlds he'd conjured up, theology and the plunge into thousands of years of history, lonely old men poring over brittle parchments trying to decipher the meaning of the world hidden in the obscurities of text, and she thought of Mother Angelica and her book and what a challenge and rude shock it would have been to the church to have such ideas put forward, but, more than that, to have them put forward by a woman.

She entered the station to update the incident log and type up the notes from her interview. It was early afternoon and she was glad everyone was out, her feet still a little unsteady as she walked down the long carpeted corridor towards the incident room.

She saw him walking towards her and it was too late to pretend she hadn't.

DS Karlson nodded curtly as he passed, then she heard him stop and turn. She wanted to disappear into the ladies but it was three doors down.

'Miller? I was just looking for you . . .' Karlson was wearing a neat three-piece worsted suit and a tang of bitter aftershave. He stood right next to her, leaning into her space, defeating her obvious and pointless attempts to turn away. 'I need you to sign some of the report sheets,' he said, hovering over her as she squirmed and tried to answer him without opening her mouth.

'Can't it wait?'

'No, Branch wants everything up to date.'

She walked a couple of paces ahead of him. She could hear Karlson trailing behind her. She sat down and started signing off forms, Karlson standing only a foot away, wrinkling his nose and trying very hard not to smile. She gave him the completed sheets and was about to leave when he said, 'Can you smell something?'

'No,' she replied, trying to talk down to the table.

'Funny, smells like someone knocked over a bottle of cheap wine.' Karlson shook his head in a gesture of mock bemusement, winked and walked away.

28

Hyde Park was a blaze of white. Fat clumps of dirty snow hanging on the branches of skinny trees. A cold snap in the wind as it came careening down from the pond. Carrigan bunched up his jacket and lowered his face against the stinging air as he made his way towards the Serpentine.

He was thinking about Emily as he trudged through the snow. How did she fit in? Was her presence at the convent no more than coincidence? A cruel synchronicity to send them spinning off into dead ends? She didn't fit into the theory that the nuns had irked Duka and garnered his displeasure. She didn't fit in with Geneva's ideas on Peru. Either Emily had nothing to do with the case or she had everything to do with it.

The gallery's foyer was almost empty, only a grungy student sitting behind a desk, desperately trying to keep his eyes open on the book he was reading. It was too cold to see art, too cold to stand and stare at paint and canvas and the student must have thought Carrigan had wandered in here by mistake, perhaps assuming there was a cafe, somewhere to sit and escape the wind.

'Hi.'

He turned from the rows of artfully designed magazines and saw her. Donna was standing to the right of the front desk, one leg slightly crooked, her brown leather boots dark with snow. 'I wasn't sure you'd come.' Her hair was loose and kept getting into her eyes and she brushed it away and said, 'I'm glad you did.'

They entered the gallery, several interlinked spaces, empty of everything but them and the art on the walls. Square light-boxes filled the first room. Chunky plastic devices, about two feet by two with bulbs blazing behind them, illuminating a set of fast food images. As they shuffled mutely into the room, Carrigan was blinded by luminescent photos of Big Macs, golden fried chicken, anaemic pizzas and glistening kebabs, and he realised that these images were the ones used as menus above the tills of takeaway places. The room was covered in them, sweating light and colour, these everyday images now isolated and reframed and made faintly mystical. Carrigan didn't know if it was art but it was making him hungry.

'I hope you don't mind meeting here,' Donna said. 'I just needed . . . God . . . I didn't realise how much I needed to get out of the house until . . .' She reached for a handkerchief and dropped it on the floor and got to her knees and stumbled as she picked it back up. He could see the broken blood vessels in her eyes that hadn't been there yesterday, the soft downward curve of her lids chapped and red-rimmed. She smelled of lavender and wine and something else beneath it all – a sharp and lovely citric fragrance, some expensive perfume or moisturiser. 'I'm sorry I couldn't speak earlier, back at the house . . . it's like I'm still expecting her to call . . .' Donna's lips were stained blood-red and he could tell she'd been drinking before coming here. She turned away from the wall and faced him. 'I just can't believe I'll never see her again.'

'I know,' he replied, remembering a day twenty years ago when he'd first entered the country of grief and never-again. 'I could tell you you'll get over it, that time heals all wounds and all that, but I'm not going to lie to you. Your life will never be the same. You'll always look back and see a clear demarcation. Everything will take place in reference to before or after. You should maybe think about seeing someone . . .'

Her sudden laughter surprised him. 'That's the last thing I need. I grew up with psychiatrists for parents.' Her smile collapsed and he saw the years crash up against her. 'Been there, done that, and it's not worth the paper it's written on. Besides, Emily's dead, there's nothing that's going to change that, is there?'

'We'll find out who did this.' Carrigan moved closer until he could feel the heat and burn of Donna's breath against his skin. 'I know that's not going to be much of a consolation, that Emily will still be gone, but I promise you she will be avenged.'

Donna placed a hand on his arm. 'Thank you for saying that but . . . I still don't understand it . . . any of it. What was she doing in a convent? That's just not like Emily at all.'

He pulled away and turned to face the opposite wall, a succulent burger in pornographic close-up, each sesame seed and bead of moisture visible under the relentless light. 'The more you can tell us about her, the more likely we are to find out why she was there.'

'I lied to you.' Donna put out her hand and steadied herself against the wall. 'When I said I hadn't talked to her for a couple of years that wasn't true.'

'Why didn't you tell us when we were at the house?' Carrigan said as gently as possible.

'Because I didn't want my father to know,' Donna replied, and she seemed embarrassed by this somehow. 'Because Emily swore me to secrecy.'

'When did you last speak to her?'

Donna looked anyplace but at Carrigan, her eyes restless and heavy. 'She called me a couple of weeks ago.'

'A couple of weeks ago?' Carrigan tried to control his breathing. 'What did she want?'

'The usual,' Donna sighed. 'She only ever called when she needed help. She was always getting into trouble and we were always getting her out of it.'

'What kind of trouble?'

Donna shrugged. 'You name it, Emily . . . well, you probably know by now that Emily had problems. She'd had problems since we were little girls and we all thought that as she got older they would go away but they didn't, they only got worse.' Donna reached into her handbag and took out her phone. She pressed several buttons then tilted the screen towards Carrigan. 'I took this a couple of weeks ago when we met.' Donna's eyes shaded as she realised it had been for the last time. 'You never know, do you?'

'No you don't.' Carrigan took the phone and stared at the photo under the flickering fluorescents.

Emily was sitting in a pub, her arms propped up against the table, a nearly full pint glass cradled in her right hand. She wore heavy powder-blue eyeliner and had a piercing through her left nostril, a small bronze hoop. Her hair was pink and the sudden blush of colour was shocking against her white skin. Her expression was soft, a world away from the bitter scowl of the mugshot, and you could tell she wasn't looking at the camera but at her sister. 'Did she say what kind of trouble she was in?'

Donna put the phone back in her handbag. 'She sounded really strung out. We met at King's Cross. She was always calling me when she was in trouble but normally she only needed money. This time was different. She was scared and Emily was never scared and when I said something about how it'd all work out in the end, she laughed and told me that some things cannot be righted no matter how hard you try. She said she'd done something very stupid but she wouldn't tell me what. I asked her if she needed money. She said money wouldn't solve this.' Donna twirled a lock of hair round her finger, her lips tight and pale.

'But she didn't tell you anything about the trouble she was in?'

Donna shook her head, 'I should have known, damn it. I knew her better than anyone else and I thought she was just being melodramatic, I didn't . . .' She hung her head and stared at her shoes. Her body seemed to fold in on itself.

'Can I have a copy of this photo?' It was the most recent image he'd seen of Emily and would be much more useful to them than a four-year-old mugshot.

Donna nodded. 'I'll email a copy to your phone.'

'I wouldn't even know where to begin with that.' Carrigan pulled out his mobile and showed it to her. It always managed to raise a smile and this time was no exception. She stared at the chunky black box, already an antique, and smiled.

'What happened between your parents and Emily? Why haven't they spoken for a couple of years?'

The question took Donna by surprise. She looked up at Carrigan and he could see the screaming arguments, slammed doors and sleepless nights burning through her memory. 'The things she stood for . . . the things she said . . . you know how families are . . .'

Carrigan nodded but in truth he had no idea. His father had disappeared from his life when he was sixteen and his mother certainly wasn't like any of his friends' mums, not with her rosary beads and *Reader's Digest*s, her spotted half-blind Jack Russell and the permanent scowl etched on her face by her husband's abandonment. 'She must have been very angry and hurt by your father disinheriting her.'

Donna laughed a thin, harsh laugh. 'The will? She didn't care about that, money meant nothing to Emily.'

Carrigan nodded, thinking only someone who'd grown up with too much of it could ever think that. 'What were the disagreements with your father about?'

'What weren't they about?' Donna replied as they entered the second room and Carrigan was surprised to find the fast food images replaced by the illuminated face of Mohammed Atta in each light-box, his expression subtly altered between one and the next. 'Everything she said or did our father saw as some kind of failure on his part. Remember, both our parents are child psychiatrists – when your kid grows up to be something other than you expected, it becomes a professional failure as well as a personal one.' She raised her voice and changed pitch and stressed certain syllables to ironise what she was saying and distance herself from the memory of it, but Carrigan thought it only enmeshed her deeper in her own inescap-

208

able history and he felt bad because he'd imagined her life a gilded one, money and breeding and good luck. He should have known better, should have known that sorrow and pain lurked everywhere and came for everyone.

They left the gallery and crossed the winding strip of road that bisected the park, heading towards the small cafe overlooking the Serpentine pond. Carrigan bought them both coffees and, as he walked out onto the terrace, the trees silver and still, the lake almost frozen, he saw Donna sitting and facing the water, her hair wind-blown and aswirl, eyes lost in wistful haze.

'Thank you,' she said, raising the cup to her lips and blowing on it, white wispy vapours escaping into the chill air. A Labrador puppy came bounding up the path and stopped, tail wagging, by Donna's feet. She ran her hands through its thick downy fur and stroked it and, for the first time, Carrigan saw her as she'd been before he'd come and broken the news and it pierced him deeply that she would only ever be this carefree and giddy in fleeting moments and that the memory of her dead sister would be like a lens through which she would forever view the world. He thought of his own dead, voices whispering to him in the crackle of night, the friends and lovers gone to earth and silence.

'You said that Emily was always getting into trouble. When did this start?'

'From very early on,' Donna replied. 'She was always in trouble at school, with her teachers, classmates, even her friends. It only got worse as she got older. She kept skipping classes, smoking and drinking during lunch breaks, seeing boys, getting caught – always getting caught as if that had been the intention all along. Everything that life threw at her just made her more furious and she would go off into these week-long depressions, sit in her room with the lights out, under the covers, moaning and crying. As she got older these periods got longer. Father and Mother tried everything, sent her to behavioural specialists, tried all sorts of pills – you can imagine what it did to them, having to send their own child to a specialist. It was the greatest sign of their failure as professionals and as parents.

'She . . . she made several attempts at taking her own life. The usual teenager slashing her wrists, cries for help . . . but Father and Mother ignored her, believing that was the best way to deal with it. And then, one day, when she was sixteen, everything changed.

'She'd gone to a summer camp the school had set up for kids who'd fallen behind. She'd been to these kind of places before and always ended up running away or assaulting a teacher, but this time something extraordinary happened. She stayed the whole length of the course and came back and it was like she was a new Emily.'

'How do you mean?'

'She'd met a couple of older students at the camp and they'd introduced her to the world of politics. At first we were all so relieved she'd finally found something which motivated and interested her, but what we didn't realise was that she'd only managed to find a new receptacle for her rage and fury at the world.

'She began going to student meetings, small groups in dusty after-hours classrooms watching atrocity videos and international news reports, rolling thin cigarettes and drinking cider, discussing capitalism and exploitation. She would sit at the dinner table and rant non-stop about America and imperialism, spinning wild conspiracy theories, believing that everyone who didn't agree with her was complicit.

'You have to understand, Emily grew up in that house surrounded by all that money and in the streets she saw men sleeping in doorways and fishing their dinners from bins outside restaurants and it made her angry and ashamed and determined to do something about it. She was so passionate and brave and principled, I always envied her so much for that.'

'And you?' Carrigan enquired gently. 'After all, you grew up in the same house.'

'I was always a little less engaged with the world than Emily and I also learned early on that the world isn't fair and nothing we can do will change that.'

She looked away, as if Carrigan had caught her in some shameful act. 'We were still close though, she and I, and we went to university at Leeds together, but it was never the same. I chose to study English, she took courses in politics and history. She began going on marches and protests, getting into trouble with the police. She joined a radical animal rights group and went on hunt-sab missions. I rarely saw her any more on campus, and she barely ever came home.

'Then things got worse. You never think they can but they always do.' A slow baleful smile appeared on Donna's face for a brief moment. 'It was the Easter break of our final year. I'd prevailed on her to come home for the holidays. We were having lunch and a massive argument blazed between Father and Emily, over something stupid and meaningless, foreign policy, oil, something that had nothing to do with our lives. She called him a hypocrite. Father ordered her out of the house. In the middle of Easter lunch. She took her things, dropped out of uni and disappeared. It was the first of her many disappearances. We didn't hear from her again for almost a year.' Donna took a deep breath and brushed the tears from her eyes. She finished her coffee and wiped her top lip.

'I'm sorry for bringing all this back.' Carrigan reached his hand out, then, thinking better of it, pulled it back.

'Don't be,' Donna replied. 'They might be bad memories, but they're still memories.'

He could see a deep sadness settle behind her eyes and he changed tack. 'Did you know any of her friends? Boyfriends? Anyone she was especially close to?'

Donna shrugged as she watched a squirrel lean and quiver in the wind. 'I tried to avoid them when I could. They were not the kind of people I liked socialising with. Always so angry and bitter about the world and so full of unrealistic expectations and empty slogans. They just depressed me. Besides, people came and went all the time, found other things to get angry about. The only constant was Geoff.'

'Geoff?'

'Geoff Shorter. He was Emily's first proper boyfriend. They met in her second year at Leeds and moved in together during her finals. They broke up last year. She told me he was acting all weird about it.'

Carrigan leaned forward, the chair legs scraping against the gravel. 'Weird in what way?'

'She didn't say. But it doesn't surprise me. When I first met Geoff I thought he would be good for her, drag her out of the swamp she'd sunk herself into, but if anything he only made her worse.'

'How?'

Donna sighed and crossed her legs. 'Geoff's one of those identikit guilty rich white boys. His parents own some massive castle in Herefordshire, been in the family for centuries and all that, and he dabbles in all this activism and protest as a way to get back at his parents and his upbringing and to convince himself he isn't exactly like them.' She snuffled and finished the remains of her drink. 'They never realise that for other people it's a matter of life and death.'

'I take it you're not his biggest fan?'

'He was a bad influence on Emily. He encouraged all her craziness and rage, I think it even turned him on. You should talk to him,' Donna said, facing Carrigan. 'He spent much more time with her in London than I did, he'd know who she hung out with, what she was up to . . .' She looked down at the green water and hung her head. 'Whatever trouble Emily got herself into, I wouldn't be at all surprised if Geoff was behind it.'

29

She'd always hated this pub, which, of course, was why he chose it.

He was late and that wasn't anything new either. Geneva waited, a White Russian cooling her palms, the day's notes and typed reports spread out in front of her. Before talking to Father Spaulding she was almost ready to be convinced that Carrigan was right, but the monk's story had changed that.

All she knew for certain was that Holden had lied.

He'd told her the dispute between the convent and diocese was nothing important and yet Spaulding had said that the nuns were on the verge of being excommunicated. What could have led to such an extreme measure? She thought about the bank transfers, the trips to Lima, the missing nun, ignoring the swelling noise and merriment surrounding her. She reread interview transcripts as people laughed and kissed and bought each other drinks, their faces red and bright, clothes smeared wet and shiny with snow. She closed her notebook and pulled out her phone.

'We know about Chiapeltec,' she said, and heard Holden inhaling sharply on the other end of the line. 'We know that the nuns weren't travelling to Peru for conferences and we know about Sister Rose's disappearance. We need to talk to Father McCarthy. He was a regular visitor and can tell us what the convent was up to. He was also the last person to be seen leaving the building.'

'I'm afraid that's impossible,' Holden replied.

'There are other ways to find him,' Geneva said. 'Ways you may not like.' There was a pause, a staticky silence which made her think he'd hung up. 'Why do I get the impression you're not dying to know who killed your nuns?'

'Your impressions are of no concern to me,' Holden replied. 'And Father McCarthy is on retreat and therefore cannot be disturbed. This is something we take very seriously in the church.'

'And we take the murder of eleven people very seriously, Mr Holden. Why has he suddenly decided to go on retreat? What kind of retreat are we talking about?'

There was a measured silence, thick with hum and crackle. 'It's a delicate matter,' Holden finally said, and his voice now seemed to be coming from further away.

'So is the case of a missing nun which the diocese refuses to acknowledge.'

'Damn it,' Holden snapped. 'You won't give up, will you?' She could hear him sigh and tap something against his desk. 'Father McCarthy has taken time off to face up to certain issues.'

She was about to answer, then stopped, realising what Holden was saying between the words. 'Are you telling me he's in rehab, not on retreat? That he just decided to check in the day after the fire?'

'I'm not saying anything, Miss Miller, I'm just explaining the situation . . .'

'Then why can't we just speak to him?'

'These facilities are private, and can only function if they remain so. Now, if you . . .'

Geneva was no longer listening. A date caught her eye in one of the files, a date she'd not paid attention to before. Something tripped, some switch in her brain, and she ended the call and pulled out the papers from her files until she found the one detailing the nuns' recent trips to Peru. She checked the dates against the travel documents.

'I'm glad to see you're finally going through the papers.'

She snapped her head up and was startled to see Oliver peering down at her, a smile that was all teeth spread across his face. She quickly cleared the pages off the table, almost spilling her drink, Oliver catching it just in time, grinning, saying, 'What would you do without me, Geneva?'

She was about to answer but there was no point. Everything she said Oliver would use as further ammunition against her. Three years of marriage had taught her that if nothing else. 'It's work,' she snapped, not making eye contact, shuffling the papers back into her bag, wishing she was anywhere but here.

Oliver sat down and took a long sip of his bitter, the foam covering his top lip, his perfect fingernails tapping against the glass. Just looking at him made her feel queasy, the eroded years and restless nights coming back to her – the time they'd spent up north, her thinking this was the thing she'd been waiting for all these years, and then seeing him for what he really was and knowing she'd made the worst decision of her life. That long year of fretting and plotting and getting the nerve up. Telling him one night, her bags already packed, a friend outside waiting to collect her.

And, yes, that night – the screaming, fists and hurled accusations. Then came the threats and ravaged pleas, running out of the house and into her friend's car, Oliver's voice receding as they wound through the narrow streets of the spa town towards the train station where she hid in a photo booth, hoodie covering her face, until the train arrived, then the slow stifled journey south and the final humiliation, asking her mother if she could stay with her for a while.

'You're looking good,' Oliver said, tearing her from the onrushing past. 'Not easy for a woman to keep up with the years.'

Like all his compliments, even when they were still in love, this one came with hooks and barbs attached. 'Can't say the same for you,' she replied, and though she'd said it to spite him, she realised that he really had aged, his good looks forming a hard shell over his bones, the youthful glimmer of danger in his eyes now sublimated to something feral and cunning, something you know to get away from as soon as you see it.

'Always the charmer, Geneva. Good to see you haven't changed.' He had a packet of cheese and onion crisps ripped open in front of him. He stuffed a handful into his mouth and continued talking. 'You remember the last time we met like this?'

Geneva nodded, hoping it would end this part of the conversation, but Oliver wasn't prepared to let it go. 'I think you said you loved me and we'd be together forever.'

'That was a long time ago.'

Oliver crunched some more crisps and his voice turned hard and cold. 'You left me, Geneva. Jesus. You left me. You don't know how much that hurt.'

'This is what you called me up for?' She splashed the glass down, the liquid sloshing and spilling all over the table but she didn't care. She was certain everyone in the room was looking at them, all these happy celebrating couples watching her and Oliver bicker and blame across a pub table. 'Look, Oliver, I'm busy. You called me up, said you wanted to sort this thing out, just you and me, no lawyers or any of that, and all you're doing is fucking reminiscing.'

'Being a cop hasn't exactly made you into a nice person.'

'Who the fuck wants a nice person, Oliver? I am what I always was. You call me up out of the blue last year, tell me you're taking the house away from me, what the fuck do you expect?'

He took a folded sheet of paper from a leather briefcase by his feet. He carefully smoothed it out on the table. 'I expect you to sign this, is what I expect. It's the best deal you're going to get.'

She took the paper from him, scanned it quickly and saw that nothing had changed, his lawyer suing for the proceeds of the house even though they'd bought it together. Oliver had paid the deposit and she'd paid the monthly repayments. The divorce had finally come through a couple of months ago, the house sold, but the money was still locked in litigation.

'I need that money, Oliver,' she said, immediately hating herself for having revealed so much to him.

'I know you do,' he smiled, flecks of crisps dancing across his teeth. 'Sign now and you'll get ten thousand pounds.'

'You're joking?' She stared up at him and saw that he wasn't. 'The house sold for half a million.'

She glanced back down at the contract, reading through the dense technical language, feeling her face burning up with each word. She wanted to be through with this, to never see or hear from Oliver again, but her equity in the house was the only savings she had. Without it she'd never be able to buy another flat. She looked up at him and saw that he was enjoying this, a gleeful spark animating his face.

'You should do it for your mother, Geneva, if not for me.'

The sudden change in topic threw her off balance and she wrapped her fingers tightly round her empty glass. 'What's Katrina got to do with it?'

'How much money do you have in your savings? How long do you think it'll last?' Oliver asked. 'I can drag this through the courts for months and if I win, which I will, you'll be liable for all costs and, since your mother was your guarantor on the house, what you can't pay will be taken from her.'

She stared at him, stunned. 'You looked into our finances?'

'It's what I do, Geneva, remember? It's my job.' He leaned forward across the table and she could smell his breath and see the curl of satisfaction on his top lip.

She closed her eyes and felt her stomach lurch. She thought of her mother fleeing from Czechoslovakia, working nights behind the counter of a cheap hotel to save for a flat. She picked up the contract and ripped it in half. Then ripped it in half again. 'Good enough for you?' She threw the shredded paper across the table, oblivious to the stares and startled looks she was receiving from the other drinkers. 'Take me to court if you want,' she said. 'Bring as many lawyers as you can, but I'm telling you now, watch your back.'

'Are you threatening me?' Oliver said in mock outrage, the tone he'd increasingly used in those final months of their marriage.

Geneva smiled a thin pale smile. 'Yes. Yes I am. You do one thing wrong, you slip up in any conceivable way, and I'll make sure you'll go down for it. I may not have your money or connections but I have friends up there in North Yorks as well as the Met. They'll be watching you, remember that.'

The wet slap and pound of her shoes on the pavement beat in time with her heart. She'd come to the meeting prepared and unwilling to lose her composure and yet five minutes with Oliver could undo all her best intentions. She felt a rippling fury running through her body, as if a layer of skin had been stripped off. She stopped at the corner of the high street, pulled out her cigarettes and lit one. She dragged hard and felt her heart rate slow, the buzzing in her brain begin to settle. She watched the clasped forms of couples drifting in and out of pubs or huddling in freezing bus stops, their arms wrapped tightly around each other, and she looked away. She had no one she could turn to for advice, no one she could tell.

There was a dive bar a few streets away and it made a whole lot more sense than going back to her empty living room and falling asleep on the sofa again. She walked past the swarming pubs and all-night grocery shops, then cut down an alley which connected the two high streets, thinking about the case so that she wouldn't keep thinking about Oliver. She knew Carrigan had been right when he'd said that the intersection of the nuns and Emily would prove to be the key. How had they made contact? Geneva couldn't even begin to imagine. They came from such different backgrounds but at some particular moment in time they had met and that meeting had resulted in eleven dead bodies. She was still thinking about this when she looked up and there he was.

Fifty feet ahead of her, motionless, blocking the alley.

She squinted against the bright streetlights but could make out only his shadow. She should have known Oliver wouldn't let her get away so easily, that had never been his style, but this was something else, an escalation she'd glimpsed in his face earlier – sending letters, bombarding her phone, and now following her out here.

She stopped and waited for him to move but he did not move. She waited for him to speak, to light a cigarette, pull out his phone, anything that might explain why he was standing still in the middle of an alleyway, but there was no tell-tale flicker of light or comforting series of digital beeps. Sirens wailed and faded into the night behind her. She felt for her belt but there was nothing there, she'd checked in her truncheon and mace when she'd signed off for the day. 'Oliver?' she said, trying to keep her voice steady. 'What the fuck do you think you're doing?'

She took a couple of steps forward. The angle of the streetlights shifted. The man standing in the alley wasn't Oliver.

She stood struck and still as his shadow emerged from the blinding glare and she saw that he was both shorter and wider than her ex-husband. Her heart started beating in her ears, a loud tidal pulse she tried to drown out. The man hadn't moved but he was looking directly at her, a faint smile on his face. She turned around, ready to retreat, and saw that another man was blocking her exit. He was much taller than the first man and he was coming towards her.

She spun around and froze and looked at the short man, the eagle tattoo spreading down his neck. He returned her look, grinned and took a step forward. She glanced up at the fences bordering the alley, topped with glass or razor wire, impossible to scale, and knew that her only chance was in making the first move.

The men were getting steadily closer, taking their time, teasing it out, knowing she had nowhere to run. Eagle-neck looked fast and vicious but the other man looked slow and clumsy despite his height. There was no time to reach for her phone. No one to hear her screams.

She tensed her legs and fists and ran at the tall man, seeing a gap to his side, her feet slipping on the pavement as she faked right and ducked left, but the man had anticipated her and he twisted and shuffled and blocked her run. She felt as if she'd slammed into a brick wall, all the air exploding from her lungs in one crushed breath. She swung uselessly with her fist but the tall man effortlessly trapped it in his palm, gently crushing all the resistance out of her.

Eagle-neck's breathing turned erratic and heavy as he approached, the hot animal smell of his presence making it all seem suddenly very real. Geneva looked in his eyes and could tell that her life didn't mean anything to him and that he would just as soon snuff it out as he would a burning match and she realised she was scared, scared as she'd never been before in the job, knowing she was looking at a new kind of adversary.

The tall man let go of her fist and secured her arms, making it impossible for her to move. Eagle-neck came to a stop beside her and lit a cigarette, the smoke curling through his dark stubble and disappearing into the night.

'Let go of me!' She struggled and writhed and twisted but the tall man's grip didn't falter. 'I'm police.'

The two men both laughed, a thick guttural sound that echoed through the alley. A million horror-film deaths flashed through her brain and it was too late to wish she'd never seen all those movies as her vision filled with chainsaws and blood, the sharp glitter of knives and fragile delicacy of human skin.

Eagle-neck leaned in until his nose was almost touching hers, and inhaled deeply as if drinking the air. Geneva tried to scream but he placed his oily palm across her lips and she could suddenly taste his cigarette and smell his breath, garlic and beer, the rough feel of his skin against her own. He held her mouth and moved her head from side to side as if assessing a dog's pedigree.

Gently, he inserted three fingers into her mouth, pushing past her teeth and gums. His fingers probed and stroked the inside of her cheeks, his thumb holding down her tongue so forcefully that she could feel his pulse beating in her mouth. She flinched at the sharp rub of his stubble as he pressed his face against hers and then she saw him reach down and unzip his fly.

She could hear buses hissing to a stop down the high street, only a hundred yards away, TVs blaring game shows from the flats above her, raised voices shouting into mobile phones, and then all she heard was a faint trickling on the pavement and suddenly her right leg was warm and wet.

She opened her eyes and looked down to see the short man directing a long stream of piss at her legs. It smelled rank and sour. It seemed to go on forever. She closed her eyes but she could still feel the hot gush of his urine and hear it splashing against the pavement under her.

When he was finished, he shook off the last few drops and zipped himself back up. He let out a long sigh of relief then took a step closer, his face less than an inch from hers. 'There are no second chances.'

She spat in his face, and was glad to see the shock and fury in his eyes. He grabbed her hair and used it to pull her head down, twisting the strands until she thought she was going to pass out. He punched her once in the stomach. The other man let go of her arms and she fell heavily to the floor, her eyes fluttering and fading from focus as her face hit the cold pavement.

30

The relentless muffled drumming of the shower echoed through the walls of the flat. Carrigan stared out the window at the falling snow and tried to ignore the sound. He made himself instant coffee in the kitchen, rooting through the unfamiliar cupboards and products of another person's life, made her tea, turned on the heating and kept his mouth shut.

He'd found her in the alley, crouched into a ball, shaking and holding tightly onto the phone she'd called him from. She couldn't meet his eyes as her voice trembled, stumbled and stuttered, telling him what had happened, the men in the alley, the fight with Oliver, and he'd said it was okay, putting a finger to her lips, lifting her off the wet floor and placing her into the back seat of his car.

She'd been in the shower for nearly an hour. She'd had several successive showers. Every so often he could hear the wet scamper of her feet and cessation of noise, only to be replaced by the swirling rush of water rolling down the drain as she brushed her teeth over and over again.

It had seemed rude to leave. It had seemed wrong. And so he'd sat and watched the snow swirl and spin, and made hot drinks, trying to swallow the red hot spike burning through his chest – the fact they would do something like this to one of his officers. The fact they would do this to Geneva.

She came out towel-wrapped and skin-wrinkled and looked at him and looked at the flat and went back into the bathroom and locked the door behind her. There were copies of the convent investigation file spread across her coffee table, scribbled notes, typed reports, photos from the morgue. She wasn't supposed to have made copies or brought them home with her but Carrigan understood.

'Thank you.'

Her voice startled him, the way it didn't sound like her at all. She was wearing a red robe and her hair was loose and smeared wet across her face. 'We should call this in . . . if you're ready,' he said and it was too late for him to take it back as he saw a sharp flicker ignite the corners of her eyes.

'I can't do that.'

He didn't want to push her. He knew these moments were not like other moments, but he also knew that if she were to change her mind and report it later, vital forensic evidence would be lost. 'No one will think any different of you.'

The look she gave him made the words die in his throat, useless and empty.

'You don't really believe that, do you?' She went over to the fridge, her wet feet slapping against the floor, and took out a litre of duty-free tequila that looked like bottled starlight. She picked up two mugs and poured herself a large measure and swiped it back, her eyes turning fuzzy for a brief moment.

'Everyone will be super nice to me, which is fucking terrible, but worse, behind my back, when I'm not there, in the canteen or the pub, they'll be talking about the incident – you know that as well as I do. They'll start with how awful it is, then they'll get to speculating what *really* happened, what those brutes did to me, and then they'll have had a few drinks and start wondering was there something I could have done to help myself, because no one, least of all cops, wants to admit that there are some situations where there's nothing you can do.' She refilled the mug and took three quick sips. 'And don't forget I'm a woman. They'll use that as their excuse. This is what happens when we put women on the front line and all that crap. I'm not going to report it and I don't want to talk about it any more.' She slumped down on the sofa beside him and passed him the other mug. 'I want to drink away the fucking memory of tonight, all of it, the taste of his fingers, Oliver – I want to forget it happened – for a few hours, at least. If you want to join me that would be nice.'

They drank the alcohol neat and fast. It burned and flamed as it rolled down their throats. 'Can we talk about it, at least? Just you and me?'

She refilled the mugs. 'What do you want to know?'

'Did you recognise them?'

Geneva turned towards Carrigan and nodded. She lifted the mug to her lips but her hand trembled and most of it spilled down the front of her robe and she didn't seem to notice. 'The one with the eagle tattoo . . . he was the one who did . . .' She looked down at her legs. 'Who did this. The other man I didn't recognise.'

'Shit.' Carrigan slammed down the drink, coughing and shaking and gripping the edge of the sofa. 'What did they say to you?'

Geneva tucked her feet underneath a small tartan blanket as if she could make herself disappear within its folds. 'There are no second chances.'

'It must mean we're getting close,' Carrigan said, looking down at the floor.

'You're still hanging on to the theory this is over the nuns' involvement in cleaning up the neighbourhood?'

He looked at her sharply, then muted his eyes. 'We know Viktor works for Duka, an Albanian crime boss who runs drugs in our area. The nuns were mobilising the community against drug dealers and petty crime. Viktor and Eagle-neck attacked me in the ruins. Eagle-neck just assaulted you. I think that speaks for itself.' He looked at her and smiled. 'I know you disagree and that's fine. It's always dangerous to stick to only one avenue of investigation. That's how mistakes get made. But we also need to judge the evidence accordingly. Viktor has to be our main priority and, through him, Duka. We have to get him before something like this happens again.' He saw her body shake at the mention of what had occurred earlier. 'Twenty years I've been doing this and this is the first time something like this has happened.'

She looked at him as she poured another drink. 'You say that like there's a code? A line even criminals shouldn't cross?'

'I used to think there was.'

She raised an eyebrow at that, and said, 'You think things are getting worse?'

Carrigan nodded.

'Every generation thinks that.'

He took the bottle from her clenched fingers and held it between his hands. 'Maybe every generation's right and it's getting steadily worse all the time.'

'Do you really believe that?' she said, intrigued and a little unsettled by the resignation in his voice.

'We have these great new technological advances – DNA, CCTV, all the rest – but none of it stops the crime. It's only good to us afterwards. Sometimes I think all we are is janitors, clearing up the mess after everyone else has gone home. At least the nuns were doing something.'

She leaned across the sofa and reached for an ashtray. 'God, you approve, don't you?' she said, unable to hide the surprise in her voice.

'The neighbourhood improved after they began their community work. Residents became more involved. Property prices went up and street crimes were down fifty per cent until the nuns decided to stop it all a year ago. They were putting into practice what they believed in. In their minds, they weren't breaking any laws. The laws they subscribe to, ultimately, are God's laws, not man's.'

'But that's exactly the justification everyone uses – vigilantes, illegal downloaders, terrorists . . . you name it.'

Carrigan nodded in agreement. 'We have to face up to the fact people don't trust our laws any more. There's a growing discontent, don't tell me you haven't noticed? A disillusion with the prevailing structures of law and government the likes of which we haven't seen before. Look at how many empty shops there are on every high street, construction projects left unfinished, people sleeping in doorways and bus stops. Look at people's faces and you see a stunned desperation there – it all happened so quickly, money fell and no one understands quite how or why it did, only that their lives had been staked and lost over a financial roulette wheel.'

'I don't know if you're being extremely cynical or extremely prescient.'

Carrigan shrugged and Geneva watched him as he worried the dulled ring on his left hand, seemingly unaware of what he was doing, turning it between his fingers as if it were a rosary. 'How come you still wear it?' she said before she could think twice about it.

'Never had a reason to take it off.' He glanced down at the small gold band and twirled it twice more to ease the pressure.

'You loved her a lot,' Geneva said, and it wasn't a question.

'Far more than I thought I did . . .'

'What happened?' she asked, then quickly brought her hand up to her mouth. 'I can't believe I just said that. I'm so sorry. I must be a lot drunker than I realise.'

'Don't be.' Carrigan knocked back the remainder of his tequila, his eyes burning fierce and bright. 'Louise made a decision. That was all there was to it,' he said, thinking of the days following her death, the way the flat seemed both larger and smaller, expanding and contracting with the hot burning shock of his loss. 'She'd planned it carefully. I only found out later when I talked to her doctor. A couple of months previously she'd been to see him about an ache she kept having. He sent her for tests. The tests returned and he sat her down and talked to her and gave her two years as his best prognosis. She went home and thought about it for a month and made her decision. She wanted to spare me the agony of watching her slowly wither and die.

226

'I had no idea. The last year had been such a good one, and then I came back from a conference and she was gone, instantly and for ever. She'd made sure to tie up all the loose ends and make it as easy for me to deal with her affairs as possible, and then she took a handful of pills and died.'

Geneva looked at Carrigan and didn't say anything for a long while. 'You found her?'

'I found her,' he replied and his eyes ached with the memory of that day, the strange smell in the kitchen, the sound of blackbirds shrieking, a certain foreboding on opening the door. 'It doesn't get worse than that,' he said and looked up and let out a dry choked laugh. 'At least I hope to Christ it doesn't.' She passed him the bottle and he took a sip and looked into her eyes and knew now was the time to broach the subject. 'Since we're getting personal and confessional and all that crap, I'd really like to know what's going on with you at the moment, Geneva . . . and I'm not talking about what happened tonight.'

'Nothing,' she said, her body turning into shadow and angle. 'Nothing in particular.'

The droop of her eyes and curve of lip told him this was somewhere she didn't want to go. 'You don't have to tell me anything. Your life is your life. Absolutely. But I know there's something bothering you. Something serious. I'd like to think that in the last year we've developed some trust, maybe enough to be able to share these things.'

It took her a long time to answer and when she did she said, 'Are you asking as my boss or as a friend?'

'Whichever you prefer.'

'I think, tonight, a friend is what I need,' she replied, and told him about Oliver, the whole sad story, the solicitor's letters piling up on her table and darkly whispered threats against her mother.

'Bastard,' Carrigan said. 'You want me to talk to him?'

'Thanks,' she replied, hiding her surprise and shaking her head.

'I appreciate the offer, but this is something I need to do for myself.'

'Have you thought about hiring your own lawyer?'

Geneva laughed coldly. 'That's exactly what he wants me to do. He's a lawyer. He can keep this going for as long as he wants and there's no way I can afford that. He knows he'll win either way. He wouldn't have proposed it otherwise.'

She got up and weaved unsteadily as she made her way to the kitchen, coming back with two large glasses of water. 'I know it's asking a lot . . . but if you could stay? I just . . . I just don't want to be alone tonight.'

Carrigan took the glass and nodded. 'The sofa looks comfy enough.'

Her smile unfroze and he saw relief tear through her face.

'Besides, I'm going to stay up for a bit . . . I don't get much sleep these days.'

She thanked him again and said goodnight and disappeared down the small dark corridor and the room felt colder and smaller without her.

After a while, he got up and moved the armchair so it faced the window. He stared up at the shadowed landscape and there was no light nor sign of human habitation as far as the eye could see, only a sky berserk with snow and behind him, somewhere, a woman sleeping in a bed, the light in the corridor the only illumination in all that rolling darkness of night.

31

Carrigan was waiting for his morning coffee to dispense when he felt a shadow fall over him. He looked up to see Karlson leaning up against the wall, smiling contentedly to himself.

'Yes?' He had no time for this, not now. He could feel the rush of facts swirling inside his head, the leads multiplying and diverging, the need for more coffee, more time, the nagging awful sense that he was missing something.

'I was wondering where DS Miller was?' Karlson said in that fake-nonchalant way you ask a question you already know the answer to.

'She's taken the morning off,' Carrigan replied, hoping his voice didn't betray him.

Karlson made a show of looking behind him, a quick glance back, then said, 'I didn't want to bring this up in front of everyone else but I thought I ought to talk to you before I go any further with it.'

Carrigan snatched the drink from the dispenser, his fingers burning on the plastic cup, and tried to decipher Karlson's tone. He took a cautious sip and grimaced at the muddy taste of powdered coffee. 'I wish you'd just say what you mean, John. I've got no fucking time for playing games today.'

Karlson stepped closer and all Carrigan could smell was his aftershave, spicy and pungent, like walking into the front of a department store. 'I'm not playing games, believe me. I was just extending the courtesy of telling you before taking this higher.'

Carrigan crushed the cup in his hand and flung it into the bin. 'Taking what higher? What the fuck are you talking about?'

Karlson's voice dropped conspiratorially, 'I saw DS Miller yesterday . . . and she didn't seem right.'

For a brief moment, Carrigan wondered how Karlson had found out, then realised the sergeant meant something entirely different.

'I'd keep my eye on her if I were you,' Karlson continued, scratching his cheek and flashing his gums. 'Wouldn't want the brass to find out one of your detectives arrived at work drunk. Guess that's why she had to take the morning off.'

'What did you just say?' Carrigan felt his fingers clenching, a bright sharp twitch blossoming in his left shoulder.

'The other day she came back from lunch reeking of booze. Don't tell me you haven't noticed her recent mood swings? If you don't report it, then I will, which means I'll also have to report you for not reporting it once I'd informed you of the situation.'

Carrigan was about to say something, then realised there was nothing he could say. Karlson had him – either he passed on this info about Geneva to the super and betrayed her trust, or he'd be up in front of Branch himself. He pulled his hands out of his pockets, turned towards Karlson and slammed him against the coffee machine.

He saw the raw shock in Karlson's eyes. 'You have no idea what she's been through.' He realised almost immediately it had been the wrong thing to say by the subtle shift in the sergeant's expression.

'You seem very eager to defend her,' Karlson replied, recovering his grin.

'She's part of the team. I'd do the same for any of you.'

'You sure it's just that? That it's not personal? After all, you're wearing the same clothes as yesterday and look as if you haven't slept. If I were a detective I'd surmise you spent the night at her place.'

Carrigan pushed Karlson hard against the drinks machine. Images of Geneva flashed before his eyes – Geneva curled up on the wet pavement, the phone she'd called him from still clutched in both hands, the stumble in her words as she told him what had happened. He blinked and he was back in the room, his hands locked around Karlson's neck, fingers pressing deep. 'You ever do something like that again and you're finished,' he said, but he was out of breath, and the words came out faint and false.

'*You're* fucking finished if you're covering up for her.'

Carrigan's fist crashed into Karlson's jaw at the same moment that the door to the refreshment room was flung open.

'What in fuck's name is going on here?'

Carrigan turned and saw Branch standing in the doorframe, his mouth hanging half open, his eyes blazing behind smudged glasses.

'Nothing,' Carrigan said, moving a step back, trying to force the adrenalin down, his eyes never leaving Karlson's.

'Nothing?' Branch repeated. He shook his head as he entered the room. 'What do you have to say about this, DS Karlson?'

Karlson rubbed his jaw, his eyes lingering for a long moment on Carrigan, then turning to Branch. 'It's nothing, sir, just a few flared tempers . . .'

'Jesus Christ – now you're both lying to me.' Branch shook his head in dismay and disgust. 'Carrigan – my office now, and you, Sergeant, go and clean yourself up for God's sake, you look like some yobbo on the wrong end of a Friday night.'

Branch didn't say anything as Carrigan followed him through the winding corridor and into his office. The super sat down, un-clipped his phone and began texting furiously. The buzzer on his table lit up. He looked at Carrigan. 'Just make yourself presentable, Quinn's due any moment.'

Carrigan ran his fingers through his hair and adjusted his shirt and tie, all the time watching Branch texting on two phones at once. The door opened and ACC Quinn came in, dressed in a gravestone-grey pinstripe, snowflakes melting on his shoulders and eyebrows.

'Carrigan,' he said, as Branch got up and gave the ACC his seat. 'Good of you to come in. I know this investigation is keeping you busy so I won't delay you long.' He cleared the front of the desk, pushing papers and phones aside, and laid his arms across it. 'So, where are we on this? Please tell me you're about to wrap it up. The press are becoming intolerable, and I'm getting calls from the Home Office every morning.'

Carrigan took a deep breath, still rattled and adrenalin-jumpy from the fight. Quinn was staring expectantly at him. Even at the start, Carrigan had known the case would come down to such moments but it didn't make it any easier now. 'We're following some promising leads but it's a lot more complex than we first thought.'

Quinn wrinkled his brow. 'What's so complicated? Someone set the fire and you need to catch that person.'

Carrigan sighed inwardly; it was always like this with the brass, as if they'd forgotten everything they'd learned on the street or had it surgically removed on promotion. 'We have no forensic evidence of any use, the fire made sure of that, so the only way we're going to catch who did this is by knowing why they did it – the motive will lead us to the suspect,' he said, noticing his voice turning defensive, hating it but unable to control it.

Quinn sniffed and tapped one finger three times on the surface of the table. 'Okay, Carrigan, explain it to me. Pretend I'm some idiot who can barely string a sentence together and tell me what we have.'

'We're trying to work out why Emily Maxted, the eleventh victim, was at the convent that particular night, and what her connection to the nuns is. We're interviewing her ex-boyfriend later today and he may shed some light on this.' He saw Quinn wrinkle his brow and continued. 'The more we look into the convent's affairs the more anomalies we find, and the diocese is being less than helpful with our inquiries.' Carrigan stopped and waited a beat, knowing his timing had to be just right. 'We're trying to figure out if the nuns' political activities in South America in the early 1970s have anything to do with the fire. They were also involved in neighbourhood clean-up schemes that may have pissed off a local dealer, Agon Duka,' Carrigan said, noticing how each new piece of information produced a different physical reaction in Quinn, his jaw tightening, eyelids fluttering, lips twitching and pursing. 'They were also embroiled in a dispute with the diocese; the entire convent was on the verge of being excommunicated, and we're looking into that too.'

'Enough!' Quinn slammed his palm down on the table, a hard resounding crack that made Branch jump almost an inch off his chair. 'I wish I could just press a button and go back in time and not have heard any of that. But we can't do that, can we? And you, Carrigan, can't go around flinging about wild rumours and innuendoes hoping something will stick. These nuns have suffered enough and now you want to besmirch their reputation and drag it through the dirt?'

Carrigan kept his mouth shut, having expected this and counted on it.

'And now I'm getting calls from the diocese's press secretary saying you treated him like a suspect and that two of your men gained unauthorised entry into the archives.'

'Women,' Carrigan said.

'What?'

'They were women, not men.'

Quinn's eyes turned narrow and dark. 'You're walking a very high wire here, Carrigan. I would advise you not to look down.' Quinn paused, his hands entrenched in his jacket pockets. 'Desist on the nuns, understand me? No more digging up the past, that's not going to lead you to the arsonist. You mentioned the nuns pissing off a drug dealer – what's your feeling about that?'

Carrigan leaned forward, knowing the time had come, trying to keep his face blank and neutral, trying not to think about what the men had done to Geneva last night. 'Very much in the picture, sir,' he replied. 'I'd like to shift the investigation's focus to Duka. We've had certain developments over the last couple of days that point strongly in his direction.'

'So why aren't you focusing your energies on Duka rather than digging up dirt on the nuns?'

Carrigan shrugged. 'We're not equipped to deal with that. I need a clear remit and no interference from the drug squad or Organised Crime. I need more overtime allocations, surveillance vehicles, an armed response team at the ready, and more uniforms. I also need my warrants to be fast-tracked so the trail doesn't go cold. These people are highly sophisticated and electronically aware – we need to move fast on any info we get.'

Quinn scratched his cheek, and looked at Branch, then back to Carrigan. 'And if you had all this, you'd be prioritising Duka and not the nuns?'

'Yes, sir. With these added resources I can pile some pressure on him and his business.'

Quinn put his hands together, closed his eyes and nodded. 'Okay, Carrigan. Send my secretary a list of what you need and I'll make sure you get it. And for God's sake, do something about that hideous black eye – it's very unbecoming in a policeman.' Quinn gave a curt nod, stood up, brushed the creases from his suit and left the office.

'Why do I get the feeling you just let him play into your hand?' Branch was staring at Carrigan, his expression somewhat unreadable, maybe even a little amused.

'I have no idea why you'd think that, sir.'

32

'Can you please stop asking if I'm okay?' She turned back just in time to see the oncoming bus hurtling towards them. With a quick flick of her wrist she pulled the car out of danger at the last possible moment. Carrigan gripped the edges of his seat and felt a trickle of sweat run down the back of his neck.

'I'm sorry.'

'And stop saying you're sorry.'

It had been like this since morning. A cold hard wall had formed around her, layers of silence. She seemed veiled in shock as if she were watching him and the road ahead at one remove. He was going to tell her about his altercation with Karlson, but decided against it. Perhaps it was better she didn't know yet. There were still a few cards he had left to play and maybe the issue could be resolved before she found out. He sat back and kept his mouth shut and watched the silent ballet of last-minute shoppers through his window, trussed-up bodies trudging wearily through the clumpy streets, the snow turned from wonder to nuisance almost overnight.

'DC Singh looked through Emily's Facebook site,' Geneva said as they stopped at a red light.

Carrigan nodded, happy to change the subject and happy that someone else was doing this, knowing how lost he was in the electronic mesh and sprawl of lives on the Internet. 'And?'

'And nothing. Not for almost two years. Before that, apparently, she was quite active, used her site to organise protest marches and online petitions against this or that corporation, and then it all stops dead.'

'Just like the nuns' charity work?'

'Yes, but the timing doesn't match. The nuns stopped their outreach work a year ago. Emily went off the net about twenty months ago. Singh said Emily wasn't following any religious organisations and when she cross-checked her friends list with the convent's there wasn't any overlap.'

'It's a connection even if we don't yet understand it.' Carrigan looked at Geneva, noticing how crumpled she appeared, a tightening of her muscles and a persistent tic below her right eye, the small betrayals of her body. 'We need to find out what happened to Emily in the last year – we need to know what steps she took that brought her into collision with the nuns but, having said that, I think we need to be very careful with Emily. She was involved with the nuns, possibly stayed at the convent and was there that night, but I'm not so sure her presence has anything to do with the fire.'

'A few days ago you were sure Emily was the key.'

'I know,' he admitted. 'I've changed my mind. The facts have changed. We still need to find out more about Emily. I'm not quite ready to drop her yet. We'll talk to her ex-boyfriend, see what he has to say, but we need to be careful we don't let a good story get in the way of evidence.'

Geneva found a parking space outside Geoff Shorter's office. After what Donna Maxted had told him, Carrigan had been surprised that Shorter had no criminal record but even more so by the fact that he now owned his own business.

The offices of Green Solutions were situated above an exclusive children's clothes store on Kensington High Street – Carrigan glanced in the window and saw a toddler's gingham dress that cost more than his entire wardrobe put together. He stood in the swirling snow and watched the blanketed streets as Geneva smoked a hurried cigarette. Despite her reservations, he felt a quickening as he walked up to the front door. He looked at Geneva climbing the stairs behind him and wondered what was going through her head.

The woman who opened the door had clearly been expecting someone else and she didn't bother to hide her disappointment at the sight of them. She looked liked she'd only left school yesterday, all zits, puppy fat and a blank bored expression. She wore a dark black blouse and black miniskirt, her hair cut short and severe, and she smelled of hairspray and the chewing gum she was pounding between her teeth.

'Geoff's busy in a meeting.' She tapped something on her iPhone with a long false nail. 'Maybe you should come back after Christmas.'

'Thanks for your help,' Carrigan said, walking straight past her, up the stairs and through the lobby into Shorter's office.

Geoff Shorter had his legs up on the desk and was watching a cricket match taking place in some hot dusty city half a world away. His eyes shot up when they entered, lingering a second longer on Geneva, then went back to the game. Carrigan heard the announcer's flat voice running off statistics, batting tallies and legendary stands from times long gone. He saw a jug of Pimm's on the desk, three thumbed and ragged copies of *Wisden*, various papers and scrawled notes, a disarranged set of playing cards and a laptop.

'We need to talk to you about Emily Maxted,' Carrigan said, studying Shorter, trying to gauge his reaction, but the man's face was impassive and bland, impossible to read, his eyes fixed dreamily on the screen in front of him. Shorter's hair had receded halfway up his skull. To compensate, he'd grown what was left into a shaggy blond afro and he now ran his hand across it as if to make sure it was still there. 'Emily? God, I haven't heard from her for ages. How is she?'

'Emily was killed in a fire five days ago.'

They both watched carefully as Shorter processed the information. His eyes flicked from Carrigan to Geneva and then his eyebrows shot up and he began to laugh, a series of semi-articulated *haha*s emerging from deep in his throat. 'She put you up to this, didn't she? I sincerely hope you're not going to start stripping now.'

Carrigan kept his mouth tight. 'No, Mr Shorter, I am not going to strip, rest assured. But this isn't a joke, Emily is dead, and we are investigating the circumstances surrounding her death.'

Shorter had been rocking back on his chair and now he stopped, using his arms to anchor himself to the desk. 'Emily? Dead?' He looked down at the papers and print-outs and shook his head. 'I knew it,' he whispered. 'I knew it would end like this.'

Carrigan and Geneva exchanged looks. The more people they spoke to, the more it seemed that Emily had fulfilled the destiny everyone expected of her. It was only the location and circumstance that surprised them.

Shorter was silent for a couple of minutes, facing away, and when he turned round they could tell he'd been crying.

'How long were you and Emily together?' Geneva asked, moving her chair just a little forward of Carrigan's. They'd agreed in the car that she would lead and the way Shorter's gaze tracked the line of her cleavage only confirmed that decision.

Shorter quickly looked away and stared at the glass of Pimm's in his hand as if surprised to find it there. 'We were together about eleven years, give or take. We met at Leeds then moved down here.' He downed the remains of his drink. 'What . . . what happened to her?'

'We'll get to that,' Geneva replied.

Shorter glanced up, then back down at his hands. 'Do I need a lawyer?' he said.

Carrigan and Geneva looked at each other, blood beating in their eyes. 'Why would you think you need a lawyer?' Geneva asked.

Shorter shook his head, his hands fidgeting at his sides. 'I don't know if I should be talking to you,' he said.

'Well, that's entirely up to you, Mr Shorter, but if you decide to do that, we'll have to arrest you on suspicion of the murder of Emily Maxted.' Carrigan knew they had nowhere near enough evidence to do that but the look in Shorter's face told him it wouldn't get that far.

'Murder?' Shorter looked momentarily disoriented, as if waking to find himself in a strange bed. 'Someone murdered Emily?' His voice turned high and crackly. 'That's not why I didn't want to talk to you. I don't know anything about that.'

'Then why?'

'You're only interested in Emily's murder?'

'Yes.'

'Because if I tell you about Emily and me, well, some of the things we did in those days weren't legal – we thought we were doing the right thing at the time and that the laws were wrong – I don't want any of this coming back at me . . .'

'Mr Shorter, when was the last time you saw Emily?'

Shorter seemed to sag, the question hitting him like a punch to the guts. 'Nearly two years ago,' he said in a flat, distant voice. 'She decided we were over, packed up her stuff and left.'

'And you haven't heard from her since?'

'Not a word.'

Geneva thought about the timing of this. Nearly two years ago. 'Did she leave out of the blue or were you going through a difficult time?'

Shorter laughed unexpectedly, a small dry strangled choke of air. 'Difficult? With Emily everything was difficult.' He picked up an oversized paper-clip and started kneading it between his fingers. 'She was different when we first met, of course . . . or maybe . . . I don't know . . . maybe it was me who was different back then.' He put down the unfolded paper-clip, pulled open a drawer and took out a pack of cigarettes, an ashtray and a lighter. 'You see, we didn't meet like a normal couple does,' Shorter explained, coughing on the smoke of the cigarette as he tried to light it. 'We didn't hook up at the uni bop or in smoky pubs or at lectures. When I first saw Emily she was wearing a black balaclava, a vinyl jumpsuit and she was covered in horse's blood.' Shorter let out a bitter little laugh. 'I guess you could say it was love at first sight.'

'Where was this?' Geneva enquired, feeling the slightest twinge of . . . what? She couldn't quite name it, some pale and minor envy at the lingering devotions in other people's lives, perhaps.

'We were on a hunt-sab mission. This was the late nineties, early 2000s. Students were marching against the poll tax, against fees, against foreign intervention. It was an exciting time. The world was changing and we believed we were the instruments of that change.' Shorter took a deep breath and let it out slowly. 'That day, when I got out of the van, I saw her. I actually stopped, stopped in my tracks, unprepared for such a vision. She was standing under a tree, pouring ball bearings from a cardboard box into small sandwich bags.'

'Ball bearings?' Geneva asked.

'We'd leave them dotted around the route of the hunt and when the horses' hooves made contact, the bags would burst, spilling their contents. Once the first horse goes down it's like dominoes.'

'I guess you weren't too concerned about the horses' rights, or did you see them as collaborators?'

Shorter shot Geneva a sharp glance, not quite sure if she was asking him a question or making a statement. She noted a faint flaring in his eyes, a rush of blood to the cheeks, as if something had come to the surface and been instantly snuffed out.

'I know . . . I know,' he admitted. 'It's funny how easily you can convince yourself of the necessity of violence when you're fighting to obliterate it.' He shook his head. 'We shared the same van on the way back. It had been a successful sab but a costly one. The riders had attacked us with whips and clubs. But that just made the atmosphere on the ride back even more electric.

'The van was everything.' Shorter's eyes glowed with sparks of resurfaced memory, his whole body shuddering into animation as he continued, and Geneva could tell this was a part of himself and his past he romanticised and used as a bulwark against his fading present. 'You have to understand that. When we were in the van the constant hum of the world disappeared. We no longer worried about the essay we were due to hand in, the girl who may or may not call back, the raging slammed-door argument with parents . . . none of that mattered. In the van there was just us and the task at hand. There was only now. The next hunt, the next bend of the road, the next police stop. Names were not important. History and background were not important.

'We lived in the van that summer. We slept and talked and cooked and fucked and argued in the van. We knew every rivet and dent and bump and where to sleep without waking up bruised and cramped, and where to hide our stashes when we got pulled over. We criss-crossed the country that summer, up and down motorways and rural two-lanes. We went to marches and protests and sit-ins. Wildcat strikes in medieval stone villages and anti-war rallies in the heart of the capital. There was always somewhere to go to, new drugs to take, the clamour of massed voices, the tingled anticipation of trouble, the bloodrush of the cause. There were five of us in the van but really there was only Emily and me.'

'That doesn't sound to me like someone who would spend their time in a convent?'

'A convent?' Shorter's eyes rattled in confusion. He picked up another paper-clip and was pulling it apart between his fingers. 'I couldn't think of a less likely place for Emily.'

'How about nuns? Did Emily ever mention being involved with nuns?'

'Nuns?' Shorter shook his head. He caught his thumb on the point of the paper-clip, winced as a bright red dot bloomed from his skin.

'What else was Emily involved in?'

'Whad'ya got?' Shorter said in a weird accent.

Carrigan looked up from his notes.

'Like Brando in *The Wild One*,' Shorter explained. 'It's how I always used to think of Emily back then. Didn't matter what the cause was, she would throw herself headlong into it. It's partly what made her so attractive, that unswerving dedication and wild-eyed zeal. She wasn't like the rest of them, you have to understand that, for her it wasn't a posture, a way to make her life seem more meaningful than it really was – she actually meant it, meant it too much, that was the problem. She became so consumed by the troubles of the rest of the world and so enmeshed in its grievances that she somehow lost her self, and it wasn't long before I discovered another Emily residing just below the surface.'

'Another Emily?' Geneva said, seeing flashes of pain settle in Shorter's eyes.

'I began to see that there were two Emilys. There was the Emily I'd met – the midnight warrior dressed all in black, ready to go out any time of day or night and right injustice, who came back from meetings flushed and excited, who couldn't get the words out fast enough, who sat on the couch and brilliantly analysed and dissected the problems of the world.

'And then there was the other Emily. The days and weeks when things quietened, when even the most strident of activists had to go to the library, put their heads down and revise for finals. This was the Emily who stayed in bed all day with the curtains closed, who spent evenings telling me over and over how much she detested her parents, who locked herself in the bathroom for hours at a time, who looked in the mirror and saw only saggy skin, an ugly nose, bitten nails and fat legs. I took her to Florence, to Amsterdam and New York. I wanted her to see some of the other side of life, to let her hair down, but wherever we went she would just sit there and simmer, finding injustice in the smallest thing.'

'But you still moved down to London together?' Geneva asked.

'I thought that once away from the buzz of student life she'd get better, realise the world was much bigger and more complex than she'd painted it. But London only made Emily worse. She no longer had the constant rush of meetings and seminars to go to. She was now in the real world and the real world came crashing up against her. She hardened in turn, became less communicative, except when railing against something or other she'd read on the Internet. Those were not good times. We argued all hours, furiously, with our words and with our hands, at the top of our voices. She'd call me a stooge, a collaborator, a capitalist pig. She spent entire evenings putting my family on trial. She would storm out, lose herself in the London night, be gone for days at a time and come back with a strange vacancy in her eyes and a small offering – a cake she knew I liked, or a paperback, or a bottle of wine – for the worry she'd caused me.'

'Do you have any idea where she went?'

Shorter poured himself a fresh drink. 'No, but she found what she was looking for in London, meetings and action groups, angry young men and women whose lives had left them with nothing but hate.

'We stopped sleeping together. We stopped talking to each other. We set up a couch in the living room and on the nights Emily did return, she would sleep there. She began hanging out in the squats of east London. These Dickensian hell-holes, no water, no electricity, rats, and food left rotting for days. These people wanted to save the world but they couldn't even keep their own house in order. They pretended that cleanliness was a bourgeois concept, that washing and changing clothes were just another surrender to the system.' Shorter lit a cigarette and blew the smoke at the ceiling.

'She began to get more secretive. She disappeared for days at a time, often coming back bruised and bloody, her eyes burning fiercely.' Shorter paused, took a deep breath and his eyes drew hard and tight. 'And then Nigel entered the picture.'

'Nigel?' Geneva looked up from her notes, catching the shift in Shorter's tone.

'He called himself Nigel the Nail – he used to say he didn't want to be a thorn in the side of the government but a great big fucking nail. That tells you as much as you need to know about how Nigel saw himself. He was the self-appointed guru of the squat set, older by a generation, regaling them with stories of manning the barricades during the strikes of the Thatcher years, his time in prison, his days in Belfast and the West Bank.

'Emily had been so uncommunicative for so long and suddenly she was talking all the time, about Nigel and how he did this and did that, and it was obvious she'd fallen in love with him.

'A month or two after she met him, she told me it was over. Nigel came to help her pack her things, to make sure I didn't cause a scene, she said – as if I even cared enough by that point. Nigel stood there sneering and making remarks about my furniture, my accent, the kind of coffee I had in the cupboard. Emily took her clothes and very little else. That was the last time I saw her.'

Shorter sat back in his chair and stared vacantly at the wall, slumped and drained. 'It's easy to see now she was in a downward spiral. But at the time you always think this will pass, that things will get better. But they never do, and every day you become a little less blind, and it freezes your heart to look at the only person you've ever loved and see no future at all in their eyes.'

There was nothing to say to this. They thanked him and left him there, his face white and his Christmas ruined.

*

As soon as Geneva was back in the car she immediately began typing into the onboard computer. Carrigan waited, the screen angled away from him so that he couldn't tell what she was looking at. Instead he watched her face as it changed from worry and frown to a quick delicious smile.

'What is it?'

'Nigel the Nail's got some previous.'

Carrigan nodded and started the car. 'From what Shorter told us about him, that doesn't surprise me in the least.'

'Well . . .' Geneva said, drawing it out. 'Does it surprise you that four of those charges were for arson?'

33

Nigel Burton, AKA Nigel the Nail, had been remarkably easy to find. 'Amazed you didn't see him on telly last week,' a gruff sergeant from the Public Order Unit had explained. 'He's marshalling one of those anti-Tesco protests. Loves the camera, our Nigel does, loves getting arrested too, good for his image and all that.'

Carrigan let Geneva do the driving so he could study Nigel's file on the way over. He didn't even notice Geneva's music or the spiralling south London snow, his eyes and thoughts completely ensnared by Nigel's arrest sheet.

He'd been in trouble since the age of fifteen. Burton, or Nigel the Nail, as he was now legally known after a deed poll change, had been arrested seventeen times. He'd spent a total of thirty-eight months in various low-level prisons and each time he was released he wasted no time before reoffending.

Nigel's first arrests were nothing unusual – possession of class B drugs, a minor infraction in a pub at closing time, the charges later dropped – but then he had got serious and most subsequent arrests were for public disorder issues, mainly stemming from his participation in violent protests and riots. However, what Carrigan was most interested in were the four counts of arson Nigel had been charged with. Two Starbucks, a suburban branch of NatWest and a synagogue. None of the charges had been proven; witnesses had backed out, evidence got misplaced, and Nigel always had a crew of cohorts on hand to provide him with a timely alibi. According to the sheet, Nigel was now living in a squat in Balham and leading the protest at the new Tesco Express.

Carrigan looked down at the print-outs, confused, feeling a

slight judder of disorientation. His mind reeled back through the last few days. They'd been digging deep into the convent's secret history. They'd been following up the drugs in the neighbourhood angle. They'd been tracking the Peruvian connection. He didn't know where or how Nigel fitted in, but his form for arson, and his relationship with the eleventh victim, changed everything.

They turned into a narrow high street and Geneva pulled the car to a stop outside a row of cracked and leaning terraces. A huge hand-daubed banner was spread along the facade of three of the houses. Red paint read Tesco Brings Nazism to Your Street and Smash the Supermarkets. The lettering was crude and a misspelling had been painted over twice. Across the road, in the middle of a small parade of shops, was a Tesco Express, one window covered by a sheet of rough splintered plywood.

'Democracy in action,' Carrigan said as he pulled on his jacket and headed for the squat's front door.

Except there wasn't a front door. The council had removed it and replaced it with large grey Sitex screens. The screens had been pulled open and now stood flapping in the wind. Carrigan heard the dull thump of electronic music echoing from inside and could see the shadowdance of people flickering across the windows.

'Ready for this?' he asked Geneva.

'No,' she replied, 'but that never stopped me doing anything before.' She smiled and then her mouth curled up into a frown.

'What?'

'You look way too much like a copper,' she said.

'I don't know whether to take that as a compliment or not?'

She looked him up and down, 'I know we're not exactly undercover but it would help if we didn't immediately look like the enemy.' She made him take off his jacket and put it back in the car. His tie was similarly disposed of. 'Lucky you got a beard,' she said, shuffling closer to him. 'But it's too neat.'

Before he could react she leaned forward and ran her fingers through his beard, fluffing and messing it.

Carrigan smiled, feeling . . . he didn't quite know what . . . as they stepped through the Sitex screen and into a dark corridor reeking of weed and booze and body odour. Music was seeping from every corner of the house, several different tracks clashing and crashing in a dissonant caterwaul.

He couldn't believe people lived like this, life reduced to the bare essentials and often not even that, no water or electricity or heating. And yet what were your options if you were young and starting out in London? The rents so high that an entire segment of society was now kept off the property ladder. He looked around the crumbling corridor. The squatters had followed their own logic and beliefs – they didn't think it was morally just that buildings should be vacant – but they missed the bigger picture, and Carrigan thought back to last night's conversation. If every marginalised group took the law into their own hands, society wouldn't last very long.

'You want to try in there?' Geneva shouted above the dull thump of drum and bass, nodding towards a door on their left.

Carrigan went in first and was greeted by a thick fog of cannabis smoke. The room was shaking with the music, the walls convulsing and throbbing like beating ventricles. Sweat popped on his forehead and under his collar, the heat and musk of fifty or sixty bodies dancing and swaying to the deep rhythmic pulse, the room itself seeming to breathe in time with the beat.

They let their eyes and ears adjust and tried to spot anyone resembling Nigel but it was impossible, and they left, their bodies still vibrating with the deep rumbling bass drones. They passed through a dangerously leaning partition wall that had come loose and ducked through a hole into a large hallway. The walls were painted in bright lurid colours, daubed with monosyllabic slogans and the ubiquitous anarchist sign. Carrigan heard something behind him and stopped. He thought he saw a flash of yellow hair but when his eyes focused there was nothing but the empty hallway. He turned and followed Geneva through the winding labyrinth, realising they were in the house next door now, that all the houses were connected and that the squatters had erected makeshift walls and corridors to guide them through.

In the next room, people were slumped on sofas and bean bags, listening to music that seemed to consist of nothing but fire alarms, fax screeches and klaxons calls. The occupants were passing around a large cylinder of gas between them. A face mask was connected to a white rubber tube and each person took long hungry pulls, their expressions distorted by the mask. Geneva went around asking if anyone knew Emily or had seen Nigel but it was hard to tell if the people in the room even registered her or merely thought she was part of their shared hallucination.

They left the room and realised that they were now lost, not sure how many of the connected houses they'd passed through. Carrigan felt his head swell with the roar and scream of the music and quickened his step, leading Geneva down a long reeking hallway and into a dead end.

'Christ!' he said, turning round, and that was when he saw the girl.

She was blonde and small, her T-shirt dark against her flat torso. She had large green eyes and a slender neck that didn't look like it could support the weight of her head. She didn't say anything but beckoned them with her hand and, before they could stop her, she'd turned away and they had little choice but to follow.

Through the darkness and muck, through corridors and barriers, through noise and heat and broken walls until the girl ducked under a low-hanging beam and into a dark cramped room. Carrigan went first, Geneva following, watching their back.

'Close the door.'

They did as they were told and stood in total darkness, every muscle and fibre of their bodies attuned and tense.

'I'm sorry, I didn't want anyone to see me talking to you . . . I saw . . . I saw it on the news,' the girl said, switching on a small electric light which radiated across her face, making her look like a gilded angel. 'I'm not doing this for you,' she made clear to them, her accent rough and common and slightly exaggerated, a distinct middle-class burr underneath. She looked all of fourteen, a slim nothing of a girl, long blonde hair matted and split, her face a mask of scary blankness. Another one of those girls, Geneva thought, who created a web of chaos around them, shiny black ravens in a hurricane. 'I'm only doing this for Em.'

'You knew Emily?' Geneva asked.

The girl nodded. 'Yeah, we used to hang out a bit when she was staying here.'

'She lived here?' Geneva took a step forward and looked around, realising that this was the girl's bedroom, the hairdryer on the chair, the crumpled magazines and pillows and empty food cartons. 'How long ago?'

The girl sniffled and lit a cigarette, the smoke filling the room and shrouding her face. 'She first turned up, I think it was March of last year. She was one of Nigel's.'

'One of Nigel's?'

The girl looked at Geneva, totally ignoring Carrigan. 'You know, one of his girls? He always has a new one around. The ones he can mould, the ones that fall under his spell. He turned up with her one night, likes showing off his new recruits. Introduced her to everyone.' The girl took quick, angry drags off her cigarette. 'We started seeing her more and more and one day she was crashing here, permanent like, and before we knew it she was doing all the talking and planning. Nigel found a right one when he found her.'

'What kind of stuff are we talking about?'

The girl ground out her cigarette and glared at Geneva.

'It's okay, we're not interested in anything but finding out who killed Emily.'

'You mean that?' she said, and when Geneva nodded, the girl

seemed to accept it. 'Nigel's part of what he likes to call the movement. He organises and mobilises people for protests – war, student fees, human rights violations, doesn't matter what.' The girl's lips were thin and pinched and it was hard to believe she was so young. 'Emily was just like him. She lived for the moment we hit the streets, came up against the cordons and looked into the eyes of the enemy. She was one of those people who only found themselves in the crowd, in the flash and roar of running battle. She was only ever happy when she was fighting. That's why Nigel loved her, she was his mirror in so many ways.'

Geneva lit a cigarette for herself then another for the girl. 'How long did she stay here for?' she asked, trying to get a sense of the timeline, the blank space between Emily leaving Geoff Shorter and the fire in the convent.

'She was here six months, maybe a little less. Then they went abroad, her and Nigel, and when they came back she'd changed.'

'Abroad? Where?' Geneva tried to keep the excitement out of her voice, tried to tell herself this was probably nothing, just another step out of many that Emily had taken to get to the convent on that particular night.

The girl looked down at the floor or at her torn trainers, the toes poking out, it was hard to tell. 'I think it was Nigel's idea. He'd come into some money. No idea where they went but they were gone three weeks and when they came back Emily was different.'

'Different how?' Geneva and Carrigan looked at each other.

'More focused. As if all her stray particles had finally come to rest. She began to miss meetings and marches, went out for days at a time, never telling anyone where she'd been. She started criticising Nigel and the things we were doing. He confronted her one night, both of them screaming at each other in the kitchen, Emily laying into him for not having enough commitment, for only being interested in causes that got him on TV. The next day she was gone. Left all her stuff and didn't bother telling anyone.'

'Her stuff?' Carrigan said.

'Just left it here. I kept it in case she came back but she never did.'

'Do you still have it?'

The girl went over to a corner of the room. She reached behind a thin mattress that lay flush against the wall and pulled out a small canvas bag and handed it to Geneva.

Geneva opened the flap and gazed down at the contents. There was a toothbrush and an electric razor, a couple of faded paperbacks, a stack of scratched CD-Rs, a few blurry photos, a packet of cigarettes, a lighter and a black notebook.

'We'd also really like to talk to Nigel.'

'So would I.' The girl shrugged and scratched her wrist. Geneva saw that the skin was red and dry, striated with white crescents and old cutting scars. 'He was supposed to be here for the protest party but never showed up . . . first I ever heard of Nigel missing a party.'

'How long has he been gone?'

The girl thought about this, her lower lip pressed between her teeth. 'I haven't seen him for five days. The news people were back yesterday, I'm surprised he missed that.'

Five days, the day of the fire. 'Did Nigel or Emily ever mention anything about nuns?' Carrigan asked.

The girl looked at him as if he were mad.

Geneva handed her a card, said to call if she remembered anything else and thanked her. The girl whispered, 'Good luck,' but when they turned, she'd already disappeared back into the darkness.

When they made it back through the connected rooms and corridors to the main hallway, they saw them.

Two men stood against the front door blocking their path. They were young but heavily muscled, one with a green Mohican, the other shaved except for one black lock, gelled and twisted around his neck in the shape of a noose. They both wore torn T-shirts, snarls, and old scars across their faces.

Carrigan instinctively moved closer to Geneva. He looked at the door, then he looked at the men. Mohican was reaching into his pocket. Noose extended his arm across the door in a challenge. Carrigan could see Geneva gripping the bag with Emily's things tightly in one hand, the other resting on her hip. He glanced behind him and saw that others had left the party and were gathering to watch the action. A group of men and a couple of women stood a few feet away, swigging cider, laughing, and blocking their escape.

Carrigan quickly ran through their options. He knew they'd been stupid in coming here alone but he'd also known that coming in with a full team would have ruined whatever chance they'd had at finding anything. He felt his body tensing, his hand reaching down for the snap stick he wore on his belt.

'C'mon then,' Mohican snarled. 'I can't wait to fuckin' have you.'

Carrigan saw him smile then pull something from his back pocket. It took him a few seconds to realise it was a chunky black padlock. It was tied to a long rope and the man began to swing it in front of him in long extended arcs. Carrigan heard Geneva breathing heavily beside him, the rumble of her fear, the tightness in his own throat.

'Step away from the door now!'

The two punks laughed and Mohican swung the padlock and just as quickly snapped it back. When Geneva flinched, he burst out laughing. 'You cunts,' he said. 'Think you can just come in here and there'll be no consequences?'

Carrigan glanced down at Geneva, saw her face reddening, her hands twitching at her sides. She tightened her grip on Emily's bag. Carrigan looked behind him, noticing that the crowd was becoming more animated and that there would be no way out in that direction. The two punks and the door were their only option.

He was trying to decide the best course of action when Geneva launched herself at Mohican. The man swung with the padlock as she entered his space. Carrigan saw her duck, missing the ridged metal by only a few inches, then swing upwards with her baton, smashing it hard into Mohican's crotch as the padlock crashed into the wall.

Carrigan was already moving on the other man, using the full weight of his body to force him back. A sharp stinging pain burned through his ear as the man's jaw clamped shut over it. Carrigan felt something rip, turned to see Noose grinning with bloody lips and smashed his truncheon into the man's stomach. Noose went down without a sound and Carrigan placed his shoe on the man's neck, pinning him to the floor.

He could see some of the others starting to creep up on them, not sure whether to join the fight or just watch, and then all he could see was Geneva in a blur of motion as she swung her truncheon at Mohican's neck, causing him to stumble, grab his throat with both hands and drop the padlock. She used one foot to shunt it away, delicate as a dancer, and then swivelled and kicked Mohican in the chest. He tried to grab her legs and she took out her pepper spray and pressed down hard on the nozzle. Mohican let out a long agonised scream but Geneva didn't stop, bent over him, aiming the stinging mist directly into his eyes.

Carrigan took his foot off the other man's neck and grabbed Geneva. 'That's enough!' he shouted, pulling her away with one hand while using the other to open the front door.

The street light and cold air rushed in and Carrigan took a couple of deep breaths as he pulled Geneva through the door. She looked back once, her face twisted into a scowl. Carrigan remembered Karlson's comments from yesterday, felt his body start to ache and moan with pain, the sudden enervation as the adrenalin disappeared from his system.

Something exploded on the path next to them, spilling its contents onto the cracked paving stones. Carrigan looked down and saw a trail of baked beans splattered across his shoe, the tin torn and twisted on the ground. Something else hit his shoulder. He looked up and saw an ashtray spinning through the air and ducked just in time.

'Run!' he shouted, grabbing Geneva by the hand as more items began raining down from the high windows of the squat. They wove through the front garden avoiding chair legs and potted plants, empty tea mugs, planks of wood and a shopping trolley which just missed Carrigan, buckled and bounced and glanced his thigh. He saw Geneva stagger as a stone stung against her shoulder and he grabbed her and pushed her through the gate.

They made it into the car, shaking, breathing heavily, staring blankly at the road ahead. They both jumped in their seats as something smashed against the roof of the car. Geneva started the engine and was about to release the handbrake when the back window exploded in a shower of glass and noise. Carrigan looked through the gaping hole and saw a hundred people, maybe more, spilling into the street – a few were chasing after them but the rest had turned their attention to the Tesco Express, hurling objects and piling against the windows, and then he heard more breaking glass and the sharp stuttering whine of the shop's alarm system as the mob piled in.

'Fuck. Fuck. Fuck,' Geneva shouted, smashing her fist into the dashboard.

Carrigan turned towards her but she was staring back at the squat.

'I can't fucking believe it,' she said, reaching for the door handle.

Carrigan grabbed her arm. 'What the hell are you doing?'

'I've got to go back there. I dropped Emily's bag. Shit.'

Carrigan eased his grip and when Geneva turned in her seat she saw that he was smiling.

He slipped his hand into his jacket pocket and pulled out the small black notebook.

Geneva's eyes widened and a smile cracked her face. She took the notebook and turned it over in her hand, tilting it so that it caught the overhead bulb-light. The notebook was a Moleskine, bound shut by a piece of black elastic. Geneva slid her fingers underneath the strap and snapped it open. The pages smelled of damp and hairspray. She flicked through pages of scrawls and lists, internet addresses, random notes, phone numbers, and then she stopped.

This was a different section of the notebook, demarcated by several blank pages before it. She stared at the page on the right. There were only seven words, written in large chunky letters, a heading of sorts:

Em & N's Peru Trip – September 2011

He's with me, by my side, but I don't really see him nor feel his presence. He may as well be a tree, or a dog that follows you around because no one else will love it. But even dogs can be useful. Sometimes it's the dogs that tell us where to look.

That first night we slept on the rocky ground, as far away from the hanging trees as possible, and in the morning we set off along the road, hoping to find help at the next village.

He has a map and a tattered guidebook and a sure sense of where he is going. He says if we leapfrog across the highlands, village to village, we'll be able to catch up with the bus. Otherwise, it's a two-week wait until the next one. Of course, all he wants to do is go back to the bars and alleyways of the town to drink and tell his tale to gape-eyed college girls and gap-toothed Scandis and watch them swoon and melt but it doesn't bother me any more, at least not in the way it used to.

We hitch rides in the backs of ancient pick-up trucks, the kind of thing you expect to see in a museum, belching black smoke and diesel stink, us rolling around in rusty beds among straw and farm equipment and animal shit. Each truck or car only goes as far as the next hamlet. These are the limits of their lives. The rest of the world seems cut off from this high arid plateau but, of course, that's only a romantic illusion – something we like to tell ourselves – if you look closer, if you can be bothered, you can see it seep through every crack of rock and bend of river.

It didn't take us long to understand that this wasn't an isolated incident. That the trees of the high country carried familiar fruit and that many villages were empty and abandoned like the one we'd stumbled upon.

On the second day the smell came back and this time there was no mistaking it for some natural occurrence. The back of my throat was sore within minutes. My skin felt hot and prickly. He coughed and popped some pills and pretended not to notice but I could see him fighting back tears.

The villages are strung out along these impossible peaks, fifty or seventy or a hundred miles between them, small groupings of mud huts and tin shacks, crumbling alleyways reverting to dust, leaning brick buildings and always, at the bottom of every ravine, the skeleton wrecks of smashed cars, a constant reminder of what we all want to forget.

The villages are beautiful in their simplicity and setting but most of them are deserted.

There are old men sitting on stones in town squares and stray dogs that bark and sneer when they see us approach. But everyone else is gone. Most of the villages are empty and the ones that aren't, all slammed doors and dark suspicious glares. The old man we spoke to, or at least I tried speaking to in my crappy guidebook Spanish, just shrugged and flickered his fingers and waved as if to say they'd all flown away.

There's something very wrong here. He refuses to admit it, refuses to even have that conversation and the few people we do stumble on seem to share his reticence. He keeps telling me how much he hates it here. Hates everything about it – the food, the backpacks digging into our sides, the miles of stumbling up and down hills, the endless sun-baked hours waiting for a truck or car to come by.

But I don't feel like that at all. This thin meagre air suits my lungs perfectly, the twisting hills and treacherous slopes strip the fat and drift I accumulated in the city. It's as if every part that was not a true part of me is finally slipping free into the high clean air. I feel something strange and exciting and I don't quite know what it is or how to express it. With each place we stop at, with each broken conversation and whispered warning, with each new story, I begin to understand what is happening here and why.

I try to interest him. In London this is exactly what would goad him into action but here, in Peru, Nigel has become remote and distant and as different from his normal self as this landscape is to the glass and concrete of the city.

There is barely any life here at all. It is almost like the surface of another planet. Barren and cold and stark. The thin air and rocky ground deter everything but the hardiest weeds, the animals all look like shrinkwrapped skeletons and the people too seem stunted, closed in on themselves, each like a fist. Their mouths are tight but their eyes give them away. The shrugs and grudging smiles hide a deep unreckonable desperation and you feel that anything can happen at any time.

But people like to talk. People like to tell stories. We are such a curiosity to them we may as well be from another galaxy and, eventually, words are spoken, stories told.

We hear about the mines. That's all we hear. How

the mines have taken over the region. The foreign mines where no one understands what the foreman says but they all understand the cruel smack of his stick. We sit and listen as they tell us of rivers that float with death and strange shiny chemicals that swallow the sun. They say men come at night and take their children. That there are things in these mountains woken up out of millennia-long slumber. They talk of seeing the paramilitaries again, the rumble of boots and cruel smiles and bloodstench. How they thought these days would never come again but here they are.

Everywhere we go we hear whispers and rumours of a fenced compound high in the mountains and people say the days of war and blood are coming back and I can tell from their faces and the agitation in their muscles that they've waited their whole lives for this. They tell us about death threats and assassinations. They speak of the disappeared, ghosts walking the silent hills, demons roaming the Inca night. They complain about their persistent bloodcoughs, the black dust they bring forth every morning from their lungs, and they shrug and look up at the sky as if it owed them an answer and then they look back down at the holy ancient ground that has been stripped from their very feet and it makes me feel mad and restless and pale-eyed and he's not even interested, he just skulks in corners and sits on the backpacks and smokes his cigarettes.

He makes me sick. I can't stand to be near him any more. Even the way he moves his hand up to his jaw, that slow deliberate gesture, repeated through hours and days, in buses and sleeping bags, drives me crazy.

But he makes me understand myself better. He's like a mirror in which I can see my former life. All those long and wasted years behind me. The posturing and pretending in small hot flats as if we, us, were the ones who were going to change the world. In the light of other people's suffering our own seems so petty and small and pointless. In London we got angry about library closures and low pay rises. In London we protested against health cuts and housing benefits – but here in the wind and blood it is easy to see what is important and how, even in our worst moments, our lives are a million times better than these people's. They would swap with us in a heartbeat.

I left Nigel in that village last night. He'll wake up, shrug, catch tomorrow's bus and be in town by nightfall where he can go back to his act and tell his stories and drink his beer and feel good about himself.

Without him I feel free. Without him I feel new and unknown to myself. A mystery slowly unravelling after so many years of blindness. I talk to people in the villages, people on the highway, people out in the stony fields. They all tell the same story. They keep mentioning the compound in the hills. Their faces shade and they look behind them as they say this. A place where gunfire is regularly heard, and chanting, and the cries of strange animals. They moan about the mine diverting their water for its machines, the constant blasting of the dynamite, the last fish seen in the river several months ago. They talk of doing something. Of getting back at the bosses. But you can see in their sunken eyes and defeated mouths that there is nothing left in them but talk.

I collect rumours, stories, and outrageous fabrications from each village I stop at. *Are the men from the compound responsible for this? Are they soldiers?* I ask them, but they pretend not to understand or not to hear or not to care. But I knew I was getting close to the compound when people became less willing to talk, when doors got slammed in my face or the ground in front of me flecked by spittle. They say it lies on a hill. A gated fortress. A palace. A monastery. A torture centre. Take your pick. The stories varied but the fear and apprehension didn't.

A young man in a bar made of aluminium siding and old beer cans told me where it was. He was slow and hunchbacked and seemed to be retreating into himself even as we spoke. Around us farmers stared into their drinks, flies buzzed, the world went on. I paid him his price and wrote down the directions he gave me.

I can see it long before I reach it. Twenty-foot walls surround the building and stand stark and ugly against blue sky and silver peaks. The trail is well used and it doesn't take me long to make my way up the hill, through a pass in the mountain and onto the headland.

Two armed guards track me from their watchtowers. They swivel their mounted guns lazily and follow my progress up the hill. I can feel my heart beat, my skin itch, but I put one foot in front of the other because there is nothing else I can do.

The soldiers are no longer slouching against their guns. They are up and jabbering into walkie-talkies and sighting down their barrels at me. I keep walking and taking deep breaths, trying not to stumble on legs that feel as though they're made of rubber.

I hear the squawk and crackle of their radios, the eerie howling of the wind as it skips through the trees, and then a great wrenching as the main gate to the compound swings open.

I stand, ten feet from the entrance, and wait. The soldiers are right above me, their guns pointing down at my head, but I ignore them and keep my eyes fixed ahead.

I expect more soldiers. More guards. But there is only an old man with a straggly white beard, a priest's collar, and a mischievous smile on his face. He holds his hands out and says in English, 'Welcome, my dear. My name is Father McCarthy and I'm so glad you found us.'

34

Carrigan called an emergency briefing. Constables came in from days off or paperwork or street patrol. There was a sense of purpose and anticipation in the air as they took their seats. There was none of the usual moaning, bickering and fidgeting.

Carrigan tapped his pen against the table as he waited for everyone to settle.

'Emily Maxted met Father McCarthy in Peru last year.'

It got their attention the way he'd known it would. He remembered the look in Geneva's face when she'd finished reading the diary, a stunned comprehension creeping into her features. 'Father McCarthy was in charge of some kind of gated compound in the San Gabriel region. We don't know yet what this compound was up to, what it was for, but it seems almost certain this is where the convent's funds were being channelled.' Carrigan stopped and waited for them to finish writing their notes. 'We now know what connects Emily Maxted to the convent, but whether this has anything to do with the fire, I'm not so certain.' He glanced briefly at Geneva and continued. 'We're maybe a step closer to understanding what the convent was involved in but, given that, I'm not sure we should be concentrating so hard on Emily Maxted. I think she's a red herring. Yes, she knew the nuns. Yes, she was there that night. But that could be all there is to it.'

No one said anything, all trying to take this in, to realign the case along new parameters.

'I really think that's a bad idea,' Geneva ventured. 'We've just found the connection between Emily and the nuns and it all links back to Peru – the money, the visits, the missing nun. I think we should be focusing more on Emily, not less. I don't think the nuns pissing off some dealer is enough to explain all this.'

He could feel them waiting for him to answer but he took his time, measuring what she'd said, testing it against logic and probability. 'That's all well and fine, Miller,' he finally replied, lowering his voice. 'But we have only a limited amount of resources, as you know, and we have to choose. We have to go with the odds.' He wanted to see how she was taking this but her eyes were glued to her notebook.

Carrigan pointed to the photos of Viktor and Duka pinned to the whiteboard behind him. 'We know the nuns had run-ins with local dealers in the alleyway behind the convent. We know the nuns were organising neighbourhood watch schemes and were leafleting outside known drug houses. A few weeks before the fire we have a lieutenant in Duka's organisation visiting the convent three times. That same man was also watching the fire and assaulted me the next day in the ruins. Duka and Viktor are our main suspects and remain so. They have motive, means and opportunity, and we know from experience that this is how these kinds of organisations tend to settle their problems.'

He turned back to the whiteboard and unscrolled a large-scale map of W2. He pinned the map to the wall, then stuck four red pins into it. 'I talked to someone in Organised Crime and what he tells me about Duka fits the profile of the type of killer we're looking for.' He pointed at the pins, a rough square marking the perimeter of Queensway. 'Duka owns four properties on our patch, each a suspected stash-house, according to the drug squad. They don't know which house he's using at the moment. The Albanians change up every month or so to avoid being tracked. That said, if we can find which house Duka is using, it'll get us closer to Viktor. If nothing else, a raid will rattle Duka, cut into his profits, and maybe make him realise that giving us the firestarter makes more sense than having us come back every week.'

'Yeah, fine, but how are we going to find out which house is the current one?' Karlson asked.

Carrigan shot him a dark look. 'That's the problem. We haven't got the resources to hit all four simultaneously, and if we get the wrong one, it'll give Duka and his men plenty of warning to clear the real house.' He studied the map. 'Four houses. All standard terraced properties on quiet streets. All single residences. One on Gloucester Terrace, one on Queensborough Terrace, one on Hatherley Crescent and one on Prince's Square. Now, if we . . .'

'Shit.'

Everyone turned to stare at Geneva. She looked down at her notes but there was nothing there. She flashed back to those moments outside the house and gathered her thoughts together.

Carrigan leaned forward, a curious concern darkening his face. 'Miller?'

'Hatherley Crescent. You said Hatherley Crescent, right?' Geneva thought of the man behind the door, his silver teeth and black eyes.

Carrigan nodded.

'That's the one,' Geneva said. 'That's the house we're looking for.'

Now it was Carrigan's turn to be surprised. He looked at the map, the red pin on top, as Geneva explained about the parking tickets issued to the SUV. She told them about ringing the doorbell the previous day, the expensive security set-up, the man who'd answered the door.

'Are you sure?' Carrigan asked.

'It would be a pretty big coincidence if it wasn't.'

Carrigan agreed. 'Karlson? Get a surveillance team set up outside the house. I want them in place by tonight, when activity's likely to be at its highest. If Viktor makes an appearance then we've got him.'

Geneva sat at her table and went through the convent files as the team mobilised and gathered, their excitement suffusing the incident room but making it hard for her to concentrate. She hoped the answer would lie behind those flaked painted doors on Hatherley Crescent but she felt the tug of the information at her fingers, the Peruvian connection now made real and immediate by Emily's diary. She knew she couldn't let it go just yet. There were more things to uncover, more stories and secrets and hidden lives to unravel. She thought about Father McCarthy visiting the convent a couple of hours before the fire, his sudden decision to check into rehab, and picked up the phone.

The editor of the *Catholic Tribune* remembered her and she remembered that something in his voice which had so beguiled her the first time.

'We're trying to locate a Father Callum McCarthy. The diocese told us he's checked into a rehab centre and I was thinking the church must have its own facilities? They wouldn't use public ones, right? I don't suppose you would happen to know of any such centres or where I could find this kind of information?'

'No . . . that can't be right . . .' Staples said, sounding faraway and confused, as if she'd just woken him from deep slumber.

'What? They use public facilities?'

'No, not that,' Staples replied. 'It's just, well, I don't see what Father McCarthy would be doing in such a place. As far as I know he's teetotal.'

35

Carrigan got to the incident room early the next morning, avoiding the chattering constables and ever-growing pile of messages, and shut himself off in his office. He scanned through last night's serials, scheduled the day's actions, then picked up the phone.

He hadn't heard the voice on the other end of the line for a long time, but the laughter that greeted him instantly erased all the lost years. They got through the pleasantries quickly, both knowing that Carrigan would only call if this was important.

'You're stationed in North Yorks now?' Carrigan asked, though he already knew the answer.

'Swore I'd never come back . . . but here I am.' DI Lesh laughed but it was one of those laughs that held an edge to it, as much incredulity as mirth.

'I need you to look at a name for me.'

'Work or personal?'

Carrigan said nothing.

'One of those, then?' DI Lesh replied, the coded assent contained in the ensuing silence. 'What's the name?'

Carrigan looked down at the page in his notebook where he'd written Geneva's ex-husband's name. 'Oliver Jones . . . anything you have on him, even rumours, suspicions . . . anything at all.'

'I'll call you back.'

Carrigan thanked him and put down the phone. He felt slightly bad for what he'd done, a little ashamed and grubby, but he knew that would pass. Geneva had told him she would deal with it herself, and that was fine and as it should be, but there was no harm in having a little back-up, just in case.

He began sorting through his in-tray, reams of useless leaflets and best practice lists, all the things he hadn't got round to doing or had forgotten to, and then he saw what Berman had left for him, the convent's donor list, several sheets of print-outs, the type smudged and barely legible. There was a further note attached, Berman saying he'd been looking deeper into the convent's financial records and that the account the nuns were transferring the money to was held by something called the Tomorrow Foundation. Carrigan peeled off the Post-It note and went back to the donor list.

The list was made up of over four hundred names and the amounts donated were more often than not in the thousands. Holden had been right about that, at least. The convent had a lot of influential friends and deep pockets they could count on. Carrigan ran his eyes down the list, making a mental tally of the amounts, figures multiplying in his head, and he realised they'd been wrong in thinking that the convent's finances were the result of some illegality – it was all here in black and white, legitimate and accounted for. As he went down the list, he recognised some of the names – names glimpsed in the society pages of the *Standard*, names of prominent backbenchers and sports stars, newspaper editors and property tycoons – a cross-section of London's Catholic hierarchy, and then one name stopped him dead.

He stared at it, feeling his mouth go dry. The amount was not particularly high nor particularly low, but in keeping with the donor's salary, a generous but not overly extravagant tithing. Carrigan separated the page from the others and read it once more as if unsure of his own eyesight, then folded it neatly in half and put it in his pocket.

He was thinking about what to do with this information when Geneva burst into his office.

'Yes?' He looked up from the screen, his eyes taking a moment to focus.

She took a step forward, a smile appearing at the corners of her mouth. 'The surveillance van outside the house on Hatherley Crescent just spotted Viktor entering the premises.'

Carrigan got up from his seat, loose papers fluttering to the floor, his shirt catching on the end of the table. 'Are they sure it's him?'

Geneva nodded.

Carrigan crossed the room and picked up his jacket. He was about to put it on when he noticed a long jagged tear he'd not seen before. 'Get a car and some uniforms.'

'Already done it,' Geneva said. 'I told the surveillance unit to arrest Viktor if they see him leaving the premises but otherwise to wait for us to get there.'

'Good work,' Carrigan replied, examining the lining and the rip, his fingers running along the stitching, a frown creasing his forehead. 'So what are we waiting for?'

She looked down at his jacket and said, 'You.'

36

Carrigan stepped back as one of the uniforms swung the enforcer and splintered the door open, the sound strangely muted in the chill air. The front hallway of the house on Hatherley Crescent was gloomy and dilapidated, the paint chipped and cracked, the carpet peeling and measled with stains but four brand new CCTV cameras were mounted at regular intervals along the ceiling.

There were three doors on the ground floor, indistinguishable from each other, another hallway branching off and a wide staircase leading to the upper levels. Carrigan studied the surveillance cameras and saw that they were all angled towards the staircase. He looked down at the carpet, noting it was far more worn leading up to the stairs. He heard something move, a faint whirring susurration and he snapped his head up and looked at the cameras. They were no longer pointing towards the stairs. They were all pointing at him.

They rushed the stairs, the uniforms following, all pretence of stealth discarded. The stairs ended in a solid wooden door. Just as he got there, Carrigan heard the lock being engaged on the other side. He gestured behind him and one of uniforms shuffled past and swung the ram in a long deliberate arc. The door was no match for the enforcer, the wood and metal shearing away like tissue paper.

Two men were standing on the other side of the door. Neither one of them was Viktor.

One had a shaved head, a drunken sleepy grin on his face, and his fly was undone. The other man was wiry and sinewed as an old piece of leather, with a widow's peak that dipped towards his nose. Both men had their arms up high in the air. The only other person in the room was a middle-aged woman sitting behind a desk and staring at a computer screen.

Carrigan was momentarily disoriented. Had they somehow got the wrong house? It looked more like a dentist's waiting room than a stash-house. There was calm pastel wallpaper and dimmer lights, potted plants and deep couches. A variety of pillows and coloured throws had been added to soften the atmosphere. Framed reproductions of Manet and Picasso prints hung on the walls. The uniforms were all looking at each other, their confusion transmitted in raised eyebrows and puzzled frowns.

Carrigan turned and saw the man with the widow's peak studying him with a mild amusement, as if he'd bumped into an old friend after many years in some unexpected circumstance. The man's top row of teeth were capped in silver and looked like shiny bullets lined up in a magazine. He was looking at Geneva with an easy familiarity and smiling.

'Where's the other man?' Carrigan said. 'Viktor? Where the fuck is he?'

The two men stared at him as if they didn't understand English.

Two of the uniforms came running up the stairs. The sergeant looked tired and confused and angry. He told Carrigan they'd searched the basement and ground floor but there was no sign of Viktor.

'Did you find any drugs?'

The man shook his head.

'Upstairs it is then,' Carrigan said, addressing the uniforms. 'You find anything that looks like drugs, don't touch it, radio me or DS Miller immediately. And make sure no one gets anywhere near a toilet. We don't want the evidence flushed away.' He waited until he was sure they'd understood and started up the stairs. The smell of cheap perfume and bleach made his sinuses swell as he reached the second-floor landing. There were three doors to either side of him and a staircase leading up to another floor. Carrigan told one of the uniforms to watch the stairs, then pointed to the door on his left.

They stormed into the room and stopped, and almost walked straight back out again.

The room was small and narrow with a single bed up against one wall and an armchair against the other. Loud shrill pop music screamed and wailed from a small radio. A woman was kneeling in front of the bed. A man was sitting on the mattress, head flung back and eyes squeezed shut, still wearing his suit jacket, trousers bunched around his ankles. There was a stack of neatly folded towels on the edge of the bed and a box of tissues. The girl continued for a few seconds then stopped abruptly, turning her head and finally noticing the policemen. She blinked twice and gulped and scampered on hands and knees to the far corner of the room.

The other two rooms on the floor and most of the rooms on the floor above were also occupied. The men were surprised, then indignant, quickly turning solicitous and sorry when they realised what was happening. The girls cowered and whimpered, seemingly more scared by the police than anything which had occurred within the room.

'Something's seriously wrong here.' Geneva stood next to him. He hadn't heard her come up and the sound of her voice made him jump.

'I know,' Carrigan scanned the long dark corridor. 'We haven't found any drugs yet . . .'

'That's not what I mean.'

Carrigan took the last door on the third floor by himself as the uniforms led the women and their pale-faced clients down to the waiting patrol cars.

He knocked but there was no answer so he tried the doorknob. On first glance he thought the room was empty and was about to turn back when he saw a slight ripple disturbing the sheets. A young girl with short black hair slowly unfurled from the blankets, rubbing sleep out of her eyes with tiny hands and stifling a yawn. She looked about thirteen. There was a grey raggedy Snoopy under her pillow and she clutched it tightly with her outstretched hand. She managed a faint smile then cast her eyes down to her feet and began unbuttoning her pyjamas. Carrigan told her to stop, repeating it softly when he saw the look of confusion and panic spreading across the girl's face.

'You not like me?' she said, looking up, her eyes small pleading things.

'Please, stop that.' He took a couple of steps back to give her some space and then he saw her pouting her lips, jutting out her chest, and he turned away and slammed the door behind him. He told Geneva to call in social services then saw the uniformed sergeant coming down the attic stairs.

'Your man's not up there but I think you'd better take a look,' he said, a dark rage boiling in his eyes. He was gripping his truncheon so tightly it looked like the skin on his knuckles was about to pop and Carrigan couldn't help but like him a little bit more for that.

'He's got to be somewhere,' Carrigan said. 'He can't have just disappeared. Find him.'

The officer nodded sombrely and Carrigan climbed the last set of stairs alone.

The door at the top had two five-inch deadbolts affixed to it. The metal looked worn and flaked and well used. Carrigan slid the bolts back slowly, his hands shaking. There could be nothing good behind a door which locked from the outside.

The attic had been converted into the girls' sleeping quarters.

There were seven mattresses dotted across the bare wood floor and a cracked sink in the far corner. Next to it stood a portable toilet, the kind you would find on building sites or at music festivals. The smell was the same too, mulchy and rotten, hanging flat in the stale air. The mattresses were old and thin, overlaid with a patchwork of stains and bereft of sheets. The pillows still held the shape of their occupants' heads and the blankets were worn and frayed. There were two skylights but both had been panelled over with thick planks of wood, the nails hammered in tight against the window-frames. The room smelled of bad bone-shaking nightmares and four-in-the-morning agonies and he tried not to breathe the thick air, tried not to notice the stuffed rabbits and plastic Madonnas standing guard next to each mattress, the rolls of band-aids and lubricants.

DC Jennings came up behind him and took one look at the room. 'Oh my God,' he said, his face turning red and bright and his eyes blinking rapidly. 'We've been through the whole house,' he continued, getting his breath back, 'and no sign of Viktor any-where.'

'What do you mean no sign of him?' Carrigan turned so quickly that Jennings had to take a step back. 'He can't have just disappeared, can he?'

Jennings looked down at his shoes. 'I'm afraid that's what it looks like, sir.'

Carrigan sighed and tried to control his breathing. 'Fuck! How can that happen?'

'But we did find the drugs,' Jennings said, his voice rising in pitch.

'How much?'

'Maybe four or five ounces, all bagged in individual wraps, quite a haul.'

Jennings seemed pleased but Carrigan wasn't. 'That's not what we're looking for,' he snapped. 'There should be much more. Unbagged. There should be scales and cash. I want you to go through everything, especially the office, any computers, hard drives. They're going to say fuck all unless we have something on them we can use.' He watched as Jennings walked slowly down the stairs, his body folded in on itself as if all the air had been punched out of it.

Carrigan closed his eyes, took a deep breath then snapped on a pair of gloves and started searching the makeshift bedroom.

At least seven women had spent their nights here. The mattresses were crowded together in one part of the room as if the proximity would allow them some kind of protection against their keepers, or maybe it was just warmer that way. There were no heating appliances in the attic, the breath emerging from his mouth in thick foggy clumps.

The girls had tried to make it home with what little they could scavenge and it gave even the most quotidian of objects a sense of pathos. He tried to imagine the lives these girls had led, the constant dread and physical pain, the any-time-of-day call to go downstairs and do whatever some man who paid his money wanted them to do. They would close their eyes and think of the fields back home just before Christmas, their parents hunched over the stove, the pet dog they'd left behind. Then, when it was over, they'd fake one of a million fake smiles and silently trudge to the bathroom, rinse themselves, and go back to this drab and dusty room to drown themselves in their pillows.

37

The detainees from the raid were already sequestered in separate interview rooms when Carrigan got back to the station, their details being checked by constables and the attendant analysts recently brought into the case. Carrigan had gone through the interview strategy with his team earlier, his voice curiously detached. They all knew him well enough to know it was better to keep quiet when he got like this.

They'd watched the surveillance tapes until their eyeballs ached. There was no doubt it was Viktor who'd entered the premises a few minutes before the raid. The house had been searched top to bottom but no trace of Viktor had been found nor any way he could have escaped. Carrigan couldn't fucking believe it – the one man who had a definite link to the case had somehow managed to disappear right before their eyes.

They didn't have an Albanian translator but they didn't need one as the two bouncers didn't say a word between them. The first man spent the whole interview shaking his head genially and throwing his arms up in the air. The second man, the one with the widow's peak, was different.

Carrigan and Karlson sat opposite him in interview room number two. He was in his early thirties, his skin puckered and pitted with old acne scars. He smelled of lamb and wood-smoke.

'Where is he?' Carrigan sent the photo of Viktor spinning across the table.

The man could have been deaf for all the reaction he showed. His absolute stillness was unnerving. He leaned back in his chair and didn't answer any of their questions. His top row of silver teeth gleamed like spent shell casings in the stark white light of the inter-view room.

'We know he went inside. We saw him. Did he take the drugs with him?'

The man kept smiling, his eyes fixed on Carrigan's. They'd been in the room for forty-five minutes and he'd barely blinked. Carrigan could feel a drop of sweat making its way down his spine. It was no wonder the girls had been so terrified.

Carrigan took out the photos nestled in the green file beside him. The first was of the convent before the fire. He slid it across the desk. The man looked down at it as if it were a scrap of litter, then back up, his expression unchanged. 'The nuns warned you not to sell drugs in that alleyway, right? But you didn't listen and you didn't like them telling you how to run your business. You made several visits and, when they refused to stop, you burned down the convent and got rid of your little problem for the price of a box of matches.'

There was no reaction. If he looked closely, Carrigan could see his own reflection, fuzzy and upside down, in the man's gleaming wall of teeth. 'We know Duka was involved. We have Viktor on tape, visiting the convent.' He took out Emily's photo and flicked it across the table. 'What do you know about her?'

The man picked up the photo, looked at it, then crushed it in his hand, sending the crumpled ball spinning back across the table.

The woman was sitting by herself in a separate interview room. They'd left her there for the last hour and a half so that she could take stock of her situation. It was a general rule that the longer someone sat in an interview room by themselves the more compli-ant they became. They stared at the walls, at the constantly buzzing video camera, at their own faces in the one-way mirror. Expectation was often worse than reality.

Carrigan entered, followed by DC Singh. 'Do you understand why you're here?' he said, taking his seat.

The woman was wearing a lace top and short leather skirt. Her hair was in a tight, intricate bun that looked glazed. Her lipstick was smeared and her nails clattered rhythmically on the table.

'I've done nothing wrong,' she said, sounding almost as if she meant it.

'I'm not so sure about that,' Carrigan replied. 'You were caught in a house that was being used as a brothel. The girls, at least a couple of them, are underage. It's obvious you were the manager, madame, whatever.' He paused and watched as her face twitched and reacted, this last piece of information sinking in. 'Now, maybe we can't prove the rest. Maybe your bodyguards don't say anything, probably the girls will deny it all. But you were still found in an house with underage girls and that's a very serious offence here.'

The woman kept drumming her nails on the surface of the table. Under the harsh glare of the lights you could see the wrinkles and hard years etched on her face, all the small and not-so-small things she'd had to do to survive. Carrigan suspected she'd been a trafficked girl herself, working the endless night shift until she got too old, her skin too loose, her body wasted, and then instead of selling her off to someone else, they turned her into procurer and jailer. He rested his head in his hands, appalled by this cruel and logical cycle.

'I told you, I know nothing, now why you keep me here?'

'That might work if we hadn't found a thirteen- and fourteen-year-old girl on the premises.' He took out the photos and laid them flat on the table. 'This man assaulted a police officer. He's also wanted in connection with a murder and arson we're investigating,' Carrigan said, seeing the slight flicker of dread pass through the woman's eyes as she glanced at the photo of Viktor.

'He was sent by Duka to burn down the Sisters of Suffering convent last week, wasn't he?' He saw something in the woman's expression shift. 'I know you wouldn't have had anything to do with the murder of ten nuns but maybe you overheard something. Tell me what you know and I'll make the charges go away.'

The woman looked down at her hands, the skin folded and wrinkled like topography. 'There's nothing you can threaten me with that they won't deliver a hundred times over.'

'We can protect you,' Carrigan insisted, sensing a tiny crack in her wall. 'We can have you moved to a different city, give you a different name, you'll be untraceable and you'll be free.' It was his best shot. It was all she understood and all he could offer her.

But the madame only laughed that thin derisive wheeze again, empty of any human referent. 'You can protect me?' she said. 'You think so? Well, answer me this, detective, can you protect my son? My ten-year-old son who I haven't seen for three years?'

Carrigan was suddenly confused. He saw a spark in the woman's eyes that had previously been absent, a slight awakening from the torpor and crushed fatalism of a few minutes before. 'Son?'

'You think you know how this works but you know nothing,' she replied. 'Can you protect my son? Can you? My son who's being held by these men back home? You think I do this for fun? For money? The longer you hold me here the more likely it is they will do something to my son, so please, I do not know anything, I do not see anything, either lock me up or let me go before they think I have talked to you.' She looked him directly in the eyes, her last and everything in that naked glare.

*

Brothels in Bayswater were nothing new. The area had always been a conveniently located carnal playground, a pocket of anonymity and licence snuggled deep inside the heart of the city; a place where Victorian gentlemen had frequented the lavender-scented parlours of Porchester Terrace, returning soldiers had celebrated their survival in dusty Praed Street walk-ups, and where Rachman had ruled over a vast empire of sex and cold-water flats. The oil boom sheiks of the 1970s and wayward minor Gulf royals had gentrified the business at the same time as introducing a new undercurrent of medieval slavery and micro-audited profit margins. The break-up of the former Soviet Union had turned it into a finely tuned production line. Every building in the city had a story to tell and it was seldom a happy one.

Geneva sat at her computer, reading up about this, trying to control the rage racing through her. The girls they'd taken in had ranged from thirteen to seventeen years old. They were scared and broken. They whimpered and cried in the van on the way to the station. They'd been raped daily for as long as they could remember. And the men who'd made sure they did their job, who knew where to place a fist so that the bruise wouldn't spoil a customer's pleasure – those men were sitting in the room behind her.

She bumped into Carrigan in the corridor. He looked pained and drawn and she wondered, not for the first time, how long he could keep this up.

'SOCOs found a hidden door in the kitchen pantry,' he said. 'It leads out into the back alley. That's how Viktor got away. Bloody uniforms didn't spot it.'

'What about the girls?'

'I want to try talking to them,' Carrigan said. 'Then we'll speak to someone in immigration, see if we can get them sent back to their families. There's no way I'm releasing them back into the arms of those men.'

Geneva felt a little bit better as they headed back to the interview rooms.

The girls they'd found had all been seen to by FLOs, social workers and other support staff. Their reports made Carrigan's eyes water. They were mainly from Moldova, Belarus, the Ukraine. Trafficked through Sofia and Tirana, those beautifully named cities of sin and suffering. They were all in an advanced state of psychological distress, their bodies riddled with hidden bruises and cigarette burns.

Carrigan entered the first interview suite and saw the girl he'd discovered sleeping. She was the youngest one they'd found. She was sitting cross-legged in the corner of the room, her back against the wall, and she was crying and talking to herself, nodding vigorously, then shaking her head in mute disagreement. The social worker was sitting on a folding chair and when she saw Carrigan she gave him a look that spoke of profound sadness and frustration.

'I've got something for her,' he told the social worker, slowly making his way across the room. The girl flinched at each footstep, burying her face deep in her hands. Carrigan leaned down and took out the Snoopy he'd retrieved from under her pillow. She looked up, her eyes red and wet, and hesitated. Then she quickly grabbed the stuffed dog and clutched it tightly to her chest, sniffling into its downy fur. Carrigan got up, nodded to the social worker and left.

He stood in the corridor and thought about what he'd seen and what he'd heard. He didn't want to think about the possibility that they'd been wrong but he knew they were. He searched the incident room and interview suites until he found Geneva.

'I think we've got this all wrong,' he said.

Geneva was nodding before he could finish. 'We have,' she replied. 'Come . . .'

He followed her into the second interview suite. He kept his distance this time, sitting at the back of the room as Geneva took the chair opposite the girl.

At least she was a bit older, this one, maybe sixteen. Geneva placed a can of Coke in front of the girl, then said, 'Please tell us what you just told me.'

The girl opened the Coke and took a long sip. She was obviously a teenager but her eyes looked as weary as an old woman who'd seen several husbands and most of her children die.

'We talk to each other a lot,' the girl said, her voice heavily accented and hesitant. 'There is no one else we are allowed to speak to. Girls are moved from house to house, every week sometimes, so that we do not form any bonds, do not get comfortable and because . . .'

'Yes?'

'Because the men, they like, how you say? Variety? So yes, they switch us from house to house. I myself have been in about fifteen different houses since I came to this country. You never know when they'll take you somewhere else, how much worse it will be, what kind of men keep guard in the new place. But the girls talk and there are always rumours.'

'Rumours?'

The scrape of Carrigan's chair as he edged forward startled the girl.

'They say that if you manage to escape there are people who will help you hide.'

Carrigan felt the skin tighten against his bones and tried to keep as still as possible.

'What kind of people?' Geneva asked.

The girl laughed derisively. 'This, you understand, is like saying if you win lottery you can buy a new house. Escaping is almost impossible, only a few girls manage it. They make sure of that.'

Carrigan remembered the bolts on the door to the upstairs room, the two bouncers whose job wasn't to keep the customers in line but the girls. He couldn't stop thinking about these young women, the dreams they'd have nurtured about England, the rock bands and nightclubs and glamour parties, and then they finally make it here and all they see of the country is the interior of a locked room, the sweating overweight face of the bank manager pummelling their thighs.

'But there is this rumour that everyone keeps repeating,' the girl continued. 'That if you manage to escape there is a place near here where you can find shelter, a safe house, where they will keep you hidden from the men that will be sent to find you.'

'Do you know where?' Carrigan asked.

The girl shook her head. 'No. These are rumours, like I said, but the one thing they all seem to agree on is that if you manage to escape there is a group of women who will provide sanctuary and that these women are not ordinary women but women of God.'

'Women of God?'

The girl frowned. 'Yes . . . you know . . . ?'

Carrigan leaned forward, the pulse hammering in his neck. 'Do you mean nuns?'

The girl's eyes lit up, 'Yes, exactly. Nuns.'

III

'Many of the rebels had no weapon except sand.'

Vasily Grossman

38

The nuns had been sheltering escaped women and if the women knew about it, it was almost certain their captors did too. Geneva sat, thought about this, made notes, avoided going home. She told herself it was the case pressing against her, the spinning puzzlement of facts rolling through her brain, but when she closed her mouth she could still taste eagle-neck's fingers and feel the hot wet pulse of him on her tongue, and knew it was nothing to do with the case.

She spread the files and papers and interview transcripts across her desk. The incident room had been chaos all afternoon, the subjects from the raid being processed and booked, and now the girl's story about the nuns sheltering escapees had changed everything yet again. Geneva looked at the grainy photos from Peru, the picket lines and clenched fists, and wondered whether she'd been wasting her time – worse – whether she'd convinced Carrigan to allocate personnel and resources that could have been better used elsewhere. She scratched her wrist until the itching stopped and opened a fresh can of Coke. She hadn't thought it would be like this. She'd been on the murder squad just over a year now. It was what she'd thought she'd always wanted, but she hadn't realised the responsibility embedded in every choice she made, the lives and futures dangling in the balance. She knew she had to do better – work longer hours, read through everything again – whatever it took.

She printed off a large-scale map of Peru from the Internet and spread it out in front of her. The country looked hunchbacked and folded, an afterthought in the shadow of the Andes. She remembered from Emily's diary that the compound was located in the San Gabriel province and she quickly found the region, nestled between mountain and river. The nearest big town was Cusco. These coincidences no longer surprised her. The money from the nuns' bank account was funding Father McCarthy's compound.

It took her half an hour to find the right number. Another forty-five minutes to get clearance to make the call. Countless forms to fill out and endless waiting. She didn't know what she was expecting. She didn't know if the person on the other end would even speak English.

Commander Gamboa of the Cusco police force spoke English extremely well. He spoke it in that formal, almost stilted way that people do when they've learned it from old TV shows and news reports and it made her feel curiously homesick, the ghost of her mother rising through every inflection and malapropism.

'I was on my way out,' he said.

'Lucky I caught you, then.' She explained who she was and what she was working on. Gamboa kept saying *yes yes yes*, his impatience mounting, but when she mentioned the Tomorrow Foundation his tone changed completely.

'We have been very interested in that,' he said.

When Geneva told him about the convent and the money transfers he suddenly forgot the meeting he was rushing off to.

'We suspect the nuns were funding some kind of compound through this foundation but we have no idea why or what its purpose is.'

She heard something that might have been a chuckle on the other end of the line but there was so much static and buzz that it was hard to tell. 'So, you know about the compound?'

Geneva felt her stomach tumble. She wondered whether to bluff him but ended up going with the truth. 'Yes, we do.'

'Wait just one minute,' Gamboa said and disappeared off the line. He came back and told her he had the files up on his computer. 'As you can imagine,' he continued, his voice steady and soothing and so far away, 'we have been keeping an eye on this place for the last couple of years.'

'Do you know what it is?'

'We're not sure,' Gamboa admitted. 'It first came to our attention four years ago. No one knows how it started. One day there was just the bare ground and the next there was a small wooden shack. The fence went up first. The villagers asked the workmen what they were building but the workmen didn't know. The fence was laid over a large parcel of land. The land, when we traced it, was owned by the Tomorrow Foundation. Soon villagers reported construction day and night, power tools and diggers and bright lights.

'In town they began to notice a steady stream of outsiders passing through. They would stop for a night then disappear into the compound and were not seen again. We, the police, began to get interested. We saw priests and bishops, lawyers and soldiers come through town heading for the compound. A very curious collection of people. No one would tell us what it was or why they were headed there. The army provided us with some aerial shots but all we could see was how well organised and constructed it was.

'Shipments were being delivered by truck almost daily. We stopped several of these trucks and searched them but all we found were sizable quantities of food, tinned food, enough for years, even for a large group of people. There was no law against buying food so we had to let them go but then, roughly a year ago, we noticed that activities at the compound had stepped up and we began to hear rumours of priests making large purchases of guns and ammunition in Cusco and that was when we became really interested.'

Geneva thought about the timing of this, the £240,000 coming in from the convent every year. 'Did you come across any English nuns during the course of your investigation?'

'We came across many nuns and priests,' Gamboa replied. 'Did you have anyone in particular in mind?'

She told him what she knew of Sister Rose, her trip to Peru and subsequent disappearance.

'I know of the case,' Gamboa said. 'We never found out who killed the priest she was travelling with and we never found her body. Unfortunately, this is not so rare here as to warrant further inquiry.' Gamboa paused and she could hear a fan spinning somewhere in the room behind him.

'Do you have a person named Emily Maxted in your records?'

Gamboa was silent but she could hear him punching keys. 'Yes, here we go,' he said. 'She was arrested for taking part in an anti-mining protest in the Altiplana. When it was discovered she was a foreign national she was released and deported from the country.'

'When was this?' Geneva asked.

Gamboa took a minute to look it up. 'October 2011.'

'Any record of her linked to the compound?'

'No, not that I can see,' Gamboa replied. 'You know, I went up there one time. They had armed guards at the gate but they let me and my partner in. We met the English priest, Father McCarthy, and he showed us around and told us that the compound was there to help minister to the spiritual needs of the people, but I saw the locked doors, the safety provisions and alarms, the frightened look in people's faces.'

She heard the slow pulse of the phone's static holding all the words Gamboa hadn't been able to say. 'What happened?'

'We were taken off the case.'

Geneva gripped the phone tightly between her fingers. 'Why?'

'The federal police took over,' Gamboa replied. 'It's standard procedure when these kinds of issues are involved.'

'Issues? What do you mean?'

There was a pause and she thought he'd said all he was going to say and then she heard him light a cigarette, the slow sizzle and exhale. 'The compound had been mentioned in connection to a spate of incidents.'

'Incidents? What kind of things are we talking about?'

'I'm afraid that is classified. You'll have to go through Lima to get that information.' He paused and she could hear him scratch his stubble. 'Or you could use the Internet,' he whispered, and hung up.

39

Roger Holden was on the phone, laughing at something in a boom-
ing baritone as he watched Carrigan and Miller barge into his office, his expression unaltered except for a quickly subsumed frown.

'I would say what a pleasant surprise, Inspector.' Holden put
down the phone. 'But somehow, I don't think this is going to be all
that pleasant.'

'That would be entirely up to you,' Carrigan replied.

Holden looked down at the folder on his table then carefully
closed it. 'Yes, quite,' he answered. 'May I ask how the investigation
is going?'

'As well as can be expected,' Carrigan said. 'We're just trying to
tie up some loose ends and there are a few questions you can help
us with.'

Holden smiled but this time there was no warmth to it. 'Fine, but
I'm afraid we'll have to keep this short. I have a video conference
with the Vatican all day tomorrow and I need to prepare . . .'

'Why did you lie to us?' Geneva interrupted.

Holden turned towards her. His face was expressionless but a
small muscle jumped under his right eyelid. 'I don't believe I lied to
you, Miss . . . ?'

'It's Detective Sergeant Miller, as you well know,' Geneva
replied, taking a thick handful of papers from her bag. She took her
time shuffling through them. They'd talked about their strategy on
the way over. She would present her latest findings on the nuns,
press Holden for why the church was covering up, and then Carrigan would come in swinging with the final blow. She took a little
more time than was necessary finding the right papers and coughed

and took off her glasses and wiped them on her blouse and put them back on. 'You told us you only had a minor argument over theology with the convent but that wasn't true, was it?'

Holden twirled the ring on his finger, mouth pursed. 'What exactly do you mean, Miss Miller? I'm afraid you'll have to be more specific if you expect me to answer you.'

Geneva bit the inside of her lip. Since talking to Father Spaulding she'd been doing further research, staying up late, long scratchy hours on the Internet, waste-of-time phone calls, digging and delving into old files and dusty archives. 'You said that it was a minor dispute but I've heard it was much more serious than that.' She passed over a photocopied page of the *Catholic Tribune* from last July. 'It says here that the convent was involved in a dispute not only with the diocese but also with their own order. It says the dispute went up the chain all the way to the Vatican.'

Holden considered her silently for a moment. 'And you believe everything you read in the press?'

'No, Mr Holden, I do not. Which is why I sent an official request for information to both the Vatican and the order's headquarters in Rome. I didn't think they would get back to me but they did. I was told that the convent, Mother Angelica in particular, had been censured three times in the last five years. When I dug a little deeper, I discovered that there's a motion floating around the Vatican to excommunicate the nuns. It looks as if – had the nuns not been murdered – they would have been excommunicated from the church at the beginning of the new year.' She passed across the relevant papers and typed transcripts. Holden picked them up and perused them slowly, stroking his chin and nodding his head as he did so.

'You must understand that we in the church like to keep things in house,' he finally said. 'I imagine it's not too different from the police force. You have your own internal investigation department and so do we; likewise we do not publicise every little coming and going within the church.'

'You haven't answered my question.'

The edge of Holden's mouth crumpled slightly. 'Yes, the convent was under investigation and yes, there was a motion for excommunication that the order was going to vote on after Christmas, but I can't see how that has anything to do with your case.'

'Everything that happens has something to do with the case,' Geneva said. 'And the fact you lied to us in the initial interview is something we do not forget. You made this seem as if the nuns were just innocent victims of some crazed arsonist – wrong time, wrong place – yet the more we find out the more that theory flies in the face of every bit of evidence. The nuns had secrets, Mr Holden. These secrets leave traces. We're giving you one last chance to explain before we take this further.'

Holden stared at her, a silent calculation clicking away in his eyes. 'What exactly did you want to know?'

Geneva smiled to herself, relieved and a little surprised that she'd read him right. 'What did the nuns do to get themselves excommunicated?'

'They took things into their own hands,' Holden said, and this time there was something else in his expression other than the usual disdain. He blinked, then pressed a button and told his secretary to hold all calls for the next fifteen minutes. 'I wasn't lying when I said it was a matter of theology.' He leaned forward, sighing, his arms crossed in front of him. 'Mother Angelica was stationed for several years in South America. I'm sure your research has led you to an understanding of this thing called liberation theology? Mother Angelica became too involved in the worldly sphere when she was in Peru. She got herself into a little trouble and had to be transferred.'

'You're talking about the Chiapeltec massacre?' Geneva pulled out a set of grainy black-and-white photos and spread them across the table. 'I would call that more than a little trouble.'

'There were death threats against her,' Holden conceded. 'We moved her to England to save her life.'

'And to save your reputations, right? You put her here, right under your noses where she couldn't get into trouble.'

'You really don't know what you're talking about, do you?' Holden said, a slight amusement in his tone. 'You have no idea.'

'Then tell us.'

'We had to relocate Mother Angelica because of the death threats. I wasn't lying about that.'

'Death threats from whom? The government?'

Holden nodded. 'There was that, but we were more worried about the threats coming from the other side, from the workers and survivors of Chiapeltec.'

Geneva felt something in her chest pop. 'Why . . . why would they want to kill her?'

'You know about the bomb which killed all those people, derailed the strike and led to the massacre? We got word that rumours, credible rumours at that, were spreading through the villages that Mother Angelica had brought in the Scarlet Fire. That she'd okayed the use of the bomb. We had no idea whether this was true or not but it was enough that people believed it to be so. We had to get her out of there.'

Geneva sat back, stunned. She let the words run through her brain and nothing in there contradicted them. 'Do you think it's possible what happened at the convent is a direct consequence of that?'

Holden shrugged. 'People kill each other for nothing, Detective Sergeant, you know that. For something like this, who's to say?'

'So, you brought her back here to get her out of harm's way, but it didn't work, did it?'

Holden leaned back, eyes plagued with useless hindsight and careful deliberation. 'We monitored her closely and, for many years, it seemed that the change of location had served its purpose.

Mother Angelica poured herself into outreach work, into helping the homeless and drug-sick and many other worthy causes. The church lifted the censure, happy that she'd focused her liberationist tendencies on more fruitful ground.

'Then we began to hear rumours. That she was recruiting nuns who'd fought alongside her at Chiapeltec. That she was withdrawing from her missionary work. That she'd finally finished the book she'd been working on for so many years.

'One of the nuns who left the convent after a dispute with Mother Angelica told us about this book – a calculus of violence – a mathematical procedure which would tell you whether violence in any particular situation was justified or not. You can imagine the furore this caused when news of its contents leaked out. The church does not sanction violence under almost any circumstances, certainly not violence by an individual.' Holden shook his head, in resignation, despair or disapproval, Geneva couldn't tell. Maybe all three. 'What these people failed to understand was that Jesus was not some bearded anarchist liberator saving the oppressed from the tyranny of the state, but a spiritual liberator who saved them from the tyranny of their own hearts.

'We approached Mother Angelica and voiced our concerns but she wouldn't listen to us. She was called to the order's headquarters in the Vatican and told about the excommunication ruling. She refused to recant the book's teachings and stop publication. The excommunication was only a formality after that.'

'This was all about a book?' Geneva said, surprised, despite herself, at what some people chose to stake their lives on.

Holden laughed. 'Isn't everything?' He sipped carefully from his glass. 'The difference here is that Mother Angelica's book wasn't theoretical – it was meant to be used as an instruction manual in direct action. Its publication would have been a severe embarrassment to the church.'

'More so than what they were doing in Peru?'

Holden stared at Geneva. 'I'm afraid I don't know what you mean.'

'No, of course not,' Geneva replied. 'We, however, do know that Father McCarthy was involved in running a compound in rural Peru that the convent was funding. We know Emily Maxted met him there.'

'I have no idea what you're talking about,' Holden replied. 'Our remit is London, not Peru or anywhere else.'

'Still, kind of convenient for you that they all disappeared in a puff of smoke,' Carrigan said.

Holden turned slowly towards him, his face pale and rigid. 'What, exactly, are you insinuating?'

'I'm not insinuating anything, I'm just making a statement. The excommunication of the nuns would have been bad press – and you've had a lot of bad press recently. This solves the problem rather neatly.'

'You're not seriously suggesting . . .' Holden paused. 'I'm going to speak to ACC Quinn about this. He's a good friend of the bishop, as you well know. It'll be interesting to see what he has to say about your theories.'

'At this point,' Carrigan continued, knowing he was almost halfway there, 'all we know is that these nuns of yours were not the perfect, saintly beings you made them out to be. They made enemies in South America. Five of them had been tortured for their beliefs. They were involved in things we're only just beginning to grasp. And we now have strong indications that this may have led to their deaths.' He paused, watching Holden carefully. 'The eleventh victim, Emily Maxted, was spending a lot of time at the convent. She even slept in a room downstairs. We need to know why she was a regular visitor and what she was doing there that particular night. We know she knew Father McCarthy. He's the only one left alive who knows what linked Emily and the nuns. And you keep telling us he's unavailable, on retreat, whatever. It almost sounds like you're trying to cover something up. We need to speak to him, Mr Holden.'

Holden's gaze drifted to the grey filing cabinets lined up against the far wall, then back towards the two detectives as he considered this, or pretended to be considering it, his fingers tapping against the armrest. 'No,' he finally said. 'I'm afraid I'm not at liberty to divulge his whereabouts. I suppose you could try and get a warrant but you'll have to go through ACC Quinn first.'

'I thought you'd say that,' Carrigan replied. 'So, you see, we have a back-up plan . . .'

'Back-up plan?'

'We need to find Father McCarthy and we need to find him ASAP. As you're not willing to give us the information, we have no choice but to go public with our inquiries.' He stopped and waited, faintly aware that he was holding his breath.

'Public? Do you mean . . . ?'

Carrigan tried not to smile. 'A full press conference, this time telling the public everything we know about the nuns.'

'You can't do that.' Holden was leaning forward, his arms clenched against the table, fingers pressing tight against the edges.

'It's the only option you've left us with.'

'What . . . what are you going to say?'

'Exactly what we have. That we believe the nuns were sheltering escaped prostitutes. That they were running a safe house for these women and that the Albanians weren't particularly happy with this turn of events and burned down the convent to teach them a lesson.'

Holden's face had gone white. The phone on the table started ringing but he barely looked at it. 'Whores?'

'We believe the nuns were no longer happy to feed the homeless or minister to the junk-sick, that they had stepped up their "work" and were running a shelter for escaped women, women who'd been trafficked as sex slaves.'

'Oh my God,' Holden said, his head collapsing into his hands.

'You can imagine what the papers will do,' Carrigan continued, feeling the crackle and buzz running through each word. 'Full-page spreads, shocked commentaries, calling you up non-stop for quotes. With Christmas only a few days away, this will be their big story. Now, I know how much bad press the church has garnered over the last few years, seems you can't open a paper any more without reading about a paedophile priest or some former altar boy suing the pope. As press officer for the diocese, I'm sure it's the last thing you or your bosses would want.'

Holden stared at Carrigan, motionless as a marble statue. He finally looked down at the table and picked up the phone. He spoke briefly to his secretary then typed something on his keyboard. 'I have to step out for a moment. I'm sure you two can see yourselves out.' He stood up, looked down at them, frowned and left the room.

Carrigan got up, closed the door and walked over to the row of filing cabinets lined up against the far wall.

'What are you doing?'

'Each time I mentioned Father McCarthy's whereabouts, Holden glanced in this direction,' he explained, pulling open the top drawer of the nearest cabinet. The metal screeched against the sides, making Geneva jump. 'Keep an eye on the corridor,' Carrigan told her as he bent over the cabinet and started flicking through the folders.

She opened the door and looked out, then ducked back in. 'We shouldn't be doing this,' she said, but he could hear the lack of conviction in her tone.

'It's the only way we're going to find Father McCarthy,' he replied, opening the bottom drawer. 'And that's more important than confidentiality issues right now.' He went to the next cabinet, stopped and looked at her. 'You have a problem with this?'

She shook her head and he turned back to the cabinet.

The files were arranged alphabetically. There were several Father

McCarthys and it took Carrigan a couple of minutes to find the right one. A burst of footsteps sounded from the corridor outside. Carrigan quickly replaced the file and waited until they receded, holding his breath. Geneva stuck her head out the door, then gave him the all-clear.

The folder was thick and bulging with stray papers, photos and official documentation. It would have undoubtedly made for very interesting reading. A door slammed somewhere outside, followed by raised voices echoing down the corridor, getting closer. Carrigan flicked to the back of the file and looked at the last entry. It was a transfer form for Father McCarthy, dated 15 December and signed by Roger Holden. Carrigan scanned the photocopied sheet until he saw the address stamped in the bottom left-hand corner. He took out his notebook and started copying it down. Geneva glanced out the door and immediately popped her head back in, signalling that someone was coming. Carrigan finished writing and replaced the file in the cabinet. He crossed the room and showed Geneva the address.

She stared at it for a long moment and was about to say something when her phone rang. Carrigan's beeper went off at the same time. They looked at each other silently. Geneva scanned the text Jennings had sent. She saw Carrigan fiddling with his phone, trying to access his inbox, and turned towards him. 'They've found Nigel.'

40

They sat and waited on the cold metal benches while the pathologist got the body ready. Carrigan had booked their train tickets to Yorkshire for tomorrow and he was impatient to talk to Father McCarthy, his feet tapping the tiled floor. Orderlies came and went, their faces turned into blank expressions of boredom as a shield against the mounting horror of their days. Like emergency rooms, Christmas was the busy period in the morgue.

Geneva's phone broke the silence. She ignored the sharp looks and narrowed glances and checked the display. There were no messages from Oliver. There were no messages from Lee. She'd sent Lee a text in reply to his. And then she'd sent another one because the first wasn't quite what she'd wanted to say. But he hadn't answered and she wondered if that part of her life was over too.

Milan was waiting for them downstairs, drinking from a large mug of milky coffee and flicking through a book in French. A radio was sitting on a shelf behind him, blaring fuzzy football commentary in what sounded like Serbian, a shock of cracking consonants and garbled imprecation, spluttered, spoken and shouted.

'Ah, Mr Carrigan,' Milan said, brushing back his hair and getting to his feet. 'I didn't think I'd be seeing you again so soon. I sent your superior the latest . . .'

'This is about the body that came in a couple of hours ago,' Carrigan interrupted, his eyes scanning the humped tables, each corpse a mystery to itself and others.

'Of course, I should have known that would be one of yours too,'

Milan said. 'They all like this, your cases?'

'That's what your predecessor thought.'

'And look where that got her.'

Carrigan closed his eyes. He felt frazzled and enervated, so tired he could barely stand straight. He knew it wouldn't be long. Could feel it in every twitch and ping of muscle. Too much coffee, too little sleep and the spiralling data from the case all burning through his synapses like runaway horses. 'Just tell me what you've got.'

'Okay. Yes. Very interesting. I only managed to have a quick look but that tells me almost all I need to know. Your man did not die easy, someone certainly had their fun with him.'

Geneva exchanged glances with Carrigan, the giddy exuberance of only an hour ago replaced with a raw dread in her eyes as Milan walked over to the nearest gurney and pulled the sheet. Both Carrigan and Geneva had to swallow down their revulsion as they stared at what remained of Nigel the Nail.

It didn't look much like a human body any more. There were small red marks and huge black swellings dotted across his torso and legs. He was missing two fingers, four toes and his right eye. His mouth had been sewn shut with fine white thread and in the dazzle of lights it looked as if he'd swallowed a spider-web. He vaguely resembled the man in the mugshots and photos. He barely resembled a man.

'Are you sure it's him?' Carrigan asked.

Milan laughed disdainfully and lifted the corpse's arms, the skin quivering like jelly as the broken bones settled within. Milan turned the arm around and they could see that the burns and marks stopped at Nigel's fingers. 'They made sure to leave his fingertips untouched,' Milan said, 'the fingers they left him with, that is.'

'How long has he been dead for?'

'Between twelve and twenty-four hours.'

Carrigan noticed the pathologist seemed distracted even as he was talking to them, his head tilting in a tell-tale gesture towards the radio whenever the announcer's voice suddenly rose in pitch as it did now. Milan's whole body stiffened. The radio blared and roared and the announcer shouted – *GOAL!* – a punctured holler that almost blew the speakers, the one word repeated like a burst of machine-gun fire, transcending all language and culture. Milan squeezed his eyes shut and sighed and turned back towards the body.

'They took their time with him,' he said, pointing to the long serrated ridge of scars and wounds along Nigel's torso, a tapestry of burn and blister, the colours blending from pink to yellow to stark black. 'This was done over a period of days, not hours, understand?'

Geneva's head was spinning. 'Tell me exactly what they did to him,' she said, her voice distant and brittle.

'What didn't they, young lady?' Milan sniffed, his lips disappearing behind his bushy black beard. 'The people who did this, they were artists in their field. The Tintorettos of torture. The Picassos of pain. See those black and brown marks?' Milan pointed to a set of curiously uniform wounds on Nigel's torso. 'Best guess is they used a cattle prod, and they used it repeatedly, mainly down below,' he said, indicating Nigel's groin. 'There is not much left of the private areas,' he pointed to the dark smear of bruises spiralling up both thighs. 'They spent a lot of time on this region . . .'

'Jesus.' Geneva looked away but the bright gleaming metal surfaces and gargled sound of blood sluicing down the drain wasn't much better. 'How can anyone's body stand so much pain?'

'You'd be surprised at how much the body wants to survive even long after the soul has given up,' Milan said. 'Of course, it helps that whoever did this kept reviving him.'

'Reviving him?' Carrigan leaned forward, shocked by his own capacity to still be shocked by the acts of men.

Milan indicated a faint line of bruises along Nigel's chest. 'Those are from a defibrillating machine. This man was artificially revived several times so that he could face more torture. He was . . .' Milan blinked, cocking his head towards the radio, his attention snared by the commentary. Carrigan glared at the pathologist, walked over and turned it off.

'There's only ten minutes left,' Milan protested.

'Good,' Carrigan replied. 'Gives you an incentive to hurry up and tell us what we need to know.'

Milan stared at Carrigan, then shook his head and turned towards the corpse. 'They tortured this man with a variety of instruments. We'll send the tool marks off to the lab but there's not much doubt they'll find these men used screwdrivers, chisels and pliers, as well as more sophisticated electrical devices. We'll know better once I open him up, but it's not going to be pretty in there, that I can tell from the outside.'

'They did all this to get information?' Geneva asked.

Milan shook his head, his eyes almost disappearing behind the black bags of skin couched underneath his lids. 'You still don't understand, do you? This has nothing to do with information. This kind of torture is way too extreme for that, the man wouldn't have been able to speak. No, this was for fun, or for what some people call fun, or for something I don't even want to think about.'

'You've seen this kind of thing before, though?' Carrigan said.

Milan looked down at the floor. 'I thought that by coming to this country I wouldn't see such things again . . . but nowhere is really different from anywhere else, is it?'

'It was a professional job, then, in your estimation?'

'Oh yes. Whoever did this has had plenty of practice.'

Carrigan flashed back to videos he'd seen of what the Mexican cartels did to their enemies – faces of children flayed and stitched to soccer balls left in their parents' front garden, men naked and mutilated hanging from underpasses in the city centre, rows of severed heads in the desert. The cruelty and level of sophistication Milan was describing fitted. It felt like Duka's work and it made

304

him wonder if they'd underestimated Nigel's role in this all along.

'There's something else,' Milan said as he walked over to a silver wall-mounted table and picked up a small pair of scissors. 'We did an initial X-ray and that's when I noticed it.' He squeezed his fingers through the tiny hoops and began to cut the thread which held Nigel's mouth closed. His movements were delicate and fleet, belying his size and bearing. He unsnipped the last piece of thread and gently lowered the jaw, then angled the lights until he was satisfied. He bent over the gurney and carefully inserted his fingers into the corpse's mouth. Carrigan and Geneva watched as he pulled his hand back out and opened it to reveal several burnt matches.

41

She sat in the canteen and tried to focus on the food in front of her but all she could see in the red tangles of pasta were the twisted and torn remains of Nigel, the smell coming off his body, sour and earthy, the pathologist's last words as he flipped the corpse over. She pushed the plate away, finished her coffee and went back upstairs.

Carrigan was in his office, the door shut. She checked on the constables and uniforms, making sure they each had their assigned tasks and duties for the day, then made her way to her desk.

She couldn't stop thinking about what the Peruvian policeman had told her over the phone, that last whispered comment of his. She thought about the particular words he'd used and emphasised – *incidents* and *federal* – and then she was typing into the search box, her finger hitting the return key with a satisfying thunk.

She scrolled down the search results, surprised at how many there were. She opened a separate window for each article and spent the next hour reading about strikes and sabotage – pipelines vandalised in the high mountain night, mine equipment monkey-wrenched into obsolescence, bombs strapped to the backs of donkeys in the marketplace. There were articles saying that the Shining Path were back and the old ways about to resume. Other articles argued that the Shining Path were a spent force and that these incidents were nothing but random grievances played out under hot sun and pale sky. She read about corpses dipped in battery acid and children's skulls placed along the highway like traffic markers. She learned about the cocaine corridors running across the dark jungle and threading through the ancient mountains, rival gang shootouts, army incursions, the endless and familiar spiral of blood and revenge.

She wrote down dates in a separate page in her notebook. Bombs, strikes, assassinations, kidnappings, drug hauls. She ordered the dates chronologically, then brought up the file for Sister Glenda's trips in a new window. She remembered the dates she'd noticed in the pub before Oliver had turned up, before . . . she shook her head, took three deep breaths and focused back on her task. Her eyes flicked across the screen. Her pulse strained against her skin. Her mouth went dry. She felt the tug and urge for a cigarette but she ignored it as she compared the two sets of dates.

During the week of Sister Glenda and Sister Rose's trip to Peru, a mine in the San Gabriel region had been shut down for three days due to a sabotaged generator. On Sister Glenda's first return trip, a pipeline in the remote Acarilla range had been destroyed by a home-made explosive device. Sister Glenda's third trip coincided with the kidnap of a company executive.

Geneva double-checked the dates. Each of Sister Glenda's subsequent visits fell during a week in which an incident had occurred in the province. She looked up the incidents and saw they were all directed at mine and logging operations. She began to discern a pattern – a peaceful strike broken with hoses and tear gas and bullets, followed by an act of sabotage against that company's property. She saw the gradual escalation, the inexorable drift from strikes and walk-outs to vandalised equipment to murder, and she wondered, once again, just what on earth had the nuns been up to?

42

The city never ended. You could look in any direction and there it was, chasing the horizon. And yet Carrigan could think of no other place he'd rather be than up here on the roof, alone, in the spray and slash of wind, twelve floors of activity below him and only the dark sky above.

He'd hated the new building when they'd moved in last year. The ergonomically planned cookie-cutter offices, the persistent smell of new carpet and paint, the constant hum of the air conditioners and computer monitors. And then he'd found the roof. No one else seemed to know about it, or care. You took the lift to the top floor, past Branch's office and up a set of stairs, then through a door that said Do Not Open, and suddenly the city was gone and you found yourself alone in sky and wind.

He'd spoken to Karen again, a conversation rendered in hushed tones and silent expectation, and they'd made a tentative arrangement to meet up for Christmas dinner at her flat. It left him feeling a bit better as he unwrapped a bar of chocolate and watched London lying hidden under a soft blanket of snow. Days like these, you could almost forget the daily evils and petty feuds which occurred in the city's shuttered houses, the lost and broken people dragging themselves through its cold closed streets.

The snow had begun again, small round fluffs falling at his feet and turning the air into a random dance of particles. Behind him, cars flashed on the elevated motorway, fleet and shiny, on their way to somewhere else. He remembered how Louise had always insisted he come outside with her at the first sign of snow. They would huddle in the hallway, donning thick coats and hats, and

God, how he missed the electric sting of her excitement as they stepped out onto the street, her eyes and heart instantly ensnared by the wonder of falling things.

But he couldn't make the memory last. The case came roaring back, scuttling his thoughts. The girls hadn't talked. They'd had to release the suspects from the brothel raid for lack of evidence. Carrigan had contacted immigration and detailed Jennings to make sure the girls would be processed and fed and sent back to their own country and kin. It wasn't much but it was better than nothing.

He thought about Geneva, how the state of Nigel's body had shocked her – he could tell by her silence in the morgue and the way the skin above her cheekbones rippled as she stared at the torn remains. The torture bore all the hallmarks of Duka and the matches seemed a message directed at them. But what kind of message was Duka sending? Were the matches an indicator of Nigel's guilt, Duka having heard about the raid and wanting no further interruption of business? Or were they a big fuck-you from the Albanian boss? And what did Duka and Nigel the Nail have to do with each other? Carrigan didn't want to contemplate the possibility that if Nigel was indeed the arsonist then the trail and the case were, literally, dead.

But Nigel didn't make sense. And he didn't make sense just when things were beginning to make sense. If the nuns had been sheltering escaped women then the fire was an act of retribution and a warning to others. But Nigel kept poking at Carrigan like a stray burr. Nigel and Emily – the two pieces of the puzzle that didn't fit. Tomorrow he would go with Geneva to a small monastery high up on the North Yorkshire moors and finally talk to Father McCarthy and maybe he would understand a little more. He finished his last piece of chocolate as the stairwell door slammed shut, a harsh burst of sound ripping through the clean crisp air. Carrigan turned and saw DS Byrd coming towards him, a dark deranged figure flecked by blowing drifts of snow.

'You bastard,' Byrd yelled when he was twenty feet away, 'you fucking bastard.' Byrd was speeding up now, feet slapping against the asphalt, his face twisted and canted, arms raised wildly at his sides. 'Idiot.' Byrd leaped and threw himself against Carrigan.

Carrigan flew backwards, his arm scraping painfully against the rough gravel, pain shooting up his back, his vision blurring.

'Get up, you cunt,' Byrd screamed.

Carrigan's head was a foot away from the twelve-storey drop down into the waiting snow. The wind felt like razor wire as it whipped across his torn skin. He rolled over on his side, away from the yawning ledge, and got to his feet warily, fighting a burst of dizziness and straightening his collar. 'What the fuck do you think you're doing?'

'I should be asking you the same question.' It was obvious that Byrd had been drinking and that he'd been drinking for a long time. His face was flushed, his jacket flung open, his zip half undone. His breath was sour and rank and his hands were curled into tight fists.

Carrigan slowly moved away from the edge and steadied himself against the adjoining wall, getting his breath back, all the time keeping his eyes on Byrd. 'What the hell are you talking about?'

Byrd hovered over him, the muscles under his shirt popping and flexing, his eyes blinking rapidly. 'All fucking innocent now, aren't you? You piece of shit.' Byrd dived at him and Carrigan managed to sidestep most of the impact but not all. Byrd's shoulder caught him on the collarbone and sent him spinning against the wall. The hard concrete crashed against his spine as Byrd pressed his left arm crosswise against Carrigan's throat.

'You screwed everything up. Jesus! Where the fuck was your head? I told you to tell me if you were going to do anything like this and what do I get? Fuck all from you and then I read the serials and see you've gone and busted one of the places we had under surveillance, one of the places I told you we had under surveillance.' Byrd jammed the side of his arm deeper into Carrigan's throat, the bone pressing hard against his Adam's apple.

Carrigan was about to say something, then stopped.

'You wanted me to go in, didn't you?' The realisation ran down his body in soft shuddered jumps. 'You wouldn't have been so free with the addresses otherwise.' He looked for Byrd to deny it. 'What? You couldn't get enough for a warrant? You knew that once I spotted Viktor I'd go in, didn't you? You were hoping I'd rattle Duka's cage for you.'

Byrd pushed against him harder, his knee pressing deep into Carrigan's thigh. 'I don't know what you're talking about. You screwed up a major operation and you got everyone killed. Happy?' He backed off and Carrigan managed to get his breath back, doubling over, his hands planted on his knees so that Byrd wouldn't see them shaking.

'What do you mean, I got everyone killed?'

Byrd shook his head, depleted by his efforts or by Carrigan's ignorance, it was hard to tell which. 'What the fuck's the point now? They're dead and you killed them.'

'We closed down a brothel with thirteen-year-old sex slaves in it. That's what matters. That's what I care about.'

Byrd turned and spat on the ground, his breathing heavy and laboured. 'Those bouncers you arrested – you know what's going to happen to them? Haven't talked, have they? Kept their mouths shut, denied everything, right? You've probably already had to let them go – tell me, how am I doing?'

Carrigan didn't need to nod, the expression on his face confirming everything Byrd had said.

'You know what's going to happen to them the minute they're released? Duka's never going to be sure how much they said or didn't say in that interview room. Better safe than sorry is how Duka got where he is. They're probably dead already or strapped to a chair in a warehouse somewhere, getting more intimate than they thought possible with a Black and Decker. Frankly, I don't give a shit about them, it's what they deserve. But they'll do the same to the madame, can't trust her now, can they? Maybe she made a deal with you.'

Carrigan shook his head but he knew that Byrd was telling the truth and that he'd been too rash or too naive or just too damn stupid to realise this before he'd gone charging in. He thought of the madame's son locked away somewhere in Albania and the way she couldn't stop tapping her fingernails against the table as if she needed a constant reminder that this was all real and not some nightmare conjured up from fear and ancient dread.

'We saved the girls,' Carrigan protested. 'While you were doing your surveillance and gathering evidence, those underage girls were being raped in there. We got them out and we're going to make sure they get back home.'

Byrd seemed almost sorry for him when he replied. 'Do you have any idea what's going to happen to those girls when they get home?' He laughed, a cruel derisive wheeze scraped from the back of his throat. 'Home is run by these thugs. Guess what they'll do to them when they reach Albania?'

'I don't want to know.'

'Well, fuck that, this is on your head.' Byrd grabbed Carrigan's collar and cinched it between his fists. 'Those girls will be picked up from the airport. They'll be taken to a safe house somewhere in the country. They'll be beaten and tortured for a month, maybe two, both as punishment and to see what you guys said to them, what they may have said to you. Then comes the good part. They're damaged goods now, so they'll be sold off for the hard stuff – you know, the guy who likes to bite off nipples when he comes, the one who likes to get inventive with instruments, to use animals and get off on the screams – they've entered the lowest rung of whore hell, thanks to you. Believe me, they'll wish they were back there in the brothel.'

Byrd shoved Carrigan hard against the wall, shook his head in disgust and walked away, disappearing into a blind haze of dirty snow.

43

Carrigan and Geneva picked the car up in Leeds. The train station was swarming with young men wearing tight white T-shirts, their arms clasped around tawny blondes in pencil skirts and impossible heels. They were coming in from the outlying towns to buy presents, get drunk and fight. Carrigan thanked God he was no longer working street patrol.

The car was tiny, not at all what he'd booked over the Internet. It looked more like a rich kid's toy than something that could get them to Burnham monastery.

Carrigan was squeezed into the driver's seat, the steering wheel crashing against his knees with each bump of the road as Geneva smoked quietly out the side window. They left the high-rise apartment blocks and grey flyovers behind them and entered a blank and featureless world, devoid of form and shape, as if some creator had wiped the slate clean, unsatisfied with his creation.

As they climbed away from the city the snow started falling in heavy spiralling drifts, the wipers working frenetically, screaming and squeaking against the windscreen. Carrigan saw Geneva texting, reading an incoming message and smiling, then trying to hide it, her brows knotted together in a tight squiggle above her eyes. He was glad there was someone whose texts could make her smile and clutch her phone a little tighter but the look in her eyes was complicated by a fleeting shadow that crossed her face.

They drove in silence for the next thirty minutes, the motorway deserted as it humped and straddled the rolling sea of moors. It was a landscape without feature, made doubly so by the thick layers of snow. Silence enveloped them so that all they could hear was the wet slap of the tyres and their own ragged breathing.

A few minutes later Geneva pointed to an unmarked road curving off from the motorway and Carrigan swerved into the narrow opening. The car heaved and groaned as the surface of the road deteriorated. The snow had been cleared overnight, great ridged humps on either side of the tarmac, but the wind was blowing it back in slanted drifts that twirled and scurried along the surface of the road.

The monks had seen their approach for miles, a tiny black speck on the horizon steadily growing in size. One of them was standing by a big wooden door built into the surrounding wall. Carrigan got out of the car, put on his jacket and rubbed the feeling back into his hands. They trudged through deep drifts, the trees sleeved with snow, the wind howling at their backs, forcing them to walk bent over, and he was out of breath by the time they reached the gate.

'Bit far from home, aren't you?' the monk said, peering through old-fashioned Coke-bottle glasses at his warrant card. Despite the thin robe and bitter wind, he didn't seem at all affected by the weather.

'We're here to speak to Father McCarthy,' Carrigan said, watching his breath cloud and fog in the frigid air. 'We've come up from London.'

'You'll be wasting your time, then,' the monk replied, not discourteously. He looked like some minor functionary in a vast system, an apparatchik without conviction, grey and remorseless. 'We don't allow visitors.'

'We're not visitors, we're investigating a murder.' Carrigan's feet were beginning to turn numb and he could feel the first dull throb of a bad headache. 'Roger Holden gave his express permission,' he said, his voice steady, eyes unblinking.

'This is a private facility. There's no visitors.' The man tried to sound firm but the jitter in his eyes gave him away.

'Call Holden,' Carrigan said. 'Ask him yourself. I don't have time to waste.'

The monk was undecided for a moment, then, surprisingly, plucked a mobile from the folds of his gown. He looked up at Carrigan and dialled. Carrigan watched as the man talked to Holden's secretary, his voice turning deferential and unctuous.

'Mr Holden's in a video conference and unavailable all day,' the monk said, a smile appearing on his face. 'And without talking to him, I can't let you in.'

Carrigan took a step forward, until they were breathing the same air. 'This is a murder investigation,' he said. 'This is about ten dead nuns and whether we find out who killed them or not, do you understand?'

The monk gave the slightest of nods.

'You can let me in,' Carrigan continued in his most reasonable voice. 'Or you can come back with me to the nearest police station on an obstruction charge.'

The monk didn't reply. He stared out at the white wasteland behind them, then nodded imperceptibly and turned, leaving the gate open.

They followed him into a large courtyard surrounded by huge stone walls. They had expected it to be empty and were surprised to see seven or eight priests working the frozen fields. They wore threadbare gowns and no gloves, sandals on their tiny gnarled feet, and they were wielding shovels and scythes, digging and furrowing the hard icy ground. None of the priests showed the slightest interest in them, their eyes fixed on their hands and the tools they held as they swung in some unspoken rhythm, their faces flushed and perspiring freely despite the cold.

As they neared the main building, Carrigan could see more priests milling around the grounds, each one attended by an orderly. The priests ranged in age from very young to shrivelled figures lost in their wheelchairs but they all seemed to share a certain expression, a commonality of suffering, the puffiness around the cheeks, the sadness in their eyes, a dishevelment of body and soul.

The monk led them through an airy and dark vestibule. The walls were bare stone and the cold and wet seeped through the cracks like smoke. They passed several monks kneeling in front of a large wooden crucifix, their heads almost touching the floor, and then went up a set of stairs that creaked and swayed under their feet and into another long corridor with doors evenly spaced along both sides, the smell harsh and sharp, industrial cleaning products and antiseptic mixing with the odour of confined men. The door to Father McCarthy's room was locked from the outside and the monk reluctantly selected a key from the large silver ring hanging at his belt and turned the lock, the jambs creaking and shrieking like wild cats as they retracted.

Father McCarthy was sitting on a hard-backed chair facing a white plastic table. He didn't look up as Carrigan and Geneva entered and introduced themselves, his eyes focused on a large bowl resting between his enormous hands. The room was small and sparse. There was a narrow metal-framed bed up against one wall, a simple table with books lying stacked and splayed on it, a jug half filled with water and a large black crucifix, the wooden floor below it worn and sanded smooth by the constant rub of knees and shins.

'You took your time,' Father McCarthy said, taking a big mouthful of stew, his lips smacking against the spoon. He was eating some kind of broth, a thick blood-red gloop with dark kidneys and pellets of grey meat floating inside. His face was almost perfectly rectangular and it was huge, a concrete slab of a head framing deep-set eyes, his wrists almost the width of Carrigan's hand. His beard was wild and unruly and totally white and, when he turned his head, Carrigan thought he could see the sheen of old scars on his puckered skin. McCarthy ignored his scrutiny and continued staring down into his soup.

'You weren't easy to find, Holden made sure of that.' Carrigan paused and stared at the old priest. He was somehow everything the stories and rumours made him out to be. 'Why did he put you in here?'

'Why do you think?' McCarthy replied. 'The church wants to protect its image. When they heard about the fire, they knew you would find me and maybe the press would too, and that their precious little secret would end up as tabloid fodder. So, here I am. But it's good you finally found your way to me. I knew you would. I need to get out of here,' he said. 'I need to resume my work.'

'And what work is that, Father?'

McCarthy put down his spoon. 'You know exactly what kind of work I'm referring to, detective, otherwise you wouldn't be here.'

Carrigan suppressed something that was close to a smile. 'We're aware you knew Emily from Peru and we know what the nuns were up to.' He took out Emily Maxted's photo and handed it over to the priest. The paper disappeared in McCarthy's hands as the scored and wrinkled flesh caressed the image. 'Emily . . .' The priest nodded softly and handed the photo back. 'Emily was our saviour.'

Geneva tapped her pen against her notebook. 'What do you mean by that?'

McCarthy went back to his stew, stirring the juice with his spoon. 'When I first met Emily I knew immediately she was the one I'd been waiting for.'

'Waiting for?' Geneva asked, the pen sticky between her fingers.

'They only come along once in a while. People like her. People with the true fire burning within them. The ones who'll do anything for what they believe in.'

'Including breaking the law?'

Father McCarthy looked at Geneva and smiled. 'There is only

one law and that is God's law. Tell me, what import do your jails and life sentences have against eternity?'

'Is that what you were doing at the compound? Following God's law?'

'I was doing what I've always been doing. God's work. The work the church has forgotten about in its haste to catch up to the twenty-first century. You've heard about the book Mother Angelica was working on the better part of her life? The moral calculus?'

They both nodded.

'The compound was an experiment in putting those theories into practice.'

'I thought the book had been suppressed by the Vatican?' Carrigan said.

Father McCarthy nodded slowly and took another slurp of his soup. 'That it was, but random chapters, lost pages, abstracts and glosses had crept out over the years. People in the church, priests and nuns on the ground, read these fragments avidly and collected them and passed them around.'

'Why Peru?' Geneva asked.

'I'd been involved in Peru since the summer of '73, and if anything, the situation's worse now. Sure, the dictatorship is gone, the civil war engendered by the Shining Path is over, there is a president who was voted in – but nothing has changed. The mines are operating with impunity. The rivers polluted with cyanide. Entire species are dying off. Workers are being exploited. The mine company has even bought up all the local medical clinics so that reports of toxic poisonings and industrial accidents never see the light of day. And then, on the other side, you have the drug barons. Ex-Shining Path men now forcing villagers to grow coca. Burning their fields and taking their women. The church pretended it wasn't happening. The world was more interested in other wars. Something had to be done.'

Geneva leaned forward. 'The sabotage and bombings? Is that

what you mean by *something had to be done*?'

'These things are sometimes necessary to stop a greater evil,' McCarthy replied. 'That's what Mother Angelica's book was about. That's what the point of the compound was.'

'Did you and Mother Angelica set it up together?'

Father McCarthy shook his head. 'I wrote to Mother Angelica a few years ago and told her how we'd organised the camp according to the principles outlined in her book. I thought she would be pleased but she was a long way away, both in time and space, from what was going on in Peru, and she'd lost her fire in the intervening years. She was content with helping the homeless, handing out leaflets and sheltering escaped prostitutes.

'We were running out of money. We needed a steady and constant tithing if we were to fulfil our mission. I wrote to Mother Angelica again and begged her to come and see what we were doing but she refused.

'Then I met Emily. She'd become very interested in the plight of the local people. She wanted to know what she could do to help. She reminded me of Mother Angelica the first time I saw her, forty years ago on that dusty dirt road leading up to Chiapeltec. The same spirit and fire, an equal ferocity. And I knew Mother Angelica would recognise it in her too.'

'You sent Emily back to London to galvanise the nuns into action? To help fund your compound?'

'They had lost their way. Someone needed to show them how to get back. Like I said, Emily was our saviour. She possessed the very thing the nuns had lost – the excitement of youth and the unwavering belief in one's own power to change the world. The nuns had already fought their battles, in South America, in Africa, in all the world's dusty forlorn places, and they had lost. Emily spoke to us of her time in the protest and anti-war movements, the screaming barricades and late-night beatings, and there was a sparkle in her eyes as she said it – oh yes, a touch of trouble and madness too, but beneath all that lay a pure white flame of indignation. All the nuns recognised it. Emily reminded them of who they'd been and what they'd lost.' Something in the priest's eyes mellowed when he said Emily's name, intoning it as if it were a benediction.

'It all sounds very high-minded but I don't see how these ideas led to bombed-out buses, blown pipelines and dead executives?' Carrigan said.

'Every action the compound took was in strict accordance with Mother Angelica's moral calculus. Every action was weighed and discussed and deemed necessary and proportional and more likely to do good than harm.'

'So what went wrong?' Carrigan asked and it was hard to tell if he was being sarcastic or not.

It seemed for a moment as if McCarthy wasn't going to answer, his eyes locking onto Carrigan's with such a piercing glare that it felt as if he were weighing his soul. 'Where does anything go wrong, Inspector?' The priest smiled. 'You know as well as I do that there are no hidden meanings scribbled in the margins of ancient texts or obscured in the mathematical pattern of letters and spaces. There is no meaning in planetary motion or the disposition of tea leaves. Nor is there meaning in coincidence and similarity. There is nothing but actions and their consequences.

'It didn't take Emily long to do what she was sent to do. She convinced the nuns that sheltering escaped prostitutes wasn't enough. That they should stop being so passive in the face of evil. She told them about the compound and the conditions she'd witnessed in Peru. A couple of the nuns came and visited. They saw what we were doing and they saw what the mine companies were doing. They embraced the cause whole-heartedly. They reported back to Mother Angelica and the money started flowing in.'

'But Sister Rose McGregor never reported back.' Geneva's voice was clipped and low.

Father McCarthy looked momentarily stricken and for the first time Carrigan could see how old he really was. 'I blame myself for that,' the priest said. 'It was the last day of her trip and we were conducting masses for the local village. Sister Rose kept asking to see one of the mines we'd talked so much about and Father Ramirez offered to take her.' Father McCarthy looked down at his shoes. 'Two weeks later we found Father Ramirez's head in the front yard of the local church. Sister Rose was never seen again.'

'One of the nuns, Sister Glenda, kept coming back, though,' Geneva said. 'I also noticed that her visits often coincided with incidents occurring in the region.'

Father McCarthy nodded. 'As time went on, the nuns wanted to see if they were getting their money's worth. If we were making a difference. Of course, we also showed them the free clinics we'd set up, the new schools and missions, defence lawyers we had on hand for the workers and the fund we kept for striking miners' families. That was our job, to fight back on the side of the poor, by whatever means were judged necessary and proportional. As you can imagine, after Sister Rose's disappearance, the nuns' commitment to the cause increased greatly.'

'So this was all about Mother Angelica taking liberation theology too literally?'

McCarthy's eyes creased. 'It's meant to be taken literally. That's the point.'

'Then why didn't they try to escape the fire if their mission meant so much to them?'

'Would it have done them any good?' McCarthy said with a flat stony stare.

'No,' Carrigan conceded.

'No. Exactly. And they knew that. They had nothing to fear from death, Inspector, on the contrary . . . they would have realised their situation and would have stayed sitting at the table and preparing for the life to come.'

'Would they have had their rosary beads out?'

'Yes, it's quite possible they did.'

'It sounds to me like they knew they'd done something wrong, gone too far, and were making amends.'

'Ah, wouldn't you like to believe that?' McCarthy said. 'It would make it so much easier, wouldn't it? But you have to remember the compound was an experiment. An experiment in direct action, in accordance with the Bible and Jesus' teachings. We weren't revolutionaries or rebels, we were priests and nuns doing God's work.'

'And it got them killed.'

McCarthy turned to face Carrigan. 'I don't know that it did.'

'What do you mean?'

Father McCarthy smiled. 'Well, you've asked me a lot of questions about Peru and the compound but you still haven't asked me about the night she came back with blood on her clothes.'

44

'What do you mean she came back with blood on her clothes?' Carrigan said. 'Are you talking about Emily? Emily Maxted?'

McCarthy nodded and pushed his bowl aside. He reached for a packet of Senior Service lying on the table next to him. He grimaced as he lit the cigarette, the scent instantly filling the room as he exhaled a spiralling twist of smoke from his nostrils.

'I told you the nuns had been sheltering escaped women? They'd bring them in through the back garden and hide them in the priesthole. Emily persuaded them to take it a step further – not to wait until the lucky ones managed to escape but to snatch them from the hands of their captors. It didn't take much persuading. I suspect it had been Mother Angelica's unspoken conviction all along. Emily watched the Albanians and got to know their routines. The women were only ever let out when they were being transferred to another brothel. Emily and her accomplice would wait outside, then grab the woman and be out of sight before they even knew what had happened.'

'Accomplice?' Carrigan said, reaching into his file and pulling out the mugshot photo of Nigel the Nail. He passed it to the priest, watching him nod, a slight curl of distaste appearing on his lips.

'Not the kind of person you would want to have dinner with, but the right kind for the job.' He handed back the photo, evidently not wanting to hold onto it any longer. 'He'd been travelling with Emily in Peru. Back in London, Emily talked him into helping the nuns snatch women from the Albanians. He was enamoured with her, that was clear to see. This man was not interested in saving the women, he only craved confrontation and battle, but sometimes we use tools that do not fit our hands and yet who's to say they're not good tools?' The priest dragged hard on his cigarette, a wisp of regret flickering in his eyes then just as quickly disappearing.

'What about the blood? You said she came back with blood on her clothes.'

McCarthy looked down at his hands and sighed. 'Something went wrong the third time they tried it. When Emily came back she was screaming, all wild-eyed and hysterical. She was clutching a bag to her chest, blood all over her.

'The nuns hid her in the priest-hole. They'd used it previously to shelter the escaped women and it was comfortable, if a little damp. For the first few days Emily refused to even come out – there was a new look in her eyes and it took me a while to realise that I'd never seen her scared before. She left a week later without saying a word to anyone. We saw her less and less after that. The nuns curtailed their snatch work for the time being, battened down and hoped it would go away. Then the visits began.'

'The Albanians?' Carrigan's fingers were pressed tight against the stem of his pencil as he wrote down the information, all these missing blanks rushing in like mad whirling flakes of snow.

'They'd somehow worked out who was behind it, I have no idea how. Two thugs came to the convent and asked to see Mother Angelica. They told her they only wanted Emily and the man who was with her that night. They didn't know their names but they knew everything else. They came twice more, each visit with a new ultimatum to hand over the girl and Nigel. Mother Angelica held firm. They probably expected some spineless nun and had no idea of the torture and suffering she'd endured in South America.

'But she wasn't through with Emily. The next time Emily turned up Mother Angelica took her off to the kitchen. I remember hearing them screaming and arguing and shouting over each other's words. Mother Angelica told her it was over, that she was no longer welcome in the convent. That if Emily didn't turn herself in to the police, the nuns would be forced to. Emily called her a coward, a fraud and a fake and then—'

The door crashed open, spilling harsh white light into the room. Two huge orderlies entered, ignoring Carrigan and Geneva, and made their way directly to Father McCarthy, their strides long and brisk and full of purpose. Carrigan rose from his chair and saw Roger Holden standing in the doorway. The two orderlies flanked McCarthy and, at a nod from Holden, grabbed him by both arms and lifted him out of the chair.

Carrigan took a step forward and one of the orderlies detached himself from the priest and moved towards him, arms tensed, an unspoken challenge in his eyes.

'Put him down,' Carrigan ordered, reaching for the baton on his belt. The orderly threw a short right and Carrigan ducked and spun and grabbed the swinging fist in his own, twisting the man's arm behind his back in one quick move. The other orderly let go of Father McCarthy and was coming to his colleague's aid, fists squared and ready.

'Wait, Norman,' Holden said. 'We don't need to do that – do we, Detective Inspector Carrigan?'

Carrigan looked at the orderly, the ripple of muscles snaking down his arms, the funky smell of his fear-sweat. He saw Geneva up and ready, the can of pepper spray clutched in her small fist.

'After all,' Holden continued, 'you're trespassing. You used false pretences to gain entry. You took information from my office without permission. You've broken several laws, all of which I'm sure ACC Quinn will be very interested to hear about.'

Carrigan took a step back, realising that Holden was right and even if he somehow managed to overpower the orderlies, he would never be able to get McCarthy out of the building.

He let go of the man's arm, catching his breath. The orderlies grabbed the priest and frogmarched him out of the room. McCarthy looked back at Carrigan once, then disappeared through the grey metal door.

'Where the fuck are they taking him?' Carrigan said, moving closer to Holden, breathing the words into his face.

Holden took a step back. 'Don't you worry about that,' he replied. 'Father McCarthy has to prepare himself for a long flight tomorrow. He needs his rest.'

'A flight?'

'He's being transferred to a small parish in the South Pacific. Somewhere that needs a man like him. I'm sure he'll find it a very interesting posting, a lot of challenges . . .'

'You set me up, didn't you?' Carrigan said. 'You left the room knowing we would . . . you even kept glancing in the direction of the filing cabinets every time I mentioned Father McCarthy . . .' And then he stopped and leaned forward. 'How long?'

'How long what?'

'How long have you known? From the very beginning? Or did you stumble on what the nuns were up to in Peru by accident? That's the real reason you were having them excommunicated, isn't it? Not over some book that no one would ever read.'

Holden resisted the temptation to take a further step back. 'I don't know what you're talking about.'

Carrigan grabbed Holden's lapel and held him firm, cinching the material in his fists. 'You suddenly have a very good reason for getting rid of the nuns.'

Holden pulled himself out of Carrigan's grip, smoothing down the lapels of his jacket and shaking his head. He looked at his watch and smiled. 'You have only a few hours left to enjoy your last day as a policeman – I suggest you don't waste them here.'

45

He'd never seen the ACC like this. Normally undemonstrative and calm, Quinn was pacing back and forth behind Branch's desk, the super nowhere to be seen, the grinding of Quinn's teeth the only sound in the room. 'What the hell do you think you're doing?' Quinn was pulling out Branch's chair, leaning on it, putting it back, his hands seemingly not under his control.

'Sir?' Carrigan kept his face impassive, a sinking in his stomach, the way you know something before you know it.

'I will not tolerate your continued disrespect to the church and the position it's put me in. I spoke to Roger Holden just now and he's furious, on the point of pressing charges against you. You're bloody lucky you're not suspended. What did you think you were doing, Carrigan?' Quinn's eyes shot up, cold and piercing. 'No, don't answer – there's nothing you can say to make this better. You entered Burnham monastery yesterday under false pretences and harassed a patient. I really thought someone with your background would be more discreet.'

'My background?' Carrigan repeated, lost words and conversations rattling through his head, that horrible sensation of things clicking into place. 'You put me on this case because I'm a Catholic?'

'Enough! Just listen to yourself, Carrigan. It's how it looks that matters. Now, tell me, is the case wrapped up? Or have you been wasting time again?'

Carrigan took a deep breath and ran through what Father McCarthy had told them. Quinn's face was rigid and unblinking. 'Whores?' Quinn said, shaking his head.

'Nigel's murder makes sense now. His death – the torture, mutilation and prolongation of suffering – is consistent with a revenge killing by the Albanians. Duka was getting payback. The way he saw it, Nigel and Emily had stolen from him. Duka's men made three visits to the convent, demanding that the nuns hand over Emily and Nigel, and when the nuns refused, Duka sent someone to torch the place.'

Quinn sighed. 'You have this gift of making something very complicated sound so simple, Carrigan. I wish it were so. If this really was Duka, you'll never tie him to it. You know that as well as I do.'

Carrigan was silent, the same thought circling his brain for the last few hours. 'Maybe we can't tie him to the fire but that doesn't mean we should just forget him. He's running a brothel on our patch, drugs, guns, God knows what else. Money is all he cares about and that's where I want to hurt him. Raid his premises every other day. Station surveillance vans in plain sight outside his brothels. Make him give us the firestarter.'

Quinn shook his head and planted his hands deep in his pockets. 'No. The last thing the Met needs right now is another harassment suit. You already have your culprit in the morgue.'

Carrigan wasn't sure he understood quite what Quinn was suggesting. 'Nigel?'

'The man was scum. I want to go live with this tomorrow lunchtime. You know what to say. Emily had broken up with Nigel and he wasn't too happy about it. He followed her to the convent, killed her and set the fire to hide the evidence.'

'Nigel didn't do it,' Carrigan said. 'The man was trash but he's just as much a victim of Duka as the nuns. I'm not going to let Duka get away with this.' He said it with as much conviction as he could muster but he could tell by the ACC's eyes that it wasn't enough.

'I thought you'd say that, Carrigan. Which is why I called you in here to inform you that as of tomorrow I'm transferring the case to

DI Malone.'

Carrigan had been expecting this, but not so soon. He stopped, took a deep breath, thought about what he was about to do and said, 'Perhaps it would be wise to think about that before you ...'

'Are you threatening me?' Quinn snapped.

'Absolutely not.' Carrigan eased forward on the chair, taking his time. 'It's just that if DI Malone takes over, I'll have to hand him all my files, including the one detailing donors to the convent.'

Quinn stopped mid-stride and turned and stared at Carrigan. His hands gripped the back of the chair, the fingers turning white, his lips almost disappearing. 'Donating money to a charity isn't a crime.'

Carrigan allowed himself the faintest hint of a smile. 'No, you're correct – but it's how it looks that matters, right?'

Quinn was breathing deeply, his fingers digging into the chair fabric, the rest of his body absolutely motionless.

'You knew what they were doing, didn't you?' Carrigan stared into the ACC's eyes and saw no flicker of denial or surprise. 'You knew and you still gave them money.'

Quinn pulled out the seat and sat down heavily. He closed his eyes for a moment, eventually opening them to reveal small shrunk stones bereft of light. 'Okay, Carrigan. What do you want? You want to be back on the case?'

'I want a lot more than that.'

Quinn looked up and eyeballed him for a full minute before speaking. 'Don't for a minute think I'll forget this, Carrigan.'

*

Geneva called out to Carrigan as he was leaving the building. She was sitting on a ledge outside the main gate, a cigarette clamped between her lips. She pulled out her earphones and crushed the butt under her shoe.

'Problems with Quinn?'

Carrigan walked over and stood beside her. She looked tired and frayed, her eyes sunk deep into their sockets. 'Nah, he just wanted to tell me what a great job we're doing.'

It brought out a smile. He sat down on the ledge beside her, letting the adrenalin of the meeting course through his veins. 'You done for the day?'

She nodded. 'Was going to go home and watch a DVD.' She hesitated, her mouth slightly ajar. 'Don't suppose you fancy joining me?' She looked down at her shoes and the still smoking butt beside them.

'I'd love to,' Carrigan replied, 'but I have to go meet Donna.' He noticed a flicker of something on Geneva's face, quickly subsumed. 'I owe her Emily's story. She'd finally turned her life around and the family needs to know that.'

Geneva didn't say anything for a few moments, her eyes searching his. 'Are you sure it's because of the case you're going?'

'Of course,' he replied, but as soon as he said it he knew he was partly lying and that it wasn't the only reason. He watched as Geneva walked away and disappeared under the grey overhang of the motorway, only a couple of crushed cigarette butts to remind him she'd even been here at all.

46

Donna was sitting at a corner table staring blankly at the snow, a cup of coffee going cold in her hands. When she saw Carrigan enter the cafe, her eyes softened and she brushed back a twist of stray hair as she got up. She was wearing a blue-and-white jumper and a brown skirt that curved and clung to her figure. They stood there for a long moment not saying anything, their eyes locked together, and then Carrigan coughed and broke her stare. 'Thanks for meeting me.'

Her smile was deep and warm. 'I was so glad when I got your call,' she said, and stepped aside to let him sit down. Their bodies brushed lightly against each other as he shuffled past her.

They sat and sipped their coffees and watched the people stop and drink and make jokes with the baristas and wish them happy Christmas. He told her about Emily and what she'd been up to. 'She was trying to do good in her own way and she was killed because of it.'

Donna wiped her eyes and smiled and took a sip of her coffee. Carrigan rested his palm on her elbow. 'I'm sorry.'

Donna shuddered, a slight tremor that Carrigan could feel leaking through her arm. 'Thank you for telling me about Emily. I know it's a small thing but you don't know how much it means to me.' Her mouth was close to his, her breath sweet with coffee.

'She was a brave girl,' Carrigan said and, before he could react, Donna leaned forward and planted a kiss on his cheek, her lips soft and warm and wet against his skin. 'Thank you,' she whispered, leaning back, her face blushing. 'You know, that day by the pond, that was my only good day since . . .'

'I know.' Carrigan smiled softly, got up and walked away.

He waited for the bus but was too impatient to stand around so he started walking, trying to burn off the excess energy in the gathering storm. He could barely see a few feet in front of him but he didn't mind, enjoying the sting and melt of the snow against his face and thinking about Donna's last words, the residual heat of her kiss on his cheek. He didn't notice the SUV stopping fifty feet ahead of him nor see the man get out.

He looked down at the man's hands and all thoughts of Donna's long hair and shy smile were instantly erased. The gun was pointing at his stomach and Viktor's eyes were hard and sharp. 'Get in.'

Carrigan stood frozen.

'I said get the fuck in.' Viktor used the gun to gesture to the passenger seat. Carrigan saw that it had been pushed back to its limit. He felt the barrel press up against his flesh and he leaned in and was about to sit down when Viktor shouted, 'On the floor!'

He crouched down on his knees in the scant space of the SUV's footwell, knowing that this was the crucial moment. Once they were both in the car his chances of escape were virtually zero. His only opportunity would be when Viktor made his way across to the driver's side.

Carrigan steadied himself and rehearsed how he would do it. Wait until the Albanian sat down, when his body and aim were out of line. He started a deep breathing cycle to calm his heart and still his hands.

Viktor looked down into the car, smiled as if he'd just read Carrigan's mind and smashed the butt of the gun against his head.

47

The feel of the gritted road beneath him. The swelling pressure in his head. The smell of crushed cigarettes and cracked leather.

Carrigan opened his eyes and looked around. He was crouched in the footwell, squeezed into a space too small for a man half his size. His wrists had been secured with a plastic snap-tie, his fingers already numb and swollen.

'Viktor.'

The man didn't flinch or react to his own name. The effort to speak caused a new wave of nausea to rise through Carrigan's throat and he fought hard against the weight of his own body as it tried to sink back into blackness. The dark smeared sky stretched above him. He could see individual snowflakes smash against the passenger window and dissolve like tears.

'What the fuck do you think you're doing?'

Viktor turned towards him for a split second and hissed, 'Shut up!'

Carrigan tried to ignore the pain creeping up his legs. His knees were almost touching his chin and the enforced position was starting to pull at muscles he never knew existed, torquing his spine and chest, making each breath something to be gasped and fought for. He could taste his own blood in his mouth. He thought of what had been done to Nigel and wondered if they had a special place for that sort of work and if that was where Viktor was taking him.

The sudden pull of gravity told him they were ascending a motorway ramp. A bitter taste filled his mouth as he realised they must be heading out of London, the ramp most probably the M40 scrolling out to the darkened west. He tried to identify the buildings as their roofs passed in a blur through the passenger window, but they were only flashes in the night, dim and unrecognisable.

The road levelled and their speed picked up. Carrigan felt the sour taste of vomit in his throat and swallowed it back down. His heart was hammering away, a deep rumble through his chest. He remembered the feel of Donna's kiss on his cheek, the sadness weighing down her eyes, the way he'd walked into Viktor's trap.

'The police will be following you,' he said but he knew they wouldn't even realise he was missing until morning.

'Shut up,' the man repeated.

The fact that Viktor was unconcerned about showing his face made Carrigan uneasy – he remembered DI Byrd's warnings about what Duka and the Albanians were capable of and that snowy morning in the pub, the smell of beer and damp wood and old men, seemed like a lifetime away.

The car began to decelerate, a deepening hum as Viktor spun the wheel, and they were suddenly bumping along an unpaved track, the darkness swallowing everything.

Viktor stopped the car, looked down at Carrigan and gestured with the gun.

'Get out slowly,' the Albanian said. 'Don't do anything stupid,' he added. 'Don't make me have to shoot you.'

Carrigan wondered if this was the moment, if this was to be his last and only chance. He uncurled slowly and stepped out of the car. He lost his footing on the soft ground, expecting concrete not earth, and righted himself just in time, about to make his move, when he felt the cold kiss of the gun against his head and he didn't know how Viktor had got out of the car and across so quickly.

'Over there.' Viktor pointed towards a dark form at the edge of their vision. Carrigan began walking towards it, the man at his back, the snow falling softly on his face.

They were in an allotment in the middle of a large field. Carrigan could see the dividing fences and square lots to either side. He saw the shed they were heading towards, a rickety wooden structure pitched at the end of the allotment. He felt the snow melt through his shoes and soak his feet, the chill wind cutting through his clothes. He walked slowly, grudgingly, knowing he'd been wrong, and that the chance had come and gone and now there was only him, the man, the gun, and the dark interior of the shed.

'Stop here.' Viktor took a step forward, reached into his pocket and pulled out a long serrated knife. He thrust the blade at Carrigan and cut. The blood flowed back into Carrigan's fingers in white-hot needles as the broken snap-tie fell to the ground.

'Open it and step inside slowly,' the man commanded and Carrigan did what he said.

The shed smelled of wet soil and mould, a deep fungal stench. Viktor closed the door behind him and suddenly the world was muted and all Carrigan could hear was his own heart.

'Sit on the floor. Cross your legs underneath you and sit on your hands.'

Carrigan winced as he followed the Albanian's orders. In this position it would be almost impossible for him to make any quick movements or try to escape. Viktor knew exactly what he was doing. All around them tools were hanging on the walls, rusty scythes and pruning shears, spades and rakes and hammers, root vegetables black with mould stacked up high in one corner.

'What do you want from me?'

Viktor pulled a folding chair from where it was propped up against the wall and sat down opposite him. 'I want you to listen,' he said, his voice slow and measured.

Carrigan dropped his head, his eyes searching the floor for anything he could use, a loose nail, a piece of garden equipment, a sliver of broken glass, but there was only the bare earth.

'You need to stop this thing you're doing,' the Albanian said.

'You need to stop right now.'

'Stop what?' Carrigan stalled.

'This investigation of yours. The raid on our premises. We had nothing to do with the fire, understand? You're getting in the way of business and no one is happy about this. Now you plan to do more raids, more trouble, this is something I think you need to reconsider.'

Carrigan wondered how Viktor knew about the forthcoming raids, planned only that morning. 'I have a job to do and I'm going to do it until it's done.'

'I thought you'd say that.' Viktor sounded exasperated as the wind shook the timbers of the shed, moaning and whistling through the cracks. 'But maybe you care for your partner more? The blonde woman? She can be halfway across Europe by tomorrow morning if I give the order. The men back home in the villages, they will greatly appreciate her, I think.'

Carrigan said nothing, his tongue frozen, his eyes hooded. He looked up at Viktor. 'You expect me to believe you had nothing to do with the fire and yet you threaten me? We know what happened. We know what you did and why you did it.'

'You know nothing,' the man sneered.

'We know that the nuns were sheltering escaped women. Women your organisation was selling and raping. We know you made several visits to the convent, we even have you on tape. Emily Maxted and the nuns were helping girls escape from your clutches and you couldn't bear that, could you? Women getting the better of you, ruining your business? So, you sent one of your men to the convent and solved your little problem.'

Viktor's laugh was deep and sonorous as it reverberated around the dark interior of the shed. 'That's what you think?'

'That's what I know.'

'Really?' Viktor shook his head. 'This Emily you talk about, your victim, well, did you know that she killed one of my men?'

Carrigan's eyes widened. 'What did you just say?'

'Your victim, your *innocent* victim, is a murderer. She killed Bratislav and she had to pay.'

'What the hell are you talking about?' Carrigan thought back to Father McCarthy's words, how things had gone wrong, the blood on Emily's clothes.

'These nuns and this girl, you were right, they were helping women who'd escaped. But that was not enough for them. They decided to take it a step further. Emily and her friend jumped my men twice and took the girls from them. We started using two-man teams. Emily and her accomplice appeared outside one of our properties on Old Street. They surrounded my men and demanded they release the girl. As you can imagine, my men refused. Then, this Emily of yours, from nowhere she leaps forward and suddenly she has this knife in her hand, this big kitchen knife, and she stabs my man. Not once, but several times.'

'How do you know this?' Carrigan said, feeling his stomach drop.

'I was there. I saw my friend get stabbed, holding himself in, his guts pouring out, and Emily didn't stop. Her mouth was open and she was grinning. Her eyes were blazing as she plunged the knife in again and again. Her accomplice held me, the woman ran off, but Emily wouldn't stop until her friend had to grab her, wrestle the knife away and slap her face to calm her down. Bratislav crashed to the ground. Emily picked up the bag he was carrying, then ran back to the van. I stood there and watched my friend die because of her.'

'Jesus.'

'Yes, this is your innocent little victim. This is the kind of woman she was. I do not get scared of much but I was scared of her. She was crazy, she loved it, you should have seen her face.'

'The bag? What was in the bag?'

'Cocaine,' Viktor replied. 'For the customers. Bratislav was dropping off the brothel's weekly supply.'

'You're not exactly convincing me of your innocence,' Carrigan said, the images whirling through his brain, half-remembered conversations with the priest and the Maxteds. 'Everything you've told me just gives you more reason to have wanted her dead. If you're so innocent, what were you doing in the ruins of the convent the night you attacked me?'

Viktor shrugged. 'Duka had us watching the convent. He wanted to know what was happening, what the police were doing, whether there was anything there that could lead back to us. We saw you that night, we didn't know who you were, it was too late for an official visit and you were alone. We thought you might be Nigel, the man who'd helped Emily.'

'You're digging yourself a deeper hole as we speak.'

'Wrong, my friend. You think we're stupid? You think we're *that* stupid? We wanted the girl, this Emily, and we wanted the man with her, but the nuns were not our concern.'

'The nuns were helping shelter your women.'

The Albanian laughed. 'Girls are cheap, detective, in fact you could say they are less than cheap, they're free. So what if a few escape? This is the price of business. It is much easier for us to get ten new girls than chase down one escaped whore.'

'But you would want to teach them a lesson? Isn't that how you work? You would want to teach the nuns a lesson so that others don't get the same idea.'

'Believe me, if we had wanted to teach them a lesson, you would know about it. We would not give them the easy option of dying in flames. We would make their deaths long and drawn out and we would leave much evidence of suffering on their bodies.'

'Like you did with Nigel?'

'He was involved in the killing of one of our men, he got exactly what he deserved. But to burn down a convent? It would be a stupid business decision, put the spotlight on us and bring us unwelcome attention. We went and talked with the nuns. We told them we knew what they were doing but that we were prepared to forget that. We talked to the old one, the head nun, and we told her what Emily had done. I thought we would have to convince her of the truth of this but she needed no convincing. I could see that she had feared exactly such a thing. Yet she refused to give up the girl. We visited three times but she wouldn't budge. We knew it didn't matter, we have long memories and a lot of patience. We would wait and Emily would show herself, then we would take back what we were owed.'

'You expect me to believe that?'

'I can see that you already do,' Viktor said. 'Whoever set the fire stole Emily from us. She belonged to Duka. If we find this person before you do, I can promise you he won't be bringing his lawyer with him.'

'Why all the charade of kidnapping me and bringing me here?'

'If someone sees me with you, detective, then I am dead and my family back home are dead. It is that simple.'

'Then why do it?' Carrigan asked. 'Why tell me all this?'

'Because we are businessmen and your crusade is bad for our business.'

'Bullshit. You wouldn't take such a risk if that were true. Kidnapping a police officer is much worse for business than a few raids.' Carrigan stopped. He thought about how Viktor had known about the upcoming raids, a stray sentence Byrd had said a couple of days ago, the risk the Albanian was taking being here, and then he knew.

'You're not really one of them, are you? You're working with Byrd. That's why you know about the raids.'

Viktor looked at him without blinking. 'Repeat those words ever again and I will find you and I will kill you, understand?'

Carrigan smiled. 'I understand.'

Viktor walked away, leaving himself unprotected, the gun hanging loosely at his side. As he opened the door, he turned back towards Carrigan. 'You want to know what happened that night?

Then I suggest you think about what Nigel was trying to tell you.'
He nodded once, then shut the door behind him.

Carrigan didn't get up. He sat and tried not to think about what
Viktor had said. Because if Viktor and Duka weren't behind the
fire, then he'd been wrong all along.

48

The next morning he dismissed the entire team. He pulled down the action sheets, scrawled lists and minutely delineated graphs from the walls, and shut down the incident room. He sent the HOLMES analysts away and rotated the uniforms back to regular duty. He told everyone to go home and enjoy their Christmas holidays.

He'd explained his reasons and they'd been surprised, some even outraged, but Carrigan could see that they all accepted it with the same snap of logic he had. There were stunned looks, evident relief and many questions, but Carrigan shut himself off in his office, the door, for once, closed. The snow was falling thickly outside, obscuring the buildings and greater city beyond, and he spent the rest of the morning going through the case files again, trying to find any way he could be wrong, any other answer that would fit the facts, any other option but this. He focused on the interview statements, reading and rereading each phrase and sentence, then listening to the recordings, hoping to isolate any peculiarity of intonation or tone that would give lie to the printed word, but everything he read and heard only made him more certain.

Geneva was knocking on the door. The sound registered but only obscurely, as yet another minor distraction, a faint tap at the edge of consciousness. He looked up and saw her standing halfway into his office, tall black boots reaching almost to her knees. She took out her earplugs and looped them around her index finger, a fluent and practised gesture that nonetheless carried a hint of irritation about it.

'Can you please explain to me what's going on?' Her voice was sharp and fierce.

'We've been wrong from the start,' Carrigan replied, thinking back to last night, the smell of wet soil and ice, the way his body had shaken uncontrollably for a long time after Viktor had left. He'd walked out of the shed and trudged through the snow-bound fields until he'd reached the motorway. He'd walked a further mile before he found a service station. Back home, he'd paced the rooms of his flat, unable to sleep, to stop the incessant flickering of his eyelids, thinking about what Viktor had said, running it through his head, trying to find a fault or crack that would split apart the man's story, but no matter how hard he tried, how many ways he looked at it, he could not. As dawn filtered through the gaps in his curtains he'd slowly and unwillingly come to the realisation that the case had been over before it had even begun.

'You're shutting down the investigation?' Geneva was looking at him, perplexed and a little piqued. She'd forgotten to turn off her iPod and he could hear a faint hiss coming from her top pocket.

She listened intently, didn't say a word, didn't blink, but bit down on her lip as he told her Viktor's story.

'Emily killed someone?' She couldn't hide the tremble of disappointment in her voice, a muzzy deflation of pitch dragging down each vowel. 'Jesus Christ.'

Carrigan closed his eyes and shrugged. 'I've been going through it all night, running the different scenarios, trying to see where we went wrong. All morning I've been rereading the witness statements and forensic results, going over them so many times I could recite you the exact height and weight of each nun along with their favourite saints.' He stopped, took a sip of coffee. 'Viktor's story is the only explanation that makes sense of what we know.'

She hadn't heard him, or was pretending not to, her body tilted forward, a hard bright gleam in her eyes. 'What else is he going to say?' Her voice trembled. 'You need to report this, and then we can get a warrant for Viktor and arrest him and find out what the fuck

343

he has to do with the fire.'

He could see the rushing excitement in her face, the scent of prey, and felt bad for deflating it. 'I'm not going to report it.'

She glared at him, a strange rumbling in her eyes. 'You have to.'

'Like you reported the other night?'

She stopped her pacing and frowned. 'That's not fair.'

'No, you're right, it wasn't,' Carrigan admitted. 'But I'm not reporting it.'

Geneva drummed her fingers against her thigh. 'You're not telling me something. I can tell by the way you won't look at me.'

He thought about it, had been thinking about it all night. 'Viktor's not who we think he is.'

'Who the fuck is he? Santa Claus?'

He ignored her comment. 'Viktor's undercover, working for or with Byrd. He's been in Duka's organisation for three years. We nearly blew his cover. He told me they had nothing to do with the fire and at first I didn't believe him either, but when I subtracted Duka from the equation everything suddenly fell into place.'

Geneva shook her head. 'You're going to have to do a better job of convincing me than that.'

'Think about what Father McCarthy said.' Carrigan felt a delayed rush of energy exploding in his chest. It was always like this when she challenged him, when he had to put his own inchoate thoughts and suppositions into the thin bindings of language, and he loved to see her eyes spark as she made the connections.

'McCarthy said that the third time Emily tried to rescue one of the women, something went wrong, and she came back with blood on her clothes. And we know the visits from Duka's men started right after that.' He picked up Emily's arrest sheet and glanced at it, that first contact he'd had with her, the snarled look she'd hurled at the camera and the black tunnel of her gaze. 'Besides, the Albanians would have wanted Emily alive. They'd want her to suffer and to make an example of her. An anonymous body found in a possibly accidental fire wouldn't serve their purposes.'

Geneva sat down, pulled out her cigarettes, looked at the packet, then put them back, realising that everything she knew about the case was wrong. She tried to fight the rush of logic and reason pouring in from all directions but it was hopeless. She could feel things clicking, an almost physical sensation of interlocked threads – the loose ends and anomalies suddenly resolving themselves – yet there was something about it that felt too neat, that felt wrong, and she couldn't quite figure out what it was. 'If Duka didn't set the fire, then who did?'

Carrigan looked down at the table and didn't reply. This was the part he'd been dreading – he knew that once he uttered the words there would be no going back. He rubbed his fingers through his beard, noticing he'd forgotten to trim it recently, and leaned forward. 'All along we've been thinking that the fire had something to do with the nuns' activities in Peru. The more we looked into it the more certain we became, the more the clues pointed in that direction. We got swept away by the pull of narrative – it makes sense so it must be true. We focused too narrowly and ignored the other possibilities.' He knew it was his fault, he was to blame, no one else. The case had been his and he'd led them all down the wrong path.

He stood up, the failure rushing hot and tight in his throat, and turned to the whiteboard. One by one he peeled off the photos of Viktor, Duka, Eagle-neck, Father McCarthy and Geoff Shorter, then he took several steps back.

The board looked bare and stark. Geneva stared at Carrigan then at the whiteboard. She looked down at the floor, then out the window at the snow-dazzled sky. She didn't want to say it but she did.

'You're not seriously suggesting . . . ?'

She stared at the whiteboard again, then at Carrigan.

'There has to be another explanation . . .'

She looked at the one face left pinned up on the board as she tried to fight the thoughts tumbling through her head.

'Emily?' she finally said, her voice pinched and flat and disbelieving. 'Emily Maxted set the fire?'

Carrigan nodded almost imperceptibly. 'Put yourself in her shoes.' He pulled out a sheet of paper so cross-hatched with scribbles and jottings it looked an impenetrable slab of black. 'Emily is in major trouble, easily the worst of her life. She's killed someone and now the Albanians are looking for her. She knows they do not forget, that they will hunt her down for however long it takes. She goes to the nuns, perhaps seeking sanctuary, but they turn against her. They're threatening to go to the police and report the murder if she doesn't hand herself in first. She's in an impossible position – on one side there's the prospect of torture and a very bad death, on the other a life sentence for murder.'

Geneva shook her head vigorously as if trying to rid herself of some buzzing insect. 'You think she committed suicide?'

'No, I don't,' he replied. 'Remember how Mother Angelica told her she wasn't welcome any more? Maybe one of the nuns spotted her and there was an altercation. Maybe the pricket stand got knocked about in the struggle.'

'Then how did she end up in the confession booth?'

'I don't know,' Carrigan admitted. 'It's likely we'll never know what exactly went down that night.' He glanced over at the photo of Emily that Donna had taken a few weeks ago.

'What are you going to do now?' Geneva asked.

'I'm going to pack up the files, put them in a box and go to Quinn with this. Tell him we've closed the case and that Emily set the fire. He won't like it but that's the way it is. Then I'm going to drive over to the Maxteds and tell them before they find out about it in the press.'

'Some Christmas . . .' Geneva said, and Carrigan saw her eyes crumple and fall, the drag and slant of her mouth, a hundred emotions whirling through her skull.

'Some Christmas, all right . . .'

He started putting the cascading mountain of papers, interview transcripts, statements and photocopied reports back into the large box file at his feet after she'd gone. His movements were slow and grudging, his head aching with the fatigue of too many days and too little sleep.

They had looked for complexity and collusion but in the end there were only the actions of one damaged individual who'd kept closing doors on herself until there was only one door left.

In that sense, it had turned out well for everyone, Carrigan thought sourly. Holden and the bishop would be happy that the nuns' activities in Peru remained a secret. Quinn would be pleased that the solution hadn't opened up an entire can of worms containing Albanian people-smugglers and young girls enslaved and raped in the heart of London. No one wanted to read about that in their Christmas papers and no one would, but the girls would still be sold, the brothels running at full capacity over the holiday season, new recruits coming in all the time, a quivering legion of the silent and the damned.

Carrigan picked up some more sheets of paper and placed them in the long cardboard case box and it felt as if he were filling a grave. There was always something bittersweet about closing a case but this time it was different – he didn't feel happy, satisfied or even relieved.

He drained the last of his coffee and cleared the last of the papers. He stared again at the photos of the fire – the dining room, bodies curled up like children, dripping walls and cracked statues, the confession booth's dark interior, the collapsed floors and smouldering crucifixes. Then he put them away, glad he wouldn't ever have to look at them again.

There would only be a skeleton crew operating from the station over the next few days, the city hushed in snow and festivity, and then it would start up all over again, the arguments and stabbings and pub fights and petty murders and phone calls waking him in the middle of the night. He thought about Geneva and how he'd need to have a serious chat with her in the new year, sort out the problem before it was too late, but, in spite of all that, he'd been impressed by her yet again, her rugged determination and needle-sharp instincts, the way she could see clear through his blind spots.

He put the lid on the case box, ready for it to be shipped to some mouldy basement. He thought of his own flat, the dark silent rooms and boxes of memories packed away in the attic, the squandered years sequestered behind cardboard and cobwebs. When he was finished he longed for a cigarette but those days were gone. He emailed his report to Branch and Quinn, then got up and faced the whiteboard. There was only one photo left and he gently peeled it off, the snap that Donna had taken of her sister two weeks before the fire.

He stared at Emily's face, those deep piercing eyes and slanted mouth, and then he noticed something in the bottom right-hand corner of the photo and his breath stopped.

He stared at it for a long moment, everything else forgotten.

A stray conversation echoed through his head. He strained to hear the words and understand their significance. Time seemed to contract and slow. Sentences ran jumbled through his brain, inflections and facts, things that didn't mean much at the time now magnified to disproportionate size. His mouth felt dry, his hands slick and clammy. He knelt down and started taking the files back out of the box, throwing them onto the floor, going through the reports and statements until he found what he was looking for.

He pulled out the printed transcript of Geoff Shorter's interview and started reading it again. Halfway through he came upon that suddenly remembered phrase and he stopped and his whole body shook as he realised what it meant.

For a moment, it seemed he couldn't move, and then he put the report down and pulled out the photos of the burnt-out convent. He flicked through them until he got to the one he wanted. He stared at it and couldn't believe he hadn't noticed it before.

But he had to be sure, absolutely sure.

He wrenched open his desk drawers, pulling them all the way out and upturning them onto the tabletop. He started going through months of accumulated junk – stray staples, Post-It notes, coffee loyalty cards, half-filled forms and bus tickets – flinging everything onto the floor, and he was getting more desperate and frenetic as he neared the bottom and then he saw it, lodged between the pages of a week-old newspaper.

He reached for it, but pulled his hand away just in time and snapped on a pair of gloves from the nearby dispenser, realising how his impatience had nearly ruined everything.

He picked it up, placed it carefully in an evidence bag, and called the lab.

49

He texted Geneva early on Christmas Day. He'd gone straight home from the station the previous night and hadn't slept or eaten or done much of anything until the lab had called back. When the first faint light of Christmas morning lit up the motorway ramp outside his flat, he knew it couldn't wait.

He called Karen and apologised for having to cancel Christmas dinner. There was a long silence and then she said she understood, and he knew she did.

He picked Geneva up from her mother's house. She was dressed in clothes he'd never seen her in before, sedate and somehow formal, and it took him a moment to recognise her. An older woman was leaning out the front door, staring in his direction.

'My mom wanted to come out and give you hell,' Geneva said, but Carrigan could tell she was only half as pissed off as she was pretending to be.

The city was empty, the shops closed, the roads stripped of the constant honk and whine of traffic. As they headed north through the abandoned streets and holiday hush they could feel the muted sense of anticipation leaking from every Christmas tree-lit window, eager young faces pressed against the glass, watching the skies, their features distorted like stockinged bank robbers. It had been snowing for ten days but it hadn't yet snowed today.

'This is all very nice,' Geneva said. 'But where exactly are we going?'

'It's Christmas,' Carrigan replied. 'And I have one good deed left to do.'

She knew there would be no point pressing him further and so she sipped her coffee and stared out of the window, recognising streets and junctions they'd passed through less than a week ago, the large houses rising out of the mist like the prows of doomed ships, the high street gloomy and shuttered, the sprawling expanse of heath blanketing them on both sides.

'I feel like such an idiot.' Carrigan shook his head. 'Two days ago I was telling them their daughter died trying to do something good.'

The maid opened the door and led them into the dining room. The scene looked as if nothing had changed from a few days ago, as if it were a painting slowly drying in its frame.

What was left of the Maxted family was gathered around the table, in the middle of Christmas lunch. Miles Maxted sat at one end, Lillian at the other. Donna, wearing a red dress, was stranded in the yawning gap between them.

The Maxteds hadn't started on their main course, the food still steaming from the oven, the maid laying out the final pieces then silently taking her place in the corner of the room. Lillian was twirling a lock of hair in her fingers and didn't even notice their arrival, but Donna looked up and her eyes grew wide and soft as she recognised Carrigan.

Geneva caught the look, the longing in it, and felt a hot rush of something she couldn't quite name.

'What do we owe this pleasure to?' Miles Maxted's voice was already thick with alcohol.

'I'm sorry to intrude like this,' Carrigan said quietly. 'But something's come up.' Carrigan kept his face blank. The food smelled wonderful but it was obvious no one was eating, their plates full, contents untouched, the cutlery still perfectly arrayed on either side.

'The investigation into the fire at the convent is about to be officially closed. There's going to be a press conference tonight but I thought it best you hear it from me first.'

Miles Maxted looked up. 'Just tell us what you have to tell us and leave us in peace.'

'Remember how I said that Emily was working with the nuns and that she was killed by the Albanians because of this?'

'You caught them?' Donna asked breathlessly.

Carrigan shook his head. 'I was wrong,' he said. 'The Albanians were involved in all this but not in the way we thought. They didn't set the fire.'

'Then who did?' Donna asked.

Carrigan took a deep breath. 'I hate to be the one to say this, but we now believe Emily set the fire herself.' He watched the reaction on Miles Maxted's face, the sudden darkening in the man's eyes, the twitch that made his lips snap against one another.

'What on earth would she do that for?'

Carrigan had put the last details into place as he'd sat waiting for Geneva that morning. 'We don't know for sure. It could have been an accident. Emily was helping the nuns shelter escaped sex slaves, as I told Donna, but since then we've found out that Emily had taken it a step further.' He ran through what Viktor had told him about that fateful night. 'Emily killed one of the men in the ensuing struggle, stabbing him.'

'Oh my God,' Donna blurted, her face white as a candle. 'No . . . no . . .' she kept repeating to herself, 'Emily would never . . .'

'I'm afraid she did,' Carrigan replied. 'But, if it's any consolation, the man she killed was probably trying to do the same to her.' He watched Miles taking this in, eyes blinking rapidly. Carrigan could see that however much he didn't want to believe it, his heart was pulling him in the opposite direction. Donna was quietly sobbing and she reached over and took her mother's hand as Carrigan continued.

'The Albanians didn't take kindly to the murder of one of their own. They obviously didn't go to the police either.' Carrigan explained about the visits to the convent and demands to hand over Emily.

'Oh God, poor Emily,' Donna said, her arms dropping to her sides and hanging there uselessly like a rag doll's.

Carrigan stared at her, the beauty he'd noticed the first day not diminished but somehow ennobled by her grief. 'But, you see, I have this annoying thing where I can't sleep very well when I'm on a case, and I kept thinking about this, thinking about Emily, what we knew about her, pacing my room, making myself coffee after coffee, but no matter how I looked at it, it just didn't make sense.'

He turned to see Geneva's eyes wide and alert, her gaze focused exclusively on him, a slight rebuke in the tilt of her head. 'Emily was a survivor, everything we know about her tells us this. So, I had another coffee and looked out the window and knew that someone who'd defend herself so aggressively against one of Duka's gangland thugs would never give in so easily. And it kept bugging me – why didn't she run away? Why didn't she simply disappear? From her years in the protest movement she would have known a lot of safe houses and hiding places, a lot of comrades who would ask no questions and gladly help her vanish.' Carrigan stopped pacing the room and turned towards the table.

'The next morning it was still there, in fact the nagging feeling had got stronger, but there was nothing I could do about it and so I started to clear the incident room, taking the photos off the wall, and as I peeled off Emily's picture, the one that Donna took, I noticed something I hadn't seen before and that's when I knew.'

'What on earth are you talking about?' Miles Maxted said.

'When I looked closely at the photo I realised Emily couldn't have been the eleventh victim.'

He paused, watching everyone's expressions freeze and flicker, Geneva shooting him a dark stricken look that spoke of deep frustration and backhanded betrayal. 'And then I remembered something. It was barely there but I could sense it, buried under layers of useless information. I pulled up the transcript of the interview we did with Emily's boyfriend, Geoff Shorter, because I was sure he'd said something that we'd not taken in at the time. I scanned through the transcript and found it. But I had to be sure,' Carrigan continued, 'and I knew one way I could be certain. I was only worried I might have thrown it away but it was there in my desk, the small white card that Donna gave me last week. I had the lab look at it and they managed to get a usable print from it.'

'But . . . but why on earth would you do that?' Miles protested and, despite all the bluster and front, Carrigan could see he was upset.

'We had Emily's fingerprints on file from her arrest. We couldn't compare them to those belonging to the body of the eleventh victim because the skin had been too badly burned, but I did a comparison between Emily's arrest record and the print found on the piece of paper Donna gave me. They were the same.'

'I don't understand,' Miles said.

'No, neither did I,' Carrigan replied. 'So I got on the phone to someone at King's College who's an expert on these things and he told me something very interesting. Apparently, twins have identical DNA but not identical fingerprints. Your fingerprints are shaped by what you do, how you use your hands during the formative years of childhood. I guess you never knew that, did you . . . Emily?'

50

'You need to get out of my house right now, Inspector.' Miles Maxted shot up, his chair flying back, his face tight and flushed, eyelids fluttering like maddened butterflies. 'I can see what you're trying to do and I won't allow it.'

'I'm afraid I can't do that. Please calm down, Mr Maxted, I haven't finished yet.'

'How dare you . . .'

'Sit down, Mr Maxted, and I promise I'll explain it to you or, perhaps,' Carrigan looked across the table, 'perhaps Emily can explain it better than I can.'

'You don't know what you're talking about, Jack.'

Her voice sent a shiver down his spine, coarse and rough, the way she used his name like an insult hurled in a fit of anger. It was a voice he hadn't heard before. Emily's voice. He forced himself to look at her but it was a totally different woman who was now looking back at him. 'It won't be hard to prove. We can take your fingerprints right now and settle this.'

She held his stare and said nothing.

'What on earth happened to you?' Carrigan said, and Geneva could hear the concern and mystification in his voice. 'You seemed to have turned your life around, to have started doing something good.'

Emily looked at her parents but they refused to meet her stare. She turned towards Carrigan. 'It wasn't supposed to happen like this.'

'It never is,' he replied, thinking of all the times he'd heard that line. 'What was Donna doing in the convent the night of the fire?'

'She followed me there. I told her to stay at home and wait for me but she didn't.' Emily shook her head and stared down at the table. 'I was going to return the cocaine. I don't even know why I took it that night, everything was so crazy. I knew it wouldn't get the Albanians off my back but I thought it might be a useful bargaining tool. And I didn't want the nuns to find it. Donna insisted she come with me. I tried arguing with her but it was no use.' She kept scratching her forearm and taking shallow quick breaths, trying to catch her parents' eyes.

'Nigel was waiting for us at the convent. I'd talked to him the night before. Told him that, if we used the cocaine as a bargaining chip, the Albanians might let us go. He laughed and said I was nuts. He wanted us to sell the coke and use the money to get out of the country before the Albanians found us. I didn't expect him to turn up at the convent. He was halfway out of his head, all amped up on speed and fear and adrenalin. He told me the nuns wouldn't be disturbing us, he'd made sure of that by locking the door. He said the cocaine would help us start a new life. I knew any life I began with him would end up exactly the way this one had.

'We argued and screamed at each other. I had the bag in my hand and I swung it at his head. The bag caught the candles and pricket stand as I threw it. Nigel staggered backwards. I started to run but he caught me and pinned me up against the wall and started to strangle me. I heard Donna scream as she jumped him. He turned and punched her in the face and she spun and fell forward and hit her head on the side of the pricket stand as she crashed to the floor. She didn't make a sound. Nigel started coming for me again. And then he stopped. He was staring wide-eyed at the niche behind me. I turned and saw that the candles had ignited the drapes. Big shooting flames ran up the walls and were spreading across the ceiling. Nigel took one last look, laughed and ran out through the back window and into the garden.'

Emily shook, her entire body crumpling as she continued. 'I

went to where Donna was lying. There was blood circling her head. I couldn't find her pulse. The flames were spreading across the room. I tried lifting her, tried slapping her face to wake her up but there was no reaction. I tried dragging her but the flames were all around us now. There was nothing I could do. If I hadn't left that moment the fire would have got me too.'

'And as you knelt there and saw Donna you realised how convenient this would be,' Carrigan said, his voice calm and reassuring, belying the words coming from his mouth.

Emily shook her head. 'It wasn't like that. There was nothing I could do. Donna was dead.'

'She was alive,' Carrigan said. 'She woke up.'

'What?' All the blood drained from Emily's face.

'She came to before the fire reached her. She crawled into the confession booth thinking she'd be safe there. She was burned alive inside, screaming and flailing and ripping her fingernails against the hissing metal,' Carrigan explained. 'It's my fault. I should have seen it earlier. Her long nails scratched and tore at the interior of the booth as she was burning to death. But you, Emily, you bite your nails. They wouldn't have made a mark. Geoff Shorter mentioned in his interview that it was a bad habit of yours. And it reminded me of something I heard a few days ago – how there are no hidden meanings, only actions and their consequences.'

Emily's hands slid under the table but her face told Carrigan all he needed to know.

'Why didn't you tell us?' Lillian's voice was cold and dismissive, the same tone Carrigan had heard her use with the maid.

A single tear ran down Emily's cheek. 'I was going to, I swear, but then you were so nice to me when you thought I was Donna and I didn't want that to change. I'd never felt that from you or Dad. I knew that Donna's death would break your hearts and, despite the way you'd always treated me, I couldn't bear to do that to you. I knew you'd far prefer it if it was me who was dead.'

She looked at both parents but neither said a word nor denied her accusations. 'I just wanted you to love me like you did her.' Emily's arms reached across the table into empty space. 'I thought if I pretended to be her . . . If I said the things she said and did the things she did then maybe I would grow to be a bit more like her . . . I hoped . . .' Emily stopped and looked up as Miles and Lillian Maxted rose from their seats. 'Please? . . . Mum? . . . Dad?'

Lillian followed her husband out of the room. Emily watched them disappear down the dark hallway. She kept staring long after they'd gone, and continued to do so as Carrigan handcuffed her and led her outside to the waiting police car.

*

He walked through the snow and howling wind until his feet were numb and he kept walking, oblivious to direction or purpose, a solitary man trudging through the deserted city, and as he walked he turned his face away from the lighted windows, silhouetted Christmas trees and happy screams of children opening their presents. He pulled up his collar and buttoned his jacket as the wind came careening down the long empty street. The temperature had suddenly dropped and he could feel his wrist, broken five years ago in a bar fight, begin to throb and ache with the memory of that night. He wanted the wind to rip through his skull and blow everything away – all the years and nights and days, the dreams and disappointments, memories and missed chances – but most of all he wanted to forget this case and all its dark and twisted layers.

He walked as if the very act of walking could shake off the last two weeks as easily as it did the snow gathered in the folds of his raincoat. He walked in ever decreasing circles, traversing the shuttered shops and barren canals, the darkened office buildings and silent motorways, losing all track of time and space as the snow began to fall on Christmas Day, until he realised he was back at the station and that's when he saw her.

She was sitting on a ledge, smoking a cigarette. The snow had woven ribbons of white through her hair and, unaware that he was there, she was swaying silently to the music, the twirled straps of her earphones framing her neck.

Carrigan felt a rush of heat and memory flood his chest and quickened his step.

Acknowledgements

Lesley Thorne, without whom none of this would exist . . .

Angus Cargill, the best editor any writer could hope for . . .

Rebecca Pearson, Katherine Armstrong, Alex Holroyd, Hannah Griffiths, John Grindrod, Neal Price, Miles Poynton, Alex Kirby, Lisa Baker, and everyone at Faber.

Sally Riley and everyone at Aitken Alexander Associates.

Matt Thorne, Richard Thomas, Alan Glynn, Damian Thompson, Milo Yiannopoulos, Nick Stone, Dreda Say Mitchell, Andrew Benbow, Luke Coppen, Ed West, Madeleine Teahan, Mark Greaves, Ali Karim, Mike Stotter, Mike Ripley, James Sallis, Rhian Davies, Eleanor Rees, Bix (Woof! Woof!), Kevin Conroy Scott, Sean, Chris Simmons, Michael Malone, Daniela Petracco, Kent Carroll, Jake Kerridge, Claire McGowan, Sophie Hannah, Erin Kelly, Chris Ewan, Chris Simms, Luca Veste, Willy Vlautin, Paul Dunn, Robert Clough, Neil Biswas and Jim Butler.

My parents.

Mother Angelica's calculus is based on William T. Vollmann's seven-volume meditation on violence, *Rising Up and Rising Down*, one of the most remarkable books of recent times.

Twitter for finally (virtually) getting me out of my room.

And all the readers and bloggers who were so kind and enthusiastic about *A Dark Redemption* – thank you! It really does make all the difference.